Books 5-8

EMILY RODDA

SCHOLASTIC INC.
New York Toronto London Auckland Sydney
Mexico City New Delhi Hong Kong Buenos Aires

Contents

DELTORA QUEST

Dread Mountain

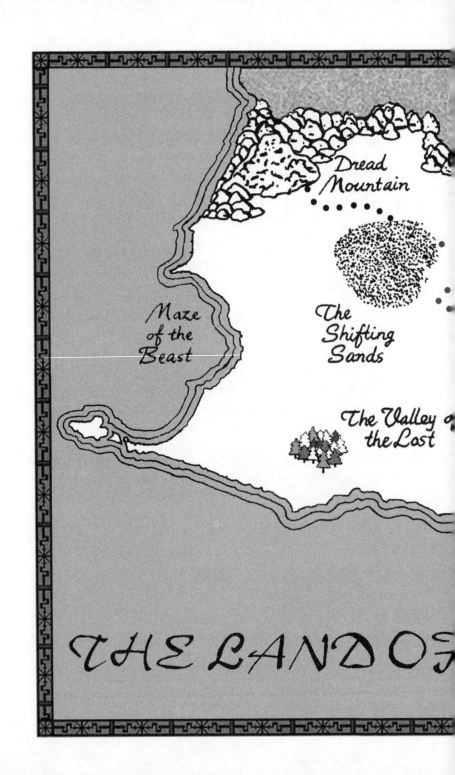

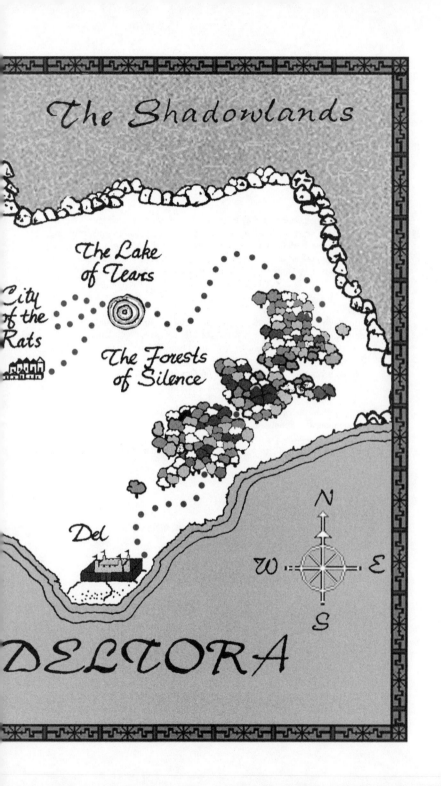

ISBN 0-439-25327-6

All rights reserved. Published by Scholastic Inc., 557 Broadway, New York, NY 10012,
by arrangement with Scholastic Press, an imprint of Scholastic Australia.

12 11 10 9 8 7 6 5 4 3 2 1   5 6 7 8 9/0

Printed in the U.S.A.   23

This edition created exclusively for Barnes & Noble, Inc.

2005 Barnes & Noble Books
ISBN 0-7607-9580-0
This edition first printing, May 2005

Contents

The story so far . . .

Sixteen-year-old Lief, fulfilling a pledge made by his father before he was born, is on a great quest to find the seven gems of the magic Belt of Deltora. The gems — an amethyst, a topaz, a diamond, a ruby, an opal, a lapis lazuli, and an emerald — were stolen to open the way for the evil Shadow Lord to invade Deltora. Hidden in fearsome places throughout the land, they must be restored to the Belt before the heir to the throne can be found and the Shadow Lord's tyranny ended.

Lief's companions are the man Barda, who was once a Palace guard, and Jasmine, a girl of Lief's own age who they met in the fearful Forests of Silence.

On their travels they have discovered a secret resistance movement led by Doom, a mysterious scar-faced man who rescued them when they were captured by the Shadow Lord's brutal Grey Guards.

So far the companions have found four gems. The golden topaz, symbol of faith, has the power to contact the spirit world and to clear the mind. The ruby, symbol of happiness, pales when danger threatens, repels evil spirits, and is an antidote to venom. The opal, gem of hope, gives glimpses of the future. The lapis lazuli, the heavenly stone, is a powerful talisman.

To find the fifth stone, they must travel almost to the border of the Shadowlands itself. To the fabled Dread Mountain.

Now read on . . .

1 ~ Refuge

The day had been fine and clear and there was a slight chill in the air. It was perfect weather for walking, but nothing is pleasant when you are thirsty, tired, and afraid. Lief trudged along, his head bowed, his limbs aching, only dimly aware of Barda and Jasmine moving beside him.

The water bottles were almost empty. Ever since leaving the Shifting Sands the companions had been existing on a few mouthfuls of water a day. But still the flat brown countryside stretched away from them with no sign of river or stream, and the sky, flooded now with the orange of the setting sun, was huge and cloudless.

Lief was walking with his head bent so he would not have to look at the ragged horizon. Dread Mountain was still far distant. It would be weeks before the companions reached it — if they did not die of thirst first, Lief thought grimly — but the very thought of it filled him with fear. The knowledge that every step he took brought him closer to the Shadowlands border was more terrifying still.

He hunched his shoulders, thinking with wonder of the boy who had left Del so filled with excitement at the thought of the adventure ahead. That boy now seemed absurdly young. And that time seemed very long ago.

Yet it was not so long — just a few months — and much had been achieved in that time. Four gems now glowed in the Belt of Deltora hidden under Lief's shirt. There were only three stones left to find. Lief knew he should feel happy, hopeful, and triumphant, as Jasmine did. Instead, he was battling gloom and despair.

For, as he looked back, it seemed miraculous to him that the gems had been secured at all. It seemed miraculous that he and his companions had survived the terrors they had faced. For how much longer could such good luck last? Lief's spirit shrank at the thought of what was ahead.

So far too they had escaped the attention of the Shadow Lord, but this time had surely ended. Doom, the scar-faced leader of the Resistance, had said that word was spreading about them. And if Doom had heard whispers, the Shadow Lord had certainly heard them too. Yet here Lief, Barda, and Jasmine walked, in the open air, under the open sky, with Kree flying ahead of them. What did it matter that no one knew their names? The description was enough.

Lief jumped nervously and nearly stumbled as a black shape flapped beside his head. But it was only Kree, landing on Jasmine's arm. The bird screeched. Filli poked his furry grey head out of Jasmine's jacket and chattered excitedly.

"Kree says there is water ahead," Jasmine cried. "A small pool — a spring, perhaps, for he could see no stream leading to it. It is in a grove of trees not far from the road."

The thought of water made them all quicken their pace, and it was not long before Kree took flight again and led them off the road. Dodging bushes and rocks, they followed him until at last they entered a grove of pale, odd-looking trees.

And there, sure enough, right in the center, was a small round pool surrounded by white stones. Eagerly they ran towards it. Then they saw that fixed to one of the stones was a dull brass plate with words engraved upon it — words they could just make out in the dimming light:

DREAMING SPRING

DRINK, GENTLE STRANGER,
AND WELCOME.

ALL OF EVIL WILL BEWARE.

The companions hesitated. The spring was clear and tempting. Their thirst was very great. But the words on the brass plate made them all nervous. Was the water safe to drink?

"Jasmine, what do the trees say?" muttered Barda. Once Barda had doubted Jasmine's ability to talk to growing things, but this time had long passed.

Jasmine frowned. "They do not say anything," she said, looking around. "They are completely silent. I do not understand it."

Lief shivered. The grove was green and still. Lush, soft grass grew underfoot. It was like a little paradise, yet there was a strange feeling in the air. He ran his tongue over his dry lips. "It might be better if we do not drink from this spring," he said reluctantly. "It could be enchanted — or poisoned."

"We are not of evil will," Barda protested. "Surely it will be safe for us."

But he remained where he was, and did not approach the spring.

Filli chattered impatiently on Jasmine's shoulder.

"We are all thirsty, Filli," Jasmine murmured. "But we must wait. We are not sure — Filli! No!"

The little creature had leaped to the ground. He scuttled to the pool, ignoring Jasmine's cries. In a moment he had dipped his head into the crystal waters and was drinking deeply.

"Filli!" called Jasmine in despair.

But for once Filli was not listening. He was lost

in the joy of quenching his terrible thirst.

And he did not become sick. He did not fall.

Kree was the next to fly to the spring. He, too, drank, dipping his beak and tipping back his head over and over again. He too showed no ill effects. And after that, Lief, Barda, and Jasmine could wait no longer, but ran to the pool themselves.

The water was cold and sweet. Never had Lief tasted anything so good. At home in Del the water was just as cold, but always tasted of the metal pump.

When at last they had drunk as much as they needed, the companions filled their water bottles to the brim in case they had to make a quick escape in the night. The grove seemed safe, but they had learned that it was unwise to trust appearances.

They sat on the grass and ate as the moon rose and stars appeared in the sky above them. It was cold, but they had decided against making a fire. Even a small blaze would be like a beacon, signalling their presence. Also for safety's sake, they moved well into the cover of the trees before unrolling their blankets. Others might know of the spring and come to drink from it in the night.

"How careful we have become," yawned Jasmine, gathering her blanket around her. "I remember a time when we were bolder."

"Things are different now," muttered Lief. "Now they are looking for us." He shivered.

Barda glanced at him quickly, then turned away

to mask the concern in his eyes. "We will sleep in turns. I will take the first watch," he said.

Kree squawked.

"You need sleep too, Kree," smiled Jasmine. "You are very tired. You cannot guard us all night long. You and Filli and I will watch together when Barda wakes us."

She turned over and closed her eyes, her hand in Filli's soft fur. Drowsily Lief watched as Kree began to flutter up to a tree branch above her head. Then the bird seemed to change his mind, wheeling and dropping back down to the grass. He hopped close to Jasmine and settled there, tucking his head under his wing.

Lief felt a small flicker of fear. "Barda," he called softly. "Look at Kree."

Barda, hunched beneath the blanket he had thrown around himself for warmth, stirred and turned around.

"Why is he sleeping on the ground instead of perching on a branch?" Lief whispered.

"Perhaps he does not like the trees," Barda whispered back. "Jasmine said they were silent. And certainly they are strange. Have you noticed that they look exactly alike?"

Lief looked around him and realized that Barda was right. That was one of the reasons why the trees looked so odd. Every single one had the same straight, smooth trunk, the same three branches pointing to the sky, the same thick clusters of pale leaves. His spine tingled.

"Lief, stop worrying, I beg you!" Barda growled after a moment. "Whatever is troubling Kree, it is not enough to stop him from taking his rest. I suggest you follow his example. You will regret it if you do not. Your turn to keep watch will come soon enough."

Slowly Lief pulled his blanket more tightly around him and lay down. For a minute or two he stared up at the star-spangled night sky framed by the pale leaves of the strange trees. Not a breath of wind stirred the leaves. No insects chirped. There was no sound at all except for Jasmine's soft breathing.

His eyelids grew heavy. Soon he could not keep them open, and he did not try. If Kree is not afraid to sleep, neither am I, he thought. After all, what can befall us while Barda is keeping watch?

In moments he was asleep. So he did not see Barda's head droop gently to his chest. He did not hear Barda's quiet snores.

And he did not feel the passing of silent feet as the dwellers of the grove moved softly to the Dreaming Spring.

2 - Before Dawn

L ief was dreaming. The dream seemed very real. He was standing by the old pump in the forge yard. The yard was dark and deserted. It is night, he thought. Mother and Father will be inside at this hour. But the house was dark too, and though he called from the door, and again from the kitchen, no one answered.

Confused, but not yet frightened, he walked into the living room. Light from the full moon shone through the window. The curtains had not been drawn. That was odd. And things were lying on the floor: books and papers, scattered everywhere. His parents would never have left them that way.

Their bedroom was empty, the bed tumbled and unmade, clothing lying on the floor. There was a jar of dead flowers on the chest. Now he knew that something was wrong. In fear, he ran outside once more.

The moon shone down on the empty yard. The forge gate was swinging. There was a mark on it. He could not quite see what it was. He moved closer, his heart thudding. Then he saw it.

Lief woke with a start. Sweat was beading his forehead, he was breathing fast, and his hands were trembling. He told himself that he had been dreaming, dreaming. There was nothing to fear.

Slowly he realized that the sky above him was pale and the stars had almost disappeared. It was nearly dawn. He had slept the night through. But — surely Jasmine, who had taken the second watch, had not forgotten to call him?

He glanced over to where he had seen Jasmine settling to rest the night before. She was still lying there, breathing quietly and evenly. Kree was huddled beside her. And not far away sat Barda, his back against a tree, his head on his chest. He too was sleeping soundly.

Lief almost laughed. So, despite their sensible

plans, they had all slept. Perhaps it was as well. They needed rest, and as it happened, nothing had troubled them in the night.

He felt very thirsty. Silently he unrolled himself from his blanket, got up, and moved through the trees towards the spring. His bare feet made no noise at all on the soft grass. That was something else about the grove that was unusual, he realized — the trees seemed to shed no leaves or sticks at all.

He had almost reached the spring when he heard it: a soft splashing sound. Someone — or something — was drinking.

Lief's hand crept to the hilt of his sword. He half-turned, thinking to wake Barda and Jasmine. But he was so near to the spring now that it seemed foolish not to at least peep at whatever had entered the grove. Holding his breath, he stole around the last tree and looked.

A plump shape was bent over the water, lapping. It was an animal of some kind — about as big as a large dog, but far rounder than any dog Lief had ever seen. Lief narrowed his eyes, struggling to see it clearly in the dim light. The creature was a rich, chestnut brown. It seemed to have no fur, and its ears were small and set close to its head. It had short, stubby back legs, and slender front paws. The skin on its back and sides was oddly marked, folded, and rippled.

What was it?

He took a step forward, and at the same moment

the creature straightened, turned, and saw him.

Lief gazed at wide, startled dark eyes, whiskers stiff with fright, a pink, open mouth, and small front paws clasped together in fear, and the strangest feeling of pleasure and peace flowed through him. He could not understand it, but he knew one thing clearly: the creature was harmless, gentle, and very frightened.

"Do not be afraid," he said in a low, soothing voice. "I will not harm you."

The creature still stared at him. But Lief thought that some of the fear had left its eyes, to be replaced by curiosity.

"I will not harm you," he repeated. "I am a friend."

"What is your name?" the creature asked in a squeaky voice.

Lief jumped violently. It had not occurred to him that it could speak. "My name is Lief," he said, without thinking.

"I am Little — I mean, Prin, daughter of the Kin," said the creature. She stood upright and began waddling towards Lief, her short legs toiling across the grass, her front paws bent, her mouth curved into a sweet and hopeful smile.

Lief's jaw dropped in astonishment. Waves of memory were flooding over him. No wonder he had felt that feeling of peace when first he saw Prin's face. How could he not have realized before what she was?

Kin! The fabled flying creatures that every child in Del knew of. Had Lief not had a toy Kin, Monty, to sleep with from his earliest days? His mother had made Monty out of soft brown fabric stuffed with straw, and over the years the little creature had grown worn and battered. Now he was kept hidden away in a drawer with other treasures, well out of sight of teasing friends. But once he had been Lief's trusted companion and comforter, carried around everywhere. How often in those days had Lief wished that Monty would come to life?

And this creature could be that wish come true, Lief thought. It could be Monty walking towards him over the grass. But surely — surely he had been told that the gentle, kindly Kin died out long ago? Surely they only existed now in old tales and picture books?

Lief swallowed, and for a moment wondered if he was still dreaming. But Prin was standing in front of him, large as life. Now he could see that she did have fur after all — a silken fuzz like fine brown moss. Her folded wings were covered with the same velvety stuff. He longed to stroke them, to see if they were as soft as they looked.

"Will you play with me, Lief?" asked Prin, twitching her whiskers and bouncing up and down on her toes. "Will you play hide-and-find?"

Lief realized then that she was very young. And of course she must be! Standing upright she only reached his shoulder. But fully grown Kin, he had been told, were so large that people in the old days, looking up and seeing them in the sky, had sometimes taken them for dragons and tried to shoot them down.

"Where is your family?" he asked, looking around. "Should you not ask — ?"

"They are still dreaming!" said Prin scornfully. "They will not wake till long after the sun comes up. See?"

She pointed to what Lief had taken to be groups of huge rocks scattered among and beyond the trees. To his amazement, Lief saw that they were not rocks at all, but Kin, curled up so tightly that all that could be seen of them were their hunched backs.

"I am supposed to stay curled until they wake," said Prin, lowering her voice. "But it is not fair. I have nothing interesting to dream of. I would rather play. Now — you hide and I will sing. I will not cheat, I promise! I will sing slowly, and I will close my ears as well as my eyes. Ready? Go!"

She put her paws over her eyes and began to sing.

"You can hide but I will find you,
My sharp eyes will seek you out . . ."

Lief quickly realized that the song was used by Kin children instead of counting. At the end of her song Prin would open her eyes and expect to find him gone. Not wishing to disappoint her, he ran away quickly and hid behind one of the trees in the thickest part of the grove.

It was not a very clever hiding place, but he did not want to stray far from where Jasmine and Barda were sleeping, and at least it would show the little Kin that he wanted to be friendly.

Flattening himself against the trunk of the tree, he smiled to himself as he listened to her voice squeaking on towards the end of the song.

". . . You can hide but I will find you,
Flap your wings and you'll be out!
You can hide but I will find you.
My sharp eyes will — oh!"

With a choking squeak the song broke off. There was a burst of loud, harsh laughter.

"Got it!" roared a voice. "Yo, help me! It's putting up a fight."

Horrified, Lief crept out from behind his tree and peered back to the spring. Two Grey Guards were bending over a struggling bundle on the ground. The bundle was Prin.

They had thrown a jacket over her head, and now were winding her round and around with rope.

"Give it a kick, Carn 4," the second Guard growled. "That'll teach it."

Lief smothered a cry as Carn 4 kicked savagely and the bundle stilled.

3 - Evil Will

L ief took a step forward, then jumped as a hand gripped his arm. It was Barda, his eyes swollen with sleep. Jasmine was right behind him.

"Come away, Lief," Barda whispered under his breath. "They are going to rest and eat. We can be long gone by the time they are ready to leave."

Lief shook his head violently, his eyes still fixed on the figures by the spring. "I cannot go," he hissed. "I cannot let them kill my friend."

He saw Barda and Jasmine exchange glances and knew that they must think he had lost his wits. "There is no time to explain. Where are the blisters?" he breathed. "Go and get them."

Without a word Jasmine slipped away into the trees. She might think Lief was being foolish, but she was not going to let him face the Guards with only a sword to protect himself.

With Barda close behind him, Lief began moving closer to the spring, running from tree to tree until he was very near to where Prin was lying.

"Pig for breakfast," Carn 4 was crowing. "Nothing better."

"It's not a pig," the other one said. "Look at its feet."

"It's fat, whatever it is. It'll be good eating." Carn 4 straightened his back and went over to the spring, taking the cap off his water bottle.

"We smelled out this water just in time, Carn 5," he called, tipping up the bottle and shaking it to show how empty it was.

Lief heard Barda draw a sharp breath. "They are members of the Carn pod," Barda breathed. "Like . . ."

"I know," Lief whispered in reply. "Like the Guards who caught us in Rithmere."

His hand was slippery on the hilt of his sword. Did Carn 4 and 5 know or guess what had happened to their brothers in the Shifting Sands? Had they taken over where Carn 2 and Carn 8 had left off, to save their pod from disgrace?

Carn 5 strolled over to join his fellow at the spring, rubbing his nose with the back of his hand. "This place stinks of ticks," he complained.

Lief held his breath.

"Not ours, though." Carn 4 bent to fill his bottle. "Our two and their friend went straight on. That big ugly one — the one they call Glock — he drags his feet. You can smell every step he takes. He didn't come in here."

Lief's heart was thudding wildly. So Doom had released Glock and Neridah, as he had planned. Carn 4 and 5 must have been Glock and Neridah's captors. Now they were pursuing them just as Carn 2 and Carn 8 had pursued Lief and his companions after their escape.

The Guards were both facing the spring. Now was the time to try to get Prin away. Lief glanced urgently over his shoulder. Where was Jasmine with the blisters?

"We'll get them by nightfall," Carn 5 said confidently, kneeling down beside Carn 4 and plunging his own water bottle into the water. "Them and whoever let them go. And won't we make *him* sorry for himself?"

"We'll have some fun with him," the other agreed.

They both laughed and bent to drink, sucking and lapping noisily.

Lief knew he could not wait. He could not miss his chance. Ignoring Barda's restraining hand on his arm, he darted into the open, seized the limp bundle that was Prin, and began dragging it away.

Afterwards, he cursed himself for his stupid thoughtlessness. He had just assumed that Prin was unconscious. But Prin was very much awake, lying motionless in an agony of fear. Feeling unknown hands upon her she squealed in terror.

Instantly the Guards leaped to their feet and whirled around, still swallowing the water in their mouths, their blisters and slings already in their dripping hands. They saw Lief bent over Prin. Snarling, they rushed towards them.

"Lief! Run!" Lief heard Barda roar, as the big man lunged forward trying to push him out of the way. But Lief was frozen to the spot. He was gaping in shock.

For the Guards were screaming. They were staggering, stopping. Their feet were sprouting roots that snaked into the earth, tying them in place. Their legs were drawing together, hardening into a solid trunk. Their bodies, arms, and necks were stretching towards the sky, and pale leaves were forcing their way through skin that was becoming smooth bark.

And in moments, two trees stood in their places. Two new trees for the grove — as silent, still, and perfect as all the others.

Jasmine came running, with Filli chattering in fear on her shoulder. "The rocks are coming alive!" she panted. "They are coming this way!"

✳

Half an hour later, still dazed, Lief, Barda, and Jasmine were sitting among a group of huge Kin. Filli was staring, wide-eyed, at the great creatures. Prin, complaining bitterly, had been made to climb into her mother's pouch.

"You must stay curled until we awake, Little One!" her mother scolded. "How many times have I told you? Now see what has happened. Those evil ones might have killed you!"

"They drank the water, Mother," sulked Prin from the depths of the pouch. "I knew they would."

"You could not know that they would drink before they did you harm!" her mother snapped. "Be still. Your side is badly bruised."

"We drank the water also!" exclaimed Barda, who was gazing from the Kin to the motionless trees in pure amazement.

Prin poked her head out of the pouch and twitched her whiskers. "Those who mean no harm can drink without harm," she chanted, plainly repeating something she had been taught.

Her mother ignored her and turned to Barda. "We knew you were of good heart when you drank from the spring and remained unharmed," she said in her slow, deep voice. "Sure that you were not a danger to us, we dreamed peacefully last night — little knowing that our child would be a danger to you in the morning. We are sorry."

Barda bowed. "It was my friend who helped the little one," he said, gesturing to Lief. "But for my part, it is a privilege to meet you. I never thought to see the Kin in my lifetime."

19

"We are few now," said an old Kin standing beside Prin's mother. "Since we left our Mountain — "

"Dread Mountain! You lived on Dread Mountain once, did you not? Why did you leave?" Lief interrupted, able to keep silent no longer.

The old Kin stopped, and looked at Barda.

Barda smiled. "As you see, I too have young ones in my care," he said, to Lief's annoyance. "Please forgive the interruption and continue."

"The gnomes of Dread Mountain had always tried to hunt us," said the old one. "But their arrows could not do us great harm. Our main dangers were Grey Guards and Vraal beasts, coming from the Shadowlands. But long ago something changed . . ."

His voice trailed off and he bent his head.

"The gnomes began using poison on their arrow tips," said Prin's mother, taking up the story. "It was deadly poison, and killed painfully and quickly. Many of us died." Her voice sank to a whisper. "It was a terrible time. I was very young then. But I remember."

The other Kin nodded and whispered among themselves. Plainly they too remembered.

"At last, the few of us that were left decided we could stay on the Mountain no longer," the old Kin rumbled. "This grove used to be our winter home — a good place for the growing young. Now we are here all year long. Now we can visit our Mountain — see the Boolong trees, hear the rippling streams, and smell the sweet, cool air — only in our dreams."

A feeling of sadness swept over the group. There was a long silence. Jasmine fidgeted uncomfortably.

"I had a strange dream last night," she said, plainly trying to bring a little cheer to the gathering. "I dreamed I saw the man Doom. He was in a cave full of people. The boy Dain was there — and Neridah, and Glock, and many others. Glock was eating soup, spilling it all down his chin. I called to them, but they did not hear me. It was so real!"

The old Kin looked at her. "Do you not understand? It *was* real," he said. He waved a paw at the spring. "This is the Dreaming Spring. Whatever or whoever you picture in your mind when you drink, you visit in spirit when you sleep."

"We ourselves visit our Mountain every night," Prin's mother added, as Jasmine looked disbelieving. "It comforts us greatly to see it as it is now. The Boolong trees grow thickly — far more thickly than they once did. Of course, we cannot eat the cones, but at least we are there, and together."

"Not me!" said Prin loudly. "I cannot go there. I have never seen it! I have never known anywhere but here. So I have nothing to dream of. It is not fair!"

Her mother bent over her, murmuring. The other adults looked at one another sadly.

"What I saw in my dream was *real*?" Jasmine gasped.

"So Doom, Neridah, and Glock have reached the Resistance stronghold in safety!" Barda exclaimed. He

21

looked with satisfaction at the two new trees by the spring. "And now no Guards will trouble them."

He grinned. "I dreamed of Manus and the Ralad people. I stood by the stream in their underground town. They were singing, and all was well. That is very good to know."

But Lief sat in silence, numb with shock. He was remembering his own dream, and slowly facing the knowledge that it too had been true.

4 - The Plan

At length, the gathering of the Kin broke up as each creature moved off to feed on the grass that grew beneath and beyond the trees.

"Grass is all we have here," Prin's mother explained to Lief, Barda, and Jasmine as she toiled away with her heavy young one in her pouch. "It is nourishing enough, but we have grown tired of its sweetness and long for the leaves and cones of the Boolong trees. The leaves of the trees in this grove are not fit to eat. They are not truly alive."

Kree, perched on Jasmine's arm, squawked in disgust. "Kree always knew the trees were not as they should be," Jasmine said, shuddering as she looked around her. "No wonder they are silent. It is horrible to think of them standing here, unchanging, for centuries."

"And it is fortunate for us that we passed the

spring's test," said Barda grimly. "Or we would be with them."

Lief had not spoken for a long time. When the last of the Kin had departed Jasmine turned to him. "What is the matter?" she demanded. "All is well."

"All is not well," Lief muttered. "My mother and father — " He broke off, swallowing desperately to hold back tears.

"Jarred and Anna?" Barda exclaimed, looking alert. "What do you . . . ?" Suddenly his face changed, filling with fear as he understood. "You had a dream!" he exclaimed. "Lief — "

Lief nodded slowly. "The forge is empty," he said in a low voice. "The Shadow Lord's brand is on the gate. I think — I think they are dead."

Stricken with shock and grief, Barda stared at him wildly. Then his mouth firmed. "Very likely they are not dead, but simply taken prisoner," he said. "We must not give up hope."

"To be a prisoner of the Shadow Lord is worse than death," Lief whispered. "Father told me that, many times. He was always warning me . . ." The words choked in his throat and he covered his face with his hands.

Awkwardly, Jasmine put her arm around him and Filli jumped onto his shoulder, brushing his cheek with soft fur. Kree clucked sorrowfully. But Barda stood apart, struggling with his own fear and sorrow.

Finally Lief looked up. His face was very pale. "I must go back," he said.

Barda shook his head. "You must not."

"I must!" Lief insisted angrily. "How can I go on, knowing what I know?"

"You know nothing but that the forge is empty," Barda said evenly. "Jarred and Anna could be in the dungeons of the palace in Del. They could be in the Shadowlands. They could be in hiding. Or, as you said before, they could be dead. Wherever they are, you cannot help them. Your duty is here."

"Do not speak to me of duty!" Lief shouted. "They are my parents!"

"They are my friends," Barda said, still in that same expressionless voice. "My dear and only friends, Lief, since before you were born. I know what they would say to you if they could. They would tell you that our quest is their quest too. They would beg you not to abandon it."

Lief's anger died, leaving dull sadness in its place. He searched Barda's face and saw the pain behind the grim mask.

"You are right," he mumbled. "I am sorry."

Barda put a hand on his shoulder. "One thing is clear," he said. "Time has become of the first importance. We must reach Dread Mountain with all speed."

"I cannot see that we can move any faster than we have been doing," Jasmine put in.

"On foot we cannot," Barda agreed. "But I have a plan." His face was shadowed with grief, but still he managed a small smile. "Why should the Kin dream of home, instead of seeing it with their own eyes? Why should we walk, when we can fly?"

✳

Barda talked to the Kin for a very long time. He argued well. But it was not until sunset that three of them finally agreed to carry the companions to Dread Mountain.

The three who agreed were Merin, Ailsa, and Bruna. They were among the largest in the group, and all were female, for only the female Kin had pouches in which to carry passengers.

All three agreed for different reasons: Merin because she was so homesick, Ailsa because she was adventurous, and Bruna because she felt that the Kin owed Lief a debt for trying to save Prin.

"She is very dear to us all," Bruna explained. "The only young one to be born to us since we moved here from our Mountain."

"This is because we need the Mountain air and the Boolong trees to thrive," Merin cried. "Here, we just exist. On our Mountain, we can grow and breed. We should have gone back long ago."

"Gone back to die? What foolishness you talk, Merin!" snapped the old one, who had been greatly angered by the three's agreement to go. "If you, Ailsa, and Bruna go back in flesh and blood to Dread Mountain, you will surely be killed. Then there will be three less Kin, and we will have three more deaths to mourn."

"What is the use of staying here to die slowly?" snapped Ailsa, lifting her great wings. "With no babies to carry on our line, we have no future. The Kin are finished. I would rather die quickly, in a good cause, than linger here."

"We have our dreams," Prin's mother said quietly.

"I am sick of dreaming!" Ailsa exclaimed.

"And I cannot dream at all!" squeaked Prin. She ran over to Ailsa and clasped her paws. "Take me with you to the Mountain, Ailsa," she begged. "Then I too will have seen it. Then I can go with you when you dream."

Ailsa shook her head. "You cannot come, Little One. You are too precious. But think of this: you can dream of us. Then you will see where we are, and what we are doing. Will that not be just as good as travelling yourself?"

Plainly, Prin did not think so, for she began to wail and cry, paying no attention to her mother's orders and pleadings. At last her mother hurried her away, but even when they were out of sight, the sound of their arguing voices floated back through the trees. The other Kin looked distressed.

The old one frowned. "You see what you have done?" he mumbled to Barda, Lief, and Jasmine. "We were peaceful and happy here, before you came. Now there is anger between us and Little One is unhappy."

"It is not fair to blame the strangers, Crenn," Bruna objected. "Merin, Ailsa, and I have agreed to go to the Mountain of our own free will."

"That is true," said Merin gently. "And Little One is only saying what she has been saying these past few years, Crenn. The older she grows, the more she will say it. Her life here, with no companions of her own age, is too quiet for her. She is very like Ailsa — lively and adventurous."

"And she does not have dreams to lull her, as I have had," Ailsa put in. Her bright eyes turned to Jasmine, Lief, and Barda. "I think I must thank the strangers for disturbing my peace," she added. "This day has made me feel that I am alive again."

Crenn sat very upright. His old face, the whiskers white, the eyes faded and full of longing, was turned to the Mountain. The sun had dipped below the horizon when at last he spoke.

"Of course you speak the truth, all of you," he said reluctantly. "And if this must be, it must be. I only pray that you will be safe, and beg you to take care, and return to us with all speed."

"We will," Ailsa promised. She smiled around. "I will drink from the spring now, but not again this night. Then I will sleep only lightly. One of us must be awake to call the others tomorrow morning. We must leave before dawn."

5 - The Enemy

That night, Lief dreamed again. He had planned for it, drinking deeply from the spring and thinking of his father and mother while he did so. If they are dead, then it is better to face it, he told himself. If they are alive, this is my chance to find out where they are.

As he and his companions prepared for sleep, the thought of what he was about to find out made him silent and tense. He said nothing to Barda and Jasmine but perhaps they guessed what he was planning, for they were equally silent, bidding each other good night, then saying no more. Lief was grateful. This was something he had to face alone, and speaking of it would not help.

Sleep did not come quickly. For a long time he lay awake, staring up at the sky. But at last the drowsiness caused by the spring water overcame him.

This time, the dream began almost at once. The smell was what he noticed first — the smell of damp and decay. Then there were sounds — people groaning and crying somewhere not far away, their muffled voices echoing and ghostly. It was very dark.

I am in a tomb, he thought, with a thrill of terror. But then his eyes became used to the darkness and he saw that he was in a dungeon. A figure, head bowed, was sitting on the floor in a corner.

It was his father.

Completely forgetting that he was in the cell only in spirit, Lief called out, ran over to the slumped figure, and seized its arm. His hands went straight through the solid flesh. His father remained bowed in misery, plainly hearing and feeling nothing. Hot tears springing into his eyes, Lief called again. This time, his father stirred and raised his head. He looked straight at Lief, a slight, puzzled frown on his face.

"Yes, Father, yes! It is me!" Lief cried. "Oh, try to hear me! What has happened? Where is this place? Is Mother — ?"

But his father was sighing deeply and bowing his head again. "Dreaming," he murmured to himself.

"It is not a dream!" shouted Lief. "I am here! Father — "

His father's head jerked up. A key was grating in the lock of the cell door. Lief swung around as the door creaked open. Three figures stood there — a tall, thin man in long robes backed by two huge guards holding flaming torches. For a moment Lief was panic-stricken, convinced that his cries had been heard. But immediately he realized that the newcomers were as unaware of him as his father was.

"So, Jarred!" The man in the long robes took a torch from one of the guards and moved into the center of the cell. Lit by the flickering light of the flame, his face was sharp, the cheekbones deeply shadowed, the thin mouth cruel.

"Prandine!" breathed Lief's father.

Lief's heart thudded. Prandine? King Endon's chief advisor, the secret servant of the Shadow Lord? But surely he was dead? Surely —

The man smiled. "Not Prandine, blacksmith," he jeered. "The one called Prandine fell to his death from the tower of this very palace over sixteen years ago, on the day the Master claimed his kingdom. Prandine was careless — or unlucky. Perhaps you know something about that?"

"I know nothing."

"We shall see. But where one dies, there is always another to take his place. The Master likes this face and form. He chose to repeat it in me. My name is Fallow."

"Where is my wife?"

Lief caught his breath. The thin man sneered.

"Would it please you to know? Perhaps I will tell you — if you answer my questions."

"What questions? Why have we been brought here? We have done nothing wrong."

Fallow turned to the door, where the guards stood watching. "Leave us!" he ordered. "I will question the prisoner alone."

The guards nodded, and withdrew.

As soon as the door was firmly closed, the thin man took something from the folds of his robe. A small pale blue book.

It was *The Belt of Deltora*, the book Jarred had found hidden in the palace library. The book Lief himself had so often studied as he grew up, and which had taught him so much about the power of the Belt and its gems.

Lief squirmed to see it in this man's hands. He longed to snatch it away from Fallow, save his father from this cruel taunting. But he was powerless. All he could do was stand and watch.

"This book was found in your house, Jarred," Fallow was saying. "How did it come there?"

"I do not remember."

"Perhaps I can help you. It is known to us. It came from the palace library."

"As a young man I lived in the palace. I may have taken it away with me when I left. It was many years ago. I do not know."

Fallow tapped the book with bony fingers. The cruel smile never left his face.

"The Master thinks you have deceived us,

Jarred," he said. "He thinks you kept in contact with your foolish young friend, King Endon, and at the last helped him, his idiot bride, and their unborn brat to escape."

Lief's father shook his head. "Endon was fool enough to believe me a traitor," he said in a low, even voice. "Endon would never have turned to me for help, nor would I have given it to him."

"So we thought. But now we are not so sure. Strange things have been occurring in the kingdom, blacksmith. Things my Master does not like."

Lief saw a sudden flash of hope in his father's downturned eyes. He glanced quickly at Fallow. Had he seen it too?

He had. His own eyes were gleaming coldly as he went on.

"Certain allies, valued by the Master, have been viciously killed. Certain — goods — also valued by the Master have been stolen," Fallow went on. "We suspect that King Endon is still alive. We suspect that he is making some last, useless effort to reclaim his kingdom. What do you know about that?"

"Nothing. Like everyone else in Del, I believe that Endon is dead. That is what we were told."

"Indeed." Fallow paused. Then he leaned forward so that his face and the lighted torch were very close to the man on the floor. "Where is your son, Jarred?" he spat.

Lief's mouth went dry. He watched as his father

looked up. His heart ached as he saw the deep lines of exhaustion, pain, and grief on the well-loved face that was so like his own.

"Lief left our house months ago. The blacksmith's trade bored him. He preferred running wild with his friends in the city. We do not know where he is. Why do you ask about him? He broke his mother's heart, and mine."

Lief's own heart swelled at his father's courage. The voice was high and complaining — the voice of an injured parent, no more. His father, always so truthful, was lying as though he had been born to it, determined to protect his son, and his cause, at all costs.

Fallow was examining the despairing face closely. Was he deceived or not?

"It is said that a boy of about your son's age is one of the three criminals who are roving the land, trying to overturn the Master's plans," he said slowly. "With him are a girl and a grown man. A black bird flies with them."

"Why are you telling me this?" The man on the floor moved restlessly. He seemed to be merely impatient. But Lief, who knew him so well, could see that he had been listening intently. No doubt he was wondering furiously about this mention of a girl and a black bird. He knew nothing of Jasmine and Kree, or what had happened in the Forests of Silence.

"This boy," Fallow went on, "could be your son.

You are crippled, and may have sent him on some useless quest in your place. The man — could be Endon."

Lief's father laughed. The laugh sounded completely natural. As of course it would, Lief thought. It was absurd to think of Barda being mistaken for the delicate, cautious King Endon.

Fallow's thin lips set in a hard line. He lowered the flame of the torch till it flickered dangerously in front of the laughing man's eyes.

"Take good care, Jarred," he snarled. "Do not try my patience too far. Your life is in my hands. And not only yours."

The laughing stopped. Lief ground his teeth as he saw his father once again bow his head.

Fallow walked to the door. "I will be back," he said in a low voice. "Think over what I have said. The next time I come to see you, I will come expecting answers. If you have done what we suspect, mere pain will not make you tell the truth. But perhaps the pain of one you love will be more persuasive."

He lifted a fist and thumped on the door. It opened and he went through, banging it behind him. The key turned in the lock.

"Father!" Lief cried to the figure slumped against the wall. "Father, do not despair. We have four of the gems. And now we are going to Dread Mountain to find the fifth. We are moving as fast as we can!"

But his father sat motionless, staring unseeing

into the darkness. "They are alive," he whispered. "Alive, and succeeding!"

His eyes glowed. Chains rattled as he clenched his fists. "Oh, Lief, Barda — good fortune! I am fighting my fight here, as best I can. You must fight yours. My hopes and prayers go with you!"

6 - Take-off

Lief woke to the sound of voices. It was nearly dawn. Jasmine and Barda were already stirring, taking up their weapons, buckling the canisters of blisters to their belts. Ailsa, Merin, and Bruna were moving back from the spring. Lief lay still, remembering his dream. Though he must have slept for many hours after it was over, every detail was clear in his mind.

A terrible weight seemed to be pressing him down. It was the weight of his father's danger and pain, of fear for his mother. Then he remembered his father's glowing eyes, and those final words.

I am fighting my fight here, as best I can. You must fight yours . . .

Lief sat up, determinedly shaking off the misery.

"Jarred and Anna always knew that it might

come to this." Barda was standing beside him. His face was grim and drawn.

"You saw Father?" Lief exclaimed, jumping to his feet. "You too?"

They picked up their sleeping blankets, shouldered their packs, and began walking together to the spring, talking in low voices. Jasmine followed, listening.

"I dreamed as soon as I fell asleep," Barda said. "I knew you must be planning to do the same, Lief, but I wanted to see for myself how Jarred was faring. I learned little, but I saw him. He was sitting against the wall of a dungeon — in chains." His fists clenched at the memory. "I could do nothing. If only I could have told him — "

"He knows!" Lief exclaimed. "He knows we are succeeding. It has given him hope."

"He could *hear* you?"

"No. He found out another way."

They had reached the spring. As they breakfasted hastily on dried fruit and travellers' biscuits washed down with sweet water, Lief told of Fallow's visit to the cell. Barda laughed grimly when he heard that he was suspected of being King Endon.

"My dear old mother would be proud to hear it," he said. "So they have not noticed the disappearance of the beggar at the forge gates?"

"No," said Lief. "Or if they have, they think you have just moved elsewhere in the city." He frowned.

"But I am a different story. When trouble started they went to the forge, because of Father's history. They found I was gone. They searched the house . . ."

"And they found the book," muttered Barda. "I told Jarred long ago that he should destroy it. But he would not. He said it was too important."

Lief heard a small sound behind him and turned. Jasmine was pulling on her pack. Her mouth was set and her eyes sad. He thought he guessed why.

"I did not dream of anything last night," she said, in answer to his unspoken question. "I tried to picture my father as I drank from the spring, but I was so young when he was taken away that I cannot remember his face. It is just a blur to me now. So — I missed my chance."

"I am sorry," Lief murmured.

She shrugged, tossing her hair back. "Perhaps it is for the best. Father has been a prisoner for so many years. Who knows what he suffers? It would torment me, knowing I could do nothing to help him. It is better to think of him as dead, like my mother."

She turned away abruptly. "You had better make haste. We are losing time with this useless talk."

She walked off, with Kree flying beside her. Barda and Lief quickly packed up their own bags and followed. Both knew that great suffering lay behind Jasmine's harsh words. Both wished that they could help her.

But there was nothing to be done. Nothing to be

done for Jasmine, or her father, or Lief's parents, or any of the thousands of other victims of the Shadow Lord's cruelty. Except . . .

Except what we are doing now, Lief thought, as he approached the place beyond the grove where the Kin and Jasmine were waiting. The Belt of Deltora is our task. When that is complete — when Endon's heir has been found and the Shadow Lord overthrown — then all the prisoners will be free.

✳

The Kin were waiting beyond the trees, at the top of a grassy hill. They had all gathered to bid the travellers farewell, except Prin.

"Little One would not come," her mother explained. "I apologize for her. Usually she does not remain angry for long. This time it is different."

"This time the disappointment is very great," murmured Ailsa. "Poor Little One. I feel for her."

Merin glanced up at the lightening sky and turned to Barda. "As I am the largest, you are to ride with me," she said politely. Plainly, she was anxious to be gone.

Rather nervously, Barda climbed into her pouch. Lief had to smile at the sight, and despite their fears many of the watching Kin laughed aloud.

"What a large baby you have, Merin," called Prin's mother. "And how beautiful!"

Both Barda and Merin preserved a dignified silence.

Lief was to ride with Ailsa and Jasmine with Bruna, the smallest of the three. They climbed into the pouches in their turn, Filli chattering excitedly on Jasmine's shoulder. He plainly thought the Kin wonderful, and was thrilled to be so close to one.

Ailsa's pouch was warm and velvety soft. At first Lief was afraid that his weight would hurt her, but soon realized that his worry was needless. "A young Kin is far heavier than you by the time it leaves its mother's pouch for good," Ailsa told him. "Be comfortable."

But comfort was the last thing Lief felt shortly afterwards. He had wondered how such heavy creatures could leave the ground. Finding out at first hand was terrifying.

The method was quite simple. Ailsa, Merin, and Bruna stood in a line, spread their great wings, and then began running as fast as they could down the hill. Their passengers, jolted unmercifully, could only hold on, gasping for breath. Then they saw what was ahead. They were running straight for the edge of a cliff.

Lief yelled and shut his eyes as Ailsa launched herself into space. There were a few dizzy moments of panic as the great wings beat hard above his head. Then he felt an upward rush and a surge of cool air against his face. He realized that the sound of the wings had settled down to a steady beat. He opened his eyes.

The earth below looked like a patchwork rug embroidered all over with little trees and narrow winding paths. Ahead, Dread Mountain already seemed closer. It was still hazy, but looked larger, darker, and more ominous than it had before. Behind it were the folds of the mountain range that marked the border with the Shadowlands. They too seemed closer.

"How long will it take to reach the Mountain?" Lief shouted above the noise of the wind.

"We will have to stop when the light fails," Ailsa called back. "But if we continue to have good weather, we should reach it tomorrow."

Tomorrow! Lief thought. Tomorrow we will know for good or ill if the gnomes of Dread Mountain still watch the skies for Kin. If they do, it will mean our deaths. The gnomes will shoot down Ailsa, Merin, and Bruna, and we will go crashing to the ground with them.

He shivered. His hand stole down to the Belt at his waist and he lightly brushed the four gems set in place there. They warmed beneath his touch: the topaz for faith, the ruby for happiness, the opal for hope, and the mysterious lapis lazuli, the Heavenly Stone.

Surely all will be well, he told himself. Surely these gems together will keep us safe. But even as he thought this, words from *The Belt of Deltora* flashed into his mind.

† **Each gem has its own magic, but together the seven make a spell that is far more powerful than the sum of its parts. Only the Belt of Deltora, complete as it was first fashioned by Adin and worn by Adin's true heir, has the power to defeat the Enemy.**

The warning was clear. The gems that Lief and his companions had in their charge so far could help them on their way, but could not save them.

Lief took care not to let his fingers linger on the opal. He did not want to glimpse the future. If it was fearful, he did not wish to know it. He would face whatever fate had in store when the time came.

7 - Kinrest

As the sun sank in a blaze of red, the Kin circled lower and lower, searching for the place where they planned to spend the night.

"There is water there, and food, and shelter from above," Ailsa called to Lief. "It is a small forest where long ago we always broke our journey between the Mountain and the grove. We call it Kinrest."

It was almost dark by the time they dropped to earth, their great wings beating hard as they sank between tall trees to the soft shelter below.

Lief, Barda, and Jasmine climbed unsteadily to the ground. It felt very odd to have firm earth under their feet again. They looked around. Kinrest was indeed a peaceful place. Ferns thickly edged the small stream that bubbled through it, and toadstools grew in clumps under the great trees. Somewhere near there was the sound of a waterfall.

"How the trees have grown!" Merin exclaimed excitedly, brushing leaves and twigs from her fur. "They hide the stream completely. And, see, Ailsa — the entrance to the big cave where we used to play is choked with ferns."

"Everything looks quite different," Ailsa agreed. "No wonder we took so long to find it from above. We should have visited it in our dreams long ago, instead of always going to the Mountain."

Wearily Lief, Barda, and Jasmine sat down by the stream and watched as the three Kin began to explore. Jasmine put her head on one side, listening to the rustling of the trees.

"What do they say?" asked Lief eagerly. "Are we safe?"

Jasmine frowned. "I think so. The trees are happy to see Kin again. Many of them are hundreds of years old and remember past times clearly. But I sense sadness and fear in them also. Something bad happened here. Blood was spilled, and someone they cared for died."

"When?" demanded Barda, suddenly alert.

"Trees such as these do not speak of time as we do, Barda," Jasmine said patiently. "The sadness they are remembering could have happened one season ago or twenty. It is all one to them."

Suddenly she shivered. "I think it would be safe to light a small fire," she said. "The trees will surely hide the light. And I feel in need of cheer."

※

The friends were crouching over the warming blaze of
their fire, eating dried fruit and slices of nut and
honey cake, when Ailsa called to them out of the
dimness beyond the stream. Her voice sounded odd.
Jumping up in alarm, they lit a torch and found their
way to where she and the other Kin were standing by
a large cave thickly overgrown with ferns.

"We were exploring our cave," Ailsa said in a
low voice. "We used to play here as young ones. We
found some — things inside it. We thought you would
like to see them."

The three companions followed the Kin into
the cave. The light of the torch flickered over the
rocky walls and the sandy floor, showing the objects
lying there: a few pots and pans, a mug, some old
sleeping blankets lying on a bed of dust that had
once been dried fern, a bundle of old clothes, a chair
made of fallen branches, a dead torch fixed to a
wall . . .

"Someone has been living here," breathed Lief.

"Not recently," Barda said, picking up a blanket
and dropping it again in a cloud of dust. "Not for
many years, I would say."

"There is something else," said Ailsa quietly.

She led them back to the cave entrance and
parted the ferns that grew thickly on one side. A flat,
mossy stone stood there, set firmly upright like a
marker.

"There is writing scratched upon it," whispered Bruna.

Barda lowered the torch and the three companions saw that there were indeed words carved carefully into the stone.

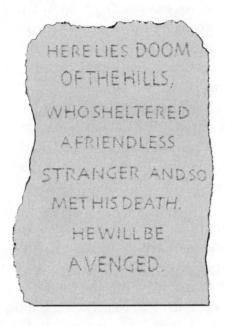

HERE LIES DOOM
OF THE HILLS,
WHO SHELTERED
A FRIENDLESS
STRANGER AND SO
MET HIS DEATH.
HE WILL BE
AVENGED.

"A strange name to find on a gravestone," muttered Barda, glancing at Lief and Jasmine meaningfully. "And a strange message to go with it."

Stunned, Lief stared at the words. "Doom of the Hills is dead!" he breathed. "But this grave is old — ten years old at least, by the look of the stone. So the man *we* know as Doom — "

"Is someone else entirely," Jasmine finished crisply. Her face was flushed with anger. "He is going by a false name. I knew he could not be trusted. For all we know he is a Shadow Lord spy!"

"Do not be so foolish! That he does not use his real name proves nothing," growled Barda. "We ourselves were going by false names when we met him."

Lief nodded slowly. "He needed to conceal his identity. So he took the name of the man who lies buried in this place."

"A man he betrayed and murdered, perhaps," Jasmine muttered. "For he was here. I feel it!"

Barda would not answer her. Gently, he began to clear the ferns from around the stone. Lief bent to help him. Jasmine stood aside, her eyes cold and angry.

The three Kin looked helplessly on. Finally, Merin cleared her throat and clasped her paws. "It is clear that our find has caused you pain, and for that we are sorry," she said softly. "We have eaten many leaves, and drunk from the stream. Now we will curl, and sleep. We must leave early in the morning."

With that hint, she, Bruna, and Ailsa moved away and disappeared into the darkness. Shortly afterwards, Barda and Lief finished their work and moved back across the stream, with Jasmine silently following. By the time they reached the fire, the three Kin were huddled together, looking like a cluster of great rocks, and apparently fast asleep.

Lief wrapped himself in his sleeping blanket and

tried to sleep also. But suddenly the forest seemed less welcoming than it had before. A veil of sadness seemed to hang over the trees, and there were noises in the darkness: the breaking of twigs and the rustling of leaves, as though someone, or something, was watching them.

He could not help thinking about the man who called himself Doom. Despite what he had said to Jasmine, he had been shaken by the words on the gravestone. Doom had helped them, saved them from the Grey Guards. That was true. But had it been all part of a greater plot? A plot to gain their confidence? To worm from them the secret of their quest?

. . . the Enemy is clever and sly, and to its anger and envy a thousand years is like the blink of an eye.

Was it by chance that Doom had appeared in their lives once more? Or had he been acting under orders?

It does not matter. We told him nothing, Lief thought, pulling his blanket more tightly around him. But still doubts plagued him, and the night seemed to press in on him, the darkness full of mystery and menace.

Tonight we have all drunk from the stream, he told himself. We have not been drugged by the Dreaming Spring. We will wake if an enemy approaches. Kree is on the watch. And Jasmine says the trees feel we are safe.

But still it was a long time before he could sleep.

And when he did he dreamed of a lonely grave and a dark, bitter man whose face was hidden by a mask. Thick mist swirled about him, now parting, now closing in.

What was behind the mask? Was the man friend, or foe?

8 - The Mountain

The travellers set off again an hour before dawn, Ailsa, Bruna, and Merin leaping from the top of the waterfall to sail through a narrow valley and up into the skies once more. Now they were flying very fast. Their time at Kinrest seemed to have filled them with new energy.

"It is the stream water," Ailsa called to Lief. "For the first time in many years I slept without dreaming — or, at least, without the special dreams the spring gives. This morning I feel like a young one again."

"I too," called Bruna, who was flying beside them. "Though I did stir for a moment in the night. I thought I felt the tribe near. It seemed to me that they were trying to tell me something. But of course I could see and hear nothing, and the feeling soon passed."

She and Ailsa spoke no more, but Lief, watching

Dread Mountain growing larger on the horizon, felt worried. The Kin must have tried very hard to communicate with Bruna, for her to sense their presence. Could they have had news they needed to tell? Alarming news?

He closed his eyes and tried to force himself to relax. He would find out all too soon what Dread Mountain had in store.

✳

By midday the Mountain was looming in front of them — a vast, dark mass filling their view. Its jagged surface was thick with cruel rocks and prickly dark green trees. Clouds were gathering around its peak. A road wound away from its base, disappearing into the range of peaks beyond. The road to the Shadowlands, Lief thought, his stomach churning.

It was impossible to see through the leaves of the thickly clustered trees. Even now the gnomes could have sighted them. They could be hiding, deadly arrows aimed, waiting for the three Kin to come within range. Lief's eyes strained for a glimpse of metal glinting, any sign of movement. He could see nothing, but still he feared.

"This is the dangerous time," Ailsa called to him. "I must begin making it harder for the gnomes to take aim. I was taught to do this long ago, but it is not something you forget. Hold tight!"

She began swooping and wheeling, zooming upward, dropping again. Gasping, holding on for dear life, Lief saw that Merin and Bruna were following Ailsa's lead, making the same sudden movements.

And just in time. Moments later, the first arrow sped towards them, just missing Ailsa. A faint chorus of shrill cries sounded from below. Lief looked down, and his skin crawled. Suddenly the rocks were covered by pale-skinned, hollow-eyed creatures, every one with a fiercely grinning face and a drawn bow. Suddenly hundreds of arrows were hurtling towards them like deadly, upward-flying rain.

Left, right, up, down swooped Ailsa, dodging and swerving but all the time moving forward. Closer they came to the Mountain, and closer, till it seemed that the tops of the trees were rushing to meet them, till it seemed that surely one of the arrows must find its mark.

"All the gnomes are up high, near their stronghold!" Bruna cried. "Land lower down, Kin, lower, where the Boolong trees are thickest. They will not venture there."

The air was filled with the gnomes' high, gobbling shrieks and the soft grunts of the Kin as they threw their huge bodies this way and that. Lief could hear Ailsa's heart pounding, and, faintly, the shouts of Barda and Jasmine, urging Merin and Bruna on.

"Cover your face!" bellowed Ailsa. And with a crash they hit the treetops, smashing through leaves and branches, shattering all in their path to the ground.

✳

"Lief, are you all right?"

Stiffly, Lief uncovered his face and blinked into Ailsa's dark, anxious eyes. He swallowed. "I am very well, thank you," he croaked. "As well as anyone can be who has just crashed through a thorn tree."

Ailsa nodded solemnly. "It was not my best landing," she agreed. "But there are no gaps in the Boolongs here. That is why we are safe from the gnomes. They do not like the thorns."

"I do not love them myself," grunted Barda, who was sitting on the ground beside Jasmine, inspecting several wicked-looking scratches on the backs of his hands. He hauled himself to his feet, went to a narrow stream that gurgled nearby, and began bathing the wounds.

Merin and Bruna had plunged into the thick of the gnarled trees that overhung the trickling water. They were joyously pulling hard little black cones from the clusters of prickly leaves that grew all over the twisted trunks, and crunching them as though they were sweets.

"So these are Boolong trees," Barda went on. "I cannot say I find them pleasing. I have never seen such spines."

"They do not hurt us," said Ailsa. She picked a few clinging leaves from her velvety fur, popped them into her mouth, and chewed with relish, despite the long, needle-sharp thorns at their edges.

"When we lived here there were not so many Boolong trees, and there were many paths winding through them," she went on, with her mouth full. "The streams were wide, and there were clearings everywhere. Without us to feed on them, the Boolongs have grown and spread wonderfully. The cones are full of seed, of course. That is what makes them so tasty!"

Above, there was the rumble of thunder. Ailsa stopped chewing and sniffed the air. Then she hurried over to where Merin and Bruna were still thrashing around, feasting. "We must go!" the companions heard her calling. "A storm is coming. Fill your pouches with cones. We will take them home for the others."

Jasmine shook her head. "The gnomes must have the gem. But I do not know how we are to climb to their stronghold through this thorn forest," she muttered. "We will be cut to pieces if we try. We can only sit here now because the Kin smashed a clearing when they landed."

"Perhaps we could clear a path with fire," Lief suggested.

Kree squawked, Filli chattered nervously, and Jasmine shook her head.

"That would be far too dangerous," she said. "We could never control a fire in woods as thick as these. The blaze could easily burn us all."

The three Kin came towards them, their pouches

bulging with cones and bundles of thorny leaves. They looked as though they had been arguing.

"We came to say farewell," Ailsa said. "We must leave now, so as to be away before the storm breaks. Storms here are fierce and can last for days."

"We should not leave our friends alone so soon!" Merin exclaimed. "There is too much they do not know."

Bruna's whiskers twitched crossly. "Merin, we promised Crenn that we would return as quickly as possible. And if we are marooned here — "

"We would not be marooned!" Merin exclaimed. "This is our place. This is where we should be, for always. I see that, now that I am here." Her eyes were bright with excitement. "We should stay, and the others can join us. The gnomes cannot touch us here, in the lower part of the Mountain."

"Merin, we landed safely by a miracle," Ailsa sighed. "Do you want our friends to take that risk? How many do you think would survive?"

"And even if only half did so," Bruna put in, "the Boolong trees would be eaten back to normal in a few years. Then the paths would be open once more, the gnomes would come back, and the slaughter would start again."

Merin hung her head. "It is cruel," she whispered. But Lief, Barda, and Jasmine could see that she knew her friends were right.

Overhead, the thunder growled. Ailsa glanced nervously at the sky. "There is a big outcrop of rock not far from here," she said rapidly. "I saw it as we landed. It will be quickest if we take off from there. It will be heavy work, but I think we are all strong enough to do it."

With Lief, Barda, and Jasmine following, the three Kin pushed a track up through the Boolong trees. Soon they had reached the rocks and were looking out at open sky. Dark clouds had rolled in from the south.

"The clouds will hide us, once we are safely inside them," Ailsa said. "And if I am right the gnomes will not be looking down here. They will be watching higher up, hoping for more of us to arrive."

"Farewell, then, good Kin," said Barda. "We cannot thank you enough for what you have done for us."

"There is no need for thanks," Bruna answered simply. "All of us are richer for seeing our home again — even for this little time. All we ask is that you take care so that one day we may see you again."

The three bent, touching their heads to Lief's, Barda's, and Jasmine's foreheads. Then they turned, spread their wings, and sprang for the sky.

For a few tense moments, wings beating frantically, they struggled just to stop themselves from crashing back down to earth. The companions watched in breathless silence, sure that at any moment the gnomes would hear the wing beats, look down, fire . . .

But all was well. There were no shouts, no arrows shooting from above, as the Kin at last steadied and began moving forward. Their outlines grew fainter as the clouds closed in around them. Then they were gone.

Barda turned away with a sigh of relief and began scrambling back down the rocks. Lief was about to follow when he caught sight of something out of the corner of his eye. He looked up and to his amazement saw a dark shape emerging unsteadily from the clouds above their heads.

"One of the Kin is returning!" he breathed. "But why so high? Oh, no!"

All of them stared up, aghast, at the Kin blundering into view right in the gnomes' firing line. It was not Ailsa, Bruna, or Merin. It was . . .

"Prin!" hissed Lief in terror.

The little Kin caught sight of the patch of broken trees that marked the others' landing place. She began flying towards it, stubby wings flapping weakly. The next moment there was a high, triumphant shriek and a gale of laughter from further up the Mountain, something was hurtling through the air, and Prin was falling, falling, with an arrow in her chest.

9 ~ Fear

Crying out in horror, Lief, Barda, and Jasmine leaped from the rock and pounded down to the clearing. Prin was struggling feebly on the ground by the stream. Her wings were crumpled beneath her and she was making small, piteous sounds. Her eyes were glazed with pain.

The arrow that had pierced her chest had already fallen out. The wound it had left was small. But the poison the arrow carried had acted swiftly, and its terrible work was nearly done. Prin's agonized eyes closed.

"Foolish child!" groaned Barda. "Jasmine, the — "

"The nectar — " cried Lief at the same moment. But Jasmine was already tearing the tiny jar from around her neck and tipping it over the little Kin's chest. The last golden drops of the nectar of the Lilies of Life fell into the wound. Three drops — no more.

"If this is not enough, there is nothing more we can do," Jasmine muttered, shaking the jar to show that it was empty. She ground her teeth in anger. "Oh, what did they suppose they would gain, shooting at her? They knew she must fall down here, where they could not get to her. Do they kill just for enjoyment?"

"It seems they do," said Barda. "Did you not hear them laughing?"

Lief cradled Prin's head in his arms, calling her back to life as once he had called Barda in the Forests of Silence. As Jasmine had called Kree on the way to the Lake of Tears. As Lief himself had been called in the City of the Rats. The nectar that Jasmine had caught as it dripped from the blooming Lilies of Life so long ago had saved three lives. Would it save another?

Prin stirred. Lief held his breath as the small wound on her chest began to close up and disappear. Her eyes opened. She blinked, looking up at Lief in surprise.

"Did I fall?" she asked.

"Prin, what are you *doing* here?" thundered Lief.

He saw her shrink back and cursed himself, realizing that he had fallen into the trap of letting fear and relief make him angry. Barda had done this not so long ago, in the Shifting Sands, and Lief had resolved that he would never do the same. So much for resolutions, he thought grimly.

"I am sorry, Prin," he said in a gentler voice. "I did not mean to shout. But we have been so afraid for you. Have you flown all this way alone?"

Prin nodded, still eyeing him warily. "I followed you," she said. "I could not bear to miss my only chance to see the Mountain."

She looked around the clearing, drinking in the sight. Her voice was growing stronger by the moment. "I slept near you at Kinrest, and you never knew," she went on gleefully. "But today the others flew so fast that I fell behind. I was so, so tired. And then the clouds came, and I was lost. Then — "

Her eyes widened in sudden terror. She clutched at her chest. Then she looked down and gasped as she saw that there was no wound to be seen.

"I thought I was hurt," she whispered. "But — it must have been a dream."

The companions glanced at one another. "It was no dream," said Lief gently. "You were wounded. But we had — a potion that made you well again."

"You should not have come, Prin," growled Barda. "What would your tribe do if they lost you, their only young one?"

"I knew I would not be lost," said Prin confidently. She clambered to her feet and looked around. "Where is Ailsa?" she asked, bouncing up and down. "And Merin, and Bruna? They will be very surprised to see me! They did not think I could fly so far."

Without waiting for an answer she jumped across the stream and began thrashing around in the trees on the other side, calling.

"She does not realize they have gone," Barda muttered to Lief and Jasmine. "No doubt she expected to return home with them. She will never find her way back alone. Whatever are we to do with her?"

"She will have to come with us," Jasmine said calmly.

"But it is too dangerous!" Lief exclaimed.

Jasmine shrugged. "She chose to come here. She must put up with what happens as a result. The Kin spoil her, and treat her as a baby. But she is not a baby. She is young, but not helpless. She can be useful to us."

She nodded over to where Prin was dancing in the stream, breaking off cones and leaves from the overhanging Boolong trees and eating ravenously. Already the little Kin had cleared a broad space among the prickles.

"You see? She can help us make a path," Jasmine said. "If we follow the stream — "

"It is out of the question," Barda broke in firmly. "I refuse to be burdened by another wilful child who has more energy than sense. Two are quite enough!"

Lief did not take offense at the grim joke as once he would have done, but he did not smile either. The idea of taking Prin up the Mountain was as unpleasing to him as it was to Barda.

Thunder growled above their heads. It had grown very dim in the clearing. The air was thick and heavy.

"Our first task must be to find some shelter," Jasmine said. "The storm — " Suddenly she stiffened, her head on one side. She was listening intently.

"What . . . ?" Lief began softly. Then he realized that the sound of the stream had become louder. It was rising every moment. In seconds it was as though water was rushing towards the clearing. A flood? he thought, confused. But there has been no rain yet, and in any case the sound is coming from downhill. How — ?

Then he forgot everything as he saw Prin standing quite still in the middle of the stream, staring, startled, in the direction of the rushing sound.

"Prin!" he shouted. "Get out! Get out!"

Prin squeaked and half-flew, half-sprang, out of the water and onto the bank. At the same moment there was a roar, and a huge, glistening man-shaped horror came leaping into view, landing exactly where the little Kin had been standing and missing her by a hair. Growling in anger at having been cheated of its prize, the thing swung around, raising its ghastly head.

"Vraal!" Prin shrieked, her voice cracking in terror as she stumbled backwards away from the stream. "Vraal!"

Lief's blood ran cold as he grabbed for his

sword. The Vraal's snakelike scales, dull green striped with yellow, shone evilly in the weak forest light. It was as tall as Barda and twice as wide, with hulking, bowed shoulders, a lashing tail, and powerful arms that ended in claws like curved knives. But the most horrible thing about it was that it seemed to have no face — just a lumpy, scaly mass of flesh, with no eyes, nose, or mouth.

Then it roared. The mass seemed to split in half like an exploding fruit as its jaws gaped red. At the same moment its eyes became visible — burning orange slits glaring through protective ridges and folds. It leaped from the stream, landing on the bank in a single movement.

Now Lief could see that instead of feet it had cloven hoofs that dug deeply into the soft, damp earth. They seemed too delicate to support such a huge body, but as it roared again and sprang forward, Lief put this thought out of his mind.

The creature was a killing machine. That was clear as day. It took no notice of the thunder that rumbled above the trees. Its evil eyes were fixed on Prin.

"Prin! Down!" roared Barda's voice. Terrified into instant obedience, Prin threw herself to the ground as a blister flew above her head towards the Vraal. Barda had hurled the weapon with all his strength, but the creature leaped aside with astounding speed and the blister smashed harmlessly into a tree, the poison inside hissing as it trickled to the ground.

Cursing, Barda threw another blister — the last he had, Lief saw in terror. The big man's aim was true, but again the creature leaped aside just in time, its hoofs digging great holes in the earth, landing firmly in another place. A place away from Prin, but closer to Barda.

Lief saw Prin scramble away and roll into the stream. She would not be safe there! He wanted to call to her to run, but did not want to turn the creature's attention to her. Then, as he hesitated, he realized that the Vraal had forgotten all about the little Kin. Its orange eyes were burning as it turned to face the man it now saw as its chief enemy. The man who had tried to kill it with Grey Guards' poison. The man who now stood facing it, sword drawn.

The creature's lipless mouth stretched in a hideous grin and it hissed as it stretched out its claws, daring Barda to fight.

10 - Fight

B arda stood his ground. He knew that to turn, to step aside, to show any fear at all, would be fatal. Behind him, Lief and Jasmine glanced at each other. The creature moved like lightning. The remaining blisters, which were in Jasmine's keeping, were useless while Barda stood between her and the enemy. The only hope was for her to creep to one side without being seen.

Without warning, the Vraal lashed out. Barda's sword flew up in defense and the creature's claws rang against the shining steel. Barda twisted and lunged, and this time the Vraal defended, hitting the flat of the sword with such a mighty thump that Barda staggered.

Lief sprang to his friend's side, his own sword held high. The Vraal hissed with pleasure. Two foes were even better than one. It had not fought for a long, long time, and fighting was what it had been bred for.

It had missed using its skills. It had missed the joy of battle and the screams of defeated enemies. Snatching squealing, wriggling gnomes from the stream as they bent to drink was no sport. Dodging arrows was too easy. But this — this warmed its cold blood.

Growling, it sprang at the two swords, beating them away effortlessly, driving the two weaklings who held them back, and back. Twice the weapons pierced its armoured skin. It cared nothing for that. It cared nothing for the black bird that dived at its head, snapping with sharp beak then wheeling to dive again.

The Vraal did not fear pain, did not fear death. Its mind was not fitted for such thoughts, or indeed any thoughts but one — that any creatures not of its own species were enemies, to be fought and defeated. In the Shadow Arena or here — it did not matter.

Once only in its life had it lost a fight. But that was long ago, in the Shadowlands. The Vraal no longer remembered the loss, or the pursuit that had left it marooned and wandering in this place. It no longer remembered the Guards who had accompanied it. Their gnawed bones had sunk beneath the earth of the forest long ago. The steel ring that hung from the back of its neck was all that remained of its old life. That, and the need to kill.

It saw that the third enemy, the small female with the dagger in one hand and Guards' poison in the other, was edging from behind the others, moving away. She was going to attack from the side, or from behind. She was moving slowly, carefully. She thought the Vraal, occupied with her companions, would not notice her. She was wrong. It would deal with her presently.

The Vraal sprang suddenly, slashed, and with satisfaction saw the smaller of the two swordsmen falter, and smelled fresh, red blood. The smell stirred vague memories of times long past. Gnomes' blood was thin and bitter, like stale green water. This was better. Much better.

The little one, the female, was clear of the others now. Where was she? The Vraal opened one of its side eyes. Deeply buried in ridges of scaly skin over its ear slits, the side eyes did not see quite as well as the eyes at the front, but they were useful.

Ah, yes, there she was. Raising her arm, taking aim. Time to dispatch her. A single lash of the tail . . . there!

As the female fell, the black bird flying above her head screeched and the injured swordsman cried out — a single word. The Vraal understood few words and did not know this one, but it knew fear and grief when it heard them. The Vraal grinned, its mouth stretching wide.

"Jasmine!" Lief shouted again. But Jasmine lay

where she had fallen, silent and still as death.

Barda cried out in warning. Lief ducked the Vraal's swinging claws just in time and staggered, falling backwards, hitting the ground hard. He scrambled to his knees. His head was pounding. The breath was sobbing in his throat. Blood was streaming from the long cut in his arm. He could barely hold his sword.

"Lief," panted Barda, leaping in front of him and beating the Vraal back as it lunged again, kicking with hard, deadly hooves. "Go! Get the Belt away!"

"I will not leave you," Lief gasped. "And Jasmine — "

"Do as I tell you!" Barda roared savagely. "You are injured. No use to either of us. Get away! Now!"

Furiously he swung his great sword, attacking with all his strength, pushing the Vraal back one step . . . two.

Lief began to crawl painfully away. Spines from the fallen, smashed Boolong trees pierced his hands, stinging and burning. He staggered to his feet and took a few more steps. Then he stopped and turned.

Flight was useless. There was nowhere to go, nowhere to hide. When the Vraal had finished with Barda it would come after him. Better, surely, to die fighting here than to die cringing among the Boolong trees, crushed into the thorns.

A flash of lightning lit the clearing for an instant, showing the scene in hideous clarity. Barda battling with the gleaming, hulking Vraal, Jasmine lying motionless on the ground. And Prin . . . Prin toiling from the stream, her eyes enormous with fear, her front paws clasped together in front of her, clutching a mess of purple slime. As Lief watched, amazed, she spread her wings.

Then the air exploded with a terrible clap of thunder. The very earth seemed to shake. Barda faltered, lost his footing, and fell to one knee. The Vraal sprang, its slitted orange eyes gleaming. With one swipe of its huge arm it beat away the big man's sword. The gleaming steel turned in the air, once, twice, and fell to the ground far out of reach, its point buried in the earth. The Vraal hissed, grinning, preparing for the kill.

"Barda!" Lief cried out in agony. He staggered forward. But Prin — suddenly Prin was springing forward and up, straight at the Vraal, landing squarely on the back of its neck and clinging there, slime-filled paws wrapped around its head, wings flapping wildly.

The Vraal roared and staggered. Its terrible claws flailed around its head, now smeared all over with purple. Prin leaped backwards, landing on her strong back legs and stumbling back to the stream, her paws, still purple-streaked, held out in front of her.

"No, Prin! Run into the trees! It will see you there!" shouted Lief.

But he was wrong. The Vraal was seeing nothing. It threw back its head, screaming in rage and pain.

"It is the moss!" sobbed Prin, frantically washing her paws. "In its eyes, its ears! The purple moss! The green moss cures, the purple moss harms. They told me! They told me so often, and it is true!"

Lightning flashed and there was another huge clap of thunder. Then, as if the sky had cracked open, rain began pelting down — hard, icy rain mixed with hail. Barda staggered to his feet and stumbled towards his sword. Lief also gathered his wits and started forward. On the ground, Jasmine stirred as Kree screeched frantically.

But the Vraal had had enough. With a final roar it turned and, as Prin jumped aside, it blundered blindly to the stream, fell into it, and splashed away.

*

Later, soaked, exhausted, and chilled to the bone, the companions crouched together in the shelter of a small cave made by a rock that overhung the stream. Stinging hail still pounded the earth outside. They had managed to light a fire, but so far it was doing little to warm them. There was not one of them, however, who felt like complaining.

"I thought our hour had come," said Barda, lighting a torch by dipping it into the fire. "That beast would not have stopped until all of us were dead. Lief — how is your arm?"

"It feels much better already," Lief said. He was

lying with his back propped against his pack. His injured arm was bound with what looked like a green bandage, but was in fact clumps of green moss taken fresh from the stream and tied in place with vines.

Having seen the moss's effect on the Vraal, and the terrible blisters it had raised on Prin's paws, Lief had at first been unwilling to have it near him. But Prin had assured him that the moss in its green state had amazing healing powers, and to prove it she had padded her own burned skin with the stuff, and asked Jasmine to bind it on tightly.

"Often I have heard the others speak of the green-purple moss," she said now, as Barda raised the torch to send light and shadows leaping around the cave. "The gnomes use it for their wounds, and Kin who were injured by Vraal in the old days could be saved by green moss also. It is only when the moss is old and water-soaked, when it has fallen under the edge of the rocks that line the stream and has turned purple, that it clings and burns. Of course, it is not a real poison, like the gnomes use on their arrows. It only troubles Vraal in their eyes and ears. And even they recover quickly. Our Vraal will be ready to fight again in a few days."

Lief glanced at her. She smiled at him, her padded paws tucked into her pouch for warmth and comfort. "You were very brave, Prin," he said. "You saved us all. Your people would be very proud of you."

"Indeed," Jasmine said warmly, and Filli chattered agreement.

Prin sat up a little straighter. "The Kin have always used the purple moss to defend themselves from the Vraal and Grey Guards who used to come here in great numbers," she said, plainly proud of her knowledge. "Mother and Crenn have told me about it, many times."

"I wonder then that Ailsa, Bruna, and Merin did not show it to us," Jasmine said, frowning.

Prin shook her head. "In their dreaming they have never seen a prowling Vraal, or a Grey Guard either," she said. "In the mornings they speak only of the Boolong trees. They think the gnomes are the only dangers on the Mountain now."

"Perhaps that is the trouble with dreaming," Barda said slowly. "You see only what the dream shows you, and then for only a little time. For example, did your people ever tell you, Prin, of seeing a traveller of our kind on the Mountain?"

The little Kin shook her head. "They say no one comes here now. They say the gnomes' poison arrows keep everyone away."

"Not everyone, it seems," said Barda quietly. He jerked his head towards the back of the cave and held the torch high.

Everyone turned to look. Lief drew a sharp breath. There were faded words on the pale, soft stone. Written, Lief was sure, in blood:

WHO AM I?
ALL IS DARKNESS. BUT I
WILL NOT DESPAIR.
THREE THINGS I KNOW;
I KNOW I AM A MAN.
I KNOW WHERE I HAVE BEEN.
I KNOW WHAT I MUST DO
FOR NOW, THAT IS ENOUGH.

11 - Mysteries

Lief, Barda, and Jasmine stared at the scrawled words on the cave wall. All of them were imagining the lonely, suffering man who, it seemed, had used his own blood to write the message.

Why had he written it? To keep himself sane, perhaps, thought Lief. To convince himself that, in the nightmare of terror and confusion that his life had become, some things were real. That he himself was real.

"Who was he?" breathed Jasmine. "Where is he now?"

"Dead, perhaps," said Barda. "If he was wounded, then — "

"He did not die here, at least, for the cave is empty of bones," Lief broke in. "Perhaps he recovered, and escaped from the Mountain." He found himself hoping against hope that this was so.

"He says, 'I know where I have been,' " Jasmine

75

murmured. "Surely that means that he came here from somewhere else, not long before he wrote the message."

"He could have come from the Shadowlands, like the Vraal," Prin put in helpfully.

"That is impossible. No one escapes from the Shadowlands," Barda growled.

Lief leaned back, his head suddenly swimming. He felt Jasmine's hand on his arm and struggled to look at her.

"You have lost much blood, Lief," she said, in a voice that sounded far away. "That is why you feel weak. Do not fight the urge to sleep. Barda and I will keep watch. Do not fear."

Lief wanted to speak — to tell her that he too would take his turn to keep watch. To say that she had been knocked unconscious by the Vraal and was also in need of rest. To beg her to make sure that Prin stayed safe. But his eyelids would not stay open, and his mouth would not form the words. So at last he simply did as she asked, and slept.

✳

The storm raged on all that night and through the next day. Thunder roared without ceasing. The hail became icy rain. Wind lashed the Boolong trees, and many crashed to the ground.

The companions could do nothing but stay huddled in their shelter, eating, resting, drinking from the stream that rushed by the cave's opening, taking turns to keep watch. By the time night fell again they were fretting about the delay. Lief's arm and Prin's paws were healing wonderfully, and they feared that the Vraal might be recovering just as quickly.

"Only if it has learned that the green moss heals," Prin reminded them, nibbling a Boolong cone. "And I do not think that is likely. Vraal are clever only in fighting and killing, Mother says."

At the mention of her mother her voice faltered, and she swallowed hard.

"It is very fortunate for us that you were with us when the Vraal came. But your mother, and the other Kin, must be worried about you, Prin," said Lief after a moment.

"They know I am safe," Prin said softly. "I am sure they visited us last night, in their dreams."

She looked around. "And now it is night again. They could be here at this very moment. They would all fit, because, after all, it is only a dream." She bent her head. "If they *were* here, I would tell them I was sorry for causing them pain," she murmured. "And I would say I missed them very much."

The others were silent. It was eerie to think that they might be surrounded by Kin spirits, yearning to speak to Prin, to touch her, but unable to do so. It was sad to realize that Prin was deliberately saying aloud the words she wanted her family to hear, just in case.

✳

By the following morning, the wind had died and the storm had retreated, leaving steady, light rain in its place. The travellers decided that it was time to move on.

They began climbing through the rain in single file, following the swollen stream, alert for the sound of the gnomes above them and the Vraal below. The way was steep, slippery, and dangerous. Prin went first, doing the best she could to beat a safe path, but despite her best efforts the companions were soon covered in scratches.

After an hour or two of this miserable tramping, the rain stopped and a few weak rays of sun began to struggle through the clouds.

"That is something, at least," muttered Barda. Then he jumped as Prin stopped suddenly in front of him and darted off the path.

"What is it?" whispered Jasmine from behind.

"I do not know!" Barda whispered back irritably. "Prin! What are you doing?"

Prin had disappeared into the trees and was thrashing around, breaking down branches with new energy and purpose. "Come and see!" she called softly to them, after a moment.

Unwillingly, shielding their faces from the thorns, they crept into the small, cleared area she had made. Then they stopped, staring.

Right in the center of the clearing was a small round stone hut roofed with bark. Two rusted metal spikes stood on either side of the low door, each crowned by a grinning skull. To the door itself was fixed a beaten metal shape.

"I am sure this is a gnome-rest," Prin whispered. "The huts where gnomes shelter if they are caught out in storms. They are forbidden to strangers. That is what the sign means. But — "

She looked at them anxiously.

"But this has been abandoned for a very long time," Barda reassured her. "You were right to un-cover it." He strode to the door and pulled at it. It sagged open and the companions went inside.

If they had hoped to find weapons, they were disappointed. The little building was festooned with webs and crawling with spiders and beetles. Other-wise it was empty except for a few mugs, some woven rugs which had almost rotted away, and a pile of what had probably once been food, but which was now black dust.

"It is strange," murmured Prin, as they backed out again with relief. "Mother told me that in the old days there were gnome-rests scattered all over the Mountain, all of them linked by paths that criss-crossed everywhere. But this is the first gnome-rest we have seen, and it was completely overgrown by the trees."

Lief looked around at the dark and silent forest that surrounded the clearing. "The Boolong trees have run wild since the Kin left. But that cannot be the only reason why the gnomes have abandoned their build-ings and their paths. Surely they would have fought to save some of them, at least."

Jasmine too had been looking around her. "Something else has happened. Some change we do not know about," she said slowly.

There was a sound behind them. Prin glanced over her shoulder nervously, then gave a start. Barda had begun pulling sheets of bark from the roof of the little hut. Already three large pieces lay beside him on the ground.

"Oh, do not do that!" she begged, hurrying over to him. "The gnomes will be angry. Do you not see their warning sign?"

"I care nothing for that," snorted Barda, pulling a fourth sheet onto the ground. "They have already shown they are our enemies. In any case, they have plainly abandoned this hut to the forest. And this bark will be very useful to us."

Prin stared at him, and Lief and Jasmine also raised their eyebrows in surprise. Smiling, Barda tapped the bark sheets with his foot. "This is Boolong bark," he said. "See how hard it is? Yet it is light to carry, and slightly curved too. With vines to bind them, these pieces will make excellent shields. Shields that will stop any arrow — and will protect us from the Boolong thorns."

They spent the next half hour binding vine strongly around the bark pieces so that they could be held easily from the back. Standing behind their shields' protection all the companions felt safer.

"You must always carry your shield in your weaker hand," Barda instructed. "Then your strong hand is left free for fighting. It is tiring at first, but you will soon get used to — "

He broke off, startled, as Jasmine suddenly jumped up and raised her finger to her lips. "I hear voices," she breathed. "And feet. Marching feet."

Lief and Barda listened carefully and at last heard a faint, buzzing, rhythmic sound, like harsh chanting or singing, coming from further down the Mountain.

"Gnomes," whimpered Prin.

The sound was coming closer, growing louder by the moment.

12 - The Way Up

They pushed deep into the trees and crouched together in a tight circle, their shields held up around them like a wall. The sound of gruff singing and feet marching in time grew louder. Yet there was no noise of cracking branches or of weapons slashing at spiny leaves, and the marching feet did not hesitate as they passed by somewhere just out of sight.

"There must be a road nearby," Barda breathed.

As the singing began to fade away into the distance, the companions crept from their hiding place and began forcing a path in the direction from which the sound had come. Sure enough, in a short time they found themselves standing on a narrow track that wound away towards the top. It was so overhung with tree branches that it was like a tunnel.

Lief groaned. "We might have known that the

gnomes would keep at least one path clear. No doubt this trail leads all the way from the bottom of the Mountain to the top! If only we had found it before!"

"That troop of gnomes must have been at the bottom of the Mountain before the storm struck," Barda said. "I wonder what business they had there? Bad business, I suspect, for the only thing at the Mountain's base is the road to the Shadowlands."

"But the gnomes are not friends of the Grey Guards," squeaked Prin, speaking up for the first time since they heard the sound of marching feet. "They hate them, and plague them with evil tricks. Mother told me about it often. Those skulls by the gnome-rest — they are probably Guards' skulls."

"Many years have passed since your mother lived on Dread Mountain, Prin," Lief said gently. "Now the gnomes are allies of the Shadow Lord."

Prin shook her head, but perhaps the last few days had helped her to grow up a little, because she did not go on arguing, insisting that she was right. Instead she simply gripped her shield more firmly and followed as the companions began the long climb towards the Mountain top.

※

The sun was going down and it was growing very cold when finally they reached the end of the road. The climb had been hard, but without trouble of any kind. Not a single gnome had crossed their path. And now, as they peered cautiously around the last bend, they could see no sign of life or movement. All was utterly still.

"Where are they hiding? Be ready. We may be walking into a trap," muttered Barda. But nothing stirred, and no arrows flew, as they began to cross the cleared space beyond the road, looking up at the towering cliff of rock that now barred their way.

There were no trees here. The earth on which they walked was bare, white chalky stuff, packed hard by the tread of feet, littered with discarded arrows. The top of the Mountain, hidden in swirling clouds, was still high above their heads.

Jasmine summoned Kree to her shoulder and drew her dagger. "It is some sort of trick," she whispered. "The gnomes we heard could not have disappeared. And the others — the ones who shot at us when we landed — were here. Somewhere, they are waiting."

The cliff rose dark and ominous before them. At first they could see nothing odd about it except for a few small holes dotted over its surface. But as soon as they drew close enough, they saw where the gnomes had gone.

There was a narrow door in the cliff, carved from solid rock. It was dark at the top, light at the bottom. No attempt had been made to disguise it — in fact, the larger pale section had been decorated with grooved lines, and at one side there was a round stone doorknob which had a deep carving in the shape of an arrow in its center. But the knob would not turn, and pull and push as they would, the door would not open.

"Gnome tricks!" growled Barda, running his fingers over the stone and pressing vainly here and there.

"Why do you want to get in?" Prin whispered nervously. "Surely this is the gnomes' stronghold. Where they eat and sleep. And where they keep their treasure."

"Exactly," Barda frowned, still testing the stone.

"The decorations are only on the bottom part of the door, the light part," said Lief. "That may be a clue."

He moved very close to the cliff and peered at the seemingly empty space at the top of the door. The dark, uneven rock blurred before his eyes, but he was sure he could make out marks that were not natural.

"There is something carved here," he muttered. "Words, I think. But they are so small, and the rock is so dark, that I cannot make them out."

He pulled his cloak and his shirt aside to uncover the Belt of Deltora and noticed at once that the ruby's rich red had faded to dull pink — a sign that danger threatened. I do not need warning of that, he thought grimly. I know only too well that we are going into danger.

His fingers moved towards the topaz. It had sharpened his wits before. Perhaps it would help him now.

But before he had even touched the gem an idea came to him. He bent, scraped up a handful of the white dust beneath his feet, and smeared it over the dark rock. Then he brushed the loose dust away. The dust that remained caught in the carved letters made them show quite clearly:

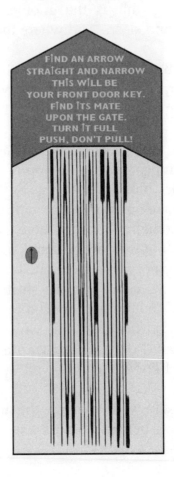

FIND AN ARROW
STRAIGHT AND NARROW
THIS WILL BE
YOUR FRONT DOOR KEY.
FIND ITS MATE
UPON THE GATE.
TURN IT FULL
PUSH, DON'T PULL!

"This rhyme is very childish," frowned Jasmine. "It reminds me of rhymes my father taught me when I was very young. And it was not difficult to make the words visible. These gnomes are not so clever."

"They are careless too," said Barda, picking up an arrow from the ground. "If arrows are keys to their door, they should not leave them lying around. And as for finding the arrow's mate upon the gate . . ."

He dug the point of the arrow into the carving on the doorknob. The arrow slid into place easily, like a key slipping into a lock. As Barda had suspected, there was a keyhole at the bottom of the carving. Gripping the shaft of the arrow firmly, he turned it until there was a slight but definite click.

"It is unlocked. Shall we go in?" he asked, turning to his companions and drawing his sword.

"No!" Prin begged, unable to keep silent any longer. "You say the gnomes are not clever, but they are, they are! They love tricks and traps. This is their door. If we use it we will die. I know it!"

"We must enter the stronghold, Prin," said Lief firmly. "The gnomes have something hidden here that we must find. But you need not enter with us. You can return to the path and keep watch."

He drew his own sword and nodded to Barda, who began to push firmly on the door. With a harsh, grating sound, the great piece of stone began to swing inward.

And just then Lief thought he heard, from somewhere high above them, a muffled giggle. He grasped Barda's arm and held it. "Wait!" he hissed.

Jasmine had heard the sound too. She was looking up, peering intently at the cliff face. "There is no one to be seen," she whispered. "But I am sure I heard someone laugh."

"It was a birdcall, perhaps," said Barda. He stood, undecided, his hand still on the door.

Kree squawked.

"It was not a bird," Jasmine said flatly. "It was someone laughing. At us."

They stood in tense silence for a moment, listening. But once again the Mountain was utterly still, as though it was waiting.

Barda shrugged, grasped his sword more tightly, and pushed the door again. The grating sound grew louder as the slab of rock moved inward. A narrow gap appeared between the door and the cliff wall. From somewhere beyond the gap, light flickered.

Jasmine peered through the crack. "I can see no one," she murmured. "Beyond the door there is a small room, with a passage leading from it. It is the passage that is lit."

She looked around at them, her small face full of defiance, her dagger glinting in her hand. "I think we should enter," she said grimly. "Then whoever is laughing at us may wish they had kept silence." She put her shoulder against the door and pushed to open it further. Then she turned to Lief. "Are you coming?" she demanded.

Lief stepped forward. But at the same moment Prin bounded in front of him. "No!" she begged. "No, Lief! You at least must not!" Taken by surprise, Lief stumbled, lost his footing, and fell heavily.

He lay on the ground, dazed, staring up at the door. The grooved lines, tall on the pale stone, seemed to shimmer above him. Then — then, to his astonishment, he suddenly saw them for what they were.

Words. The lines were words. He blinked, hardly believing what he was seeing. But it was true. The letters had been stretched tall and narrowed so much that he had not realized they were any more than decoration. But looking at them from below, he could read what they said.

IF YOU WISH TO DIE.

"Lief, I am sorry . . ." Prin was bending over him anxiously.

Barda was staring at them, his hand on the stone. But Jasmine, shaking her head impatiently, was stepping through the door.

"Jasmine — " Lief spluttered, scrambling to his feet. "Do not go in. Jasmine! It is a trap!"

He leaped forward, catching Jasmine by the wrist just as, with a cry, she plunged into the pit that yawned beyond the door.

13 - Within

Jasmine swung helplessly, Lief's grip on her wrist the only thing that was saving her from crashing to the bottom of the trap into which she had stumbled.

The pit was deep, but still Lief could see a white glimmer at the bottom. His stomach turned over as he realized they were bones — the bones of other intruders, no doubt. The gnomes had probably been watching through peepholes in the rock as the companions tried to open the door. One had laughed aloud, believing that there were about to be three more victims of the deadly joke. Lief gritted his teeth in anger.

Then Barda was kneeling beside him, and together they were lifting Jasmine up, swinging her to safety.

"We must do the opposite of what the verse

says," said Lief. "We must pull the door, not push it, if we are to enter safely."

They pulled the door until it clicked shut. Then they unlocked it with the arrow once more, and pulled again. Sure enough, the huge piece of stone grated as easily outward as it had inward.

Barda picked up a few arrows and threw them into the darkness where the pit had been. They clanged on metal.

"It is as I thought," said Lief. "The pit is usually covered. It is only when the door is pushed inward that the cover slides away."

"A devilish device," growled Barda. "If you and I had not hesitated, Lief — "

"I *told* you the gnomes were clever," Prin broke in. "They are clever, hate strangers, and love cruel jokes. We must be very, very careful. If they are still watching, they know their trick has failed. They will try something else."

This time no one argued with her.

They entered the door, tapping the earth in front of them with their shields to check it for safety, listening for any sound of movement. But all was silence. Ahead was the long tunnel they had seen from the entrance.

Their faces ghostly in the light of the flickering torches, they began to creep along the tunnel. Only Jasmine and Prin could stand upright, and even they had to bend their heads. Soon the tunnel turned sharply, and almost at once turned again. Then they came to a place where it split into three. One passage led to the left, one led to the right, and one led straight ahead.

"Which way?" whispered Lief.

"There is no way of telling which path is safest," growled Barda. "But I think we should take the one that goes straight ahead. It has a higher ceiling than the others. If we take either of the other two, I will have to crawl."

They moved on. Still there was utter silence. They saw that just ahead the tunnel once again took a sharp right turn.

"Perhaps, after all, the gnomes think we are in the pit," said Jasmine in a low voice, as they moved around the corner into dimmer light.

"Perhaps," Barda answered grimly. "But I would not depend upon it. I think — "

He broke off and halted abruptly. There were some shadowy figures ahead, blocking their path. Barda and Lief raised their swords. An answering glint showed that their opponents were also armed, and by their shape carried shields also.

"Dread Gnomes, we come in peace," Barda called. "We ask only that you listen to what we have to say. We will put down our weapons if you also will disarm."

There was no answering call, and no movement except for the gleam of steel.

"We must not let them think we are afraid," Jasmine whispered, and slowly the companions began to move forward again. The figures moved also, coming to meet them, matching them stride for stride.

"Why do you not answer?" Barda called again. "Do you want to fight? If so, we are ready and willing." He quickened his pace. Lief and Jasmine strode after him. Shuffling behind them, trying to keep up, Prin gave a muffled whimper of fear.

In moments the figures were almost upon them, still shadowy, but looming large. They are much bigger than we expected. And there are four of them, Lief thought, tightening his grip on his sword.

Hand-to-hand combat. He had not expected this. But he was ready. He lifted his shield. One of his opponents did the same. And suddenly, suddenly Lief saw . . .

"Barda, it is a mirror! A mirror fixed to a wall!" he shouted. "This tunnel is a dead end!" A chill ran through his body as he heard a clicking sound behind him. He spun around, stumbling over Prin, trying to push past her, trying to get to the metal door that was sliding from the roof of the tunnel at her back.

But it was too late. By the time he reached it, the metal door was sealed shut. They were trapped. They were locked in an airless cell. A cell as escape-proof as a tomb.

*

Hours later, they stood huddled together in thick darkness. They had put out the torch that was fixed to the wall. It was burning air they could not afford to lose.

"There must be a way out," Lief insisted. "There must!" He was swaying with weariness.

"The gnomes will come, surely," muttered Barda. "To jeer at us, if for no other reason. For what is the point of a joke no one laughs at? That will be our chance, for if they can get in, we can certainly get out."

Jasmine nodded. "We must be ready for them. We must have a plan. But when will they come? And how? If only we knew!"

"If we were at home, we could dream them," said a small voice behind them.

They all turned. They had almost forgotten about Prin. She crouched in a corner, her eyes enormous with fear, her paws clasped tightly in front of her.

"If we were at home with my tribe, we could drink the spring water, and remember the gnomes, and dream of them, wherever they are," she repeated softly. "We have seen them. Seen their faces . . ." Her voice trailed away and she began shivering all over. She heard Lief exclaim, and covered her face in shame.

"I am sorry," she whispered. "I have never been in walls before. I do not like it."

Filli chattered anxiously. Jasmine moved to

Prin's side and put her arm around her. "Do not be ashamed," she murmured. "I too fear being locked up. I fear it more than anything."

"You are very tired, little Kin," said Barda, with rough gentleness. "Lie down and sleep now. You can dream even without the spring water."

"But *with* it, how much more useful the dreams will be!" Lief burst out. As they all glanced at him curiously he grinned and held up his water bottle. "Do you not remember? I confess that I did not, until Prin reminded me just now. We have drunk from streams ever since we left the Kin. Our bottles are still full — with water from the Dreaming Spring!"

✳

Out of the mists of Lief's sleep, the dream slowly came into focus. Flickering light, dancing colors, a dull murmuring, the shuffling of many feet, clinking, chinking sounds . . . And one huge voice, terrifyingly loud, shockingly harsh, echoing, echoing . . . "MORE! GIVE ME MORE!"

Lief opened his eyes fully, stared, revolted, at the nightmare before him, and staggered back to press himself against the rocky wall. I am dreaming, he reminded himself wildly. Dreaming! I am here only in spirit. It cannot see me!

But still his heart thudded and his stomach churned. Whatever he had expected when he lay down to sleep, it was not this!

He had expected to see a cavern, though not so huge. The roof of this enormous space soared, surely, to the top of the Mountain.

He had expected to see treasure, though not in such great quantities. Great, glittering mounds of gold and jewels filled the cavern from wall to wall, rising into hills and dropping into valleys like the dunes of the Shifting Sands.

He had expected to see the gnomes he had seen on the mountaintop, though he had not thought to see them crawling, scuttling, shrinking, and afraid.

But the giant mass of lumpy, oozing flesh that squatted in the center of the cavern, its wicked eyes glazed with greed, its slimy clawed feet spread carelessly over tumbled gems and heaps of gold — this was something he had not expected. Not in his wildest imaginings.

It was a vast, toadlike beast. The hidden horror of Dread Mountain.

14 - Gellick

Gnomes crawled around the giant, collecting in great glass jars the slime that dripped from its skin like thick, oily drops of sweat. They all wore gloves and kept well away from the oozing drops, handling the jars with care.

The slime must be poisonous, thought Lief. Then, with a jolt, he realized that here must be the source of the venom that made the gnomes' arrows deadly.

As he watched, two other gnomes scuttled forward, bent under the weight of a huge golden bowl heaped high with what looked like black, glistening berries.

They knelt before the toad, heads bowed. Its long red tongue snaked out and curled in the black mass, scooping up a quarter of the contents of the bowl. As it lifted the feast to its huge mouth, scattering fragments carelessly over the gnomes and the treasure at its feet, Lief's stomach heaved. The food was not berries, but flies. Thousands — tens of thousands — of fat, dead flies.

In moments the bowl was empty. The toad gave a rasping growl of anger. "MORE! QUICKLY!" it roared.

The two kneeling gnomes cowered, glancing at each other fearfully. "Your pardon, great Gellick," faltered the one on the left, a wizened old man in a tattered brown jacket. "But — it may take some time to collect more from the breeding caves. The ready supplies are gone."

"WHAT? GONE? WHO IS RESPONSIBLE FOR THIS?" grated the toad.

The old gnome was trembling all over, but finally forced himself to speak. "It is just that you have eaten rather more today than usual, great Gellick," he quavered. "We were not prepared. We — "

His words were choked by a shriek as the toad spat at him without warning. He fell to the ground, writhing in agony. His terrified companion, wailing in grief and terror, dropped facedown beside him, clasping him in her arms as he died.

The other gnomes watched dumbly. On some faces Lief saw guilty thankfulness, because it was the old gnome who had been attacked, not them. On other faces there was sorrow and anger. But on most there was simply dull, blank hopelessness.

"Things on Dread Mountain are not as we thought," said Barda's voice behind him.

Startled, Lief swung around. Barda and Jasmine were standing near him. He could see them quite clearly, though they were shadowy and their outlines seemed to waver. Jasmine, for once without Filli and Kree, who had not drunk the dreaming water, was pale with disgust and anger.

"This is a vile thing," she muttered. "This Gellick rules the gnomes as the Wennbar ruled the Wenn in the Forests of Silence. But it is much worse. It kills not for food, but for spite alone."

"The gem we seek must be here," Barda said. "But how are we to find it? The cavern is piled high with precious stones."

Lief shook his head, amazed that he could have forgotten their quest, even for a moment. But forgotten it he had. The toad Gellick had absorbed all his attention.

Now he could feel that the Belt of Deltora had warmed against his skin. The fifth gem was here, in this cavern. But where?

"We will not be in a position to find the gem at all, if we do not get out of the prison they have us in!" Jasmine whispered fiercely.

"We must wait, and listen," Barda answered. "That is why we are here."

They watched as the body of the old gnome was dragged away by his sobbing companion. Slowly the other gnomes went back to their work of attending to the glass jars that collected the toad's slime. As each jar was filled, two gnomes carried it between them through a door near to where the companions were standing.

"Once we were a proud people," Lief heard one of these gnomes mutter disgustedly, as she passed. "Once we owned this treasure, and the Mountain was beautiful, fruitful and ours. Now we are slaves on a nest of thorns, farming flies for a toad."

"DID YOU SPEAK, GLA-THON?" The harsh voice filled the cavern.

The gnome who had spoken spun around hastily. "No. No, great Gellick," she lied. "Or, at least, if I did speak, it was only to say that the intruders — the intruders we told you about — are safely locked in the tomb-tunnel, and will not escape."

"THEY MUST DIE!"

"Oh, they will die, my lord," said another gnome, stepping forward and smoothing his red beard. "The simpler ones among us have been watching them, enjoying their feeble efforts to escape. But the sport has ended now for they have put out the light. By morning they will be dead through lack of air. Then we will drag them into the breeding caves, and the flies can have them."

He beamed, bowing low. "And soon you, great Gellick, will have the flies," he added. "It is a fine progress, is it not?"

The giant toad almost seemed to smile. "You are clever, Ri-Nan," it growled. "But not clever enough, it seems, to ensure that my food is brought to me on time, as was the bargain."

Its voice was low now, and husky. But somehow this was even more terrible than its loudest roar. Its eyes gleamed with malice. The red-bearded gnome backed away, the smile that still lingered on his lips stiffening into a snarl of fear.

"You deserve punishment, Ri-Nan," rasped Gellick softly. "But you are useful to me, so perhaps I will forgive you. Or perhaps I will not. I will think on it. In the meantime, take the rest of these miserable slaves to the breeding caves and work there with them for the rest of the night. Tomorrow there will be flies enough — or you will suffer for it."

Ri-Nan scuttled for the door, stumbling over the piles of treasure in his haste, beckoning to the other gnomes to follow him. In moments, the cavern was still.

Satisfied, the monster settled itself more comfortably and licked some stray flies from its lips. It half-closed its eyes and lowered its great head.

And it was then that Lief saw the dull green stone sunk into its brow and, with a thrill of horror, knew it for what it was.

The emerald. The symbol of honor. The fifth gem of the Belt of Deltora.

The companions woke together in the heavy darkness of their prison. It was like waking from a nightmare, a nightmare they had all shared. And yet — they knew only too well that what they had seen was real.

"Did you discover anything of use?" they heard Prin ask eagerly, as she heard them stir.

Jasmine crawled to her feet. "One thing we learned is that before we put out the light the gnomes were watching us," she said. "But how? I am sure there is not a gap or hole anywhere in this accursed cell."

Feeling her way, she began examining the walls, the roof, and even the floor again, leaving it to Barda and Lief to tell Prin the rest of the story. They told it as gently as they could, but by the time they had finished the little Kin was again shivering with fear.

"Never have I heard of such a thing," she whispered. "My people know nothing of it. So this is why the gnome-rests and paths are so badly overgrown, and why the gnomes look so sickly pale. They are underground almost all the time, collecting this toad's poison for their arrows, and serving his needs."

"I think you are right," muttered Lief.

They heard Jasmine stamping her foot in anger. "I can find nothing!" she hissed. "Not the tiniest crack."

"If there *was* a crack, there would be air," said Lief drearily. "And there is no air."

"But they *watched* us!" Jasmine insisted. "It

sounded as though many watched at once, laughing at our foolish efforts to escape. That gnome Gla-Thon spoke of it as if it was as easy as staring through a window!"

Barda gave a muffled cry, and scrambled to his feet. "Why, perhaps it was!" he whispered.

"What do you mean?" Jasmine demanded. "There is no window here!"

"No window we can see," said Barda. He edged past Lief to put his fingers against the mirror.

"I once heard a traveller tell of a miracle he had seen: a glass that was a mirror on one side and a window on the other," he said. "I thought he was just making up tall tales to earn free drinks at the tavern. But perhaps I was unjust."

"There is only one way to find out," Lief said quietly.

"Quite so," Barda agreed. "And there is no time like the present. Draw your weapons and stand back."

He set one of the bark shields against the mirror, drew back his heavy boot, and kicked with all his strength. The mirror shattered, crashing out into a room beyond the cell. Dazzling light flooded through the gap — light, and air, and a smell so foul, so disgusting, that the companions choked as they stepped forward blindly, broken glass crunching under their feet.

"What is it?" coughed Jasmine, pressing her arm to her nose. "And what is that noise?"

103

But already their eyes were growing used to the light, and their stomachs churned as they saw what the room contained. Vast, netted cages lined the walls. And inside the cages were millions upon millions of flies, buzzing around stinking piles of rotting food.

"It is one of the breeding caves," said Lief. "Let us leave quickly. The gnomes may appear at any moment."

They hurried to the door and let themselves out into a dim tunnel. The sickening smell of decay still hung in the air. They could hear voices echoing from somewhere to their right. They turned to the left, but had not gone far when a door in front of them was thrown open and two gnomes came hurrying out, each carrying one end of a large wooden box.

The companions froze, then began backing away.

One of the gnomes, who Lief recognized as the red-bearded Ri-Nan, looked around, saw them, and yelled, dropping his corner of the box. His fellow stumbled and roared in anger as the box fell, hitting the stone floor sharply and splitting open. Dead flies spilled from it in a hideous, glistening stream.

"The intruders are escaping!" shrieked Ri-Nan. He threw back his head and gave the high, gobbling cry that the gnomes had used on the Mountainside when they were shooting at the Kin. Instantly the tunnel was filled with the echoing sound of pounding feet, coming from both directions.

"Back!" shouted Barda.

They ran for the door of the breeding cave they had just left. It was very near, but by the time they reached it both ends of the tunnel were filled with running gnomes, raising their bows, closing in on them.

Arrows had already begun to fly as Lief and Barda pushed Prin inside the cave and hurled themselves after her. They were safe, but Jasmine was not so lucky. As she leaped through the doorway she gave a shriek, and the gnomes howled in triumph.

She stumbled into the cave and fell back against the door, slamming it shut. Barda sprang to slide the bolt home. Lief caught Jasmine and dragged her aside as she slithered to the ground, pulling the quivering arrow from the palm of her hand.

15 - The Dread Gnomes

The wound was slight. The arrow had caught just under the skin. But Jasmine lay back, her eyes squeezed shut, gasping in agony as the poison surged through her body. Lief and Barda crouched over her, helpless and grief-stricken, as Filli moaned and Kree screeched.

"Why do you wait?" shrieked Prin. "Give her the potion! The magic potion that saved me!"

"There is none left," snapped Barda. "You had the last of it."

Prin shrank back, trembling.

Jasmine's eyes opened. "Do not listen to Barda. Do not blame yourself, Little One," she whispered through white lips. "You had to be saved. We owed it to your people. There is only one Prin."

"There is only one Jasmine," Barda muttered. His face was tight with grief.

The gnomes had reached the door. They were kicking and beating at it. Barda raised his head. "They will pay for this," he snarled. He stood up, his sword gleaming in his hand, his eyes burning.

"Do not — try to avenge me," Jasmine murmured. "Use your wits. Save yourselves. The quest — the Belt of Deltora — is more important than . . ."

She grimaced with pain. Her eyes closed. Filli whimpered piteously. Lief felt that his heart was breaking.

"The toad's venom is killing her!" sobbed Prin.

Venom.

With a cry, Lief tore the Belt of Deltora from his waist. Prin gasped through her tears and Barda looked down, frowning furiously. "Lief, what are you doing?" he demanded.

Lief paid no attention to either of them. He was pressing the medallion that held the dulled ruby against Jasmine's injured hand, folding her fingers over it, hoping against hope as words from *The Belt of Deltora* echoed in his mind.

† **The great ruby, symbol of happiness, red as blood . . . wards off evil spirits, and is an antidote to snake venom.**

If the ruby could combat snake venom, perhaps it would have an effect on Gellick's venom also. It was a slim chance. But it was all the chance they had.

He looked up, met Barda's eyes, and saw that

the big man at last understood what he was doing.

"She is still breathing. But we need time," Lief muttered. Barda nodded and turned again to face the door. Without a word, Prin took Jasmine's dagger and crept over to stand beside him. The big man glanced at her and tried to wave her away, but she shook her head and did not move.

The gnomes were battering the door with something heavy now, heaving and shouting in time. The door's bolt was rattling and the wood was beginning to splinter. It would not hold for much longer.

Barda stood grimly, sword in hand, waiting. Beside him, eyes wide and terrified, was Prin. She winced with every crash against the door, but stood her ground.

Jasmine lay deathly still, her fingers curled around the Belt. Lief bent his head and whispered in her ear. "Jasmine, fight the poison. Fight it!" he breathed. "The ruby is in your hand. The ruby is helping you."

Jasmine's face did not change. But Lief thought he saw the sun-browned fingers move, very slightly. She had heard him. He was sure of it.

There was another crash, and the sound of cracking wood. Kree cried a warning and flew to Barda. Prin squealed in terror. Lief turned and saw that the door was shuddering violently. Its hinges were bursting. The bolt had half fallen away. One more blow, or two . . .

Beside him, Jasmine gave a long, low sigh. He glanced down, and gasped in amazement. Red light was glowing between her curled fingers.

It was the ruby. The ruby, working its magic, showing its power.

Jasmine's eyes opened sleepily. Lief's heart leaped as he saw that they were clear, no longer filled with pain. But she was weak, terribly weak.

"Lief!" roared Barda. "They have broken through!"

Lief stood Jasmine's shield in front of her to give her some protection, and ran to the door. Through the gaping holes in the shuddering wood he could see grinning gnome faces and the glinting of axes.

Barda was flailing with his sword, slashing at the holes as gnome hands and feet crept forward. Prin was by his side, stabbing bravely with Jasmine's dagger. So far they had prevented entry. But it would not be long before the door gave way completely, falling inward. When that happened, the gnomes would rush over it like water over a collapsing dam. Then all would be lost.

"Prin!" Lief shouted. "Go to Jasmine! She is reviving, but slowly. Protect her, and Filli, if you can."

He took Prin's place as she hurried to do his bidding. Barda had never stopped beating the gnomes back, but his grim, sweating face was even more determined now that he knew Jasmine was still alive.

An angry voice shrilled from the other side of

the door. A voice Lief recognized. "You cannot win, you fools! Give in now and we will be merciful and kill you quickly. Keep us waiting here and we will make you pay! We will make you suffer!"

It was Gla-Thon, the worker who had complained about having to toil for Gellick. Lief licked his lips and shouted back.

"Are you afraid, Gla-Thon, that your master the toad will be angry if you dally with us here instead of collecting flies? Ah, there was once a time when gnomes were their own masters."

"And a time, I have heard, when the halls of Dread Mountain did not stink like garbage carts," Barda called, following Lief's lead. "And when their treasure was not covered in toad slime, but was the envy of all."

"Shut your mouths!" shrieked Gla-Thon in fury.

"The great toad has made us strong!" called another voice that Lief was sure belonged to the red-bearded Ri-Nan. "It came to us and offered to protect us from the Shadow Lord and his Guards. It offered to let us use its poison, on certain — conditions. These conditions were hard, but we were glad to accept them. Gellick's venom has made us powerful."

"Oh, yes," Lief jeered. "It helped you drive away the Kin, so that now your paths and gnome-rests are smothered by thorny Boolong trees in which Vraal can lie in wait. It enslaved you, so that now you toil day and night in Gellick's service, half starved and in fear of your lives. You have indeed made a wonderful bargain."

There was silence outside the door. Lief and Barda glanced at each other. Was it possible that they were winning this battle of words?

"We could help you rid yourselves of your tyrant," Lief called, crossing his fingers for luck. "Do you not want to be free again?"

There was another long silence.

"No weapon can kill Gellick." When it came at last, Gla-Thon's voice was dull with despair. "Gellick's hide is too thick for swords and arrows to pierce. Even axes have no effect. Many have paid with their lives for daring to try to win our freedom."

"No one can survive Gellick's venom," called another, older voice. "I, Fa-Glin, leader of the Dread Gnomes, tell you this. You saw yourself what happened to your companion — through just a tiny arrow wound in her hand."

"What happened to me?" The voice rang out, strong and laughing.

As a stunned silence fell outside the door, Lief and Barda spun around. Jasmine was standing behind them, leaning on Prin's shoulder. She looked pale and weak, but she grinned at them and wordlessly held out the Belt of Deltora. Lief took it, and quickly fastened it around his waist, covering it with his shirt once more.

"The venom did not harm me, Fa-Glin!" Jasmine

shouted. "Our magic is too strong. The toad cannot kill us, but we have weapons powerful enough to kill it."

She paused, swaying. Then she made a great effort, raised her head, and called again, her voice as confident as before. "Do you want our help? If so, lay down your weapons, send in three members of your party, and we will talk."

✳

The meeting between Barda, Lief, Jasmine, and the three representatives of the gnomes, Gla-Thon, Ri-Nan, and Fa-Glin, lasted for well over an hour. While it was taking place, Prin, Kree, and Filli watched silently from a corner of the breeding cave. None of them trusted the gnomes, and the fact that the white-bearded Fa-Glin wore a fringed jacket that was plainly made from Kin skin did little to change their minds.

Discussion was difficult and angry at first. But, as Lief had suspected, in her heart Gla-Thon was determined not to let the chance of defeating Gellick pass by. Fa-Glin, astounded by Jasmine's magical recovery, was on her side. And at last even Ri-Nan gave in and a decision was reached. With the gnomes' help, the visitors would kill Gellick. In return they would receive their freedom, and the dull green stone embedded in the toad's forehead.

"It seems a poor reward," murmured old Fa-Glin, regarding them with suspicion. "And how do you know it is there, may I ask? The stone appeared in Gellick's brow only a little more than sixteen years ago."

"We have ways of knowing such things," said Jasmine quickly. "Have you not seen for yourselves how strong our magic is?"

"I have heard tell that toad-stones can weave powerful spells," Gla-Thon put in. "And this one is very large." She turned to the companions. "No doubt that is why you want it?"

Lief, Barda, and Jasmine nodded, but they could see that Fa-Glin was not convinced. Plainly he was still not sure that they were to be trusted.

"Gellick will be sleeping now," Ri-Nan said. "Entering the treasure cavern at this time is forbidden. If Gellick wakes . . ."

"The toad will not wake," Barda said firmly. "And if it does, we are the ones who will suffer. We will enter the cavern alone. All we ask is that you show us the way."

Old Fa-Glin's eyes narrowed. "Enter the treasure cavern alone? So you can pick and choose whatever you wish to steal? Oh, no, there will be none of that."

"In any case," Gla-Thon put in, as Lief bit back the angry reply that trembled on his lips, "we might as well be with you. If the plan goes wrong we will pay as dearly as you in the end, for Gellick will blame us for letting you escape."

Lief glanced at Ri-Nan. The red-bearded gnome said nothing, but his eyes, under the bushy eyebrows, were wary and hard as stones.

Fa-Glin folded his arms. "Very well," he said. "It is agreed. The six of us will go together to the cavern, and there it will be Gellick's death, or our own." He turned and looked around at the fly cages, his wrinkled face a mask of shame and disgust. "If we succeed, we can rid our halls of this filth," he said. "If we fail — at least I will never have to see it again. I, for one, am happy to take the risk."

16 ~ Do or Die

Shortly afterwards Lief, Barda, and Jasmine were following the three gnomes as they threaded their way through tunnel after tunnel, growing ever closer to the center of the Mountain. They had made Prin stay behind with Kree and Filli, with instructions that she was to do all she could to escape with the others should they not return.

They had left their packs behind too and their shields. All they now carried were their basic needs: their weapons, their water bottles — and all their remaining blisters.

They planned to use the blisters to kill Gellick. None of them shrank from the idea of attacking the monster in its sleep. It deserved no fair play from them. Their only doubt was whether they could creep close enough to it to make their aim true, without causing it to wake.

The gnomes began to move more slowly and quietly, and soon the huge entrance to the cavern came into view. Even from a distance a rainbow shimmer could be seen beyond the door, as the cavern's torches cast flickering light on the treasure trove heaped below.

Without making a sound, they stole to the entrance and peeped in. The monster was still squatting in the center of the mounded jewels and gold, in exactly the same position as when Lief, Barda, and Jasmine had seen it in their dream. Its eyes were closed. Only a slow pulse in its throat and the slow runnels of slime oozing from its skin showed that it was not a huge and hideous statue, the creation of some twisted soul who worshipped ugliness and evil.

The three companions moved forward, and this time it was the gnomes who followed, keeping well back. Slowly they climbed the mound of treasure, watching their feet, their minds focused totally on the need for silence as gold and jewels shifted under their boots like pebbles.

They crept forward, one careful step at a time. Soon they would be close enough. Gellick had not moved. Lief drew a long breath and tightened his grip on the blister he had ready in his hand. If ever I have thrown straight, hard, and true, I must do so now, he told himself.

One more step, another . . .

"Great Gellick! Beware!" The scream shattered

the silence. Lief spun around. The red-bearded Ri-Nan was rushing past him, scrabbling over the treasure, waving his arms. "I have come to warn you, great Gellick!" he screeched. "Treachery!"

The toad's eyes opened.

"Now!" Barda roared. Lief threw the blister as hard and fast as he could. It was the throw of his life. He yelled in triumph as the blister hit the monster full in the throat while in the same instant Barda's blister, and Jasmine's, burst on its chest. Lief threw his second blister, shouting as he saw it burst in the same place as before, waiting for Gellick to tremble and fall.

But nothing happened. The creature's eyes did not flicker. Lazily, its tongue snaked out and licked at the poison running, gleaming, down its chest. Its great mouth stretched wide in a mocking grin.

"Who are these foolish creatures who attack me with my own venom?" it rasped.

Thunderstruck, Lief, Barda, and Jasmine stumbled back, turning to Gla-Thon and Fa-Glin, who stood frozen in horror behind them.

"But — the gnomes collect Gellick's slime for themselves!" cried Jasmine. "How could it be in the blisters? How could — "

"We keep only a little," mumbled Gla-Thon, her lips stiff with fear. "The rest must be taken, at each full moon, to the bottom of the Mountain and left by the roadside. It was part of the bargain. We did not know — "

"RI-NAN," Gellick roared. "ANSWER ME! WHO ARE THEY?"

"They are the intruders, great Gellick!" gabbled Ri-Nan. He pointed at Gla-Thon and Fa-Glin. "And there are the traitors who set them free, and helped them find you. Kill them! I, your faithful servant, can make the gnomes work harder than that doddering fool Fa-Glin ever could. I should be leader. I, Ri-Nan, deserve your — "

He broke off as Gellick's awful eyes turned on him.

"Down, while it is not looking!" muttered Barda. "Hide under . . ."

"YOU *DESERVE*, RI-NAN?" roared the monster. "YOU DARE TO ORDER *ME*? *THIS* IS WHAT YOU DESERVE, WORM!"

It spat and Ri-Nan collapsed, screaming, rolling over and over, kicking and writhing among the gold. The toad's tongue flicked in satisfaction. Then it turned, slowly . . .

"Ah," it hissed, as it saw that the drifts of treasure now glittered empty in the flickering light. "Now you hide from me, do you, worms? You burrow under my trinkets, trembling at my rage? That is as it should be."

It lifted a huge foot, stamping with a sound like thunder, and its voice rose to a deafening roar. "I AM THE GREAT GELLICK! THE SHADOW LORD HIM-

SELF RESPECTS ME. MY VENOM ALONE DEFEATS HIS ENEMIES!"

The hideous bellow echoed around the cavern. Hidden below a glittering mass of coins and gems, scarcely able to breathe, Lief listened in terror. He knew his companions were somewhere near, but he did not dare move or speak as Gellick's voice roared on.

"HE GAVE ME THIS MOUNTAIN, AND A RACE OF SLAVES TO SERVE ME. HE KNOWS I WILL NOT FAIL HIM. HE TRUSTS ME TO KILL YOU, WORMS! HE TRUSTS ME TO GUARD THE STONE I WEAR ON MY BROW. OTHERS MAY HAVE FAILED HIM. BUT NOT I!"

Lief's thoughts were racing. The beast had been expecting them. It knew they had come for the emerald. The moment they raised their heads, the moment they moved to escape or attack, it would kill them.

Now it had fallen silent. It was waiting, watching, no doubt for any sign of movement. Long moments passed. At last it spoke again, its voice rasping, sneering, and low.

"I know where you are. I have only to wait, worms, till at last you show yourselves. But I choose not to wait. I choose instead to crush you where you lie."

There was a tumbling, clinking sound as gold and jewels were pushed aside. The toad was moving, crawling towards them, heaving its great bulk along on its vast, clawed feet. Nearer. Nearer . . .

"It will please me to feel you beneath my weight, and hear your screams, worms," it hissed. "It will please me to see what is left of your bodies dragged away at last, to feed the flies."

Lief lay very still. His sword was in his hand. He realized, almost with surprise, that he felt very calm. He had already decided that he would wait until the last moment, then spring up and try to pierce the beast's belly, whatever the gnomes had said. It would mean his death, but his death was coming in any case, one way or another.

The monster was very close now. So close that through the gaps in the jewels above his head Lief could see its shadow. The Belt of Deltora was burning at his waist. The Belt could feel the emerald — the emerald that would never shine again, but would remain dulled by the toad's evil.

Was it time yet to scramble from hiding, to make his last, hopeless gesture of defiance? No. A moment more. But no longer than that. Lief thought that Jasmine and Barda were somewhere behind him, with the two gnomes. But he could not be sure. His greatest fear now was that he would hear their anguished cries before he himself could escape into death. That he could not face.

His thoughts drifted to Kree, Filli, and Prin, waiting near the breeding cave. He hoped that the gnomes would let them go. That they would escape from the Mountain safely. That, somehow, Kree and Filli could make their way back to the Forests of Silence and Prin would return to the Kin. Prin, who looked so like the companion of his earliest childhood come to life.

He smiled slightly as he remembered the first time he had seen her, drinking from the Dreaming Spring.

Drink, gentle stranger, and welcome. All of evil will beware.

It was as though Lief had been struck by lightning. For a split second everything seemed to stand still. Then he moved his hand from his sword hilt to his belt.

The coins and jewels above him were swept away by a huge, clawed foot.

"I SEE YOU, WORM!"

The monster was above him, its great head bending low, its mouth open in a leer of triumph. But already Lief had pulled the water bottle free, and unscrewed its cap. And before the toad could jeer again, he was hurling the bottle, overflowing with water from the Dreaming Spring, straight into the grinning, open mouth, to the back of the throat.

He struggled to his knees as Gellick gulped. The giant toad hissed.

"YOU — " it choked. Then it jerked violently and its eyes rolled back in its head. It tried to move, but already its feet were fixed to the treasure hill by thick, snaking roots. It screamed. It screamed as its swollen body pulsed and changed. It screamed as its vast, spiny neck began to stretch.

Then there were some long, terrifying moments when Lief wanted to turn away, but could not. Moments when he heard Jasmine and Barda beside him, but could do no more than clasp their hands. Moments when the whole cavern seemed to flash and darken, when he thought that the monstrous, writhing thing before him would never cease its struggles.

Then all was still, and where Gellick had crouched there was a vast tree with a straight, tall trunk and three branches bearing clusters of pale-colored leaves. The tree's topmost branches brushed the soaring roof of the treasure cavern. And as Lief looked up, something fell from its tip, straight into his hand.

It was the emerald. Dull no longer, but deep, sparkling green.

Fa-Glin and Gla-Thon were watching, goggle-eyed. But Lief did not hesitate. The Belt of Deltora gleamed as he put its fifth stone in place.

17 ~ Farewell

Great was the rejoicing in the halls of the Dread Gnomes that day. The treasure cavern seethed with gnomes gazing in awe at the tree that now rose in its center. The locked doors of the food stores were opened and a great feast was enjoyed by all. Thanks and praise were heaped on the companions' heads as the story of Gellick's defeat was told and retold.

"I feared the worst," said Fa-Glin to a crowd of listeners, for the dozenth time. "I thought we were lost. Then Lief of Del wrought his great magic, and in an instant all was changed."

And for the dozenth time the crowd sighed in awe, and Lief felt uncomfortable. Fa-Glin's tale made it sound as though he had meant all along to use the Dreaming Water, and had simply waited until the time was right. In fact, of course, it was the impulse of a moment, an idea that sprang into his mind when all seemed lost.

But he said nothing aloud. He could see the wisdom of Barda's whispered advice: "It will do us no harm for the Dread Gnomes to think we can perform wonders. They are a warlike and suspicious people. There will come a time when we will need their loyalty and their trust, when we will want them to listen to our advice."

In fact that time came sooner than they expected. The feast was still in progress when there was a high, gobbling cry from somewhere near. Then there was the sound of running feet.

"Kin!" a voice shouted. "Pen-Fel and Za-Van have sighted Kin from the spyholes to the south. There are many, many. The sky is black with them!"

In an instant, food and drink were forgotten, bows and arrows were being snatched up, and gnomes were running for the door.

"No!" Lief, Barda, Jasmine, and Prin shouted at the tops of their voices. Their voices echoed around the feasting hall.

And the gnomes stopped.

"Have you not learned better than this?" demanded Lief, as Prin clung to him in terror. "Do you not realize that the Kin should be your partners on this Mountain? Do you want the Boolong trees to continue to multiply till even the streams are choked by thorns? If I am right, the Kin are coming to rescue their young one. You should rejoice, and beg them to stay! You should welcome them with open arms, not seek to kill them!"

There was a moment's silence, then Fa-Glin nodded. "Our friend is right," he said. Regretfully he smoothed the old Kin skin jacket he wore, then he took it off and threw it at his feet.

"It is a pity. But our weavers can make fine garments enough," he murmured. Then once again he raised his voice. "Lay down your weapons, gnomes. We will go out and greet the Kin in friendship. We will welcome them home."

※

At sunrise two days later, a strange group walked down the gnomes' pathway to the bottom of the Mountain. Prin walked with Lief, Jasmine, and Barda. Ailsa, Merin, and Bruna came next. Fa-Glin and Gla-Thon brought up the rear.

They spoke little as they walked, for more than one heart was heavy at the thought of the parting to come. But when they reached the road at the Mountain's base, where a bridge spanned the stream, they turned to one another.

"We thank you and will think of you every day," Ailsa murmured, bending and touching each of the travellers on the forehead. "Because of you we are home, and Little — I mean, Prin — is with us once more."

Merin smiled as she and Bruna farewelled the

companions in their turn. "As she has told us many times, Prin has grown too tall and strong in these last days to be called Little One anymore. Besides, now that we are here again, there will be more young, and she will no longer be the smallest among us."

As she stepped back, Fa-Glin stepped forward. "The Dread Gnomes also thank you," he said gruffly, bowing low. He held out his hand and Gla-Thon passed him a small carved box of Boolong tree bark. This Fa-Glin gave to Lief.

Lief opened the box. Inside was a golden arrowhead. "We owe you a great debt," said Fa-Glin. "If ever you need us, we are yours to the death. And this is a token of our oath."

"Thank you," said Lief, and bowed in his turn. "And you will follow the plan . . . ?"

"Indeed we will." Fa-Glin's teeth gleamed through his white beard as he grinned. "Next full moon, and every full moon from now on, the poison jars will be at this spot as usual. But their contents will not be the same, though the liquid will look identical. Stream water mixed with Boolong sap, I fancy, will do the trick. We and the Kin together will make the brew. It has been decided."

"And our last supplies of Gellick's venom will be kept safe," added Gla-Thon. "So that when at last our Enemy realizes what we are doing, and comes for us, we will be ready. Then, and only then, will our arrows be tipped with poison once more."

"It is our hope — " Barda hesitated, then went on carefully. "It is our hope that your Mountain will not be invaded. Before long there may come a time when the Enemy will have other concerns."

The Kin glanced at one another, confused. But Fa-Glin and Gla-Thon nodded, their eyes gleaming. They had sworn never to speak of the stone that had fallen into Lief's hand, or of what he had done with it. They had not asked for an explanation of the glittering, gem-studded Belt into which the emerald had fitted, or the two empty spaces that still glared blankly along the Belt's length. But perhaps they did not need to ask. Perhaps they knew, or guessed, the truth, for the Dread Gnomes were an old race, with long, long memories.

Lief felt Prin's gentle touch on his shoulder. "Where are you going now, Lief?" he heard her ask.

Lief looked across the bridge to where the stream continued through rustling trees, and on to where the first rays of the sun glinted on broader water: the distant river that would take them to the wide sea and the forbidden place that was their next goal.

"I must not tell you, Prin," he said softly. "But it is a long way from here."

"And why are you going? And why so soon?" she persisted, for the moment, in her distress, becoming again that more childish Prin he remembered from the time when they first met.

"Because I must," Lief said. "And because there

is no time to waste. We must finish our journey as quickly as we can, now. There are people at home who are — waiting."

And as he turned to meet Prin's eyes, to say the hardest farewell of all, he prayed that the wait would not be too long.

The Maze
of the Beast

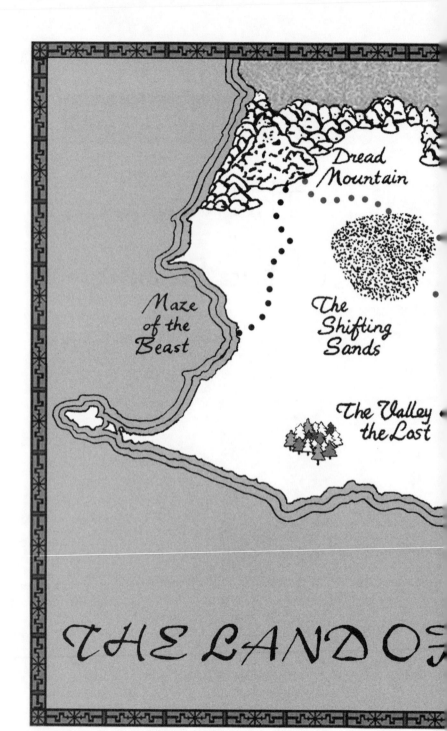

Dread
Mountain

Maze
of the
Beast

The
Shifting
Sands

The Valley
the Lost

THE LAND O

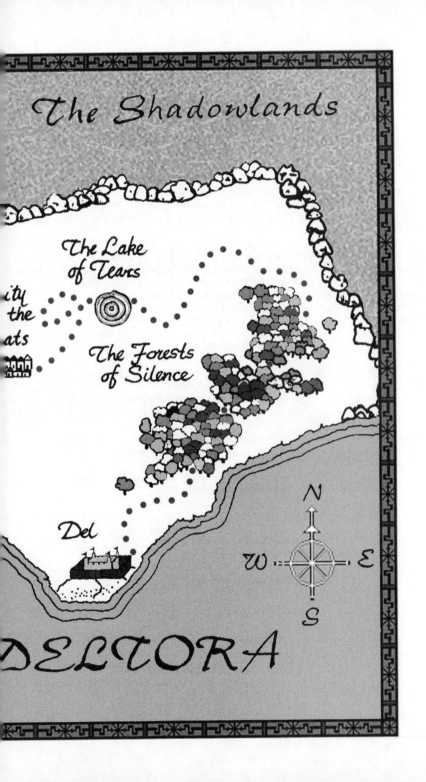

ISBN 0-439-25328-4

All rights reserved. Published by Scholastic Inc., 555 Broadway, New York, NY 10012, by arrangement with Scholastic Press, an imprint of Scholastic Australia.

12 11 10 9 8 7 6 5 4 3 2 1   1 2 3 4 5 6/0

40

Printed in the U.S.A.
First American edition, September 2001

Contents

The story so far . . .

Sixteen-year-old Lief, fulfilling a pledge made by his father before he was born, is on a great quest to find the seven gems of the magic Belt of Deltora. The gems were stolen from the Belt to open the way for the evil Shadow Lord to invade Deltora. Hidden in fearsome places throughout the land, they must be restored to the Belt before the heir to the throne can be found and the Shadow Lord's tyranny ended.

Lief's companions are the man Barda, who was once a Palace guard, and Jasmine, a girl of Lief's own age who they met in the fearful Forests of Silence. On their travels the three have discovered a secret resistance movement led by Doom, a mysterious scar-faced man who rescued them when they were captured by the brutal Grey Guards.

Five gems have been found. The topaz, symbol of faith, has the power to contact the spirit world, and to clear the mind. The ruby, symbol of happiness, pales when danger threatens, repels evil spirits, and is an antidote to venom. The opal, gem of hope, gives glimpses of the future. The lapis lazuli, the heavenly stone, is a powerful talisman. The powers of the emerald, for honor, are still to be discovered.

Following the map Lief's father drew for him, the companions are now on their way to the coast and their next goal — The Maze of the Beast. Haste and secrecy are all-important, for the Shadow Lord has become aware of them, and Lief has learned that his parents have been imprisoned.

Now read on . . .

1 - Rescue

Lief, Barda, and Jasmine moved from Dread Mountain to the River Tor in silence and in haste, glad of the trees sheltering them from the open sky. For many days they had been travelling like this, all too aware that at any moment an enemy might strike. For many nights they had slept in turns, fully dressed, with their weapons in their hands.

Soon they would reach the river. They knew they had only to follow it to reach Deltora's west coast. There, somewhere, was the next goal marked on their map — the horribly named Maze of the Beast. There, if Lief's father was right, lay the sixth stone of the Belt of Deltora.

But the Shadow Lord's servants were watching for them — waiting for them to show themselves. The Shadow Lord knew that the topaz had been taken from the Forests of Silence, that the ruby was gone from the Lake of Tears, and the opal from the City of the Rats. Perhaps by now he even suspected that the lapis lazuli had in its turn been wrested from its terrible guardian in the Shifting Sands.

If the Dread Gnomes were successful in deceiving him, it would be some time before he realized that the emerald had already gone the way of the other four gems. But his servants would be in this area by now, lurking in the mountain's foothills or searching from its skies. And the Maze of the Beast, and every road to it, would be guarded well by enemies searching for the group that fitted the description they had been given: a man, a boy, and a wild girl with a black bird.

Lief looked ahead at Kree, hunched gloomily on Jasmine's shoulder beside Filli. Poor Kree wanted to stretch his wings. But it was too dangerous for him to be seen too much in the air, in case his presence marked their position for an enemy. So he was forced to stay close to the ground, and he did not like it.

None of us like it, thought Lief. It is unpleasant to scurry like hunted creatures through this rustling forest. Unpleasant to fear the coming of night. But there is no help for it.

He jumped as Jasmine abruptly swung to one side, snatching her dagger from her belt. Kree fluttered into the air, squawking. Lief caught a glimpse of bright, dark eyes and a pointed snout in the bushes. Then there was the scuffle of tiny, escaping paws and the next moment Jasmine was sheathing her weapon once more, snorting in disgust.

"I am jumping at shadows and fighting wood mice, now," she muttered, as she held out her arm to Kree and strode on down the rough pathway. "I cannot rid myself of the feeling that we are being watched."

"I have felt it for days," Barda answered, glancing back at her. "The forest seems full of eyes."

Lief said nothing. He was very conscious of the Belt clasped around his waist. He felt that the hidden watchers must be aware of it, though it was concealed under his shirt, with his jacket buttoned closely over the top. It was far heavier than it had been when first he put it on, empty, in Del. The power and magic of the gems that now studded five of its medallions seemed to weigh it down.

Suddenly there was a faint, shrill cry and a splash from somewhere ahead. The companions stopped dead. The splashing grew louder and more desperate. At a word from Jasmine, Kree took wing and flew towards the sound.

"Marie! Marie!" screamed a high-pitched voice. "Oh, Marie . . ."

"What is it?" Lief breathed. "Barda, quickly! It sounds as if — "

"We must take care," Barda warned. "It could be a trick. Wait — "

But already Kree was flying back towards them, screeching urgently.

"Someone is in the water!" exclaimed Jasmine. "Someone is drowning!"

They began to run, their feet pounding on the narrow path, the sound of the despairing voice growing louder and more shrill by the moment, the sound of splashing growing less and less.

They burst through the last of the trees onto a broad bank of fine white sand. The river stretched, glittering, before them, deep and swiftly running. A young girl, no more than five or six years old, was drifting in the shallows, clinging to the floating branch of a tree. It was she who was screaming, vainly holding out her hand to another child who was struggling in deeper water, beside an overturned raft.

In moments, Lief and Barda had cast aside their boots and swords and were wading into the water. "You get the one nearest the shore," Barda shouted over his shoulder to Lief as he struck out for the raft. "Make haste, Lief, or we will lose her. The river is running fast."

Lief waded to the child holding the branch and managed to catch her before she was swept out of reach. She clutched at him frantically as he lifted her up and into his arms. She was deathly cold. The water lapped around his chest as he struggled back towards the shore.

"Marie!" the girl sobbed, shuddering and straining to look back at the overturned raft. "I fell in and she tried to help me and then she fell in, too! I caught hold of the branch, but she . . . Oh, where is she? Where is she?"

Lief looked around and his heart sank. Barda had almost reached the raft, but where Marie had been there was only swirling water.

Barda took a deep breath and dived. In moments he had appeared again, dragging a limp, white bundle. He began swimming back to shore, paddling with one arm, dragging the bundle after him with the other.

"She is drowned!" screamed the child.

"No. She was not under for long. She will be all right," Lief said, more confidently than he felt. He waded on, feeling with relief the water growing shallower as he climbed up to the bank where Jasmine was waiting with a blanket.

"I will see to her. Help Barda!" Jasmine said crisply, wrapping the blanket around the little girl.

"I am Jasmine," Lief heard her say as he ran to where Barda was splashing to shore, clutching his limp, sodden burden. "This is Filli, and Kree. What is your name?"

"Ida," cried the child. "I am Ida. Oh, take me away from the river! I do not wish to see it anymore! Marie is drowned. She is drowned!"

Lief plunged once again into the water and helped Barda carry the unconscious child up onto the bank. Like Ida, she was chilled to the bone. They laid her down gently. As he saw her face, Lief gasped in surprise. Straight brown hair, fine golden skin, heart-shaped face, long, curling black eyelashes — why, she looked exactly like Ida, even to the small brown mark on the left cheekbone, and the simple white dress. They were twins! Identical in every detail.

What were twin girls, so young, too, doing in this wilderness alone? Where were their parents?

Barda had turned Marie on her side and was bending over her, his face grim.

"Is she dead?" Lief whispered. Somehow the thought was even more terrible now that he knew the girls were twins. It was dreadful to think of one of them being left alone. He glanced up and was relieved to see that Jasmine was beginning to lead the sobbing Ida off the riverbank, towards the trees.

Then, as Jasmine stepped aside to let the little girl move onto the path before her, Lief saw a tiny movement in the undergrowth nearby. Before he could move or cry a warning, there was a twang and an arrow was flying through the air.

It struck Ida in the back. She crumpled and fell forward without a cry. With a shout of outrage, Lief leaped for her attacker. His sword was lying out of reach. He did not care. He was angry and shocked enough to deal with this bare-handed.

He tore the concealing bushes aside and threw himself on the dark-haired boy who crouched there. Knocking the deadly bow from the boy's hand, he hurled him out on the sand. The killer fell heavily on his face, his arm crumpled under him, and lay still, moaning in pain. Lief ran for his sword, snatched it up. His ears were roaring. There was murder in his heart as he spun around once more.

Groaning, the boy on the ground rolled onto his back. He tried to rise, and fell back again, grimacing and holding his arm.

"Do you not see — they are Ols! Ols!" he shouted.

Then Lief heard Barda's gurgling shout, heard Jasmine's scream. He looked up.

Ida's body had disappeared. And Marie, little Marie, was rising from the sand. She had Barda by the throat, her white fingers digging deep into his flesh. Her teeth were bared. And then her body was bubbling, stretching, growing till it was a tall, wavering white shadow with a black mark at its center and an enormous peaked head like a ghastly bleached candle flame. The thing's eyes were burning red and the mouth was a toothless black hole, but it laughed like a child as Barda staggered back and fell beneath its weight.

2 - Fate Takes a Hand

Gasping in horror, Jasmine and Lief both lunged forward, stabbing and tearing at the thing, trying to pull it away from Barda. The cold, wavering mass shrank and re-formed. The thing staggered, but its grip held.

"Through the heart!" the injured boy shouted. "Stab it through the heart! Kill it outright or it will finish him!"

"It is stabbed through the heart already," Jasmine shrieked. "It does not fall."

Growling, the thing turned on her. With a cry she was swept aside by a rush of white that sent her sprawling.

"Now, Lief! Strike on the right side!" the boy screamed. "The heart is on the right side, not the left!"

Lief plunged his sword home. The thing shuddered, then collapsed, its body a shapeless, writhing mass bulging horribly here and there with limbs, faces, claws, ears. Choking with disgusted horror, Lief recognized the face of Marie, the pointed snout of a wood mouse, the wing of a bird . . .

Then there was just a bubbling pool of white, that sank, as he watched, into the sand.

Barda lay shivering and coughing, the breath rasping in his throat. Already the dark red marks of the Ol's strangling fingers on his neck were darkening to purple. But he was alive.

"He was lucky. Another minute and it would have been too late."

Lief spun around and saw that the boy he had attacked had managed to crawl to his feet and was standing behind him. He heard Jasmine exclaim and glanced at her. She was staring at the boy in amazement.

"It is you!" she exclaimed. "The boy who served the drinks at the Rithmere Games. You are one of Doom's band. You are Dain."

The boy nodded briefly, then limped to where Barda was lying and looked down at him. "Your friend needs warming," he said. "He is wet, and Ol attacks chill to the bone."

He turned away and began walking slowly towards the trees.

Lief hastened to make a fire and heat water for tea while Jasmine ran for more blankets. By the time Dain returned, dragging a small backpack, his injured arm in a rough sling, Barda was well wrapped up and sitting close to a crackling blaze. The terrible shivering had eased and the color had begun to return to his face.

"Thank you," he said to Dain huskily. "If it had not been for you . . ." He winced, and lifted a hand to his throat.

"Do not try to speak," Dain advised. He turned to Lief, holding out a jar he held in his uninjured hand. "A warm drink sweetened with this will help him," he said. "It strengthens, and eases pain. It is very powerful. One spoonful should be enough."

The jar bore a small handmade label.

Lief unscrewed the lid and sniffed at the jar's golden contents, drawing in the sweet scent of apple blossom. "Quality Brand," he murmured, glancing at Dain. "The initials are interesting, but the name itself is ordinary. So ordinary, in fact, that I suspect it is false."

"As false as the names you gave at the Rithmere Games, Lief," the boy answered evenly. "These are hard times. You are not the only ones who must be careful."

Lief nodded, realizing that he had overheard them calling to one another before the Ols' attack. There was no help for it, but it was unfortunate.

He took a mug of tea and stirred a small amount of the honey into the steaming brew. Then he gave the mug to Barda, who wrapped both hands around its warmth and sipped gratefully.

"What are these Ols?" Jasmine demanded, as she passed Dain a mug of tea for himself.

"Shape-changers from the Shadowlands," Dain said, stirring a spoonful of honey into his own cup. "The Shadow Lord uses them to do his evil work. Perhaps I should not be surprised that you have not heard of them before. They are more common here, in the west, than in the east, where you come from."

He paused, watching them under his brows. Barda, Lief, and Jasmine remained expressionless. Did he think they were going to fall into so simple a trap?

Dain laughed easily and bent to draw in the sand.

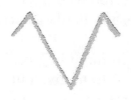

The mark of the Resistance. The companions looked at it in silence, then glanced at one another.

Dain leaned forward. "We are both on the same side, are we not?" he asked earnestly, suddenly dropping his easygoing manner. "What does it matter if I know where you live? Doom says — "

"How did you come to be here?" Jasmine asked abruptly. "How did you find us?"

Dain drew back, and his face closed once more. "I was not looking for you. I was returning to our western stronghold when I saw the Ols. I knew them for what they were. Grade One Ols are crude and cannot hold a form for very long. They are easy to recognize when you know what to look for. I followed them, waiting my chance to destroy them. And then, lo and behold, you appeared, and the Ols were plainly interested."

He paused. "They have been following you for days, you know," he added in a hard voice. "They took the shape of wood mice and watched your every move, listened to you, deciding how they would proceed. In the end, they chose to appeal to your tenderness of heart. Once they had separated you, they would have struck. You would have had no chance."

Lief, Jasmine, and Barda glanced at one another. All felt ashamed.

"We thank you for aiding us," Barda said stiffly at last. "We ask you to forgive our suspicion and secrecy. We have learned to be cautious."

"As have I," said Dain, still in that hard voice, "though for a moment I forgot myself in the pleasure of seeing familiar faces."

Lief suddenly realized that the boy was older than he had thought — at least as old as he was himself. The slight body, the fine-boned face, and the silkiness of the dark hair that flopped carelessly over Dain's forehead had deceived him.

Dain swallowed the last of his tea and stood up awkwardly, protecting his injured arm. "I will leave you in peace. Be on the watch for Ols. Grade Ones, like the two we have just dispatched, always travel in pairs. The others — well, you will probably not recognize them, anyway. It is best to trust no one."

He shouldered his pack and turned to go.

"Wait!" Lief exclaimed impulsively, jumping to his feet. "You cannot travel alone! Your arm is hurt. You cannot use your bow, or even a dagger."

"I will be all right," Dain said. "I do not have very far to go."

But Barda was shaking his head. "Wait one night, and we will escort you," he croaked, his hand on his throat. "It is the least we can do."

Lief saw Jasmine stiffen. Clearly, she did not approve of this plan. She does not want to see Doom again, he thought suddenly. She distrusts him. But Jasmine said nothing, and Dain seemed not to notice her expression.

He was hesitating. It was plain that his pride,

which urged him to leave them, was struggling with his common sense, which told him that it was madness to travel unprotected if he had a choice.

At last, he nodded. "Very well," he said, dropping his pack. "Thank you. I will wait. Then we will go together to the stronghold." He paused, biting his lip. "It is to the southeast. It is out of your way."

"How do you know? We have not told you where we are going," Jasmine snapped.

Dain's delicate face flushed red. "I thought perhaps that you may be travelling to — to Tora," he stammered.

Jasmine stared. The name meant nothing to her. But Lief was thinking furiously.

Tora! Del's great sister city in the west. He had been taught of it. But it was so long since he had heard its name that he had forgotten it existed!

Dain was waiting for an answer, leaning forward anxiously.

"Indeed," Barda said smoothly. "Well, if we are going to Tora, it will not hurt us to reach it a day or two later than we had planned."

Jasmine stood up. "I will find a secure place to camp for the night," she said. She stalked off into the trees, with Kree flying ahead. Dain gazed after her, and Lief saw a flicker of admiration in his eyes.

Lief felt an unsettling twinge of jealousy, bit his lip, and turned away. If only I had not injured him, he thought. Then he could have gone his way, and we could have gone ours.

Immediately he felt ashamed. He told himself that he was just upset because the journey to the Resistance stronghold would waste precious time. Every day of delay was another day his father and mother remained in danger, perhaps in torment, in the dungeons of the Shadow Lord in Del.

But, if he was honest, he also had to admit that he did not want Dain as a companion, even for a short time.

Dain made him uncomfortable. His gentle, polite ways were appealing, his quiet dignity was impressive, and, despite his lack of great strength, he had acted bravely in saving them from the Ols. But though he seemed easygoing on the surface, Lief could sense that there was something deep inside him that was hidden. Some secret he kept to himself.

No doubt he feels the same about us, Lief thought. And, of course, he is right. So we do not trust one another. That is the root of the problem. While we are with Dain we cannot discuss our quest, or the Belt. We cannot discuss my parents, or wonder aloud how they are faring. We cannot be comfortable.

Restless, unwilling to stay by the fire with Dain and Barda any longer, he went to help Jasmine. But as he walked into the trees, a new idea occurred to him.

Fate had played strange tricks on them before —

and somehow it had always turned out for the best. Could there be some reason for their being forced to keep Dain's company? Were they somehow *meant* to get to know him? Were they *meant* to go to the Resistance stronghold? To see Doom again?

Only time would tell.

3 - A Hard Journey

Whe they were settled under the overhanging tree Jasmine had found, Dain told them
more about Ols. Listening to his soft, even
voice, Lief began to feel that if they *had* been intended
to spend time with him, this information alone may
have been the reason.

"They are everywhere," Dain said, pulling his
blanket more tightly around him. "They can take the
shape of any living thing. They do not eat or drink,
but Grade Twos can pretend to do so, just as they can
create body heat to disguise what they are. In its natural state, every Ol has the mark of the Shadow Lord
at its core, and whatever shape it takes, the mark will
be somewhere on its body, in some form.

"The twins — the Ols we killed — each had a
mark on the left cheekbone," said Lief. "Was that — ?"

Dain nodded. "But do not expect that it will always be so easy," he warned. "Grade Two Ols are far more expert. They never have the mark in plain view."

"You are saying, then," Barda put in, frowning, "that recognizing a Grade Two Ol is just a matter of luck?"

Dain smiled slightly. "There is a way of testing them," he said. "They cannot hold one shape for longer than three full days. If you observe a Grade Two Ol, and never let it out of your sight, there will come a moment when it loses control and its shape begins to change and waver. We call this moment the Tremor. It does not last long. In seconds the Ol has regained control. But by that time, you know it for what it is."

He was growing weary, hugging his chest with his good arm as though his pain was troubling him. "There are some in Deltora who do not have to wait for the Tremor," he said. "They have developed an instinct — a feeling for Ols. Or so Doom says. When he senses an Ol he strikes at once. I have never known him to be wrong."

"We can hardly follow his example," Barda muttered. "To kill just on suspicion is a risky business."

Dain nodded, and this time his smile was broader and more real. "I agree. For such as us, suspicion should be a signal to run, not strike."

"Run?" Jasmine demanded fiercely.

He flushed at the disdain in her voice, and the smile faded. "The idea displeases you, Jasmine. You and Doom are of one mind. But it is surely better to run than to kill an innocent person."

"Or," Barda put in, "if your suspicions are correct, to be spied upon by the Ol at its leisure, or killed when you least expect it. Once those icy fingers are around your throat, you are helpless. You can take my word for it, Jasmine." He touched his own bruised throat tenderly.

Jasmine lifted her chin stubbornly and turned again to Dain. "You have spoken of Grade One Ols, and Grade Twos. Are there other grades as well?"

Dain hesitated. "Doom says that there is another," he said reluctantly at last. "He says there are Grade Three Ols. He says they are few, but in them the Shadow Lord has perfected his evil art. They can change their shape to whatever they wish — living or nonliving. They are so perfect, so completely controlled, that no one could tell them for what they are. Even Doom could not."

"Then how does he know they exist at all?" Jasmine demanded.

Lief watched, fascinated, as Dain's eyelids drooped, and he bit his lip. What was troubling him?

Jasmine saw the hesitation, too, and pounced. "Well?" she insisted.

Dain swallowed. "Doom says — he says he learned of them — in the Shadowlands," he muttered.

Lief's stomach turned over. Suddenly it was as though parts of a puzzle were falling into place. Suddenly he was seeing a tombstone by an overgrown stream. Suddenly he was back in a cave on Dread Mountain, looking at some words scrawled in blood.

"When Doom says he has been in the Shadowlands, you do not believe him, Dain?" he asked.

Dain looked up, his eyes filled with confusion. "How can I?" he burst out. "No one escapes from the Shadowlands. Yet Doom never lies. Never!"

"He lies about his name!" Jasmine snapped.

"What do you mean?" Dain was very pale. He looked exhausted. His delicate face was beaded with sweat and deeply shadowed. He swayed.

Lief caught him before he fell. Barda found the Quality Brand jar and pushed a spoonful of honey between the closed lips. Soon a little color returned to the boy's face. Lief lowered him gently to the ground and covered him with a blanket.

"Do not worry, Dain," he said softly. "Whatever Doom's real name may be, he has not lied to you. He *has* been in the Shadowlands. And, somehow, he escaped. You may not believe it. But I do."

He saw Dain's eyelids flutter. The boy's mouth opened as though he was trying to speak. "We will talk of this again with Doom himself," Lief whispered. "For now, just rest. Tomorrow, you will need all your strength."

✳

Two long, hard days followed — days in which Lief's respect for Dain grew. The fall he had taken had not only sprained his arm, but had also cracked several ribs. By the second day they were climbing rocky hills. Every step Dain took must have caused him pain, yet he did not complain. Only his eyes revealed what he was suffering.

By now, the river was out of sight. Dread Mountain rose black and forbidding in the distance. Twice, looking back, Lief saw the huge, ungainly shape of an Ak-Baba circling it, searching for signs of travellers below.

In many ways, this was a welcome sign. It meant that the Shadow Lord, for all his power, did not realize that the companions had already taken the Mountain's gem. But the presence of an Ak-Baba, even at a distance, made the need for travelling under cover even more important. As the country became rougher, with straggling bushes and great boulders taking the place of lush trees, they were forced to crouch, shuffling along in single file.

For many hours Dain had not spoken. He seemed to need all his energy just to keep walking. How would he have fared alone? Lief thought, watching the boy's bowed back ahead of him, and hearing his shallow, painful breaths as he stumbled along.

"I think Dain needs rest," Lief called in a low voice.

Barda and Jasmine stopped at once, but Dain turned a little, shaking his head.

"We must get to safety. Then we can rest. It is not

far now," the boy gasped, holding his side with his uninjured arm. "Just up above . . . the cleft in the rock. Then — three bushes in a line, and — a cave entrance, sealed with a stone. There is a password . . . "

His voice trailed off. Then, without any warning, he fell heavily to the ground.

The three companions bent over him, calling his name, but he did not wake. Even the last of the honey did not revive him.

The sun dipped below the horizon, and the light dimmed.

"We must get him to shelter," Lief said. "Another night in the cold . . . "

"He said the stronghold was near," Barda muttered. "I will carry him the rest of the way." Gently he picked up the unconscious boy. Then they began clambering upward once more.

Soon they came to a deep crack in a rock — a crack like a narrow passageway. They scrambled through it and there, as Dain had said, were three bushes in a line, pointing to a boulder lying against a sheet of rock. The boulder looked quite natural, as though it had simply fallen where it lay, but they realized it must mask the entrance to the stronghold.

"It is well disguised," said Barda. "If we had not known where to look, we would have passed it by." He moved closer to the great rock and peered at it, looking for a means of moving it aside.

"It is strange that they have left no lookout," Jasmine murmured, looking around with her hand on her dagger. "They were surely expecting Dain's return. How was he supposed to get in?"

Lief looked around also, and noticed a strip of paper lying under the last of the bushes. It must have been blown there and become caught on a twig, he

WHEN ENEMIES AT PASS, ORDERS NORMAL

thought. He pulled it free and looked at it.

"Someone has been careless," he said grimly, showing the note to the others.

"They are expecting trouble, it seems," said Barda.

"It could be *us* they are expecting," Jasmine hissed. "We have only Dain's word for it that this is the Resistance stronghold. It could be a trap."

"We shall see." Lief snatched up a stout stick and moved to the boulder. He tapped it sharply, at the same time calling out: "Hello! We are friends, and ask entry."

There was silence behind the rock, but he had the strong feeling that someone was there. He tapped again.

"Doom, hear me! We are the travellers you saved from the Grey Guards near Rithmere. We have Dain with us. He is injured and needs shelter!"

"What is today's password?" called a deep, muffled voice. Startled, Lief stepped back. It was as though the rock itself had spoken. But soon he realized that the sound had come through a tiny crevice to the right of the boulder. Like the gnomes of Dread Mountain, the Resistance had peepholes in their walls.

"I wish to speak to Doom!" Lief shouted.

"Doom is not here," boomed the voice. "What is the password? Answer, or die."

4 - The Stronghold

Barda leaned closer to the stone. "Are you mad?" he shouted. "We are not enemies! We are known to Doom. And if you could see us you would know that we have your friend here."

"You *can* be seen, believe me," answered the voice behind the rock. "There are a dozen weapons aimed at you this moment. Do not move."

Startled, the companions looked around them. They could see no one. Jasmine took a step back. A ball of flame slammed into the ground beside her, showering her with sparks. She beat out the sparks frantically.

"I told you not to move!" called the voice. "Do so again at your peril."

"Call Neridah and Glock!" Jasmine called, her voice high with shock. "They are with you, I know.

Doom saved them from the Grey Guards, as he saved us. They will recognize our faces."

There was the sound of hollow laughter. "So they may. But in these parts we know better than to judge by appearances. That is why there is a password. Do you know it or not?"

"Of course!" Lief shouted.

"Lief!" hissed Jasmine.

"If I had said no, they would have killed us!" Lief hissed back. "They would have thought we were Ols!"

"They will kill us anyway, once they realize you are lying!" Jasmine's fists were clenched with frustration and anger. "This is madness!"

Lief shook his head desperately. "Dain mentioned a password. But he could not have known the password for today, for he has been long away. He must have planned to find it out once he got here. And if he could do that, so can we! There must be a code, a sign . . ."

"Where?" Jasmine demanded.

"Perhaps they all carry a list, with one word marked for every day," Barda said.

"That, surely, would be too dangerous," muttered Lief. "Still . . ." He threw Dain's pack to the ground and rapidly began searching through it. But as he expected he found nothing printed — only travellers' supplies, a few spare clothes, and the empty jar of Quality Brand honey.

Quality Brand.

He snatched up the jar and stared at it. Suddenly an idea had come to him. He scrabbled in his pocket for the note he had found under the bush.

"I grow tired of this game. You have the count of ten to reply!" called the voice from behind the rock. "One, two . . ."

"Wait!" Lief cried. His fingers closed on the note. He pulled it out and quickly read it again, hoping against hope that he was right. The printed words danced in front of his eyes.

WHEN ENEMIES AT PASS, ORDERS NORMAL.

Yes! What he saw here could surely not be just chance. He was right. Surely he was right. He took a deep breath and let the paper fall.

"The password is — 'weapon,' " he shouted.

"Lief, how do you know that?" hissed Barda. "What — "

He broke off as, slowly, the boulder that masked the stronghold's entrance began to roll aside, and light poured through the gap from the cavern within.

In the light stood a wiry little man wearing a strange assortment of garments in every color of the rainbow. Below his striped woollen cap, grey hair twisted with feathers hung to his waist.

Lief felt Barda give a start, but there was no time to ask him what was the matter, for the little man was grinning, showing two or three crooked teeth and a broad expanse of pink gums.

"You took your time!" he boomed, in the deep, powerful voice that did not suit his appearance at all. "Does it amuse you to dance with death? I was within a hair of giving the order to fire."

He peered shortsightedly at the limp figure in Barda's arms. "So the little boy has had an adventure and come to grief!" he said. "Well, well. Who would have thought it? And him always so careful of himself!"

As the companions hesitated, he beckoned impatiently. "Well, don't just stand there!" he exclaimed. "You are letting in the cold." He turned his head. "Thalgus! Petronne!" he bellowed. "All is well. Put down your weapons and come down. You must see to Dain. He has been carried home like a babe in arms, the poor poppet."

Lief and Jasmine slipped through the entrance. Barda followed more slowly. As he stepped into the light, the little man gazed up at his face and burst into noisy laughter. "Barda!" he roared. "Barda the Bear! Who would have believed it? After all these years! By my stars, I thought you were dead! Do you know me?"

"Of course I know you, Jinks," said Barda, smiling rather stiffly. "But this is the last place I would have expected to find you."

He paused as a roughly dressed man and an equally ragged woman — Thalgus and Petronne, presumably — jumped down to the ground from somewhere high above the doorway. He allowed them to take Dain's slight weight from his arms. Then he turned to Jasmine and Lief. "Jinks was one of the acrobats at the palace in Del," he explained, his voice revealing nothing. "He knew me well, when I was a palace guard."

"A palace guard? Why, the strongest and bravest of all, so it was said!" Jinks chattered, following Petronne and Thalgus as they carried Dain towards a larger cavern from which came the hum of many voices. "But Barda, I heard that all the guards were killed the day the Shadow Lord came. How did you escape the slaughter?"

"By chance I had left the palace before it began," Barda murmured. "And you?"

The little man wrinkled his nose. "The invaders cared nothing for the clowns and acrobats!" he jeered. "We were no more important than pet dogs to them. They let us scatter as we would. We tumbled over the wall while they shed the blood of fine lords and ladies, destroyed the palace guards, and took the place apart searching for our courageous king and queen, who were hiding somewhere trembling in their golden boots."

He grinned again, and this time the smile had a touch of teasing malice. "So! You managed to run away just in time to save yourself, Barda the Bear!" he crowed. "Cleverly done! Your fellows were all killed defending the palace, but not you! You must be very proud of yourself."

Lief glanced quickly at Barda and saw that his face had tightened with pain.

"Barda did not know what was going to happen that day!" he exclaimed angrily. "He left the palace the night before because his mother had been killed, and he feared he would be next!"

"Never mind, Lief," Barda muttered. He turned to Jinks, and Lief could tell that he was forcing himself to speak politely. "You would be doing me a great favor if you would not speak of my past to anyone else, Jinks. I prefer it to be secret."

The little man opened his eyes wide. "Why, of course, Barda!" he said smoothly. "I quite understand your position — even if your young friend does not. These are hard times, and we cannot all be heroes. Why, I myself am the world's greatest coward!" They reached the entrance to the larger cavern and he stood back, gesturing gracefully for them to enter. "Mind you, *I* do not pretend to be anything else," he added, as Barda passed him.

The cavern was large, lit by flickering torches and filled with groups of men, women, and children of many different ages. Food was already cooking on several fires, and straw mattresses lined the walls.

"Why do you let him call you a coward?" Jasmine whispered to Barda angrily, ignoring the faces turned to stare at the newcomers. "For that is what he is doing!"

"I am well aware of what he is doing," said

Barda grimly, staring straight ahead. "I know Jinks of old. He was a fine acrobat, but a more gossiping, jealous, spiteful, troublemaking piece of mischief was never born. Meeting him here is ill fortune indeed. Whatever he promises, by morning every person here will know everything about me."

"Dain already knows your name," Lief pointed out.

"The name is not so important," Barda growled. "The other details — "

He broke off as Jinks came bustling up to them, clapping his hands to gain the attention of everyone in the cavern.

"Here are some friends who have come to join us!" the little man cried. "They brought poor young Dain home. It seems he decided to go adventuring, and bit off more than he could chew."

He sniggered, glancing at the pale figure of Dain, who had been put down on a mattress of straw in a corner and was at last beginning to stir. Several other people laughed in reply, and Lief felt a hot flush of irritation. He opened his mouth to speak, but Jasmine was before him.

"Dain saved us from two Ols," she said loudly. "His bravery was very great."

"Is that so?" called a voice from the crowd. "Who are you to talk of bravery, Birdie of Bushtown?"

And out of the crowd pushed the swaggering, lumbering figure of Glock.

5 - Friend or Foe?

Glock stood sneering and glowering at Jasmine by turns, his powerful arms hanging loosely by his sides, his small eyes glinting. Every line of his powerful body showed that he was looking for a fight.

"Hello, Glock," said Jasmine calmly. "The last time I saw you, you were being carried out of the Rithmere arena, fast asleep. What a pity you could not stay awake for the final."

Several people laughed. Plainly they had heard the story. Glock's heavy face darkened and seemed to swell. He growled dangerously and his fingers twitched.

Out of the corner of his eye Lief saw Jinks watching, his face alive with mischievous interest. So Jinks was the sort who loved to stir up trouble, then stand back and watch the results. A dangerous man — as dangerous as Glock, in his way.

Just then there was the sound of banging from outside the cavern. Three slow taps, followed by three quick ones. Fleetingly, Jinks looked disappointed. Then he turned and scurried out, with Petronne and Thalgus close behind him.

"What is the password?" they heard him call.

"Weapon!" came the reply. The voice was muffled, but Lief thought he recognized it. Doom had returned.

Glock took no notice whatever. He was still intent on Jasmine.

"I should have been Champion, you little piece of slime!" he snarled. "If we had fought, your dancing, jumping tricks would not have deceived me. I would have crushed you to pulp with one hand tied behind my back!"

Jasmine stared at him in disgust. "Fortunately, your greed ensured that you did not have the chance to try," she said.

Glock roared, and grabbed at her. She sprang aside, smiling disdainfully as he stumbled, his great paws clawing at empty air.

"That is enough!"

Doom was standing, scowling, in the entrance. His face was seamed with lines of tiredness, his long, tangled black hair and beard were streaked with dust, and the jagged scar showed pale on his deeply tanned skin.

"There is to be no fighting in this place!" he thundered. "Glock, you have been warned before. One more outburst and you will be turned out of the stronghold. Then you will no longer be under our protection when the Grey Guards come for you."

Glock turned and lumbered off, grumbling and casting evil looks over his shoulder. No one made a sound, but Lief saw a tall woman put her hand over her mouth to hide a smile. The woman was Neridah. She saw Lief watching, and her smile grew broader and more teasing. He looked away, his face growing hot as he remembered the shame she had caused him in the Rithmere arena.

Doom's angry eyes were now fixed on Jasmine. "And you," he added coldly, "will guard your sharp tongue, if you know what is good for you."

In the silence that followed he turned abruptly and went to the mattress where Dain was resting. By now, the boy had managed to sit up.

"So," Doom said. "You have returned at last, Dain. You were expected days ago. Where have you been?"

Dain flushed deep red. "I saw a pair of Ols, Doom," he mumbled. "Grade One only. I followed them — "

"Alone!" Doom snapped. "You followed them

alone. You went out of your way, disobeying orders, failing to arrive here when expected."

Dain hung his head. But Doom had not finished. "And I have been told" — he glanced at Jinks, who tried and failed to look innocent — "I have been told that you chose to endanger all our lives by telling these untested strangers the secret of the password."

There was an angry murmuring in the cavern.

Finally Dain found his tongue. "Indeed — indeed I did not tell them, Doom," he said.

"Then how did they gain entry?" Doom's voice was icy. "You, I gather, did not even see today's note. Yet they were able to give the word."

"It was not difficult to work out," Lief said, stepping forward hastily. "The note said, 'WHEN ENEMIES AT PASS, ORDERS NORMAL.' The first letters of those words spell the password — 'WEAPON.' "

As Doom glared at him, he shrugged and threw caution to the winds. He was not going to be bullied like Dain. "I had a clue to the code, of course," he said loudly. "I had already seen the label on Dain's jar of honey. 'Quality Brand.' There, too, initials are used to disguise the truth. Why are you afraid for it to be known that you use Queen Bee honey?"

Another loud murmur arose from the crowd. Doom barked an order and immediately Lief, Barda, and Jasmine were seized from behind by several pairs of strong hands. They struggled, but it was no use.

"What are you doing?" Lief spluttered. "I meant no harm by my question! I was simply interested."

"Then you would have done better to hold your tongue," said Doom, his eyes hard as stones. "You have stumbled on a secret we are sworn to protect. It is forbidden to trade with the Resistance. And Queen Bee honey is even more rare and valuable than Queen Bee cider. It has amazing healing powers. The lady risks much by supplying it to us. She risks not only her own life, but the lives of her sons."

Now it was Lief's turn to stare. The idea of the wild old woman they had met after their escape from the Plain of the Rats being a mother seemed very strange.

"It is nothing to us if Queen Bee supplies you with honey," growled Barda. "Who would we tell?"

"Your Master, perhaps," called Jinks, his small eyes gleaming with excitement. "Is that why you were allowed to escape from the palace, Brave Guard Barda? Had you sold yourself to the Shadow Lord even then?"

Barda lunged forward in fury, but the hands that held him jerked him back.

"Be silent, Jinks!" roared Doom. He gazed at Barda thoughtfully for a moment.

"So," he murmured. "You were a palace guard. Your real name is Barda. And where were you hiding for all those years, Barda — before you began travelling the countryside with your young companions?"

"That is my affair," said Barda, meeting his eyes squarely. "I choose to keep it to myself. As, I think, you choose to keep to yourself your own whereabouts in those early years, Doom."

"Your whereabouts — *and* your real name," Jasmine muttered.

Doom glanced at her quickly. His mouth tightened. He turned once again to Barda.

"Were you in Tora?" he asked bluntly.

At this, Dain, who had been slumped on the mattress with his head bowed, looked up eagerly.

But Barda looked blank. "Tora?" he repeated. "What is this fascination with Tora, among you? No, I have never been to Tora in my life."

Doom abruptly turned away. "Take them to the testing room," he snapped. "I will speak to them again when the three days have passed."

"Let us go!" Jasmine shouted, as they were dragged to the cavern door. "There is no reason to imprison us! You know that we are not Ols! You know it!"

Doom lifted his chin. "We shall see," he said.

✳

Locked in the small, brightly lit cave that Doom called "the testing room," the three companions spent three weary days. A barred window was set into the heavy wooden door, and at all times a face stared through it, watching their every move.

Their possessions were with them. Even their

weapons had not been taken from them. Trays of food were pushed under the door, and they had plenty of water. But there was no privacy, no darkness, no peace.

By the third day even Barda was desperate. Jasmine lay curled on a bunk, her hands over her face. Kree sat in a corner of the cell, his wings drooping. Lief paced in an agony of impatience, feeling time tick away.

He cursed the day they had met Dain — then remembered that if it had not been for Dain, he, Barda, and Jasmine would all be dead. He cursed Doom's suspicion — then remembered his own shock when sweet little Marie had changed to a specter bent on killing.

But had Dain not said that Doom could sense an Ol? If so, then Doom knew full well that Lief, Barda, and Jasmine were what they seemed. Why then, was he keeping them here?

He wants to keep us by him. The three-day test is an excuse — something the others in the cavern will accept and understand. He wants to know what we are up to. He hopes that after this we will tell him.

The idea shone clearly in Lief's mind. He knew it was the truth.

Well, you are wrong, Doom, or whatever your name may be, he thought grimly. We will never tell you of our cause. And that is because we still do not know whether you are friend, or foe.

They had lost track of time. They did not know whether it was day or night. But it was in fact exactly seventy-two hours and five minutes after they first entered the cavern that they heard a hiss from the window in the door.

Peering through the bars was Dain, no longer bent with pain, but upright, and with his arm free of its sling. His face was set and determined, though Lief saw that the fingers resting on the window were trembling.

"The three days have passed," he whispered, as the three companions gathered by the door. "You no longer need to be watched. But Doom still delays setting you free. I do not know why, and I feel it is not right. I will lead you out of here. But only if you promise me that you will take me with you. To Tora."

6 - A Change of Plans

Dain may have been afraid — may, indeed, have been guilty and ashamed — to free Lief, Barda, and Jasmine from the cell and lead them in silence down the dark passage beyond. He may have trembled as they moved into another tunnel and on to a small door that opened to the outside world. But still, he did it. And when they stood at last in the open air, under stars that sparkled like jewels scattered over the black velvet tent of the sky, he heaved a sigh of relief.

"We are safe, now," he whispered. "They are all eating and drinking. No one will visit the testing room again until it is the hour for sleep. By then, we can be long gone."

They wasted no time with words, but together began scrambling away over the rocks, slipping and sliding on loose stones, catching hold of rough bushes to stop themselves from falling.

Only when they were well away from the stronghold, when they were on flat ground again, did they stop to rest, and talk.

"Tora is many days' journey downriver from here," whispered Dain. "We will have to take great care as we go. Bandits and pirates haunt the River Tor, and Ols patrol the area in great numbers."

"Why?" whispered Lief in reply. "What is so special about Tora, Dain? And why do you want to go there?"

Dain stared at him. Several expressions seemed to chase themselves across his face: surprise, bewilderment, disbelief, and finally, anger. Slowly he clambered to his feet.

"You know very well why," he hissed, looking Lief up and down. "Can it be that still you do not trust me?" He shook his head violently from side to side. "I have betrayed my people for you. I have betrayed Doom, who has been like a father to me! Is that not enough to prove — ?"

"Be still, boy," muttered Barda. "It is not a matter of trust. We know very little of Tora."

"I know nothing of it," Jasmine muttered. "I had never heard of it until you said its name when we first met."

"But I thought — " Dain took a deep, shuddering breath and pressed his hands together till the knuckles showed white. "You tricked me. You told me you were going — "

"We told you nothing," Barda said firmly. "*You* suggested that Tora was our goal. We simply did not correct your mistake."

Dain groaned and buried his face in his hands. It was dark, and he moved swiftly, but Lief thought he saw the dark eyes shining with tears. He felt a pang of guilt, and put a careful hand on Dain's shoulder.

"We are going all the way to the coast, following the river. If Tora is on the river, or near it, we can escort you there, if that is what you wish."

Still with his face in his hands, Dain slowly shook his head from side to side. "When first I heard of you — a man, a boy, and a wild girl with a black bird, in whose presence the Shadow Lord's evil was undone — I began to think you were the answer," he said, his voice thick and muffled. "And as the months went by, and Doom brought news that you were moving west, I became sure of it."

He stifled a sob. "Then I met you. I thought it was fate. But it has all been a mistake. Another mistake. Oh, I can do nothing right! What am I to do?"

"I think you had better tell us what is troubling you," said Jasmine flatly. "No purpose is served by wailing and grieving."

Dain looked up. Her calm seemed to have brought him to himself as no amount of kind sympathy could ever do. He rubbed the back of his hand over his eyes, wiping away the tears. "For reasons I cannot tell you, I must get to Tora. But Doom forbids it. At first — when first he found me — left for dead after bandits burned my family's farm — he said I must regain my strength. Then he said I needed more training to travel in safety, though already I could use a bow. Later he said he needed my help for just a little while, and I could not refuse him. And at last, as I grew impatient, he said that Tora had grown too dangerous for me or any of our group, until we were much stronger."

He paused, shaking his head as if to clear it. "He says that to visit it now would mean certain capture, and this would be a danger to the whole Resistance. He says Tora is crawling with Grey Guards and thick with spies, because . . ."

His voice trailed off, and he swallowed.

"Because Tora has always been so loyal to the royal family," said Barda suddenly. "Of course!"

His eyes were alert and excited. In the back of Lief's mind, memory stirred. The memory was of his father, beating red-hot iron in the forge, talking of Tora, the great city of the west. He had said that it was a place of beauty, culture, and powerful magic, far away from bustling Del and its palace, but fiercely loyal to the crown. Lief remembered his father describing a painting he had seen in the palace library, long ago.

It was a picture of a great crowd of people. All

were tall and slender, with long, smooth faces, slanting eyebrows, dark eyes, and shining black hair. They wore robes of many colors, with deep sleeves that touched the ground. Their hands were pressed over their hearts.

They were all facing a huge rock from the top of which green flames sprang high into the sky. Beside the rock, his head bowed humbly, stood a big man in rough working clothes, wearing the Belt of Deltora. A beautiful, black-haired woman stood beside him, her hand on his arm.

"Adin loved a Toran woman, and she loved him," Lief said slowly. "When he was proclaimed king, she went with him to Del, to rule by his side. On the day they left, the Torans swore allegiance to Adin, and all who came after him. Other tribes had done the same, but the Torans, who were the greatest among them, carved their oath upon the flaming rock that stood at their city's heart, and set a spell upon it that could never be broken."

He met Barda and Jasmine's eyes, and the same thought flashed between them. What more perfect place than Tora to hide the heir to the throne?

"It is a long way from Del to Tora," said Barda aloud, choosing his words carefully so as not to reveal their meaning to Dain. "A perilous journey. But once there . . ."

Yes, Lief's eyes answered silently. Once there, King Endon could have been quite sure of help. The

Torans would have done anything, risked anything, to keep him, Queen Sharn, and their baby safe. And they had magic enough to do it — whatever the Shadow Lord threatened, whatever destruction he caused.

"You *do* know something of Tora, then!" Dain was exclaiming, his face brightening.

"Not as it is now," Lief said slowly. "I know only the ancient stories. No news has reached Del from the west since before I was born."

"And perhaps long before that," Barda put in. He met Dain's anxious eyes. "I think, perhaps, that it is not only the dangers of Tora that cause Doom to forbid it to his people. It is also Tora's loyalty to the crown. Doom wants no part of that. He despises the memory of the royal family. Is that not so?"

Dain's shoulders slumped. "It is so," he admitted. "And Doom wants no part of Tora's magic, either. He says we depended on magic to save us in the past, and that it failed us. He says that we must learn to stand on our own feet, and fight the Shadow Lord with cunning, strength, and weapons. But I — "

"You know that is not enough," Lief broke in. "And it is you who are right, Dain. The Enemy's power was gained by sorcery. Ordinary strength, however determined, may undo some of his evil work, but can never defeat him for good."

Jasmine had been listening, looking from one speaker to another. Now she spoke.

"Ordinary strength may not defeat the Shadow

Lord. But ordinary sense tells us how we must proceed from here. Plainly, we are about to travel into territory the Enemy is watching closely. There will be many eyes watching for the group they have been told about — a man, a boy — and a wild girl with a black bird."

She said the last words with a bitter smile.

Lief tried to interrupt, but she held up her hand to stop him. "We must separate, if we are not to be noticed," she said. "And since Kree and I are the ones who make our group obvious, we are the ones who must take another path."

She pulled on her pack. Kree flew to perch on her arm. Filli chattered fearfully.

"Jasmine, no!" Lief exclaimed.

"Do not leave us!" cried Dain at the same moment.

Jasmine turned to Barda. "I am right, am I not?" she demanded. "Tell them!"

The big man hesitated, but his grieved face showed that he knew her reasoning was sound.

She nodded briskly. "Then that is settled. All being well, we will meet on the coast, at the river's end."

With that, she lifted a hand in farewell and moved quickly off into the darkness. With a cry Lief started after her. But she did not answer his call, and he could not catch her. In moments she was just a flickering shadow among the trees. Then she was gone.

7 - Where Waters Meet

Barda, Lief, and Dain were following the river, creeping through the trees that ran along its banks.

Many days had passed since Jasmine had left them, and though Lief watched constantly for signs of her, so far he had seen nothing. It was strange and dull to be travelling without her, without Filli's soft chatter in the background and Kree squawking above their heads. Dain, though always dependable in time of trouble, could not take her place.

Lief was alarmed, too, to realize how much he and Barda had grown to depend on Jasmine's sharp eyes and hearing to warn them of approaching danger. For there was danger in plenty. Twice the companions had been forced to fight for their lives when bandits took them by surprise, leaping down on them from the trees. Four times they had hidden just in time as pirate boats sailed by — large, battered wooden craft patched with all manner of odd bits and pieces, some of them with sails made of scraps of cloth roughly sewn together.

The ruffians who hoisted the sails, lay sleeping on the rough boards, or plied the long oars, were as ill-assorted as the materials that made their craft. They were of every size, color, and shape, but all had a savage, hungry look. Their clothes were ragged and filthy and their hair wild, but the knives, swords, and axes that hung from their belts gleamed sharp and bright in the sun.

A lone figure swayed at the top of every mast, strapped in place with ropes or supported on a sling of leather. From that high perch, hard eyes, shaded with a hand, hat, or branch of leaves, scanned the riverbanks and the water ahead.

Looking for prey. Looking for travellers to kill and rob. Looking for unprotected villages, for other boats to plunder.

Here, far from the mountains and the streams that fed it, the river had grown slow, narrow, and winding. It was dark and oily, flecked with evil-looking foam. The smell of death and decay hung over it like mist. Rotting, broken timbers, rags of clothing, and other rubbish bobbed in its current.

There were more sinister floating things, too. Now and again dead bodies drifted just below the surface, the water around them swirling and bubbling horribly as writhing river creatures feasted unseen.

And Ols? Who knew which bandits, which creatures, were Ols?

One evening, when Lief, Barda, and Dain had stopped for the night, two beautiful water birds, purest white, waded through the reeds to shore, bending their graceful necks as if asking to be fed. But they ignored the scraps Lief threw to them. They simply stared. And only when they raised their wings to fly away did Lief see the black spot each bore on its side, and realize what they were.

Prowling Ols. But a man and two boys were of no interest to them. They were moving on, to seek the man, the boy, the girl, and the black bird they had been sent to find and destroy.

Lief lay back, his stomach churning, staring at the brightness of the moon. In three days it would be full, and even now it was large and gleaming, lighting the darkness. Every bush seemed bright. Every tree was open to view. There were no hiding places.

Jasmine had been right. It was her presence, and Kree's, that made their group stand out. But if the Ols found her alone, with Kree by her side, would they not strike? She was the one in true danger now.

Lief prayed she would be safe. He vowed to himself that if they all survived this test, their party would never again be separated. Prudence was all very fine. But other things were more important.

✳

The next morning they reached a bridge that spanned another river flowing into the Tor. The bridge was arched high so that boats could sail under it, and, though in bad repair, it felt safe enough to cross. On the other side was a tiny village, nestling in the corner made by the two rivers. It seemed deserted.

"This is Broad River, I think," said Dain, looking down at the slow-moving water as they began to cross the bridge. "You would have seen part of it on your way to Rithmere."

"Oh, yes," Barda answered with a grim smile. "And felt it, too — more than we would like. So this is where it ends."

They reached the end of the bridge and began to move towards the village, which they could now see had suffered some terrible disaster. Many houses had been burned. Windows were shattered. Rubble and broken glass littered the narrow streets.

"Pirates," Dain muttered.

There was a post sticking up from the ground ahead, and when they reached it they saw that it had once supported a sign. Now the sign lay on the ground, its edges broken, its brave lettering muddied.

Where Waters Meet

Welcome, Travellers!

"I have heard Doom speak of this place," said Dain dully. "He said the people were brave and full of good heart. He wanted them to join us, so they would be safe. But they refused to abandon their village to the pirates. They said they would defend it with their last breath."

"It seems they did so." Barda's voice was harsh with anger.

As Lief began to turn away, he saw that some scraps of thick yellow knitting wool had fallen on the bare ground along the board's top edge. He crouched to pick them up — then snatched his hand back as he

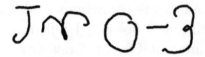

saw that they were arranged in a pattern.

"Barda! Jasmine has been here!" he exclaimed excitedly." And perhaps she is here still. This is a message for us — a message no other person would notice. See? She has made the first letter of her name. And a picture of a bird for Kree. The other signs must tell us where she is sheltering."

Barda considered the shapes on the ground. "The circle could be part of a building. But what is the 3?"

"A number on a door, perhaps!" Lief stood up and looked around, filled with new energy.

With Dain trailing behind them, they began to

explore the village. It was a depressing task, and Lief's excitement quickly died. Plainly, Where Waters Meet had once been a busy, thriving little town. Now, everywhere were the signs of violence and bloodshed. The tavern, the meeting hall, every house, every shop, had been ransacked. Everything of any value had been taken.

Some of the invaders had scrawled their names triumphantly on the walls of living rooms, bedrooms, and halls. "Nak" was one name that occurred again and again, twice in what looked like blood. But there were other names, too. "Finn" was one, "Milne" another.

Lief stared at the scrawlings with hatred. Nak, Finn, and Milne, he thought, I will remember your names. You are not Ols or Grey Guards, Shadow Lord's servants, bred for evil. You are free to choose how you act. And you have chosen to prey upon your own people. You have chosen to steal, destroy, and murder. I hope that, one day, I meet you. Then I will make you pay.

With heavy hearts they finished searching. There was a circular courtyard, and some window frames in the shape of circles, too. But there were no numbers at all, and there was no sign of Jasmine.

Lief stopped outside the last house, which had a new moon carved into the door. "Moons are circles, when they are full," he called to Barda. "Could Jasmine have meant — ?"

Then he broke off, for he had at last realized the true meaning of Jasmine's message. He shook his head, annoyed at his own slowness. "We have been wasting our time," he exclaimed. "Jasmine is long gone. The signs tell us not where she is in Where Waters Meet, but when she was here. The circle is the full moon. Then there is a minus sign, and the number 3. She was here yesterday — three days before full moon!"

"Of course!" Barda heaved a great sigh. "Then — "

Suddenly he looked alert, and put his finger to his lips, listening. Lief listened in his turn and heard the last thing he would have expected.

It was the jingling of many tiny bells, growing louder. And, even more astonishing, the merry, booming sound of someone singing.

Once there was an Ol-io,
Jolly-wolly Ol-io,
Once there was an Ol-io,
Fearsome as could be!

I said to that Ol-io,
Jolly-wolly Ol-io,
I said to that Ol-io,
You don't bother me!

8 - Steven

A shabby caravan pulled by a fat old horse was trundling towards the village along the Broad River path. At first, Lief thought there were two figures sitting on the driver's seat. But as the caravan drew closer he saw that he had been mistaken. There was only one — a huge golden-haired man with dark brown skin, singing his rather surprising song at the top of his voice.

Impulsively Lief moved forward. "Wait," Barda muttered. "Looks and words can be deceiving."

Lief nodded, and stayed where he was. But when he heard the man's song falter as the caravan drew up to the ruined town sign, and saw the sorrow on the broad face, he was not willing to wait any longer.

The man's mouth turned down as he saw the three emerge from the shadows. "Ah," he said. "This is a bad business." He climbed down from the caravan and looked around him, taking in the desolation. "But I am not surprised. Every year for many years we have come here on our rounds, and each time I have feared finding this very thing."

He shook his head. "I warned them. I said to them, 'Give it up, my friends. Move on! Life is precious!' But they were so brave. So foolish . . ."

He rubbed a huge hand over his eyes.

"You speak of your rounds," said Barda, who was still wary. "What rounds?"

The man looked up. "Why, I am a peddler, sir," he said politely. "I sell, I buy, and I trade. Steven B is my name." He gestured at the faded lettering on his cart.

To Lief's surprise, there was a movement behind him and Dain stepped forward.

"Hello, Steven," the boy said. "Do you not know me?"

The man's face relaxed into a grin. "Young Dain!" he said. "I saw you there, but I was not sure you wished to be recognized in this company."

"These are friends," said Dain. "They are helping me on my way to Tora, Steven. I am going there at last."

The grin faded. "These are bad tidings," Steven said. "Why do you not stay where you are safe? This part of the country is not kind to travellers."

"Yet you travel every day," Lief pointed out.

Steven shrugged his massive shoulders. "I?" he said, as if that was another matter altogether. "Ah, yes. But I have protection."

Lief stared. The man was unarmed, and seemed quite alone except for the old horse. He was big, certainly, but his pleasant, open face did not seem the face of a fighter. Quite the opposite.

"Steven's brother, Nevets, always travels with him," said Dain quickly, and, Lief thought, warningly.

Steven put his head on one side. "Would you like to meet Nevets?" he enquired.

"Oh, no. We would not dream of disturbing him," Dain exclaimed, before Lief and Barda could say anything. "But, before you go, my friends and I would like to buy some goods for our journey, Steven."

The man beamed. "A pleasure to serve you," he

said. He strode to the back of the caravan and threw open the doors. The space was fitted out as a tiny shop, crammed with clothes and household needs.

The brother is not hiding in here, in any case, thought Lief. And what are we to buy? For, plainly, we are expected to buy something.

He watched as Dain bought a small cooking pot he did not need. Then Steven turned to him. "And what is your fancy, sir?" Steven asked.

Lief held out a coin and gestured to a basket containing many small packets of what looked like toffee. Steven raised his eyebrows, but took the coin and tossed him two packets.

Then it was Barda's turn, and to Lief's surprise Barda pointed to a wide cloth belt embroidered with a pattern of dull gold and brown leaves. "If that is within my means, I will take it," Barda said.

"A fine choice," said Steven, removing the belt from its hook. "And to you, a friend of Dain's, only three silver coins." He measured Barda's waist with his eyes. "You could find it a little snug, however," he added.

"It is not for me," said Barda, counting out the money. "It is a gift."

Steven nodded and passed over the belt. "Ah, well," he said. "Our journey has not been quite without profit, and that is one good thing. But this place makes me sad, and that will never do. We will stay no longer."

As he turned away to close the doors, he began mumbling to himself. A strange character, Lief thought. And a little mad, for this brother he speaks of seems to exist only in his imagination. Perhaps Nevets died, and this turned Steven's wits.

Steven finished bolting the doors, and walked to the front of the caravan. As he put his foot on the step to climb up to the driver's seat, he turned back to Dain. "Give up this idea of Tora, for now, Dain, and come with us," he said, stretching out a friendly hand. "There is room on the seat for you. Soon we will be meeting with some of your friends, to make a delivery. You could return to the stronghold with them."

Dain shook his head. "I thank you most sincerely for the offer, Steven," he said. "But I cannot accept."

Steven looked regretful, then shrugged and finished his climb. When he was safely on the driver's seat again, he bent and fumbled underneath it. There was a clinking sound, and at last he brought out a small jar. This he passed to Dain. "With my compliments," he said. "May it help you on your journey."

As Dain stammered his thanks, Lief looked curiously at the jar. With a small shock, he saw the familiar "Quality Brand Honey" label.

Steven saw him looking, and put a finger to the side of his nose. "Not a word," he said. He clicked to the horse. The caravan lurched forward, and slowly turned until it was facing the way it had come.

Barda, Lief, and Dain raised their hands in

farewell. Steven grinned and waved. Then he shook the jingling reins and the caravan creaked away.

"He sells Queen Bee honey?" Lief muttered. "But I thought it was in short supply."

"He sells only to the Resistance," said Dain, looking down at the jar. "And then he charges only a fraction of the honey's worth. Do you not understand? He is no ordinary peddler. He is the son of Queen Bee herself."

Lief drew a quick breath.

"But what was this talk of a brother?" Barda demanded. "He was alone!"

A cloud seemed to pass over Dain's face. "Steven is never alone," he said. "Nevets is always with him. But Nevets is not a man you would like to meet. I have seen him only once, and I never want to do so again."

As they stared, he turned to look after the caravan. "Nevets only appears when Steven, or someone close to him is threatened. Most of the time he stays within."

Barda shook his head impatiently. "There was no one within!" he snorted. "The caravan contained only goods for sale."

"Not within the caravan," murmured Dain. "Within Steven himself."

Lief felt the hairs rise on the back of his neck. He peered along the path. The caravan was almost hidden by a fine cloud of dust. But the jingling of the bells on the horse's reins floated back to him. And over the bells came the sound of singing.

> *Colly-wobble Ol-io,*
> *Jolly-wolly Ol-io,*
> *Colly-wobble Ol-io,*
> *You don't bother me!*

But this time, Lief could have sworn that instead of one voice, there were two.

9 ~ Onward

As soon as the caravan was out of sight, the companions turned their backs on the sad remains of Where Waters Meet and picked their way down to the bank of the River Tor. There they came upon a small wooden jetty that pushed out a little way over the water. On a pole was fixed a metal sign.

River Queen

"A passenger boat must work on this part of the Tor. It must come down Broad River, carrying travellers and goods to Tora," exclaimed Lief. "That is why the bridge is built so high. Dain, have you heard of this?"

Dain shook his head, eyeing the sign suspiciously.

"It would be very nice to ride instead of walking, for a change — and faster, too," Lief said. "Should we wait?"

Barda shook his head regretfully. "I think not. For all we know the boat comes by only once a week — or perhaps no longer runs at all. This sign is not new. And in any case, we have decided to keep away from public view."

Reluctantly Lief agreed, and they trudged on.

After the joining of the rivers, the Tor broadened, deepened, and grew less winding. It looked cleaner, too, and the smell of decay was less. But Lief knew that beneath the smooth surface dark shapes, and pale ones, too, were slowly drifting. They had not disappeared, only sunk out of sight.

As the river broadened, the country on their side also changed. Gradually the trees and bushes disappeared, the reeds thickened. By the time the companions stopped for the night, the earth beneath their feet had grown marshy.

After they had eaten, Dain settled at once to sleep. The bright moon rose. Lief remembered the packets he had bought from Steven, and pulled one out, intending to share the toffee with Barda. But as soon as he had unwrapped the hard, shiny brown stuff inside he realized that, whatever it was, it was not toffee. It smelled vile, and tasted worse.

Embarrassed to have made such a stupid mistake, Lief wrapped it up again and pushed it deep into his pocket. He glanced at Barda to see if he had noticed, but Barda was busy examining his own purchase, the embroidered belt. As Lief watched curiously, wondering who the gift was for, Barda looked up and beckoned. Carefully, so as not to wake Dain, Lief crept over to him.

"I bought this belt for a reason, Lief," Barda murmured. "The cloth is double, thick, and strong. I believe we should use it — as a covering for the Belt of Deltora."

Lief opened his mouth to protest. If the Belt was enclosed by cloth, he would not be able to touch and see the gems. He would lose the value of the topaz, that sharpened the mind; the ruby, that paled at danger — and the opal, that gave glimpses of the future.

He feared the power of the opal, but for days he had been trying to screw up his courage to touch it. His father's map showed that the Maze of the Beast was on Deltora's west coast, but its actual location was unclear. The opal might provide a clue.

"The river is thick with enemies. And Dain is with us, at least as far as Tora," Barda continued. "It will only be a matter of time before he, at least, sees the Belt, however careful you are."

Lief choked back his protest. Barda was right. He felt truly sorry for Dain, but the fact remained that neither he nor Barda could yet make up their minds to trust him completely. He nodded, and Barda at once set about splitting the seam of the embroidered belt.

Lief gritted his teeth. Time was short. He could delay no longer. He slipped his hands under his shirt and ran his fingers over the gems until he came to the opal.

Eerie, bluish light. Great dripping spears of stone hanging from the roof. Gleaming, ridged walls, running with milky liquid. And something huge, white, with thrashing tail, bloodred jaws gaping . . .

Gasping, Lief tore his hands free. He screwed his eyes tightly shut, trying to dismiss the horrible picture from his mind.

"Lief?"

Barda was holding out his hand impatiently. With trembling fingers Lief pulled off the Belt. Barda slipped it inside the embroidered band and began sewing up the split. When he had finished, there was nothing to show that any work had been done at all.

Lief buckled the cloth band around his waist, under his shirt. It felt rough and strange against his skin. Father kept the Belt safe inside a leather working belt for sixteen years, he thought. This is a sensible plan.

But still he felt uneasy. He returned to the camp-fire and lay down to sleep, wishing heartily, and not for the first time, that Dain had never crossed their path.

❋

The next morning the companions struggled on, but by midday they were staggering instead of walking, plunging knee-deep into foul-smelling mud with every step.

"This is impossible," panted Barda after another hour in which very little ground had been covered. "We will have to move away from the river — get to drier land."

But by now the reed beds extended as far as the eye could see. Heavy fog blotted out the horizon. They seemed surrounded by a wet, stinking desert of mud.

It was then that they heard a faint chugging, and the sound of music. They all turned to look upstream. Coming towards them, steam puffing from its funnel, its great paddle wheel churning the water behind it, was a red-painted boat.

Lief, Barda, and Dain did not hesitate. All of them began to shout, waving their arms.

The boat came nearer. Soon it was so close that they could see the name *River Queen* painted in bright white letters on its bow. And over the music they could hear the shouts of a bearded man in a captain's cap who leaned over the side, peering at them.

"Want a ride, mates?" he roared, as the boat slowed.

"Yes!" shouted Lief, Barda, and Dain.

"Do you have money?"

"Yes!"

The man grinned. "Never let it be said that the *River Queen* turned away a paying passenger. Let alone three. Ho, Chett!"

With that, a small rowing boat splashed into the water. A strange, hunched creature with long arms and a grinning, hairy face leaped into the boat and began rowing furiously to shore.

"What is that?" whispered Lief.

"A polypan," said Dain, wrinkling his nose and taking a step back. "And if this captain uses polypans as crew, he is up to no good."

"I believe I saw something like it in the markets at Rithmere," said Barda. "It was moving around the crowd with a cup, collecting money for a woman who was playing the violin."

Dain nodded. "And secretly collecting far more than that, no doubt," he muttered, as the little boat approached. "Polypans are expert thieves. It is said that they can take the shirt off your back without your knowledge."

The rowing boat ran aground on the mud and the polypan beckoned, grinning widely. Lief saw that it was chewing some sort of dark-colored gum. Its teeth were stained brown and as the companions waded through the reeds towards it, it spat a gob of brown liquid into the river.

Lief and Dain climbed into the boat. Barda pushed it off the mud and then climbed in after them.

The polypan spat again, and then began rowing back to the *River Queen*. Though it was now carrying three extra people, the little boat ploughed through the water at great speed. The polypan's long, hairy arms were very powerful, and it seemed to have boundless energy.

When they reached the side of the larger boat, they found that a rope ladder had been lowered over the side. They began to climb upward, one after the other, very aware of the polypan's little black eyes fixed on them. No doubt, thought Lief uncomfortably, it was noting every pocket in their jackets, every fastening on their packs.

He felt glad that the Belt of Deltora was safely hidden. His only regret was that now it could not tell him if the feeling of danger that flooded over him the moment he set foot on the boat's deck was real, or imagined.

10 - The *River Queen*

The other passengers stared curiously at the newcomers. One, a hugely fat man in a striped jersey, was clutching a large painted box with a handle. A music box, Lief guessed, remembering the music he had heard from the shore. "Ho-di-ho!" the fat man cried, in a strangely light, shrill voice for one so large. "Lockie the Stripe at your service, music-lovers!"

The woman beside him giggled. She was also quite plump, and was wearing a pink dress and mittens. Her round face was framed by huge bunches of pink curls that clustered over her forehead and cheeks. With one hand she waved girlishly at Lief, Barda, and Dain. With the other she nudged the arm of a tall, thin man with a patch over one eye who stood by her side. He nodded gravely.

Two other men looked up from a table where they

had been playing cards, but made no attempt to speak. They both had shaved heads, and had broad bands tied around their brows. Their fingers were covered in rings, and each had what looked like an animal tooth stuck through one ear. They did not look friendly.

The last passenger was a haughty-looking young woman in a fine purple cloak tied at the throat with golden cord. The hands that held her golden parasol were tightly gloved in black to match her shining high-heeled boots. A scarf of purple silk was bound closely around her head. Long golden earrings swung from her ears. Her face was powdered white, her lips were painted red, and her eyes were outlined heavily in black. After one bored glance at the newcomers she turned away and stared out at the water, twirling her parasol.

Lief looked around, trying to appear at ease. But his heart was sinking. Any one of these characters could be an Ol. They could all be Ols, come to that. He began to wonder if he, Barda, and Dain would have been better off remaining in the reed beds.

The captain strode up, grinning. He was a short, chunky man with a twisted nose and grey hair in a thick braid that hung down his back like a rope. His peaked cap was pulled so low on his forehead that his eyes were in deep shadow. "Welcome aboard! How far will you be going?" he asked.

"One of my sons and I have business on the coast," Barda said pleasantly.

"Is that so?" grinned the captain. "Fishy business, I've no doubt." He nudged Barda knowingly, then stuck out a filthy hand for payment. As Barda counted out the coins, Lief saw that the captain's little finger was missing, and the ring finger was just a stump.

"A little argument with a big worm, lad," said the captain, noticing that Lief was looking at his hand. "You'll want to keep your own little pinkies out of the water as we get on. The worms, they swim up from the sea. And the farther in they get, the hungrier they get." He grinned, and the woman in pink giggled nervously.

"My younger son wishes to stop off in Tora," Barda said, raising his voice slightly. "Can you oblige him?"

"Tora?" The captain snorted with laughter. "Why, no. I can't oblige the young fellow there, I fear. A visit to Tora is not possible for us."

Dain gave a start, but instantly controlled himself. Plainly, he had decided that he had no choice but to stay with the boat, at least for the present.

Barda looked at him, then shrugged agreement.

"All right. Only two more things," the captain went on. "One, I'm offering a ride, not a guard service. This is a cruel river, and your safety is your own concern. Two, if you're Ols, that's your business. I'll carry Ols as happily as I'll carry anyone, as long as they pay. But you'll keep your hands to yourselves while you're on this boat, or you'll find yourselves overboard feeding the worms. I've dealt with Ols before, and I can do it again. Understand?"

Lief, Barda, and Dain stared, then nodded. The captain grinned, turned on his heel, and left them.

"It's all right," hissed the woman in pink. "He said that to us, too. I suppose he has to be careful. But really!"

The captain had returned to the helm in the boat's cabin. He shouted some orders, the polypan leaped to do his bidding, a whistle sounded, and the boat began moving again.

Lockie the Stripe sat down with a grunt, placed the painted music box between his knees and began to turn the handle. A piping, jigging tune began. The woman in pink and her long, thin partner began to dance, their feet thumping on the rough boards. She laughed. He remained as solemn as the grave. The two other men went back to their card game. The young woman in the purple cloak twirled her parasol and stared out at the river.

The companions sat down on a bench by the rail.

"A strange group," Barda muttered. "We will have to keep our wits about us."

"Indeed."

They all looked up. The young woman in purple had moved closer to them. She was still staring at the water, but plainly it was she who had spoken.

Lief stared at her. At the proud tilt of her head,

the painted lips, the black-shadowed eyes, the long golden earrings. Then he had the shock of his life as he recognized her.

It was Jasmine.

✳

The sun was very low in the sky. The *River Queen* chugged on, steadily moving down the river. Lockie the Stripe had at last grown tired of turning the handle of his music box, and was lying flat on his back on the deck with his eyes closed. The woman in pink and her companion were murmuring together. The two card-playing men had begun another game.

Without making any sign that she knew them, Jasmine had moved away from Barda, Lief, and Dain once more. Now she was sitting alone under her parasol at the other end of the boat. "I cannot believe I did not recognize her!" Lief whispered for the twentieth time. "How did she come by those clothes?"

"From our friend Steven, I have no doubt," Barda whispered back. "She must have tried to go inland, to avoid the reed beds, and been forced at last to double back to the Broad River path. So it was that she ended up behind us, instead of in front."

"She is very clever," Dain murmured admiringly, watching Jasmine daintily nibbling dried fruit from a small bag in her hand. "Who would describe her as 'a wild girl' now? But where is her bird?"

Lief glanced at the riverbank, and caught a

glimpse of a black shadow skimming silently through the reeds. Kree was keeping them well in sight.

*

As the sun set, the reed beds at last gave way to flat drifts of sand scattered with low bushes. The moon rose, only to be covered by cloud almost at once. The whistle blew. The *River Queen* slowed and stopped.

"We start again at first light," the captain announced as Chett threw out the anchor with a rattle of chain. "Make yourselves comfortable, friends, and get some rest. But be on guard. Remember, your safety is your business, not mine."

He stumped back into his cabin and shut the door. Everyone heard the firm click as a bolt slid home. Now there was silence, except for the lapping of the water and the creaking of timbers.

Chett ran around the deck, lighting lanterns, but they did little to pierce the darkness beyond the boat. The woman in pink leaned against her companion and closed her eyes. The men at the table threw down their cards, pulled blankets out of their packs, and settled themselves to rest.

Lief, Barda, and Dain ate a little, and drank sparingly. Then they, too, took out blankets, for the night was growing chilly. Lief yawned. The rocking of the boat was making him sleepy. He fought to stay awake.

"I will keep first watch, Lief," said Barda's voice out of the gloom. "Sleep, but be ready. I fear that this is going to be a long night."

11 - In the Night

Ashriek woke Lief. He was on his feet in an instant, his hand on his sword. He had no idea how much time had passed. It was very dark. The lanterns had gone out. The sky was black.

"Barda!" he hissed. "Dain!"

The two voices answered close beside him. His companions were also standing and alert.

The shriek came again. Lief realized that it was Kree. Kree was crying a warning. Where was Jasmine? He wanted to call to her, but knew he could not. No one must guess they knew one another.

Sleepy, grumbling voices could be heard around the deck as the other passengers stirred. "It is only a bird, my love," the woman in pink mumbled. "Go back to sleep."

For a moment, there was silence once more, except for the lapping of the water, the creaking of the boat's timbers. But surely — Lief's ears strained — surely the sounds were not quite as they had been before. They were louder. And a slight, bumping noise had joined them.

Another boat . . .

The thought had barely crossed Lief's mind when all of a sudden the darkness around the deck rails seemed to move and thicken. He could hear heavy breathing, and the tinny rattle of steel. The boat was being boarded!

"Beware!" he shouted. "Defend your — "

There was a roar of anger and a rush of feet. Someone cannoned into him, throwing him down violently. He hit the deck with a thump, striking his brow on the corner of something that chimed and jingled. The music box, he thought confusedly. He touched his forehead and felt trickling blood.

Dizzy and sick, he crawled to his knees. Lockie the Stripe was squealing in panic. The woman in pink was screaming and crying. Sounds of fighting filled the darkness. Lief could hear crashes and groans, a bloodcurdling yell, the splash of something heavy falling over the side. He could hear the clash of steel against steel.

"Give us some light, you fool!" roared a voice.

One by one, the lanterns began to glow once more. The polypan was lighting them, grinning and chewing as he swung from one to the other. Gradually, a scene of horror was revealed.

There must have been twenty invaders at least. Men, and women, too, with knives, swords, and axes. They wore a strange array of fine and tattered clothes, their wild hair was matted, their eyes glittering.

Barda, his back against the deck railing, fought two of them. Dain was beside him, fending off a third. Lockie was cringing on the deck. The woman in pink, wailing helplessly, was clutching at the thin man who was shaking her off, crawling away like a long-legged spider looking for a hole to hide in. One of the card-playing men lay dead in a pool of blood. The other had disappeared. Over the side, no doubt, thought Lief, remembering the splash.

Of the captain there was no sign. No doubt he was still locked in his cabin, and Lief was quite sure that he would not venture out for the sake of a few passengers. They had accepted his terms, paid their money, and taken their chances. He had not spent a lifetime on this dangerous river for nothing.

Lief staggered to his feet, feeling for his sword. He had to help Barda. But the deck seemed to be spinning. He could not move fast enough. With horror he saw one of Barda's opponents close in, grabbing a lantern and swinging it in Barda's face. Barda thrust himself backward to escape the flame. The deck rail groaned and began to split.

"No!" cried Lief, lurching forward. But the next second the whole section of deck rail broke away. Barda, the pirate, and the lantern tumbled into the water. There was a tremendous splashing and bubbling. Then silence.

"Barda!" shrieked Lief, stumbling to the gap. But no head broke the surface of the water. The lantern had gone out. All was darkness.

Lief prepared to jump. All he knew was that he had to save Barda, who was somewhere down in that black water. But with despair he felt himself pulled backwards by grasping hands and thrown to the deck again.

"Not until we have picked you clean, boy!" laughed the man above him, a man with a nose that reached almost to his chin, and teeth filed sharp as knives. "The worms can have you then!"

Everything was blurry. Stabs of pain shot through Lief's head as he was rolled and pushed on the deck. The cloak was ripped from his back. His sword and money bag were taken. The embroidered band was pulled from his waist.

No!

He moaned, scrambling to rise. A heavy boot kicked him in the ribs.

"Finish him off, Finn, and the other one, too," screamed a voice.

Finn. Lief squirmed at the sound of the name — one of the names on the walls of Where Waters Meet.

"The other one is valuable," a deeper voice called. "He is with the Resistance. I have seen him with Doom. The Guards will pay in gold for him, alive."

"See what I have found, trying to creep up on us!" A huge, grinning woman with streaming red hair came around the corner of the cabin, hauling Jasmine in her brawny arms. Jasmine's feet were swinging high off the ground. She was kicking and struggling, biting at the hands that gripped her, but the woman took no notice.

"Fine clothes for a fine lady!" she roared. "Would I not look beautiful in these?" She tore off the purple scarf, and Jasmine's tangled black hair swung free. Then the woman set about tearing at the golden cords that bound the cloak around Jasmine's throat.

There was a screech, and a black shadow swooped at her head. With a snap, a sharp beak struck her just above the ear. The woman shrieked and staggered and her grip on Jasmine loosened.

In a flash, Jasmine had wriggled free, leaving her cloak in the woman's hands. In a moment her dagger was in her hand, and her booted foot was kicking backwards with deadly force.

The woman howled and fell back, lurching into Lief's attacker and sending him sprawling. Jasmine hauled Lief to his feet and passed him her second dagger. "Stay behind me!" she ordered. "Where is Barda?"

"Gone," muttered Lief. Jasmine's eyes darkened. As Kree flew down to her arm she whirled to face the pirates, baring her teeth.

Lief saw them hesitate. And well they might. The

elegant lady they had thought to rob so easily had become before their eyes a fiery warrior whose dagger glinted as brightly as their swords. Even the polypan was gaping in astonishment. And the woman in pink —

Her mouth was open. Her eyes were burning, huge, fixed on Jasmine. And as she stared, something began to happen to her face. It was as though the burning eyes were melting it. The flesh was paling. The pink curls were shrivelling and drawing back, back to her swelling skull to reveal the mark high on her brow. Her arms and shoulders were bubbling and twisting. Then her whole body was writhing upward, flickering like cold white flame.

"Ol!" The cry of terror echoed around the deck. And instantly the pirates were scattering, scrambling for the rail, dragging Dain and all their booty with them. Their feet crashed onto the deck of their own boat. The polypan leaped after them, chattering and spitting in fear. Oars rattled and splashed as ruffians bent to pull away from the danger, to escape downstream.

But the Ol cared nothing for them. The burning eyes were fixed on Jasmine. The toothless mouth was grinning greedily. It lunged forward, its long, white fingers twitching as they reached for Jasmine's throat.

12 - Shadows

The chill of the Ol came before it — a breathtaking cold that froze the limbs, stung the eyes, and turned the lips to ice. Gasping, staggering back, trying to shield Lief with her body, Jasmine swung her dagger at the white, grasping fingers. Half-stunned with cold, Kree dashed himself against the thing's peaked head.

But nothing, nothing could stop it. The fingers of one hand snaked forward and caught Jasmine around the neck, lifting her from the ground. Almost carelessly, the other hand grasped Lief's dagger arm in a grip of frozen iron. The dagger fell clattering to the deck.

The moon slipped from behind the clouds. Its cool white light flooded the deck, fell over Lief's face. We are dying, he thought, almost in wonder. Time seemed to be moving very slowly.

Then the Ol jerked violently. In a dream of terror, Lief looked up at the vast, wavering body and saw something sharp and gleaming slide out of the right side of its chest, growing longer, longer . . .

The grip on his arm loosened. He saw Jasmine fall. The Ol began to tip forward.

"Get out of the way, you fool!" roared a voice.

Desperately Lief rolled to one side. The Ol crashed to the deck, the wooden pole of the long spike that had pierced its heart sticking up from its back. Its flesh bulged and heaved. Pink curls and a single blue eye bubbled hideously in the whiteness.

Grinning savagely, the captain heaved the spike free and kicked the collapsing body into the river. "Ols! I hate 'em!" he growled.

Lief crawled to Jasmine. Filli was chattering to her, trying to make her open her eyes. She was breathing, but her neck flamed red, as though it had been burned.

Dain's pack was still lying on the deck. Lief tore it open and pulled out the honey jar. He smeared some of the golden stuff on Jasmine's mouth. "Lick your lips, Jasmine," he whispered. "The honey will help you, as it helped Barda." As he said the name, his throat closed with pain.

The captain was looking around, shaking his head. The deck was littered with pirates' bodies. "Looks like your dad dealt with a few of the scum before he went over the side," he said. "They got your brother, too, did they? If he *was* your brother, which I doubt."

Lief swallowed. "They took Dain away," he managed to say. "I have to follow them. Get him back."

And the Belt. The Belt!

The words screamed in his mind and again the dreadfulness of what had happened swept over him.

The captain came closer and peered curiously at Jasmine. Filli hissed and bared his tiny teeth, his fur bristling. The captain jumped back and fell onto a pile of planks. There was a shriek, and Lockie the Stripe crawled out of hiding.

"I can't stand this river," he moaned. "Never again! I'm going to retire. I don't care if I starve!"

"That's what you always say, you cowardly blob!" snarled the captain rudely. "What about my deck rail? And my polypan? Who's going to pay for them?"

"Who cares for that?" cried Lief. "How can you talk of money when the decks are awash with blood?" Angry tears had sprung, scalding, into his eyes.

The captain turned to him, sneering. "If that's how you feel, you can get off, boyo!" he growled. "You, your wildcat friend, *and* her crazy bird. I'll be glad to see the last of you. Don't you think I know why that Ol attacked? It recognized her, didn't it? It had orders to get her. And you, too, for all I know."

He turned, snarling, to Lockie the Stripe. "Row

them to the bank," he snapped. "Get them out of my sight! We're going back to Broad River for repairs."

✳

By the time Lockie, very downcast, had dumped Jasmine and Lief and rowed back to the *River Queen*, steam was already pouring from the boat's funnel. Moments later, the anchor chain clattered and the paddle wheel began to move. The boat turned and chugged away upstream, leaving the companions with only Dain's pack and one blanket for comfort.

Jasmine was conscious, but could barely speak. She took another spoonful of honey and swallowed painfully. "What are we to do?" she croaked.

"Follow the pirates and get the Belt back," muttered Lief, with more confidence than he felt.

Jasmine nodded, her head bowed. "They have Dain, as well as the Belt," she said. "We must help Dain. Barda would have wanted us to do that."

She was shaking all over. Lief took the blanket and wrapped it around her. Then he sat close beside her, for warmth.

"If only we knew where the pirates planned to go!" he said. "The water from the Dreaming Spring would have helped us find out. But all that remains was in the packs." He looked up at the sky. The stars were fading. The pirates' boat must already be far distant.

"We must go," said Jasmine. "They are getting away!" She struggled to rise, but fell back almost at once. Lief covered her again with the blanket. His head was thumping.

"Barda would say that we should rest," he said. "He would say, 'What point is there in catching up to our enemies but being too weak to fight them?' And he would be right. He was almost always right."

"I am glad to hear you say so," growled a familiar voice.

And out of the shadows walked Barda — soaked, shivering, but alive! The shock was so great that for a moment Lief could not speak. But his joy and relief must have shown in his face, for Barda grinned and clapped him on the shoulder as he sat down with a weary groan.

"Did you think I was gone for good?" he asked. "Well, so did I, I confess. But I managed to fight off the cutthroat who went over the side with me. And the worms, if worms there are, must have been busy with other prey."

"The card-playing man," Jasmine suggested huskily. She put her hand to her throat as she spoke, but plainly her pain was already easing, thanks to the Queen Bee honey. And her spirits had soared now that Barda had returned.

Barda nodded gravely. "Perhaps so. I remember little of getting to the bank. I came to myself only a few minutes ago. There was the sound of the boat. Then I heard your voices along the bank."

"Barda, they took the Belt." It was agony for Lief

to say it. "My sword, all our belongings — and Dain."

Barda took a deep breath. "So," he said finally. "So we must deal with that."

He crawled to his feet. "But first we must warm and dry ourselves. We will start a fire — a fine blaze. And if any more enemies see it and come to attack us, they are welcome. A gang of pirates and an Ol together could not finish us — let others try if they dare!"

Lief staggered up and went to help collect wood. The terrible despair that had engulfed him had lifted with Barda's return. But as he plodded the barren sand, now slowly lightening with the coming of dawn, he still felt sick at heart.

It was all very well to speak bravely of following the pirates, of tracking them down. But by the time the companions reached the coast, the battered boat would certainly be hidden away in some sheltered bay. However were they to find it?

He saw some old planks that had washed up on the shore, and walked towards them. Then he realized that there was something else lying in shallow water just beyond the wood. It looked like a heap of rubbish and rags, but it was not. It was a dead man.

"Barda!" he called.

Barda came quickly, and together they pulled the body up onto the sand. "This is the pirate who went into the water with me," Barda said. "He, it seems, was not as lucky as I was."

Lief stared down at the gaunt face. In death, the pirate looked more pathetic than savage. He watched as Barda crouched beside the body and began pulling at the clothing, checking the pockets for weapons or anything else of value. There had been a time when neither of them would have dreamed of robbing a dead body. But that time had long gone.

Barda exclaimed and sat back on his heels. He was holding something in his hand — a thin package wrapped in oilskin. Carefully he unwrapped it. The paper inside was damp, but still in one piece. He placed it on the sand and Lief bent over it. Even in the dim dawn light, he could see clearly what it was.

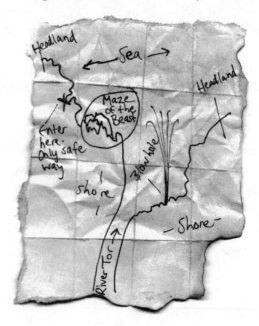

"It is the way to the Maze of the Beast," muttered Barda.

"The pirates are going to the Maze? But why? It is a place of terror." Lief's heart was thudding painfully.

"They would not care, if they had heard of a great gem hidden there." Barda gritted his teeth. "And somehow they have heard of it, Lief. They are going to seek it. And now they have the Belt to help them."

13 - Disaster

Two days later the companions stood on the shore, looking out at the vast, foam-flecked blue of the sea. Wind tore at their clothes and whipped their hair. During their cold, hungry journey they had seen several walled villages on the other side of the river, and even passed a bridge. But of the pirates there had been no sign, and even now their boat was nowhere to be seen.

To Jasmine, who had never seen the sea, the ocean was a fresh sight, and a source of wonder. To Lief, at first, it was like a breath of home. Not so much the sight, for the Shadow Lord had long forbidden the coast to the people of Del. But the sound and smell, and the taste of salt on his lips, were achingly familiar.

Yet after only a few moments the feeling melted away and a kind of loathing took its place.

This was not the coast of Del. This coast was bare

and completely silent except for the wind and the pounding waves. There was no sign of any living thing. There were no fish jumping in the swelling water, or crabs scuttling on the sand. And Kree was the only bird in sight.

Lief found himself shrinking from the hissing foam that crawled towards his feet. Into this sea poured all the filth of the River Tor. Its clean, sparkling surface was a lie, for beneath it rolled all the waste and evil the river had been forced to carry for so long. Killer worms squirmed in its depths, feeding on the bodies of the dead, crawling on the wreckage of broken boats. And at the end of the long strip of sand to Lief's left, under the headland that looked like a haggard face, was the place called the Maze of the Beast.

Abruptly Lief turned his head away so that he looked back across the river mouth to his right. Beyond the swirling water, more sand stretched away to another gloomy headland that rose from a base of flat, smooth rock. As he watched, a towering jet of spray spurted into the air from the rock. It was as though some giant creature hidden there was spitting a huge mouthful of water at the sky.

Jasmine hissed with shock.

"Do not fear," muttered Lief. "It is a blowhole. My mother has told me of such things. Water forces its way through a tunnel under the rock, then sprays up through a hole far from where it entered."

"I was not afraid," said Jasmine hastily. "Only

surprised — for a moment. But I am glad we do not have to go to that side."

This side does not hold much joy for us, either, thought Lief, as he began to trudge with his companions along the wet sand. Wind rushed around his ears. The shore ahead was bare, the headland threatening.

He, Barda, and Jasmine had been so careful, for so long. They had borne separation, they had crept and hidden. But here, where the Shadow Lord's servants must surely be watching and waiting, they had no choice but to show themselves.

There was nowhere to hide. And they no longer had the Belt to warn them of approaching peril.

Lief glanced at Barda and felt the same pang of dismay that he had felt many times over the past two days. The big man was walking with bowed head, as though he had forgotten that danger might at any time swoop at them from the skies or rise from beneath the sand. He was meekly following Jasmine, who was striding ahead, her eyes darting everywhere.

The unexpected finding of the pirates' map, which had given Lief and Jasmine a new burst of energy, seemed to have made Barda thoughtful and withdrawn. Except to urge haste, he had said little as they moved on down the river. While his companions talked of their hopes and fears, he simply listened.

Plainly, he had something on his mind. Something he would not share. When Lief took risks, he did not complain. When Jasmine stopped to pick up bits and pieces washed up on the riverbank, he said nothing. He was so patient and gentle, in fact, that Lief became uncomfortable, and longed to hear the old, irritable Barda growling once more.

Jasmine glanced behind her, and Lief saw her forehead crease in a frown as she noticed Barda's downcast head. Lief ran to catch up with her.

"Could he be ill?" she whispered. "Or has he simply lost heart?"

Lief shook his head. "Things have been desperate before, and always he has been a tower of strength. This is different. Perhaps — perhaps he senses the coming of some great disaster."

This time it was his turn to look sideways at his companion. And, as he had feared she might, Jasmine snorted and tossed her head. "Barda does not have magic powers! He cannot see into the future! And even if he could, what greater disaster could there be than what has happened already?"

She looked ahead again, her face grim. They had nearly reached the rocks. Calling Kree to her, she hunched her shoulders against the cold, waiting for Barda to catch up.

The wind-torn cliff frowned above them. The rocks rose to cruel peaks, then fell away into gaps pitted with dark holes. Waves crashed against them, spattering the companions with spray as they began cautiously to make the slippery crossing. Still there was no sign of the pirates, or of any other enemy.

How strange, thought Lief uneasily. Why . . . ?

Then he saw the cave. It gaped in the cliff face just beyond where he was standing — a dark, secret mouth, above the reach of the waves and hidden from both sides by jagged rocks.

He beckoned to Barda and Jasmine, and silently they all crept to the cave entrance. A cold, dank draught of air sighed into their faces. It was like the breath of the sea — breath tinged with salt and death.

Filli whimpered from his hiding place under Jasmine's jacket. She put up a hand to calm him and moved into the dimness.

Lief and Barda quickly followed. Lief blinked, waiting for his eyes to adjust to the dim light. But even before they had done so, he knew that the cave was empty of life. It would be impossible for any place where a living creature breathed to be so utterly still.

Yet his skin still prickled as though danger was threatening. Suddenly he heard Jasmine draw a sharp breath, and Barda give a low groan. He snatched the dagger from his waistband . . .

And then he saw what his companions had seen before him.

A gaping hole yawned in the ground — a hole that led to a ghastly darkness. You could see, by the sand piled around it, that it had been dug very recently. There were heavy boot prints everywhere.

A paper lay half-buried in the sand. Lief picked it up. It was another copy of the pirates' map.

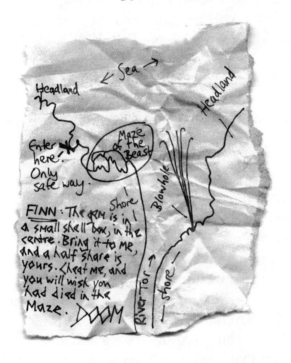

His voice shaking, Lief read the message aloud.

"Doom guessed our goal. Betrayed us!" Jasmine cried.

Lief forced his stiff lips to move. "It may not be too late. Perhaps the pirates did not find the gem. Perhaps the Beast in the Maze killed them."

"I fear that is too much to hope for." Barda had

picked up another object from the sand. It was a small box made of pearl shell. Its hinges had been broken as if rough, greedy hands had torn them apart.

"They have the gem," Barda said. "They have the gem, and they have the Belt. We are too late. It is over."

"No! We must give chase! We must find them!" Lief crumpled the paper in his hand.

"Do not deceive yourself," said Barda heavily. "With such riches in their hands, the pirates would have no need to return to the river. By now they will be far out to sea, putting as much distance between Doom and themselves as possible, and looking for strangers with whom to trade. They are out of our reach."

He put a gentle hand on Lief's shoulder. "It is a bitter blow, but we must face it," he said. "Our quest is over. We must return to Del." He kicked at the tumbled sand. "Think of this, Lief. Now your parents can be freed. You can go to the palace and show yourself — pretend that you just ran away, as your father said."

Our quest is over. Face it. Slowly, Lief nodded. Drearily, he thought of Dain, now beyond help.

Jasmine had been very silent. Lief glanced at her. She was standing on the other side of the cave, utterly still. Kree sat like a carved statue on her arm. Jasmine's face was in shadow, but in her hand something gleamed. Lief went cold.

Jasmine had drawn her dagger. But why? And why was she standing so still? As though she was afraid to move. Afraid to startle . . .

He began to turn. And at once, like a snake striking, someone who had crept up behind him lunged forward. Barda flung up his arms with a bellow of agony as a great sword plunged home, spearing him through the chest.

Lief heard his own cry echoing around the cave. His ears ringing, his heart wrung, he spun around, dagger in hand, ready to leap at the attacker.

And then his jaw dropped. For standing there, panting and haggard, pulling his bloodstained sword from the falling body, was another Barda.

14 ~ Meetings

Wildly, Lief swung to look at the figure now collapsed on the ground. His stomach heaved as he saw the face dissolving, the body collapsing into a writhing mass. The long, crooked hands of the pink-haired lady's dancing partner pushed out of the whiteness, to be quickly followed by the head of a white water bird and many other eyes and mouths that Lief did not recognize.

"Ol!" he hissed.

"Of course!" Barda's voice rumbled behind him. "How could you have been deceived?"

Hearing that gloriously familiar, irritable growl, Lief dropped the dagger with a cry of joy and flung his arms around Barda's shoulders.

"Steady," said the big man uncomfortably. But he did not pull away.

"When I saw you at the cave entrance, I could not believe it!" Jasmine had bounced over to Barda and was embracing him in her turn. "How did this happen?"

Barda shrugged. "The Ol thought I was dead. But I am not killed so easily. I crawled ashore and took much time to regain strength enough to follow your tracks."

He shook his head. "One set of tracks puzzled me. But when I reached here, I understood." He grimaced with distaste at the remains of the Ol, now just a bubbling pool on the cave floor.

"I should have known!" said Lief. "You — I mean, *it* — spoke of how we had escaped from pirates and an Ol! Yet you had gone over the side, Barda, before the Ol that was the pink-haired woman revealed itself. How could you have known about it?"

"And no wonder it was so quiet and gentle!" Jasmine exclaimed. "It could copy your appearance and voice, and learn about us from what we said. But it did not know how to behave. It had not had time to learn what you were really like!"

Barda raised an eyebrow and Jasmine realized, too late, that her words had not been very flattering. She busied herself picking up the second dagger and tucking it into her boot.

"I may not be particularly quiet and gentle by nature, Jasmine," said Barda dryly. "But on the other hand, I would not have been persuaded to give up our quest because of one small problem."

"One small problem?!" Lief exclaimed. "The pirates have the sixth gem, and the Belt! And they are far away!"

"How do you know they are far away?" Barda demanded. "Because an Ol told you so? The pirates could be sheltering in a bay just around the headland at this very moment, for all you know."

He waved a hand at the hole in the sand. "And if they have found the gem, so much the better. I would prefer to get it from them than face the Beast."

The sickening vision the opal had given him rose in Lief's mind. Suddenly he longed for fresh air. He turned and blundered out of the cave . . .

Straight into the arms of a grinning man whose hooked nose nearly met his chin, whose yellowed teeth were filed to sharp points, and whose savage eyes gleamed with triumph.

※

There were only two pirates in all, but with a sword pressed against Lief's throat, Barda and Jasmine had no choice but to surrender. Bound cruelly together, the three were hauled back across the rocks and into a rowing boat, with Kree swooping helplessly above them.

"Did I not tell you I saw movement in the cave, Nak?" chattered the man with the filed teeth. "Was it not worth making a landing?"

"They will make fine sport," agreed his companion, the huge red-haired woman who had seized Jasmine on the *River Queen*.

She twisted her fingers in Jasmine's hair and spitefully wrenched the girl's head back, so that she could stare down into her face. "You will learn not to kick your betters, fine lady!" she snarled. "We have a special fate reserved for trespassers on our shore. A little pet we want you to meet. Is that not so, Finn?"

The man sniggered agreement. As he took his place in the boat, he unbuttoned his coat. He was wearing the embroidered belt. He noticed Lief's eyes upon it, and grinned evilly. "Do you miss it?" he jeered. "I am not surprised. It is heavier than it looks — fine quality indeed! But you will not need it where you are going."

And, still laughing, he bent to the oars.

Once the boat had reached the calmer water beyond the waves, it turned and began to go back the way the companions had come. It reached the place where the Tor joined the sea and moved on, Kree battling the wind overhead, Finn and Nak straining against the current.

At last they drew opposite the blowhole, skirting the sheet of rock with care. And there was the pirate boat, rocking in shallow water, sheltering in an enormous cavern in the headland.

"Do not follow us, Kree!" shrieked Jasmine to the sky. "Wait!"

"If he does, he will wait forever," sneered Nak.

As the rowing boat slid into the cavern, Lief saw the rest of the pirate crew eating and drinking on a huge ledge above the water. The polypan ran to and fro, carrying dishes, ordered about by everyone. There was something different about it, Lief thought. It looked harried and unhappy, but that was not all. He thought about it for a moment, then noticed something else.

Dain lay in a corner, firmly bound. Another prisoner lay with him — a man in a tight blue coat.

Nak and Finn were greeted with cheers. Lief, Barda, and Jasmine were pushed and jeered at for a time, then thrown down with Dain and the other man.

"Their screams will be music to my ears!" screeched Nak, as she swaggered back to the crowd. "But it will be all the sweeter on a full stomach!"

As soon as she had gone, Lief saw Filli slip from Jasmine's jacket and scurry to her boot. With all his might the little creature tried to pull the hidden dagger free, but the task was far beyond his strength.

Dain's exhausted eyes were dark with misery. "I knew that if you were alive, you would come for me," he breathed. "At first I prayed you would — then I prayed you would not. Now what I feared has come to pass. They have you."

"What is to be done with us?" whispered Lief.

Dain licked his lips. "I do not know," he answered. "But they speak of something called the Glus."

The man in the blue coat moaned in terror.

Dain glanced at him. "This is Milne. They call him a traitor. He tried to kill Nak, when she said he was a fool for bringing me with them."

Milne, thought Lief. Milne. Nak. Finn. Well, I hoped to meet the owners of those names, and so I have. If we have to die, at least we will be taking one of them with us.

The polypan had been sniffing around them. Now it pushed its face into Lief's chest and whimpered. Lief tried to push it away. Its smell was horrible. It reminded him of something, but he could not think what.

"Are they still going to give you to the Grey Guards, Dain?" hissed Jasmine.

Dain nodded. "Yes, though there was bitter argument. Milne and the others liked the plan. But Nak and Finn were afraid."

"Afraid?" Lief looked at Nak and Finn laughing around the fire. "They seem to fear nothing."

A strange, baffled expression crossed Dain's face. "They fear Doom," he whispered. "Finn said that if Doom ever finds out that they have knowingly betrayed the Resistance, their lives will not be worth a handful of ash. Doom will hunt them down one by one, and they will never escape him."

Cheat me, and you will wish you had died in the Maze.

So that is why the pirates are still here, thought Lief. They are too afraid to run from Doom.

"We leave tonight," Dain was saying. "Nak and Finn refuse to go. They will stay here with the booty. The rest will sail with me up the river to meet the Guards near Dread Mountain."

The polypan was pawing at Lief again. "What ails you?" he said angrily, trying to squirm away from it. "What do you want from me?"

Then, suddenly, he knew.

15 - The Glus

L ief whispered urgently. The polypan listened. At first it shook its head, then, finally, it nodded and darted away.

Barda and Jasmine took no notice of it. They were concentrating on Dain.

He was biting his lip, plainly still confused and shaken by what he had heard the pirates say. "I thought I knew Doom," he muttered. "Now it seems I knew but little. Finn spoke of him — as though he had powers beyond those of an ordinary man."

"Then Finn is a fool!" Jasmine said decidedly. She raised her chin as they all glanced at her. "I fought Doom in Rithmere, remember," she went on. "I felt his danger then, and understood it. Doom does not care if he lives or dies. Whatever he has suffered has scarred his heart as well as his face. Inside him now there is only anger, bitterness, and cold."

"So he has nothing left to lose," Barda murmured.

Jasmine shivered. "That is what makes him a deadly enemy. That is the source of his power. But it is a power I should not care to have." She put up her hand to fondle Filli's soft fur.

Chett came chattering up and pulled Lief's sleeve impatiently.

"Put it on me, under my shirt," Lief hissed. "Only then . . ."

This time, Jasmine and Barda, and Dain, too, were watching. Lief saw his friends' eyes widen as the polypan, grumbling, fastened the embroidered belt around his waist. He saw them glance wildly at Finn, who was eating and drinking with his companions, quite unaware that he had been robbed.

"You are a fine thief indeed, Chett," said Lief. He rolled on his side and let the polypan take what it wanted from his pocket — the little packet he had bought from Steven. The creature unwrapped the glossy brown stuff, stuck it into its mouth, and began chewing blissfully.

"This gum is a great polypan favorite, it seems," Lief said. "Chett went with the pirates not knowing that they do not keep supplies of it for rewards, as the *River Queen* captain does. Was it not fortunate that I happened to have some?"

Barda wet his lips. "Jasmine has a second dagger

in her boot. Would Chett get it out, in return for another piece for later?" he asked.

The polypan shook its head violently.

"I have already tried that," Lief answered smoothly. "But Chett was afraid to go so far. I said that Nak and Finn would never find out who had done it — "

"Indeed!" Barda and Jasmine agreed together.

But still the polypan shook its head, casting envious eyes at Lief's pockets.

"So then I asked for my belt," said Lief, carefully looking anywhere but at Dain. "It has value for me, Barda, because you gave it to me."

"Of course." Barda nodded. "And the other little treasure? The pretty jewel found only a day or two ago? In a small pearl-shell box?"

"Chett seems never to have heard of it," said Lief. "Finn is keeping it to himself, I think."

"Treasure?" Suddenly interested, Milne rolled over and glared at them with bloodshot eyes. Dain, too, raised himself on one elbow and stared.

Not sure of the wisdom of what he was doing, Lief ploughed on recklessly. "We had a map, but we arrived at the spot too late. Finn had already been there. Wait! I will show you."

He whispered to the polypan. Chewing madly and grinning with delight, it dug its hand into another of his pockets and drew out the map Lief had found on the cave floor. It trotted over and put the map in front of Milne. Then it darted back to Lief. He rolled again so that it could claim its second reward.

Milne squinted at the paper. His lips moved as he made out the words, especially the note on the side — the note signed "Doom." For a brief moment he was silent. Then, with a sneer, he rolled over on his back again and turned his head away.

Before Lief had time to wonder about this, he was pulled roughly to his feet.

"Time to dispose of our garbage!" grinned Finn, shaking him by the collar. The other pirates, flushed with eating and drinking, swarmed over their victims and began dragging them out of the cavern and onto the great expanse of smooth rock that stretched out to sea. Dain, left behind, moaned helplessly, struggling against the ropes that bound him.

"Listen to me!" Lief shouted at the top of his voice. "Finn has cheated you! He has treasure that he has not shared! He found a great gem!"

There was sudden stillness. "Oh?" asked Nak in a hard voice, glancing at Finn. "A great gem? Where did he find it."

"In the Maze of the Beast!" shouted Lief.

To his amazement, the men and women around him, including Nak and Finn, began shrieking with laughter.

"Aha! Then you and your friends can perhaps find another one!" jeered Nak. "No doubt the Glus

242

will be happy to help you look. We will cut your ropes, so you can enjoy yourselves for longer."

There was the sound of stone grating on stone as a huge boulder was pushed away from a round black hole in the rock.

"Good hunting!" snarled Finn. Lief felt his ropes being cut through. The next instant there was a shove in the small of his back. Then he was pitching headfirst into the hole, and down, down, into darkness.

✳

There were many sounds. The sound of Milne sobbing in helpless terror. Faint laughter from above as the stone was shoved back into place. The sound of dripping water echoing, echoing through endless, winding spaces. And something worse. The sticky, stealthy sliding of something huge, stirring.

Lief opened his eyes. He knew what he would see.

Eerie, bluish light. Great dripping spears of stone hanging from the roof. Thick, lumpy pillars rising from the floor. Twisted columns, rippled and grooved, like water made solid. Gleaming, ridged walls, running with milky liquid.

The Maze of the Beast. How could he have thought they would escape it? It had always been their fate.

Lief turned, wincing at the pain in his shoulder. Jasmine and Barda were crawling upright, looking around in dazed confusion. Milne thrashed and wallowed in the water at their feet.

The sliding sound grew louder.

"It is coming," Milne sobbed. "The Glus . . ."

Jasmine snatched her dagger from her boot and swung around, facing first one way, then another. "I cannot tell where it is coming from!" she cried. "It seems all around us. Which way — ?"

The sound of monstrous, sliding flesh was everywhere.

Then they saw it — a gigantic, sluglike beast, sickly pale, oozing towards them. It filled the vast passage through which it crawled, its swollen body rippling horribly, its tiny eyes waving on the ends of stalks at the top of its terrible head.

Gabbling with terror, Milne staggered to his feet.

The Glus lunged forward, rearing its head. Its spine-tipped tail thrashed. Its bloodred mouth yawned wide. Mottled stripes lit up along its back.

A thick, gurgling, sucking sound began, deep in its chest. Then, with terrifying suddenness, a tangle of fine white threads sprayed out of its throat, aimed directly at Milne.

Screaming, Milne dodged, flailing with his arms. Most of the threads fell short of their mark, but a few drifted onto one hand and a shoulder, drawing them together and binding them like ropes of steel. He stumbled and fell, struggling to pull his hand free, rolling and kicking in the water.

"Get up!" screamed Jasmine, plunging towards him, holding out her hand. The Beast thrashed, rearing, the stripes on its back glowing like evil lights, the stalks on its head moving, dipping, as its cold, vacant eyes fixed themselves upon her. Jasmine slashed at it in a useless attempt to keep it back.

The bloodred jaws opened. The thick, gurgling sound began again. Still Jasmine reached out for Milne. Still he screamed and writhed in helpless panic.

"Jasmine, no! You cannot help him!" Barda caught Jasmine around the waist, swinging her back and aside, just as the Beast struck again. White threads cascaded from its throat, covering Milne's head and neck with a stiffening helmet of white.

Half-blinded, mad with terror, Milne floundered to his feet and splashed blindly away, one arm crooked helplessly as he blundered into the depths of the blue-lit maze.

The Glus paused, its eyestalks waving. Then, as the companions stood frozen, staring in fascinated horror, it effortlessly turned its vast body, oozed through a narrow gap between two columns as easily as though it was made of oil, and followed him.

"Now is our chance," said Jasmine urgently. "Quickly! There is fresh air down here. I can smell it. And where there is air, there is a way out!"

"Give me the dagger!" hissed Lief, pulling off the embroidered belt. Wordlessly Jasmine thrust the

245

weapon into his hands. Lief stuck the sharp point into the fabric of the belt and ripped the embroidery apart. The Belt of Deltora slid out into his hands.

For a split second he gazed at it. It was so beautiful. So precious. But the ruby was pale. The emerald was dull.

Danger. Evil. Fear.

"Lief!" shouted Barda.

Lief clasped the Belt around his waist. He gripped it with his hands, drawing strength from its familiar weight and warmth. Perhaps, now, it would never be complete. But even as it was, it had power. The topaz gleamed through his fingers, bright, rich gold.

† **The Topaz is a powerful gem, and its strength increases as the moon grows full . . . It strengthens and clears the mind . . .**

The moon was high above them, blocked by churning sea and a mountain of rock, but still its power reached the stone. Lief felt his mind clear and sharpen, as the mists of confusion and fear lifted.

"This way!" he shouted, pointing to a passage that led away from where Milne had gone. "But slowly, carefully. I think the Beast's eyes and hearing are weak, but it is attracted by movement. It feels movement in the Maze, as a spider feels insects struggling in its web. That is why it chased Milne, instead of staying and attacking us."

It was agony to move slowly, when every instinct was telling them to run, run blindly as Milne had done. They crept along, through passage after passage, twisting and turning. They wet their hands and their faces, the better to feel that breath of coolness that would warn them of a crack, a gap, a way out.

16 - Discoveries

At last they could walk no farther. They squeezed into a narrow space between two lumpy, dripping walls. There they rested, panting and shivering, one wall pressed hard against their backs, the other a hand's breadth from their faces. The sound of Milne's screams and splashes floated, echoing, in the air. He was still running, lost somewhere in the Maze.

And the terrible sound of the Glus never stopped.

"It is moving so slowly," whispered Jasmine, listening. "How can it hope to catch him?"

"It has only to follow, and wait," said Barda. "Even if he does not make a mistake, and meets it face to face around some corner, he will have to rest sooner or later."

His voice sounded odd. Lief glanced at him

quickly. Barda was looking at the wall in front of him. Carefully he raised his hand and slowly traced shapes in the gleaming stone.

A bony arm. Five fingers. A skull, its mouth gaping in a silent scream.

"Here is one who stopped to rest, and stopped too long," Barda said. He twisted his neck and looked over his shoulder. Milky drops ran slowly, ceaselessly down the wall at his back. Already they were pooling on his shoulders, setting into a fine crust of stone.

With a cry of horror, Lief and Jasmine pulled themselves forward. Drying stone cracked and slid from their backs and shoulders, splashing into the water at their feet. They edged out of their hiding place and, looking back, saw their own shapes imprinted in the wall.

"How long would it have taken before we were stuck fast?" asked Barda grimly. "An hour, perhaps? Even less? If we had slept . . ."

They began to move again. And now they saw the twisted shapes, the lumps and ridges on walls, columns, and pillars, for what they were. Everywhere they looked were the bones of the dead — clawing hands, sprawled legs, skulls that seemed to shriek of terror.

Lief felt himself shivering all over. He imagined the horror of waking and finding himself trapped by the stone of the wall. He imagined struggling, struggling . . . while the Glus moved slowly towards him.

"We must not rest," he muttered. "We must not sleep."

They crept on, and on, trying to make as little movement as possible, their faces turned to the wall, their hands held out in front of them. After a while, Lief's thoughts became a wandering haze — a haze of water, white walls, endless movement, words. *There is a way out. We must find it. We must not rest. We must not sleep.*

✳

Lief's head fell forward, jolting him awake. He blinked, confused, and realized that he had been walking in a dream. He had no idea of how much time had passed.

Dimly, he became aware that Milne's screams and splashes had stopped. Perhaps they had stopped a long time ago.

And if — if Milne had stopped running, where was the Beast? Sweat breaking out on his brow, Lief listened to the echoes, and at last made out a soft, horrible sound, mingling with the dripping water. It was not the sticky sliding he had heard before, but a still, sighing, sucking sound that raised the hairs on the back of his neck.

"Barda, Jasmine . . ." he whispered. But his friends did not answer. They moved, but their eyes were fixed and glazed. They were in a dreamlike state, as he had been.

He took a breath to speak again. Then, suddenly, it was as though a flame shot through him, from his fingers to his face.

The Belt! The Belt had grown hot! Lief stopped, shocked and disbelieving. A rounded pillar of stone stood beside him. Cautiously he moved towards it. The Belt grew even hotter. It seemed to burn under his fingers.

Barda and Jasmine were turning a corner, moving out of sight. Calling, he splashed forward recklessly, catching at their arms to stop them.

Then he froze. For straight ahead of them was the Glus. Its bloated body was rippling and heaving, its head invisible. And from the billowing mountain of flesh came that soft, hideous sound.

But in the same moment, the sound stopped. The body stilled, the head reared upright and faced them, its gaping mouth dripping with blood. The Glus slithered forward, away from the ghastly remains of Milne on which it had been feasting, towards the new disturbance. Its spiked tail curved upward. The stripes on its back began to glow.

Then it struck, lunging forward, white threads hissing from its throat.

Lief, Jasmine, and Barda hurled themselves backwards, falling into the water, scrambling up again and plunging away. The Glus moved on, a little faster.

They reached the rounded pillar of stone. Lief

caught hold of it, the Belt burning at his waist. "Barda, Jasmine, the gem is here, inside the stone!" he shouted.

Barda and Jasmine swung around, disbelieving. He nodded violently. "We have been deceived. The gem has been here, all the time."

"Lief — leave it! We must run!" Jasmine urged, tugging his arm, her eyes on the Glus, swollen and ghastly, sound bubbling deep in its chest.

"No!" Lief cried, holding fast to the pillar. "If I leave this place now I will never find it again!"

"If you stay you will die!" Jasmine shrieked. "Lief!"

Barda gripped her shoulder. His face was grim and set. "Jasmine and I will draw the Beast away, Lief," he snapped. "Stay still — still as that stone — until we are long gone. Then get the gem and do your best to find your way out. Jasmine! Your dagger!"

"No! We must stay together!" Lief shouted, as Jasmine passed him the weapon.

But already Barda was pulling Jasmine away. She was fumbling inside her jacket. At last she pulled out a ball of yellow wool. Shaking off Barda's hand, she plunged back to Lief's side, pulling out a trail of wool as she ran.

"I found this in Where Waters Meet. Hold it fast!" she cried, thrusting the loose end of the wool into Lief's hand. "It will be our line back to you."

"Beware!" Barda roared.

Lief slid behind the stone. Jasmine leaped away. Another tangle of white threads sprayed towards them, falling into the water just short of its mark. Jasmine turned and ran, splashing, back to Barda, leaving a trail of wool behind her. Shoulder to shoulder they waded on till they were lost in the maze.

Then there was only the lapping of the water, the dripping from the roof and the stealthy slithering of the Glus as slowly, slowly, it followed.

Lief crouched, holding his breath, as it passed him, its tiny eyes waving at the ends of their fleshy stalks. Its body narrowed, then bulged horribly, as it squeezed past the stone. Now he saw that its skin was covered in short, fine hairs that stuck straight out, quivering, alive to every ripple, every splash, every tiny movement in the waters of its kingdom. One mistake, and it would be upon him.

Still. Still as the stone.

The Beast crawled on. Every muscle in Lief's body was twitching, aching to move. But he held himself rigid, the slender yellow thread that was his link to Barda and Jasmine clutched tightly in his hand.

✳

Cautiously, Lief stood up. The Glus was long gone. He could hear it moving, far away. But he could no longer hear the splashing sounds of Barda and Jasmine running. They were remaining still — to confuse it, perhaps, or simply to rest. In any case, they led it away from him. They had done their part. Now he could do his.

To what purpose, Lief? a voice inside him seemed to mock. With the gem, or without it, you will walk this maze till you can walk no farther. Then the Glus will bind you with its sticky threads, and suck the flesh from your bones. What it did to Milne, it will do to you.

Lief shut the voice out of his mind. He put one hand on the Belt of Deltora, and the other on the pillar of stone. He moved his fingers over the cool, wet surface, waiting, waiting . . .

And then he felt it. The unmistakable throb that told him where the gem lay. About two-thirds of the way up the pillar.

He began to dig with the point of the dagger, holding his free hand cupped beneath it to catch falling fragments. The outer layer of the stone was soft and damp. It came away easily, and soon he had made a hole big enough to take his whole hand. But as he came to the center of the pillar, the work was more difficult. The sharp steel grated against the harder stone, setting his teeth on edge. Always he was terrified that if he worked too fast, too carelessly, he would injure the gem.

He could see nothing within the hole. He could hear nothing. He could smell nothing. So, he thought, all that is left is touch. I must be like the Glus, and let touch guide me.

He closed his eyes. He moved his hand down the dagger till the point was as one with his fingertips. He scraped delicately, calling the smothered gem in his mind, probing at the same time with his fingers for the touch that would tell him . . .

And there it was. A cool, still center within the column. The moment his fingers touched it, the coolness rolled forward into his hand, the white stone around it crumbling to powder.

Slowly, carefully he withdrew his hand and uncurled his fingers. There, veiled by a film of white dust, was a great purple gem.

The amethyst, symbol of truth.

A feeling of immense peace stole over Lief as he smoothed the dust from its shining surface, marvelling at its beauty. The Belt around his waist was burning hot, but his mind was cool and clear. He remembered words about the amethyst in *The Belt of Deltora*:

† **The amethyst, symbol of truth, calms and soothes . . .**

Indeed, Lief thought. And calm is what I need now. The calm to place this gem into the Belt, where it will be safe. The calm to wait until Jasmine and Barda return to me. The calm to believe that they *will* return.

He crouched, water swimming about him. He unclipped the Belt of Deltora and placed it across his knees. The amethyst slid into place beside the emerald and shone there steadily. Lief replaced the Belt around his waist, and carefully stood up again.

Now, I have only to wait, he told himself. He raised his wet hands to dry them on his shirt. And it was then that he felt it, cool on the back of his left hand: a soft breath of air, coming from behind him.

17 - Fight for Freedom

Lief turned. Slowly, slowly. Holding his hand in front of him, guided by the draught of air, he moved to the wall that loomed on the other side of the stone pillar.

There was a small gap at the top. A gap that could have been a fold in the stone, but was not. Through that gap, fresh, salty air streamed. Now he could not only feel it, but smell it.

He lifted Jasmine's dagger and chipped at the place. Soft stone fell into his other hand. There was the gentle whistling of a breeze. Forcing himself to be patient, he gently lowered the loose stone onto the ground at his feet. He rose and chipped again. This time a larger piece of stone came loose. Now the gap was large. Now the air was blowing into his face, and the hollow sound of rushing water was mingling with the sound of the breeze.

Lief's chest was tight. He was panting. He put his hand to the amethyst, to calm himself. It was vital, vital that he did not hurry or panic. He put down the large piece of stone, as gently as he had the first. He took another chip of rock. And another.

And that last was one too many. Water began trickling from the gap. The tunnel that was beyond the wall was half full of water. And Lief had chipped too far.

Almost with despair, he saw the trickling stream hit the water at his feet. The splashing sound seemed loud — impossibly loud. The water swirled and rippled. There was nothing he could do to stop it. As if his mind had eyes, he saw the quivering hairs on the skin of the Glus stiffen. He saw the Glus begin to turn, rearing its head. He saw it moving. Moving towards him.

He heard running, far away, coming closer. At the same moment, the yellow wool tied to his wrist tightened. He forced himself to wait, to watch.

"Lief!" the call burst out of the blue-white shadows. "Lief, what is happening? Lief, it is coming!"

Barda and Jasmine were running towards him, following the yellow thread.

Lief waited no longer. He jumped, heaving himself up into the gap in the wall, gasping as icy water rose, slapping, to his waist. There was rock beneath his feet, and above his head. But it was not the rock of the cave. It was much harder and darker. And the water was not milky, but clear, and sharp with salt.

He leaned down, holding out his arms to Jasmine. As she reached him, he swung her up beside him.

Then it was Barda's turn. He grabbed the edge of the gap. The stone crumbled under his hands and he fell back, gasping as salty water poured over him.

"Barda!" screamed Jasmine.

For the Glus was coming. It was coming, not slowly, but with tremendous speed. The sound of it was ghastly. Its mouth gaped in a snarl, a red gash in the whiteness. White threads sprayed into the air before it like a cloud.

Lief and Jasmine bent forward, muscles straining, hauling Barda upward through the pouring water. Barda's legs kicked frantically, his feet scrabbling for footholds.

He clambered into the tunnel, drawing up his feet just as a shower of threads clamped to the wall below him. He crawled, gasping, clear of the gap. The terrible head of the Glus reared up, filling the space.

"It is coming after us!" Jasmine shrieked.

But the Glus made no attempt to enter the tunnel. Instead, the head began to wag from side to side. White threads poured from the red throat, clinging and sticking to the edges of the gap. And then they realized what was happening.

The Glus was sealing the hole. The danger to the Maze, the vast lair it had built itself over the centuries, was more important than food.

"What is this place?" Jasmine's teeth were chattering. She screamed as the water in the tunnel suddenly surged, knocking her over, tumbling her forward. She came up gasping and choking, Filli squealing. Swept off his own feet by the current, Lief grabbed for her hand.

"We must be under the rock in front of the pirates' cave," shouted Barda, shaking water from his hair and eyes. "The tide is coming in. Hold on!"

With both hands he braced himself against the rock as the water was sucked back, rushing past them, gurgling like water in a drain. Gritting his teeth, Lief clung to Jasmine's hand, stopping her from being swept helplessly backwards.

"Move forward!" Barda roared. "And when the next wave comes, go with it! Do not fight it!"

Again the water swelled and surged. Again they were swept helplessly forward, their bodies tumbled against smooth walls. Again they spluttered to the surface. Again they braced themselves against the rock as the water sucked back.

"The waves are growing bigger! They will fill the tunnel! We will drown!" screamed Jasmine.

Lief tightened his grip on her hand. "We will not!" he shouted. "We have not come so far to die now."

"There!" Barda shouted.

Lief looked ahead, and saw light.

"It is the blowhole!" Desperately, Barda pushed Lief and Jasmine forward. "Go! Quickly! It is almost ready to blow. We must get out before it does. We must!"

Lief remembered the towering spout, the water crashing back to the unforgiving rocks, then sucking back with a force no one could resist. He struggled on, half-crawling, half-swimming, Jasmine sobbing and scrambling ahead of him.

The surge of a new wave overcame him, sealing his eyes, filling his ears with its roaring. Is this the one? The one that will mean our death? he thought, as he was swept towards the light. But still he gripped Jasmine's hand, and when he opened his stinging eyes there was sky above their heads. Dawn sky. They were bobbing in the mouth of the blowhole.

Lief pushed Jasmine up, up and out. She flopped onto the wet rock as he clambered after her, fighting against the water as it sought to pull him back into the tunnel. Barda followed, panting and dripping, taking great gasps of air.

Between them they hauled Jasmine to her feet and began floundering away from the hole, making for the shore.

There was a glad screech as Kree swooped towards them. Then there was a shout from behind. Lief looked back. Two figures were running from the pirates' cave, pounding across the sheet of rock towards them.

Finn and Nak, swords held high, howling in fury.

We have only one dagger, Lief thought, running, the breath rasping in his throat. One dagger against two swords . . .

There was a soft rumbling sound.

"Jump!" Barda roared.

Lief jumped. His feet hit the sand of the shore. He rolled over, breathless, Jasmine and Barda tumbling beside him. He looked back at the rock.

Nak and Finn had stopped. It was as if they were frozen in mid-stride. Their faces were masks of terror. Then, terribly slowly it seemed, they began to turn, casting away the swords, taking one step, another . . .

Too late. The blowhole gushed, roaring, throwing them onto their backs. They scrambled helplessly for a moment, like overturned crabs. Then with a mighty crash the water fell back on them, swirling them, catching them in its grip. With a terrible sucking sound it began to rush, rush back into its rocky tunnel.

Then it was gone, and there was nothing but smooth, wet rock, and two swords lying in puddles of water that gleamed in the rising sun.

✷

The companions gathered their possessions from the deserted pirates' cave, then turned their backs upon the surging waves of the shore. Exhausted and hungry as they were, they wanted nothing more than to put as much distance as possible between themselves and that terrible sea.

The sun was high in the sky when finally they found a place where they could feel safe — a long-abandoned hut by the riverside. They made a fire in the crumbling fireplace, for comfort and warmth. Then, ravenously, they ate nuts and dried fruit, traveller's biscuits, and Queen Bee honey, washed down with water from the crystal streams of Dread Mountain.

They talked little at first. None of them wanted to think of what they had seen, what they had survived. Lief's thoughts drifted to Dain. Would he live to make his way to Tora? Would they meet again? And what of Doom . . . ?

Jasmine spoke at last, echoing his thoughts strangely. "Did Doom betray us?" she murmured. "Or was the writing forged, to make us suspect him?"

Lief shook his head helplessly. He did not know.

"The map was all a lie. A false clue," Jasmine persisted.

"Planted on the dead pirate by that Ol in my shape, to lead you astray and at last cause you to abandon the quest!" Barda shook his head in disgust. "No doubt there were a hundred copies, and a hundred Ols on the river to carry them. Ols with orders to deceive, rather than to kill, if they found us."

Jasmine shuddered. "This was why no enemies waited for us on the shore. The plan this time was to cause us to abandon the quest, and to spread the word that it was hopeless, so that it would never be attempted again."

"Ols to kill. Ols to deceive. The Enemy has many plans, it seems. Plans woven together like a net, so that if we are not caught one way, we will be caught another." Lief stared at the surface of the river, that smooth, gliding surface below which horrors drifted and squirmed.

"The Shadow Lord may have plans," said Barda quietly. "But this time, they have failed. And why? Because he made an error. He did not count on the pirates. They blundered in and tore his net to shreds."

"And if we are fortunate, he will not find out, at least for a while. For who is there left to tell him?" Jasmine added. She glanced at Lief and Barda. "So does this mean that, for now, we can stay together?"

Lief put his fingers over the Belt of Deltora, now hidden under his shirt once more. He traced the shapes of the six gems in turn, and knew the answer. "We must stay together," he said. "Like the gems in the Belt, we need one another. For faith. For happiness. For hope. For luck. For honor. And for truth."

Barda nodded firmly.

They clasped hands briefly, then lay back to rest. Another long, perilous journey lay ahead of them — a journey to the place called the Valley of the Lost. The great diamond, symbol of purity and strength, the seventh and last stone of the Belt of Deltora, was waiting for them there.

Now all they had to do was find it.

DELTORA QUEST

The Valley
of the Lost

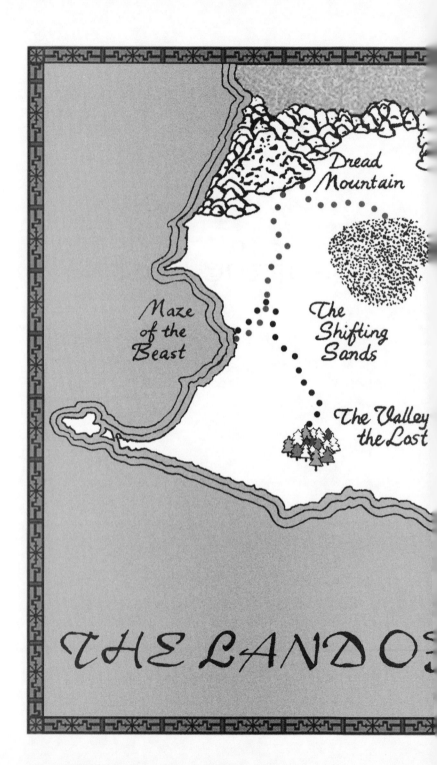

Dread
Mountain

Maze
of the
Beast

The
Shifting
Sands

The Valley
the Lost

THE LAND O

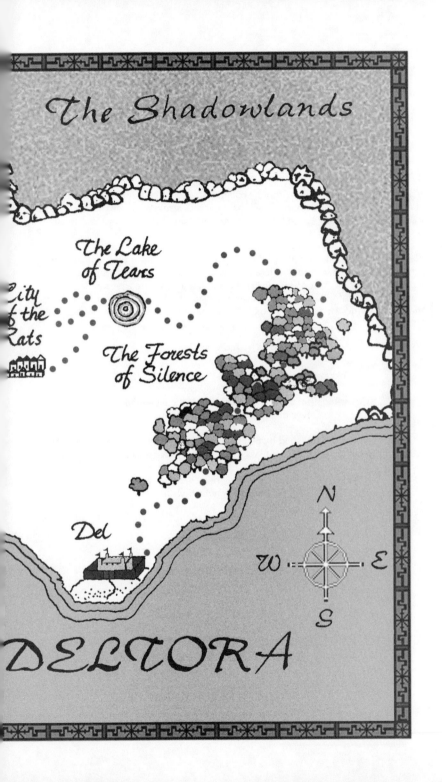

No part of this publication may be reproduced in whole or in part, or stored in a retrieval system, or transmitted in any form or by any means, electronic, mechanical, photocopying, recording, or otherwise, without written permission of the publisher. For information regarding permission, write to Permissions Department, Scholastic Australia, PO Box 579, Lindfield, New South Wales, Australia 2070.

ISBN 0-439-25329-2

Text and graphics copyright © Emily Rodda, 2000.
Graphics by Kate Rowe.
Cover illustrations copyright © Scholastic Australia, 2000.
Cover illustrations by Marc McBride.

All rights reserved. Published by Scholastic Inc., 555 Broadway, New York, NY 10012, by arrangement with Scholastic Press, an imprint of Scholastic Australia.

SCHOLASTIC and associated logos are trademarks and/or registered trademarks of Scholastic Inc.

12 11 10 9 8 7 6 5 4 3 2 1   1 2 3 4 5 6/0

40

Printed in the U.S.A.
First American edition, October 2001

Contents

The story so far. . .

Lief, Barda, and Jasmine are on a great quest to find the seven lost gems of the magic Belt of Deltora. Hidden in fearsome places throughout the land, the gems must be restored to the Belt before the rightful heir to the throne can be found and the evil Shadow Lord's tyranny ended.

Six gems have been found so far. The topaz, symbol of faith, has the power to contact the spirit world and to clear the mind. The ruby, for happiness, pales when danger threatens, repels evil spirits, and is an antidote to venom. The opal, gem of hope, gives glimpses of the future. The lapis lazuli, the heavenly stone, is a powerful talisman. The emerald, for honor, dulls in the presence of evil. The amethyst, for truth, calms and soothes.

The companions have discovered a secret resistance movement led by the mysterious Doom. Another member of the Resistance, Dain, a young man of about Lief's own age, has been kidnapped by pirates, and Lief's parents have been imprisoned.

In constant fear of the Shadow Lord's Grey Guards and hideous shape-changing Ols, the companions must now cross the River Tor and journey to their last goal, the Valley of the Lost, where the last stone lies, the great diamond.

Now read on . . .

1 - Night Terrors

It was dark and very still. Lief, Barda, and Jasmine slipped through the night like shadows, and the River Tor slid beside them, keeping its secrets.

They had decided that for safety's sake they should not travel by day. But the night held its own perils, for they did not dare to use a torch to light their way, and the moon was shrouded in cloud. As the darkness cloaked them, so also would it cloak a prowling enemy.

And it hid more than that. It hid holes, rocks, and ditches. It hid trees, bushes, and landmarks. Every step was a step into the unknown.

They knew that somewhere ahead there was a bridge. When they reached it they could at last cross the river that had caused them so much grief. Then they could begin moving towards the Valley of the Lost, where lay the great diamond, the seventh gem of the Belt of Deltora.

But in this blackness how easy it would be to pass the bridge unaware! So, though all of them loathed the very thought of the River Tor, they stayed close beside it, knowing that its dark waters must lead them to their goal at last.

With one hand Lief gripped the Belt of Deltora, hidden under his clothes. But the Belt, for all its power, could not help him as his eyes strained to penetrate the darkness ahead.

"It is not far now," Jasmine whispered suddenly.

Lief saw a faint, pale blur as her face turned to him. Filli, curled inside her jacket, made a small, sleepy sound. Kree was silent and invisible on her shoulder, his black feathers swallowed by the darkness.

"Do you see it?" asked Barda.

"No," Jasmine breathed. "But I smell people and animals, and the bridge was just beyond a village, remember?"

They crept forward, and at last found themselves moving through cleared ground. Lief thought he could make out the thicker blackness of a wall rising to his left.

Perhaps armed villagers on night watch stood behind the wall, listening for danger. Perhaps this was why the village still stood, despite the pirates that sailed the Tor's waters and the bandits that prowled its banks.

If they heard a sound, the guards would investigate. They would strike instantly, without pity. They would have learned from sad examples all along the river that to hesitate was to risk losing everything.

The companions moved on, treading lightly, scarcely breathing. No sooner had they reached the safety of a grove of trees beyond the wall, when the clouds covering the moon parted and the ground was flooded with light.

Jasmine caught her breath. "We were fortunate," she murmured. "If that had happened just a moment earlier . . ."

Barda nudged Lief's arm and pointed ahead. Through the trees Lief saw the bridge. It was very close, peaceful in the moonlight. A small herd of long-haired goats clustered around it, some standing, some resting on the grass.

The bridge was solid and broad enough to take a cart. A large sign stood beside it. The sign's lettering was faded, but Lief could still make out the words.

Lief's heart thumped. Tora! The great city of the west, so loyal to the kings and queens of Deltora. The ideal hiding place for the heir to the throne.

Tora must be near. But there had been no sign of a city as they followed the river down to the coast just days ago. At the time, Lief had thought little of it. He had too many other things to worry about. Now, however, it seemed very strange indeed. For surely Tora was set on the River Tor. Its very name made a link.

"Tora must be set well back from the river," muttered Barda, whose thoughts had plainly been running on the same lines. "But it is odd that we did not see it in the distance, at least."

Lief nodded, still puzzling over the mystery. "Perhaps we passed it at night, and it keeps no lights. In any case, we may yet be able to visit it — on our way to the Valley of the Lost."

"By all reports, we would be advised not to do any such thing, at least until the Belt is complete," hissed Jasmine. "Dain was warned — "

She broke off, biting her lip, and Lief and Barda were also silent. Memories of the boy they had last seen bound and helpless in the pirates' coastal cave flooded all their minds.

Dain had longed to go to Tora. Now he would never see it. Even now the pirates were sailing up the river with him. In a few days he would be handed over to the Grey Guards. Though Lief, Barda, and Jasmine knew they could not save him, his sad and frightened eyes haunted them all.

The boy would try his best to escape. But what hope did he have against a gang of armed ruffians greedy for the Shadow Lord's gold?

Jasmine tossed her head as if to shake away unwelcome thoughts, and turned her attention to the goats by the bridge. "We will have to move slowly, so as not to startle the beasts," she said. "If they make a sound, all is lost."

"They must be used to people." Lief stared at the goats, at the small horns gleaming, the long, smooth hair. "But we should show ourselves to them now, while the moon shines. We will frighten them if we come at them in the dark."

He took a single step forward, then stopped abruptly, his eyes widening. One of the goats — there was something wrong with one of the goats! Its body seemed to be rippling, billowing outward like a ballooning sail.

Lief blinked rapidly. What trick of the moonlight

was this? Now that he looked again, the goat was exactly as before. Yet — he felt Barda grip his arm, saw another of the goats quiver and alter, head stretching upward, body shuddering, before returning to its normal shape. Then he knew. He had just seen what Dain had called the Tremor.

"Ols!" he breathed. "They are not goats at all, but Ols!" His stomach turned over as he realized how nearly they had walked into the midst of the herd, all unsuspecting. How nearly they had met their deaths.

"They are guarding the bridge." Barda gritted his teeth in frustration. "What will we do?"

"One of us must lead them away, so that the other two can slip across," said Jasmine. "I will — "

Barda shook his head firmly. "There are far too many of them for that trick to work, Jasmine. Some will give chase, some will stay. And now I come to think of it, there were many water birds roosting on the other side of the bridge when I passed it on my way to the coast. More Ols, no doubt, though I did not realize it at the time. And surely they will be there still."

"Then we must go on," muttered Lief. "Move around the bridge, so that the Ols do not see us. Find another way across the river, farther upstream."

"But there *is* no other way!" hissed Jasmine. "I cannot swim, you know that. And even if I could, the killer worms — "

"We cannot swim, but there are such things as

boats," Barda broke in calmly. "We have money to pay for a crossing. Or we will make a raft. Anything would be better than fighting twenty Ols."

As silently as they had come, they crept away from the river and continued upstream, making a wide arc around the bridge. Now and then, through gaps in the trees, they caught glimpses of the goats still waiting, unmoving, in the moonlight.

✳

When dawn broke, the sun struggling to shine through a blanket of cloud, the village and the bridge were far behind them. They stopped to eat and rest, huddling together beneath a group of ragged bushes. Kree took flight, to catch insects and stretch his cramped wings.

Lief had first watch. He wrapped his cloak around him and tried to make himself comfortable. His eyes were prickling, but he was not afraid that he would fall asleep. His body was jumping with nerves.

Time crawled by. Kree returned, and went to roost low in one of the bushes. Sulky dawn gave way to dull morning. Clouds hung low above Lief's head, thickening by the moment. We will have rain, he thought dismally. Scuttling animals had made narrow paths through the greenery, but there were no animals to be seen now, and for this Lief was grateful. Every living thing was suspect, in a place where Ols prowled.

And Doom claimed that there were Ols who

could take the form of things that were not living — Grade 3 Ols, the perfection of the Shadow Lord's evil art. If the tale was true, and such beings really existed, the very bush on which Kree perched, or the pebble at Lief's feet, could be a secret enemy. At any moment a horrible transformation could begin. At any moment a white, flickering specter with the Shadow Lord's mark in its core could rise and overwhelm them.

Nowhere was safe. Nothing could be trusted.

Lief licked his lips, fought down the dread that clutched his heart. But still his flesh seemed to tremble on his bones. He slipped his hands under his shirt and felt for the Belt of Deltora, heavy at his waist. His fingers moved to the sixth stone, the amethyst. As they rested upon it, as its magic flowed through him, the trembling slowly ebbed.

Somehow we will find a boat, he told himself. We will cross the river. Our quest will continue. We will survive.

But still he could not rid himself of the feeling that they were caught in a net. A net that the Shadow Lord was slowly, slowly drawing in.

2 - Company

L ate in the morning Barda woke and Lief took his turn to sleep. He opened his eyes in mid-afternoon to find the sky leaden and the earth breathless. His head ached dully as he sat up. His sleep had been heavy, his dreams confused and disturbing.

Barda and Jasmine were strapping up their packs.

"We think we should move on, Lief, as soon as you are ready," said Barda. "It is almost as dark as night as it is, and if we wait for true darkness we will cover little distance before the rain sets in."

"The other village we saw on our way down to the coast cannot be far away," Jasmine added, turning away to peer through the bushes to the land beyond. "If we reach it before nightfall we may be able to persuade someone to row us across the river."

Lief felt a spurt of anger. They had been talking while he slept, making plans without him. No doubt they had been impatiently waiting for him to wake, thinking he was a sleepyhead. Did they not know how tired he was? He had slept for hours, yet he was still very weary — so weary that he felt a week of sleep would not satisfy him.

Almost at once, he realized that his annoyance was a result of that very tiredness. He looked at Jasmine's heavy eyes, and the deep, grey lines on Barda's face. They were as exhausted as he was. He forced a smile, nodded, and began pulling together his own belongings.

※

By the time they reached the next village, it was even darker, but night had not yet fallen. The companions moved cautiously through the open gate in the wall.

The place was a ruin. Everything not made of stone had been burned to cinders. The familiar names "Finn," "Nak," and "Milne" were scrawled on the walls left standing.

"They wrote their names here in triumph, thinking they were kings instead of thieving, murderous pirates," Jasmine muttered savagely. "I am glad they died screaming."

"And I," said Barda, with feeling.

Lief wanted to agree. Once, it would have been easy for him to do so. But thinking of how Milne, especially, had met his terrible fate, gibbering with terror in the Maze of the Beast, somehow he could not. Revenge did not seem sweet to him any longer. There had been too much suffering.

He turned away, and began searching the ruins. But there was nothing to find. There were no people, no animals left in this dead place. There was no shelter.

And there was no boat.

With heavy hearts, Lief, Barda, and Jasmine moved slowly on.

The rain began at midnight. At first it pelted down, stinging their hands and faces. Then it settled into a steady stream that soaked them through and chilled them to the bone. Kree hunched miserably on Jasmine's shoulder. Filli, bedraggled, hid his head inside her jacket.

They plodded through mud and darkness, trying to keep alert, watching for anything that would help them cross the river. But there were no trees — only low bushes. There were no logs or planks washed up on the shore. Nothing they passed could be used to make a raft.

At dawn they rested fitfully, finding what shelter they could under dripping leaves. But after a few hours the ground on which they lay began to run with water. They staggered up, and began to tramp again.

And so the time went on. By the beginning of the third night of rain, they had stopped looking for a way across the river, now swollen and overflowing its banks. The rain screened their view of the other side, even by day, but Lief and Barda knew that by now they must be opposite the great reed beds that had stopped their progress on the way downstream. It would be no use crossing here, even if they could find something to carry them. They knew, from bitter experience, what it was like to flounder through that oozing mud.

"Is this fiendish river forever to bar our way?" Jasmine groaned, as they stopped to rest once more. "And will this rain never stop?"

"If we can keep going a little longer, we will be opposite the place where Broad River joins the Tor," Barda said. "I know that there are trees there, at least. We can make a shelter, and rest until the rain stops. We might even keep a fire going."

On they walked, in a dream of wet, cold darkness. Then, after what seemed a very long time, Jasmine abruptly stopped.

"What is it?" Lief whispered.

Jasmine's wet hand clutched his sleeve. "Sshh! Listen!"

Lief frowned, trying to concentrate. At first, all he could hear was the pounding of the rain and the rushing of the swollen river. Then voices came to him. Rough, angry voices. Shouting.

The companions moved slowly forward. Then,

not far ahead, they saw a winking light. They had not seen it before because it was masked by trees.

Trees! Lief realized that they had at last reached the shelter they had been seeking. But others had reached it before them. The light was a lantern hung from a branch. It flickered as dark figures moved around it, blocking it now and again from view.

The voices grew louder.

"I tell you, we must go back!" a man roared. "The more I think of it, the more I am sure. We should not have agreed to leave Nak and Finn alone with the booty. How do we know they will still be there when we return?"

Lief shook his head. Was he imagining things? Had he heard the man say "Nak" and "Finn"? Could the figures in the grove of trees be the pirates who had set sail to take Dain up the river to the Grey Guards? But what were they doing here? He had thought they would be far upstream by now.

"Nak and Finn will be waiting for us, all right, Gren," growled another of the pirates. "Whatever they say, they will want their share of the gold we get for that puny Resistance wretch on the ship."

They were talking about Dain! Lief strained to see beyond the trees to the river, and thought he caught a glimpse of the pale, furled sails of the pirate boat. The boat must be at anchor quite near to the shore. And Dain was on it!

"You are a trusting fool, Rabin!" shouted the man called Gren. "If I am right, Nak and Finn have more than a handful of gold to think about! Why else would they have let us come upriver alone? Do you really believe they are afraid of this man Doom? What is he but a Resistance wretch like the other?"

"They must have stopped when the rain set in," whispered Barda. "Perhaps the river began running too swiftly for them to move against the current. They came ashore, for shelter."

"Then a rowing boat must be here, on the river-bank," Jasmine breathed.

"Nak and Finn would not betray us!" a woman shrieked angrily. "You are a traitor yourself to say it, Gren. Beware! Remember what happened to Milne."

Other voices murmured angrily.

"Do not threaten me, you hag!" snarled the man. "Where is your own memory? Do you not remember one of the prisoners in the cavern telling us that Finn had secretly found a great gem? What if it is true?"

"A gem found in the Maze of the Beast?" jeered Rabin. "Oh, yes, that is very likely, I am sure! Are you weak in the head, Gren, that you could believe such fairy tales?"

"Shut your ugly mouth, Rabin!" Gren's voice was thick with rage.

"Shut your own, you fat fool!"

There was a roar, a sudden, violent movement, and a groan of agony.

"Oh, you devil!" screamed the woman.

Something crashed against the lantern. The light swung wildly and went out.

"Keep off!" Gren roared. "Why, you — "

"Take your hands off her!" several other voices shouted furiously.

Then, suddenly, the grove seemed to explode with sound as the rest of the crew joined the fight. Over the beating of the rain rose shouts and grunts, the clashing of steel, the breaking of branches, thumps and shrieks.

"To the river!" Barda muttered. "Quickly!"

3 - Adrift

The boat, filled ankle-deep with rainwater, was bobbing at the river's edge. No doubt it had been pulled onto dry land when the last of the pirates came ashore. But the river had risen since, and set it afloat. If it had not been tied to a tree, it would have drifted away.

It took a matter of moments for Barda to untie the rope while his companions crawled into the boat, Kree fluttering after them. By the time the big man clambered to the oars, they were already beginning to move into deeper water.

Shouts and screams from the trees still pierced the drumming of the rain. Not far away, the pirate ship strained at anchor. Two portholes in its side glowed like eyes. Lief had not noticed that before. Frantically scooping water from the bottom of the boat, he peered at the ship's deck, looking for a sign of movement.

Meanwhile, Barda was struggling with the oars. But he was not expert at the task, and the swollen waters of the river surged around the boat, fighting his every movement, pushing them downstream.

"The current is too strong for me! I do not know if I can get to the ship," he roared, shaking his wet hair from his brow.

"You must!" Jasmine cried. And only then did Lief realize how desperately she wanted Dain to be saved. She had said nothing before, appearing to accept the boy's loss with the calm she always showed in the face of disaster. But now that Dain was so near, she could not face the thought of leaving him behind.

Gritting his teeth, Lief threw down the pail and crawled to the rower's bench. "Make way!" he shouted, and squeezed himself down beside Barda, seizing an oar. He had never rowed before, but he had seen the pirates do it only days ago. He thought he could copy what they had done. Together he and Barda bent forward, pulled back, bent and pulled again.

The extra weight upon the oars began to take effect. Slowly, painfully, the boat drew nearer to the pirate ship. Then there was a shout. A shout, not from the shore, but from the ship itself.

Lief glanced around. A figure was standing on

the deck, waving frantically. It was Dain. A smaller figure capered by his side, a lantern swinging wildly in its hand. Lief realized that it was the odd little thieving creature Dain had called a polypan. The pirates must have left it onboard with Dain. And somehow he had persuaded it to set him free.

Dain had lifted a coil of rope attached by one end to the boat's deck. He began swinging it, as if he was about to throw.

"Here!" exclaimed Jasmine. She staggered to her feet, holding out her hands. The boat rocked dangerously.

"Sit down!" roared Barda. "You will have us over! Lief, row!"

Then Jasmine gave a cry, Kree screeched, and the boat jerked and rolled. Lief glanced again over his shoulder. The dark shape of the pirate ship, its glowing porthole eyes staring, loomed very near.

Dain had thrown the rope, and Jasmine had caught it. The slender line stretched tightly between the two rocking craft. It seemed that surely it must snap, but though it creaked and thinned, it did not break.

"I cannot hold it!" Jasmine shouted. Already she was leaning perilously over the bow, water foaming just below her head. Filli was chattering with fear on her shoulder, unable to help, terrified of falling. Kree fluttered beside them, screeching in panic.

Barda dropped his oar and scrambled towards

them. He took the weight of the rope in his own powerful hands and heaved. The boat lurched and wallowed in the swell. Lief grasped both oars and did his best to fight the current alone.

"Go back, Dain!" he heard Barda shout. "We will come aboard!" Again Lief risked turning to look. Dain, with the polypan close behind him, was climbing frantically down a rope ladder that hung from the ship's side directly between the shining porthole eyes. The polypan still held the lantern. It looked like a third eye, an eye that flickered and swung.

But — Lief squinted through the rain — the other two eyes were flickering as well. And surely they were brighter, far brighter, than they had been before.

"Dain!" Barda roared furiously. "Dain! This boat is too small. We cannot — "

Dain must have heard, but took no notice. He turned and made ready to jump, clinging to the ladder with one hand. His hair was streaming with water, plastered to his head. His face, gleaming in the lamplight, was desperate. Above him the polypan gibbered and swung, shaking the ladder in panic.

Then Lief smelled smoke, and understood.

"Fire!" he shouted.

As the word left his mouth there was a roar from somewhere in the ship's belly. The portholes shattered and jets of flame belched from them. Great cracks opened in the ship's side, and the gaps were filled with raging fire. The rain hissed and steamed as it hit the burning wood.

Dain and the polypan leaped together, crashing down into the rowboat. It tilted sideways, a great wave of water surging over the side, throwing Lief backwards, tearing the oars from his hands.

The boat righted itself again. It wallowed in the swell, rapidly drifting sideways, weighed down by two extra passengers and the water that swirled inside it. Stunned by his fall, Dain lay slumped against a seat as Jasmine bailed frantically and Lief and Barda scrambled for the oars. The polypan screamed, clinging to the point of the bow. It knew boats. It knew all too well what could happen to this one.

Cries of rage rose from the riverbank. The pirates had heard the noise, discovered the loss of the boat and seen the fire. Lief, grimly trying to keep the boat steady, saw their shadows leaping in the glow of the lantern they had lit once more. But that tiny glow was nothing compared to the inferno that the ship had become.

It seemed incredible that fire could rage while rain poured from above and angry water rushed below. But the fire had started below the deck, and roared out of control through the stores.

"It was the polypan!" Dain shouted, pulling himself upright. "It threw a lantern into the cabin under the deck where the oil, grease, and paint are stored. The rain and the pirates' beatings have driven it mad!"

As has its longing for the brown gum it loves to chew, perhaps, thought Lief, staring at the screeching, long-armed figure clinging to the bow. Ah, how it must wish it had never left the *River Queen*.

"We must get away from the ship!" Barda roared over the rain. "If it begins to sink it will pull us down with it!"

He and Lief bent again to the oars. But their clumsy efforts were of little use. Nothing seemed to stop that perilous sideways drift. As fast as Jasmine bailed, more water splashed over the side.

The polypan shrieked, its eyes glazed with terror. Then, without any warning, it suddenly sprang from its place at the bow and leaped for Lief and Barda, thrusting them aside and seizing the oars itself.

Cursing, Barda lunged for it.

"No!" shouted Lief. "Leave it! It can row far better than we can. It can save us all!"

With two deft sweeps of the oars, the polypan turned the boat. Then, back bending, powerful arms bulging, it began to row. And as if the boat recognized that at last it was in the hands of an expert, it began to cut through the swell like a knife through warm butter. In moments it had pulled clear of the burning ship and was heading straight across the river.

Jasmine continued to bail and as the water

slowly disappeared from the bottom of the boat their speed increased. Soon the burning ship was far behind them. They knew that ahead was the broad, straight water of Broad River, and the bridge that arched over it. Ahead, too, was the sad village of Where Waters Meet, and the little jetty that bore the *River Queen* sign.

Filli chattered excitedly, snuffling the air.

"We are very close!" Jasmine exclaimed. "We are almost at the bank!"

The polypan turned, baring its brown, chattering teeth. Its arms did not stop their work for a moment, but its eyes seemed to burn as they searched the darkness.

Water swirled around them as the swollen waters of the two rivers mingled. The boat raced forward. It is like cutting through a whirlpool, Lief thought, gripping his seat. If the polypan was not rowing, we would never survive this.

But the next moment, the polypan was not rowing. It had jumped from its place, abandoning the oars. It was springing to the bow and leaping past Jasmine and Dain — out and away into the darkness.

There was a thump, and the sound of running feet.

"The jetty!" Jasmine screamed.

Wildly she leaned from the boat, snatching at the piers of the old jetty, at the pole that supported the *River Queen* sign. But the raging water snatched the boat away before she could take hold. Then the boat was being swept down the river, spinning, spinning. One of the dragging oars dug deep into the water, pulled free, toppled into the swirling tide and was lost.

Barda lunged for the other, but reached it too late. Before he could grasp it, it had followed its fellow.

Then the companions could do nothing — nothing but cling to the sides of their lurching craft, as the treacherous waters swept them away.

4 - Silence

Stillness. Silence. Pink light through closed eye-lids. Lief woke in confusion. Lay still in fear. The last thing he remembered was the boat crashing against something, spinning around, then continuing its mad, swirling dash into darkness.

Did I fall asleep? he thought. How could that be?

But he *had* slept, or else fainted. That much was clear. For here he was, waking. The rain had stopped. The terrible night had passed.

Or — was this death? This light, peaceful drifting — was it how all the struggle ended?

He opened his eyes. The sky was pink above him. Dawn.

Slowly he sat up. Before him was a lake — a huge lake, smooth as glass. Jasmine slept beside him, her cheek on the hard boards of a bench, Kree standing guard beside her. Barda lay not far away, breathing steadily. And Dain — Dain was sitting in the bow, his dark eyes filled with wonder.

Lief wet his lips. "Where are we?" he heard himself ask huskily. "What happened?"

"We hit something — a sandbar, I think, made by the flood," Dain said slowly. "It must have knocked us into a channel separated from the main river. So we floated here, into the great lake, instead of being swept farther downstream."

"But there is no lake beside the River Tor!" Lief protested. He shook his head, unable to believe his own eyes. Yet he could see in the distance the broad band of the river moving on to the sea.

"Once, it seems, there was a lake," said Dain softly. "And now, because of the flood, there is a lake again. Do you not see? These are the reed beds, Lief. Now they are a lake, as once they always were. And now there is no fog to hide what lies at the lake's edge."

He pointed. Lief turned. And there, directly behind him, was dry land and a vast shimmer of light.

"It is Tora," Dain whispered. "Tora."

Lief narrowed his eyes against the dazzling glare, and finally made out the gleaming shapes of towers, turrets, and walls. In his amazement he thought at first that the buildings themselves were shining, glowing from within by some sort of magic.

Then he realized that the shimmer was caused by the rays of the early morning sun striking thousands of hard white surfaces, polished smooth.

He looked away, rubbing his streaming eyes. It was impossible to see the city clearly. And yet, he had seen enough to feel puzzled, as well as filled with awe, at its silent, untouched beauty.

"Tora was carved by magic from a marble mountain," said Dain. "It is perfect — all of one piece, without crack or seam."

His voice seemed stronger, deeper. Lief glanced at him, wondering, and saw that he was sitting very upright. As had happened once before since Lief had known him, he suddenly looked older, prouder, and less frail. His mouth was firm. His eyes were shining. It was as though a mask had dropped from his face, leaving it unguarded.

He felt Lief's gaze and turned away quickly. "Now would be a good time to enter the city," he said, in his normal voice. "It is very early. Most people will not yet be stirring."

Without waiting for an answer, he crept gently to the end of the boat, and climbed onto the shore. The boat rocked gently. Jasmine and Barda opened their eyes and sat up, startled.

"It — it is all right," Lief stammered. "We are safe. The flood has refilled an old lake. And it seems — it seems we have reached Tora."

As Dain had done, he pointed. And as he himself

had done only moments before, Barda and Jasmine turned and blinked into the shimmering light.

"So Tora was on the river after all!" Jasmine exclaimed. "Or, at least, on a lake beside the river."

"And does Dain think we can walk calmly into the place without being stopped?" muttered Barda. "Tora is controlled by the enemy."

Lief frowned. "That is what Doom said. But — I am starting to wonder if he was telling the truth. I cannot see the city clearly, but there seem to be no Grey Guards at the gate. No mark of the Shadow Lord on the walls. No damage or destruction or rubbish lying about. And it is so peaceful, Barda. Have you ever known a place overrun by Guards to be so?"

Barda hesitated. Then he rubbed his hand across his dry mouth. "Is it possible?" he whispered. "Can it be that the Torans' magic has been strong enough to repel even the Shadow Lord's evil? If so, Lief . . . if so . . ."

Lief's heart was thudding with excitement. "If so, the heir to Deltora may be there. Waiting for us."

The city lay before them, silent, waiting, cloaked in light. The shore of the lake stretched empty and inviting before them. Yet the moment Lief set foot upon it, his excitement vanished, and he was gripped by fear.

Head bent, he slowly followed Dain, struggling with the fear, trying to understand it. Was it a natural caution, a reluctance to plunge half blinded into a place where, despite appearances, enemies might lurk? Was it fear of the powerful magic of Tora itself?

Or was it because, now that the moment had almost certainly come, he feared to meet the heir of Deltora?

He raised his head and with a shock saw that Dain was almost at the edge of the shore. The lonely figure hesitated for a split second, then stepped forward into dazzling light and disappeared. Lief squinted and rubbed his eyes as again they began to water, blurring his view.

He stumbled forward, pulling his cloak around him to hide his sword. We must not look like enemies, he thought confusedly. We must . . .

"Lief!" he heard Barda call sharply, and realized that his companions had lost sight of him. Every thread of his cloak was glittering, surrounding him with light. He answered the call and waited. Barda and Jasmine reached him in moments, their arms held over their dazzled eyes.

Together they walked the last few steps to the city's walls. Gradually they became one with the light, and it no longer blinded them. They reached the shore's end. Tora rose before them in all its vast splendor.

Tora was carved by magic from a marble mountain. It is all of one piece — perfect, without crack or seam.

They stopped for a moment, awestruck. Then,

their hands held out in front of them to show they meant no harm, they moved through the vast white archway that was the city's entrance.

At once they were swept by a tingling chill. It was like being plunged into a deep bath of cool, clear water. For a moment, time seemed to stand still, and Lief lost all sense of where he was or what he was supposed to be doing. When he came to himself he realized that his dazzled eyes had deceived him. He had thought that the arch was merely a gateway, but it was much thicker than he had thought. Instead of moving straight into the city, he and his companions were standing in the shade of an echoing tunnel. Smooth whiteness curved around them.

Kree crooned and clucked, swaying slightly on Jasmine's arm.

"What was that?" Jasmine whispered. "That — feeling?"

Lief shook his head uncertainly. But he was not afraid. In fact, he felt more at peace than he ever remembered being in his life.

Slowly they walked to the end of the tunnel, and emerged at last into the city light.

No robed figures waited to greet them. No Grey Guards jumped, sneering, into their way. The silence was eerie. Their boots echoed on the broad, gleaming street.

Turning to one side, Lief pulled up his shirt and

looked at the Belt of Deltora. The ruby glowed as brightly as ever. So they were not in danger yet. But — the emerald!

Lief stared. The emerald had lost all color. It had become as dull and lifeless as it had been when it was possessed by the monster Gellick on Dread Mountain. What did that mean? Was evil here? Or . . . he seemed to remember that something else could dull the emerald. What was it?

He and his companions paced on. Halls and houses, towers and palaces, rose, shining, on either side of them. Through tall windows and open doors, rich hangings, silken rugs, and fine furniture could be seen. Everywhere flowers in window boxes bloomed, bright and humming with bees. Fruit trees thrived in huge pots, clustered around courtyards where tables of food and drink stood ready and fountains splashed.

But no one sat by the fountains, tended the trees, or ate the food. No one walked along the streets, or peered from the windows of the houses. No one stood on the silken rugs, or rested in the fine chairs. The city was utterly deserted.

"It is like Where Waters Meet," whispered Jasmine.

"No," Barda said grimly. "Where Waters Meet was in ruins. But here — why, it looks as though the people left it only five minutes ago."

He looked over his shoulder. "How powerful is

the Torans' magic?" he muttered. "Could it be that they have made themselves invisible? And where is Dain?"

Wondering, the hair on the backs of their necks prickling, they moved on through the empty marble streets.

At last, they reached a huge square at the city's heart, and there at least one of Barda's questions was answered, for there they found Dain.

Great halls decorated with tall columns surrounded the square. The largest of these stood at the top of a sweeping flight of broad steps. A carved box lay on the top step. It looked out of place — as though it had been brought there for a purpose and then abandoned.

But Dain had not climbed the steps. He was crouched at the foot of a huge piece of marble that rose in the square's center. Lief knew at once that it was the stone his father had described seeing in the painting at the palace in Del. But no green flames flickered from the stone's peak. And it was cracked through.

Dain did not move as Lief, Barda, and Jasmine strode towards him. Even when they reached him and spoke his name he did not seem to notice they were there. His eyes, dull and hopeless, were fixed on the stone.

Words were carved on the marble. The jagged crack ran through them like a wound:

We, the people of Tora, swear loyalty to Adin,
King of Deltora, and all of his blood who follow him.
If ever this vow is broken, may this rock,
our city's heart, break also, and may we be swept away,
forever to regret our dishonour.

5 ~ The Secret of Tora

Lief stared at the dead and broken rock, his heart sinking as at last he remembered the words from *The Belt of Deltora* that described the powers of the emerald.

✝ **The emerald, symbol of honor, dulls in the presence of evil, and when a vow is broken.**

He needed no further proof of what had happened. "Tora broke its vow," he murmured. "But why? Why?"

With a groan of frustration and disappointment, Barda moved away. But Lief and Jasmine could not follow him. Not yet.

Lief put his hand upon Dain's shoulder. "Get up, Dain," he said quietly. "There is nothing for you here. Nothing for any of us. Tora is empty. Everything is preserved by enchantment, but it is empty of life. It has been so, I think, for a very long time. That is why the lake silted up, and the city was cut off from the river."

But Dain shook his head miserably. "It cannot be," he whispered. "I have waited so long." His face was drawn and deeply shadowed. His whole body trembled.

Jasmine knelt beside him. "Dain, why did you have to come to Tora? Tell us the truth!"

Dain's voice was very low. "I thought my parents were here. Mother told me, always, that if ever we were separated, they would meet me in Tora. She said she had family here, and they would shelter us."

His fists clenched. "I told Doom this, a year ago, when he found me left for dead by the bandits who attacked our farm. He said to tell no one, because when my parents arrived in Tora they would be in danger if it became known that their son was with the Resistance."

"How could it become known?" Lief demanded.

"Doom fears there is a spy in our camp. At least — that is what he told me." Dain looked up at the ruined stone, his eyes bitter. "But he also told me that Tora was filled with spies, and overrun by Grey Guards and Ols. He was lying. All the time he delayed me, making false promises, he knew that the city was deserted, and that my hopes for it were false."

He took a deep, shuddering breath. "I will never go back to the stronghold. Never."

He bowed his head and did not raise it again. Lief looked at him. Dimly he realized that at one time he might have been irritated because Dain blamed Doom for all his troubles. For, after all, Dain had not been Doom's prisoner. He could at anytime have left the Resistance and travelled to Tora alone.

But Lief did not feel irritated now. Only filled with a calm regret. Briefly he wondered about that.

"Look here!"

Barda's voice sounded strange. Lief looked up and saw that his friend had climbed the steps of the great hall. Behind him, graceful white columns reached for the sky, but he was looking down, at the open, carved box in his hands.

"Go," said Jasmine in a low voice. "I will stay here."

Lief rose, crossed the square, and climbed the steps. Barda held out the box for him to see. Inside were countless small rolls of parchment. Lief picked one out, and unrolled it.

Lief scrambled through the box, picking up other rolls and looking at them. They were all the same, except for the signatures. Some were signed by Queen

Lilia, others by King Alton, Endon's father. Still others bore the name of Endon himself.

"These are like the messages Father showed me," said Lief dully. "The messages the people of Del received when they sent requests and complaints to the king."

Barda nodded. "It seems that the Torans also sent requests and complaints, and received the same replies. I imagine that like the people of Del they felt they had been abandoned. So when the last message came . . ."

He handed Lief two crumpled scraps of paper. "These were in the box also," he said heavily. "On top of all the rest."

The scraps were the two halves of a note. Lief fitted the halves together and read the hastily scribbled message.

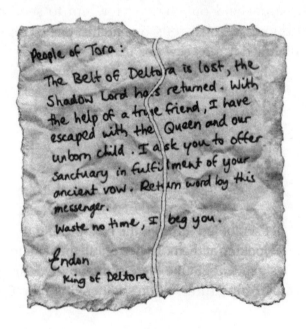

People of Tora :

The Belt of Deltora is lost, the Shadow Lord has returned. With the help of a true friend, I have escaped with the Queen and our unborn child. I ask you to offer sanctuary in fulfilment of your ancient vow. Return word by this messenger.
Waste no time, I beg you.

Endon
King of Deltora

Lief stared at the note. "Messenger? What messenger?" he stammered.

"A bird, no doubt," said Barda. "A blackbird like Kree, almost certainly. Once they were plentiful in Del, and in olden times they were always thought of as the King's birds, because of their cleverness. That is probably why the Sorceress Thaegan so hated them, and relished eating them."

"The Torans tore the note apart," breathed Lief. "They refused help, and broke the vow. How could they risk so much?"

Barda shrugged. His face was heavy, grey with disappointment. "The stone in the square dates from the time of Adin. Perhaps the Torans no longer believed in the words. But the ancient magic was still powerful. The moment they tore up the note, they were doomed."

He looked down at the carved box in his hands. "This was something your father did not count on, Lief. The king and queen left Del in haste, long before any return message could have been expected from Tora. No doubt they thought they would receive word as they travelled, and Toran magic to help them on their way. But the plan failed."

"So all this time Father has believed that the heir was safe in Tora, waiting for us," Lief murmured. "That was his secret. He thought we would meet here, and early in our travels, too. Do you remember? His plan was for the Valley of the Lost to be our first goal, not our last. If it had been, we would surely have passed Tora on our way to the Maze of the Beast."

He put his hands on the Belt. It gave him courage.

"The plan to hide in Tora may have failed, but somehow Endon and Sharn found another place of safety," he said. "The Belt is whole. Father told us that means the heir lives, wherever he may be. When the Belt is complete, it will show us the way. Father told us it would. We must believe him."

He put the two halves of the note back into the carved box, closed the lid firmly, and put the box back on the step.

When he looked up, Barda was frowning, his gaze sweeping around the great square and the buildings that surrounded it, the great columns, the statues of birds and beasts, the carved urns overflowing with flowers. Lief wondered what he was doing. Except for the cracked stone, where Dain still huddled, locked in his private misery, and Jasmine crouched beside him, there was nothing to see.

"If the city is empty, why is it still so perfect and whole, Lief?" Barda asked suddenly. "Why have looters and scavengers not destroyed it? The pirates, the bandits . . . what has stopped them from plundering this place at their will?"

He pointed at the box. "Even that is a work of art. It would be of great value to a trader. No doubt the city is full of such things. Yet no one has stolen them. Why?"

He spoke softly, but still the square seemed to echo with his voice.

Lief felt a chill run up his spine. "You think Tora is — protected?" he whispered.

"Lief! Barda!" called Jasmine.

Startled, they looked down. Jasmine was still crouching beside Dain. She beckoned urgently, and they ran back down the stairs and across the square to her side.

Dain did not raise his head, though he must have heard them come. Jasmine had wrapped a blanket around him, but still he trembled.

"He will not move," whispered Jasmine fearfully. "He cannot stop shaking, and will not take any water. I am very afraid for him."

Dain's pale lips opened. "Take me away from here, I beg you," he mumbled. "I cannot bear it. Please — take me away."

6 - The Newcomers

With Lief and Barda supporting Dain between them, the companions began to make their way out of the city. Dain's eyes were dark and blank. His feet stumbled and dragged. Cold sweat beaded his brow. The terrible shuddering still racked his slight body.

Lief was sorry to see his suffering, but somewhere in the back of his mind he wondered at Dain's collapse. Had the boy not trained with Doom and the Resistance for a year? Had he not faced Ols and other terrible dangers as part of everyday life?

Dain had hoped to find his parents in Tora, and he had not. But how could this shock and disappointment fell him so completely? It was as though his heart was broken like Tora's stone, and the light of his spirit had been snuffed out like the green fire.

They walked on, all but Dain glancing from side

to side at the houses they passed. Clearly visible through gleaming windows were the sad signs of vanished life: food as fresh as the day it was made, wonderfully painted plates and dishes, embroidered cushions and hangings. In almost every house there was a weaver's loom on which cloth of miraculous fineness hung waiting for the long-vanished weaver to return.

The looms reminded Lief of his mother. How often had he seen her sit weaving cloth for their garments and household needs? Lief knew that his mother's skill was great, because other people had told him so. But the threads she had to use were coarse and dull — nothing like the threads of Tora, which glowed like jewels.

The finest thing she had ever made was the cloak he now wore. Into that she had put her greatest skill. And love and memories besides, she had said.

Where was his mother now?

I, of all people, should understand Dain's grief, Lief thought. I know what it is to miss and fear for well-loved parents.

But you have not given up hope, a voice in the back of his mind whispered. You have not abandoned yourself to despair and become ill in body and mind. And did Jasmine give in and die when her parents were taken? Did Barda despair when his mother was killed and his friends were slaughtered?

Lief shook his head, to drive the voice away. People have different strengths and weaknesses, he told himself. I should not blame —

His thoughts took a different turn as another idea came to him. Perhaps there was something else behind Dain's collapse that he did not yet understand. All the signs were that the boy was not simply grieved and disappointed, but deeply shocked. More shocked than was reasonable, if he had told the whole truth.

The entrance tunnel was before them. They entered its cool shade and once again Lief felt that mysterious tingling run through his body. He walked in a dream, moving out into the sun with regret.

He and Barda lowered Dain gently to the ground. The boy lay shivering as if with cold, his great eyes staring sightlessly at the bright sky.

"Dain, you must try to be strong," Barda urged softly. "You are making yourself ill."

He said the words several times, and at last Dain responded. Slowly the blank eyes came back into focus. The boy swallowed, and wet his dry lips.

"I am sorry," he murmured. "Finding the city empty . . . was a great shock. But that is no excuse."

Kree screeched, flapping his wings warningly.

"Someone is coming!" Jasmine exclaimed, drawing her dagger.

Lief looked across the lake, but it remained still. The danger was coming by land, then. From the hills that rose beside and beyond the city.

Kree soared upward, preparing to investigate.

"No, Kree!" Jasmine cried. "They may have bows and arrows. Stay with us."

The bird hovered for a moment, then reluctantly came back to earth.

"Jasmine, are there many?" snapped Barda.

As she had done so often before, Jasmine knelt and put her ear to the ground. "Only two, I think," she said after a moment. "Both tall. One heavier than the other."

Dain was watching her intently, plainly very impressed. Lief saw that the trembling in the boy's limbs had eased. Having something else to think about seems to be just what Dain needs, he thought. But he found that he was slightly annoyed.

Yet why should Dain not admire Jasmine? he thought, turning his irritation on himself. Anyone would admire her skill! Then it occurred to him that if he was still inside Tora he would not be angry, but quite calm.

The city's spell is wearing off, he thought. I am almost back to normal.

And at last he understood what the tingling in the tunnel had meant. He understood why Tora remained perfect and untouched after over sixteen years of emptiness.

"Lief!" growled Barda. "Quickly!"

Lief drew his sword and hurried to join his friends. They were standing shoulder to shoulder, making a barrier between Dain and two tall figures approaching from the hills. The figures seemed to shimmer in the dazzling sunlight.

Were they bandits? Ols?

"Tora is protected by magic," Lief said rapidly. "Magic that works on hearts and minds. The tunnel drains away all evil. If we return there, nothing can harm us."

Barda glanced at him quickly, then back at the city's shining walls. Lief could see that he was measuring the distance in his mind, trying to decide if they should risk turning and making a dash for safety. But it was too late. The strangers had seen them, and quickened their pace.

Dain began crawling unsteadily to his feet.

"Dain — go back to Tora," Barda ordered. But Dain shook his head stubbornly, feeling for his dagger.

"Dain!" Jasmine exclaimed. "Go!"

"If they are Ols, I can help," Dain said, through gritted teeth. "I will stand with you, or die. I have had enough of weakness."

He moved into place beside her and frowned at the approaching strangers. Then suddenly his eyes narrowed. His mouth firmed to a hard line.

"Doom!" he muttered, and turned away.

Startled, Lief, Barda, and Jasmine realized that he was right. Now they could see that the taller of the approaching strangers was the man who called himself Doom of the Hills. Doom, who they had last seen in the Resistance stronghold. Who had held them prisoner for three long days.

To their amazement they saw that Neridah the Swift was with him. Why had he chosen her as a companion? As they drew closer, Lief could see that Neridah's lips were curved into a smile. But Doom's face was stern.

"Do not relax!" muttered Barda. "They could be Ols, trying to deceive us."

Plainly, Dain thought not, and Lief did not, either. But still his hand tightened on the hilt of his sword. Doom had shown himself to be as dangerous as any Ol, in his way. He was not to be trusted.

When he reached them, Doom wasted no words on greetings. "So, Dain," he growled. "You are where you wanted to be. Are you satisfied?"

"You knew!" Dain burst out. "You knew all along what Tora was, Doom. You lied to me!"

"Of course," said Doom coolly. "For what else was keeping you strong but hope? Has seeing that your hope was in vain made you feel better, or worse?"

Dain's face clearly showed the answer. Doom nodded bitterly. "Ever since you came to the stronghold I have been seeking your parents, Dain. I had hoped to be successful before you could find out that they were not in Tora. But you could not wait."

"No, I could not!" cried Dain defiantly. "But that

is not my fault. I did not know the truth of things. I am not a child, to be protected and fed with fairy tales! You drove me to what I did by deceiving me!"

Doom stared at him for a long moment. Then, surprisingly, his grim face relaxed into what could have been a smile. "Once you would not have spoken to your elders that way," he said. "Such a polite, obedient child you were, when first I met you."

"I am not a child!" Dain shouted furiously.

"No, it seems you are not. Perhaps . . ." Doom seemed to ponder. "Perhaps I was wrong." His lips twitched. "It does not happen often. But it is possible. If I beg your pardon, will you come back to the stronghold with us? You are sorely missed."

Dain hesitated, swaying uncertainly.

Barda, Lief, and Jasmine glanced at one another. In all their minds was the thought that many problems would be solved if Dain agreed to go with Doom. But they had to be sure he would be safe.

Lief stepped forward. "We have learned, since seeing you last, that it is not wise to trust appearances, Doom," he said in a level voice. "Before Dain decides what he wishes to do we would like you, and Neridah, too, to go into Tora."

Doom's dark eyes turned on him. And now there was no warmth or humor in them.

"You need not stay more than a moment," Lief

went on, refusing to be cowed. "The Tora tunnel discovers evil far more quickly than your Testing Room."

"So — you have discovered Tora's secret!" sneered Doom. "Congratulations! But what if I refuse to agree to your request? What then?"

7 - A Battle of Wills

Neridah moved to stand beside Doom. Barda and Jasmine stepped into place beside Lief. The two sides glared at one another. Then Barda spoke.

"If you refuse to go into Tora, then we must assume that you are Ols, and act accordingly."

Doom's sword was in his hand in an instant.

"No!" shouted Dain, thrusting himself in front of Barda. "You must not fight! You are not enemies, but on the same side!"

Doom's face did not change. "I am still not sure of that," he said grimly.

"And neither are we, twice over!" Jasmine exclaimed. "For if you are really the man Doom, you have treated us badly and we do not trust you. And if you are an Ol in Doom's shape, you are a danger to us all."

Doom's eyes flickered. Plainly, he could see the sense in Jasmine's words. Yet still he did not lower his sword.

"How can it harm you to prove to us that you are what you seem?" Lief murmured, deliberately keeping his voice low and even.

"We do not have to prove anything to you!" Neridah cried angrily. "Doom and I have been together since we left the stronghold. We can swear — "

Doom put out a hand to quiet her. "What we swear proves nothing, Neridah," he said. "Ols most often travel in pairs, do they not?"

Then, as if Neridah's interruption had somehow helped him to make up his mind, he shrugged, sheathed his sword and began to stride towards the city's shimmering light. Neridah, plainly surprised and angry, hesitated, glaring for a moment, then swung around and stalked after him.

The companions followed. When they reached the tunnel they waited as Doom and Neridah went on alone. Lief had been tempted to enter the tunnel, too, but somehow knew that this would not be wise. He could not afford all his passions to drain away at this moment. A little anger kept one alert. And one could not be too alert when dealing with one such as Doom.

So he stood and watched, and saw what he otherwise might not have seen. As the two figures walked through the tunnel, the air began to fill with colored sparks, swirling like dust motes lit by the sun.

"I saw nothing of that when we walked through," breathed Jasmine. "I only — felt."

"It must be invisible to those who are inside." Barda rubbed his hand over his dazzled eyes and turned away.

In seconds Doom and Neridah had disappeared in a cloud of dancing light. But in only a few more moments they became visible again, walking slowly back the way they had come.

As they stepped out into the sunlight, both seemed dazed. Their faces were smooth and strangely still.

"So — you are satisfied now, I hope?" Doom said. But the words held no sting, and his eyes looked lost. Groaning, he sat down, his back against the city wall.

Neridah, Dain, and the others stared at him in confusion. Wearily, he looked up.

"When anger, hatred, and bitterness have left a man who lives by little else, what is there left for him but emptiness?" he asked with a slight smile. "That is why I do not enjoy visiting Tora. I have done so only once before — and that was enough."

"Who are you, Doom?" asked Lief suddenly.

For a moment he thought the man would not answer. Then Doom's shoulders slumped and his eyes closed, as though he did not have the strength to refuse.

"I do not know who I am," he said. "I do not know what I have lost, along with my name. My memories begin in the Shadowlands. I was fighting a Vraal in the Shadow Arena. I was injured. Everything before that is darkness."

His hand moved slowly to the jagged scar on his face.

"But you escaped?" Lief prompted. Perhaps it was cruel to use Doom's present weakness to find out more about him. But it was a chance that would not come again.

"I escaped the Shadow Arena," Doom went on. "They were not expecting that. They thought I was finished. I fled across the mountains, pursued and with no clear idea of anything save that Deltora was my home. On Dread Mountain I turned and faced my pursuers. I escaped once more, but it cost me dearly."

He sighed deeply. "I travelled on, more dead than alive. At last I was found, given shelter, and healed by a good man."

"A man who lived in a place called Kinrest," murmured Jasmine.

Doom glanced at her, and again he smiled, though his eyes were filled with sadness. "So you have seen his grave, and know I took his name," he said. "He saved me, but I brought death to him. The Grey Guards who had not died on the Mountain pursued me to his cave. Doom was a man of peace. He had no chance against them. But thanks to him I was strong once more. I killed them all, and scattered their bones."

A touch of the old savagery was in his voice as he spoke those last words. Lief realized that the calming effect of the Toran tunnel was gradually wearing off. Doom was silent for a moment, and when next he smiled, it was merely a bitter tweak of the lips.

"You have taken advantage of me, I fear," he said, climbing to his feet. "I hope your curiosity is satisfied." His mouth was tightening, his eyes darkening. The grim, familiar mask was settling back onto his face.

"Doom, I knew you had been through much," breathed Neridah. "But I had no idea . . ." Her voice trailed off as Doom shot her a cold look. Plainly he did not want her sympathy or her admiration. Her face reddened. Then she tossed her head angrily and moved away from them.

"I did not pry into your affairs out of simple curiosity, Doom," said Lief in a low voice.

"No?" Doom looked into his eyes for a long moment. Then he turned to Dain. "I am due to meet Steven the peddler in a few days," he said flatly. "He has new supplies for us. Will you come with me? Or do you choose to remain with your new friends?"

"There is no choice, Doom. Dain must go with you," Barda said quickly. "We have a hard, long journey ahead of us."

Dain's sensitive skin flushed red. "I do not want to be a burden to anyone," he said through stiff lips. "I will go with you, Doom, to meet Steven."

Doom nodded shortly. Then, as though despite himself he resented having Dain so easily cast aside, he lifted one eyebrow. "And where are you travelling, that your journey is going to be so hard?" he demanded.

Even long afterwards, Lief did not know why he said what he did then. It was the impulse of a moment. Perhaps he felt the urge to give Doom some information, as a sign of trust. Or perhaps it was simply that he was tired of lies.

"We are going to the Valley of the Lost," he said clearly.

Barda and Jasmine turned to him, astonished that he should speak so freely. Dain looked curious. But Doom nodded, his face darkening.

"I thought it might be so," he said. "And I warn you with all my heart to turn your faces from the plan. The Valley is not for such as you."

"What do you know of it?" growled Barda.

Doom looked over to where Neridah sat looking out over the waters of the lake, and lowered his voice.

"It is an evil place. A place of misery and lost souls. I know of many who have entered it, seeking the great jewel that is its Guardian's prize."

Lief glanced quickly at Barda and Jasmine. Both looked startled and watchful. He wet his lips.

"A great jewel?" he asked carefully.

Doom looked at him with something like scorn. "Do not insult me by trying to pretend. I know it is your goal. A diamond, it is said, larger and more powerful than any ever seen. Beautiful. Pure. Priceless."

He shook his head. "It is no secret in these parts. Its fame has lured many before you into the Guardian's clutches. All entered the valley in hope. All came to wish bitterly that they had never seen it."

8 - A Parting of the Ways

Lief felt a chill of fear, but straightened his shoulders. Barda stood like a rock, his hand on his sword. But Jasmine tossed back her hair and lifted her chin. "Still, we must go," she said.

Doom reached forward and gripped her shoulders. *"You must not!"* he hissed between clenched teeth. "Listen to me! Your quest is already lost. If you persist, you will be lost also. And for what? For a dream! For nothing!"

Jasmine shook herself free and drew back so that she, Lief, and Barda were standing shoulder to shoulder. Doom stared at them for a moment, then raised his hands and dropped them again, in surrender.

"I have done my best," he muttered. "I can do no more. But it is a waste. Already you have a following. Together we might have roused the people. We might have stood united against the Shadow Lord. We might have saved Deltora."

"For now, we must go our separate ways, it is true," said Barda. "But when the time is right, we will join the fight together."

"When the time is right . . ." Doom turned away. "I fear that time will never come for you, my friends. Not now."

Grim-faced, he slung his pack on his shoulder and jerked his head to Dain. "Tell Neridah we are leaving," he ordered. "I have already wasted too much time here, and Steven will not wait."

With a backward glance at Lief, Barda, and Jasmine, Dain trudged unsteadily to the water's edge.

"You know more than you are telling, Doom!" exclaimed Jasmine. "If you can help us, you should do so!"

Doom shook his head. "You have refused the only help I can give you," he muttered. "You have no right to ask more."

He frowned down at her from his great height. She looked up at him, her green eyes snapping with anger. Then, quite suddenly, he gave a short laugh.

"There is one thing I can do for you," he said. He pulled a dark woollen cap from his pocket, and tossed it to her. "You and the bird are what make your party recognizable. Cover your hair with this. You are already dressed as a boy, and a ragged boy at that. Your hair is all that gives you away."

Jasmine glared, as if uncertain whether to accept the gift or not, but finally her sense overcame her pride. She twisted up her hair and bundled on the cap, pulling it down around her ears. Instantly she was transformed. It was as though a scowling young boy stood before them.

Kree squawked. Plainly, he did not like the change. But Doom nodded. "That is better," he said.

He turned as Dain approached, and frowned again as he saw that the boy was alone. "Why is Neridah not with you?" he snapped.

"She — she will not come," Dain stammered. "She says she has decided to travel on, to her home."

Doom snorted angrily. "So that is why she insisted on coming with me! I am sure she never intended to return. Life in the stronghold does not suit her. It is too hard, too dangerous, and there is no money to spare for the luxuries a spoiled athlete has grown used to."

"But — is she not afraid the Grey Guards will track her down?" asked Lief.

"No doubt she thinks that she will be able to persuade you to escort her at least part of the way. And she is convinced that once she reaches home, she will be safe," Doom shook his head. "She is a fool! Another fool who will not take heed of warnings."

Without another word he turned and began

striding away towards the hills. Dain hesitated for a moment, then murmured a hurried farewell, and went after him.

✳

As Doom had predicted, Neridah did her best to persuade the companions to let her accompany them. At last she broke down and cried in Barda's arms, wailing that she had left the Resistance only because Doom had broken her heart.

"I love him," she sobbed. "But he is cruel, and cares nothing for me. I cannot stay where I see him every day. I cannot!"

Barda patted her shoulder awkwardly. But Jasmine regarded her with cold surprise and Lief — Lief knew enough of Neridah's deceiving ways to wonder how real her tears were.

At last, at Barda's urging, they agreed to let her travel with them for a day or two. "But after that, we must separate, Neridah," Barda warned her gently. "Our goal is a dread and dangerous place."

"The Valley of the Lost," Neridah whispered. "I know. I heard its name, when you were speaking with Doom. You are so brave — braver by far than Doom realizes."

Again, Lief wondered about her. She had shown no sign that she had heard what they were talking about with Doom. She had sat quite still, staring out at the lake as if lost in thought. And all the time she had been listening. She had heard the name of the Valley of the Lost. What else had she heard?

She is sly, he thought. We must be careful of her.

✳

In the end, Neridah travelled with them for nearly a week. She protested strongly about travelling by night, and was a sulky and complaining companion. But though they passed many roads that led in the direction of her home, she refused to take them. Whenever Lief, Barda, and Jasmine tried to part with her, she cried and ran after them. She clung to them like honey, and at last she lost even Barda's sympathy.

"I have begun to think that she is not being truthful with us," he whispered one day, as Neridah sulked in her sleeping blanket. "She said she wished to go home. Why does she not do so?"

"I do not know," Lief whispered back. "But we must do something about her quickly. I do not trust her, and I do not want her with us when we reach the Valley of the Lost. According to the map, and our reckoning, it is not far from here."

"She will not willingly let us go on without her, that is certain," Jasmine said grimly. "So we have two choices. One, hit her on the head, and run. Or, two, wait until we are sure that she is asleep, then creep away."

She seemed a little disappointed when Lief and Barda chose the second course.

A few hours later they carried out the plan, sneaking away from the camping place like thieves. They walked fast all day, trying to keep under cover, and at sunset reached a range of steep, thickly wooded hills.

"The valley is within this range, I am sure of it," said Barda.

Lief looked up at the hills. "It will be a long, hard climb," he sighed. "And dangerous, for the woods are thick, and it will be very dark. The moon tonight is at its smallest. And tomorrow night there will be no moon at all."

Jasmine pulled off her cap impatiently. "I can hear nothing with this thick wool over my ears!" she complained, shaking her hair free with relief. "Now — what were you saying? That it would be dark tonight? And that the woods are thick? Quite so. I suggest we sleep the night through, for once, knowing that we can climb in the morning, well hidden by the trees."

The plan seemed an excellent one. They did exactly as Jasmine suggested. So it was not until the close of the following day that they reached the top of that ragged hill and looked down at the jagged crack in the earth that was the Valley of the Lost.

9 - The Valley of the Lost

A thick grey mist crawled sullenly on the valley floor. It lapped to the very tops of the trees, stirred by the slow movements of half-seen figures that thronged the depths. A faint, damp warmth smelling of green decay, of rotting wood, and of smothered life, brushed the friends' faces like an echo of the mist.

Jasmine fidgeted. Filli was chattering into her ear. Kree, after a single clucking chirp, sat motionless on her arm. "They do not like the valley," she murmured.

"I cannot say that I am entranced by it, either," said Barda dryly.

Jasmine hunched her shoulders and shivered. Then, without another word, she turned and returned to the largest of the trees that ringed the lip of the cliff. In amazement, Lief and Barda watched her lift Filli from her shoulder and put him onto the highest branch she could reach. Kree fluttered up beside him.

"I know you will take care of one another," Jasmine said. "Keep safe."

She turned and, without looking back, walked back to Lief and Barda. She met their questioning eyes calmly. "I told you," she said. "Kree and Filli do not like the valley. They cannot go there."

"Why?" Lief burst out. He looked down to where Kree and Filli still perched on their branch, staring after Jasmine forlornly.

Jasmine shrugged. "If they go there they will die," she said simply. "The valley is not for them. Or any creature. The mist will kill them."

A shiver ran down Lief's back. "What about us?" he asked abruptly.

"There are people down there. I can see their shadows in the mist," said Jasmine. "And if they can survive, so can we. We will go down to where the mist begins. Then we will decide what to do."

Abruptly, she swung around and held up her hand to Filli and Kree. Then she turned once more, pulled her cap more firmly over her ears, and scrambled over the edge of the cliff.

Lief and Barda followed. The ground beneath their feet was steep and treacherous, slippery with loose stones. Half walking, half sliding, always in danger of falling, they moved down and down. After only a few minutes, Lief lost the sense that he was walking of his own accord. The slippery stones, the steepness of the slope, were doing all the work for him. From the cliff edge, the valley floor had seemed very far away. Now it was growing closer by the moment.

Once, he looked back. The cliff-top towered high above them. Impossibly high. Impossibly far away. It was hard to believe he and his friends had ever stood there. Hard to believe that they had ever had the choice of descending, staying where they were, or even turning their backs and walking away from the valley.

For now it seemed that there was no choice. The closer they moved to the crawling mist, the more it seemed to draw them, and the steeper the slope became. It took far more energy to stand still than to move on. The companions clutched one another for support, but they could do little to help one another.

And before they realized it, the mist was around them. It was as if it had risen to meet them, brushing their faces with warm, damp fingers, casting a haze over their eyes. Slowly it stole into their mouths and noses, filling them with its oversweet scent, its taste of decay.

This was not the plan, Lief thought in confusion. He tried to stop in mid-stride, then slipped and fell, rolling blindly, gasping and scrambling on the stones. He heard Jasmine and Barda calling him in alarm, but could do nothing to save himself.

When finally he came to a stop, he realized that he was on the valley floor. The mist swirled thick about him. Shadowy trees, thick with mold, hung with vines, stretched above his head. Great clumps of glistening dark red fungus bulged from twisted roots beside his face. Lush ferns arched around him, brushing his face and his hands as he scrambled, panting, to his feet.

And everywhere there was a soft sighing, like wind in the trees. But there was no wind. The sound seemed to come from everywhere, from all around him, out of the swirling greyness where darker shadows slipped and writhed, moving closer.

"Barda! Jasmine!" Lief shouted, gripped with sudden terror. But the mist muffled his voice so that it sounded thin and piping. And when his friends answered, their voices sounded far, far away.

He called again. He thought he heard a cry of pain, and his stomach lurched. But then he saw his friends stumbling towards him out of the gloom. He lurched forward, gripping their arms thankfully.

"Well, we are still alive, in any case," growled Barda. "The mist has not killed us yet."

But Jasmine said nothing. She had drawn her dagger and was standing very still, every muscle tense.

The sighing, whispering sound was louder. The mist around them stirred and billowed, the shadows deepening, closing in.

"Keep back!" Jasmine hissed, raising her dagger menacingly.

The shadows seemed to falter, but only for an instant. Then they pressed forward again. And now Lief could see that they were people, crowds of men, women, and children coming through the mist, from all directions.

They did not look unfriendly. Indeed, their pale faces seemed filled with timid eagerness and welcome as they drifted forward, long, thin hands stretched out towards the companions. Their fingers were pale grey, almost transparent, and so were the long clothes that fluttered around them and the hair that hung lank down their backs. No wonder they had seemed part of the mist.

They whispered as they moved, the sound of their voices like dry leaves rustling in the wind, but Lief could understand nothing of what they said. Yet he did not feel threatened. Even when they came very close, and the first of them began touching his face, clothes, and hair with fingers that felt dry and light as moths' wings, he felt no thrill of fear, only a shrinking distaste.

And still more of the people came, and more. The colorless rags they wore hung around limbs that seemed just skin and bone. Their shapes seemed to blend and mingle, overlapping as they pressed in, each hand moving upon a dozen others, touching, stroking . . .

Barda and Lief stood rigidly still. But Jasmine quivered, her mouth set and her eyes screwed shut.

"I cannot bear this," she whispered. "Who are they? What is wrong with them?" Her dagger hung loosely in her hand. She made no move to use it. She could not do so. The people were so plainly harmless, so plainly in some sort of terrible need.

There was a stir in the crowd. It swayed and shivered like a field of long grass swept by the wind. Then the fluttering hands were slipping away, and the people were backing, whispering, into the mist, their grey eyes filled with hopeless longing.

There was fear in the air. Lief could feel it. Almost smell it. Then he saw its source. A tall, dark shadow, pierced by two points of red light that glowed like burning coals, was coming through the mist towards them.

He tried to put his hand on his sword. But his hand would not move. He tried to step back. But his feet would not obey him. A single glance told him that Barda and Jasmine were under the same spell.

The shadow gathered form and shape. Now Lief could see that the red coals were eyes, eyes that burned in the ravaged face of a tall, bearded man wearing a long, dark robe. The man held two thick grey cords in each of his hands. They stretched away into the mist behind him, as though they were attached to something, but he paid no attention to them.

His burning eyes were fixed on Lief, Barda, and Jasmine.

They struggled to free themselves, and his thin lips curved into a smile that was full of malice.

"Do not waste your strength," he purred. "You can do nothing unless I will it. As you will learn, in time. Welcome to my valley. It has been a long time since I have had the pleasure of visitors. And now I am blessed with four."

He watched with keen pleasure as Lief, Barda, and Jasmine glanced at one another in surprise. *Four* visitors? What did he mean?

"Perhaps you thought to trick me by splitting your party, did you?" he said. "Ah, that is what I like to see. Visitors who like games. That will make things so much more pleasant, for all of us."

He crooked a bony finger. And to the companions' amazement, out of the mist stumbled Neridah, her bewildered face bruised and bleeding.

She had stubbornly followed them, despite everything they had done! Now they had her to worry about, as well as themselves. Gritting his teeth in anger, Lief remembered the cry he had heard. No doubt Neridah had tripped coming down the steep slope alone.

He glanced at the woman in helpless irritation as she staggered to a halt beside him. But Neridah did not look at him. She was staring straight ahead, her eyes dark with fear and confusion.

Their tormentor was rubbing his hands.

"Who are you?" Lief demanded.

The man smiled mockingly.

"I?" he purred. "Why, have you not guessed? I am the Guardian."

With a swirl of his robes, he turned and began walking away into the mist. Just before the companions lost sight of him, he carelessly lifted one hand and crooked the index finger.

And, unable to help themselves, feet dragging as they fought to resist his command, Neridah, Lief, Jasmine, and Barda stumbled after him.

10 ~ The Palace

The mist swirled about them as they walked. Ferns and vines brushed their legs and faces. Shadows flickered at the edge of their vision. The valley's people were watching, but not daring to come near.

In front of them strode the Guardian, straight-backed and tall.

"If this Guardian is taking us to his cave, or hut, or wherever he lives, so much the better," whispered Jasmine. "That will be where he keeps — "

She broke off, glancing at Neridah, who tossed her head angrily. "I know about the great diamond!" she said, in a high voice. "Why do you think I followed you here? For the sake of your fine company?"

She stared fearfully at the Guardian's back. "I thought you would be bound to succeed, no matter who else had failed," she went on, her voice trembling. "I did not dream that you would have us captured and helpless within moments of setting foot in the valley!"

"We have been captured before, and saved ourselves," hissed Jasmine. "We will do it again. We still have our weapons."

"He spoke of games," Lief said slowly. "He likes games. What do you think he means?"

Barda grimaced. "Nothing pleasant, in any case. But surely it proves, at least, that he is a man, not an Ol or some other beast in human shape. It is humans who like games."

"And if he is only a man we can defeat him, for all his magic," said Jasmine. "Defeat him, and take the gem. We have only to wait, and learn his weaknesses."

Lief hesitated. He, too, believed that the Guardian was human beneath the trappings of his magic power. But he was not so sure that this would make their task any easier. And something was still nagging at his memory. Something that made his skin prickle with warning whenever he thought of the diamond.

They walked for what seemed a long time, crossing a deep stream and moving at last into a clearing. Abruptly, the Guardian stopped and held up his hand. Lights began to glow through the mist. As the companions drew closer, they saw that the lights were shining inside a domed glass palace.

Mist tumbled outside the glass walls, shining

eerily in the reflected light. Hundreds of shadowy grey figures shuffled in the haze. But within the palace, rich colors glowed. The many rooms were full of fine furniture, bright rugs and paintings, gold and silver statues, silken cushions and hangings. The whole glittered like a jewel.

The Guardian had stood aside so that his prisoners could better see the palace's wonder. Now he smiled proudly at their astonished faces.

"A dwelling fit for a king, you will agree," he said.

When none of them answered him, his smile disappeared and a scowl took its place.

"We will go inside," he snapped. "Perhaps that will loosen your tongues and make you more agreeable." He tugged the cords that he held in his hands and four shapes lumbered from behind him, out of the mist.

Lief heard Neridah gasp. And indeed his own breath caught in his throat as he saw the creatures emerging from the swirling grey.

Hairless, gross, and misshapen, covered in sores and boils, twisted arms hanging almost to the ground, the monsters grinned and slobbered as they stared at the prisoners. The rubbery cords that bound them to their master coiled from puffy red centers in the backs of their necks. Sickened, Lief realized that the cords were part of them. Flesh of their flesh.

"Here are my pets — my companions," said the

Guardian. "I have kept them hidden until now, not wishing to alarm you. But you will learn to love them, as I have done. Perhaps you already do so, though you do not know it. They are fine, strong monsters, are they not? They protect me, and keep me company. Their names are Pride, Envy, Hate, and Greed."

As he spoke, he lightly flicked the monsters on the head one by one. The moment it felt his touch, each creature swayed and groaned with pleasure.

The Guardian smiled. "Their names are a little joke of mine," he said. "For though each has one of the faults I have mentioned, none has that fault after which it is named. Greed is not greedy, Pride is not proud, Envy is not envious. Hate is not envious, either, not at all. But more important, it has never hated in its life. You see? Is that not amusing?"

Again receiving no reply, he turned and walked to a door set into one of the palace walls. The door swung open and he stood back.

Lief, Barda, Jasmine, and Neridah at once found themselves moving to the door. In a moment they were inside the palace, and the Guardian was following. The monsters crowded after him, grunting, their leads flopping horribly from their necks. In the crush, three of them began to snarl and claw at one another.

Their master barked an angry command, kicking out at them savagely. When at last they had quietened, he turned back to the companions.

"Like children, my pets sometimes do not agree,

and need a firm hand," he said smoothly. "The envious one and the proud one are both very afraid of Greed. But they will fight if they have to. For, after all, they are linked together and cannot escape."

The door swung shut with a soft click.

Lief looked around, blinking in the bright light. The room they had entered was vast, and furnished with every luxury. A fountain splashed and sparkled in its center. Velvet cushions lay in heaps upon the shining floor. Soft music played, though Lief could not see where the sound was coming from.

At one end of the room was a long table draped in a white cloth and gleaming with silver and crystal. Long white candles burned in exquisite candlesticks among dishes full of steaming, fragrant food.

Five places had been laid. Two on each side of the table, one at the head.

The Guardian rubbed his hands with a dry, rasping sound. "So — now we are alone," he said. "Now we can enjoy each other's company. Fine food and drink. Music. Conversation. And, later, perhaps, the game."

*

The food looked and smelled delicious, but to the companions it tasted like dust and ashes, and they ate little. They spoke little, too, for it was clear from the beginning that what their host wanted was not a conversation, but an audience.

His voice flowed on as he sat at the head of the

table, his hideous pets squatting behind his chair. The leads, Lief saw, were attached to his wrists, no doubt by bands hidden under his sleeves. This way, his hands could be free while the beasts remained under his control.

"I was born to great riches, but through the wickedness and envy of others I lost everything," he said, pouring golden wine into a crystal goblet. "I was driven out of my home. No one would raise a hand to help me. Alone, grieving, despairing, and despised, I took refuge in this valley. My only companions at first were the birds and other small creatures. But — "

"There are no birds or small creatures in this valley," Jasmine broke in. "Or none that I have seen."

The Guardian glanced at her under his eyebrows, plainly annoyed by the interruption. "They have gone," he snapped. "They had no place here once I was transformed, and the valley became the Valley of the Lost."

He leaned forward, his red eyes gleaming hotly in the candlelight. "Do you not want to know how this miracle occurred?" he demanded. "Do you not want to know how I, an outcast, gained new wealth, a new kingdom, and powers a thousand times greater than those I had lost?"

He did not wait for them to answer, but continued as though there had been no interruption.

"A voice spoke to me as I sat grieving. It whispered to me night and day. It reminded me of how I had been wronged. Of how I had been betrayed. Of what I had lost. I thought at first that it would make me mad. But then — then . . ."

The gleaming eyes grew glazed. And when he spoke again, it was as if he had forgotten the visitors were with him. It was as if he was telling himself the story — a story he had told many, many times before.

"Then I saw the answer," he muttered. "I saw that light had betrayed me, but darkness would give me strength. I saw that all through my life I had been following the wrong path. I saw that evil would succeed where good had failed. And then I accepted evil. I welcomed it into my heart. And so I was reborn — as the Guardian."

Abruptly, his eyes lost their glazed look and focused on the strangers around his table. He noted the rigid and unsmiling faces, the almost untouched plates.

"Why do you not eat?" he snapped. "Do you mean to insult me?"

Lief looked through the wall nearest the table. Half hidden by mist, a mass of longing, haggard faces pressed against the glass.

"Do not mind them," smiled the Guardian, waving a casual hand at the crowd. "My subjects do not eat or drink. They are beyond such ordinary concerns of the flesh. It is your warm life they long for."

Jasmine, Barda, and Neridah stiffened even further. Lief wet his lips, shuddering inwardly as he remembered the dry, grey fingers stroking him. "Do you mean — they are the spirits of the dead?" he choked.

The Guardian seemed to bristle with indignation, and behind him the monsters stirred and growled. "Spirits of the dead?" he snorted. "Would I rule a kingdom of the dead? My subjects are very much alive, oh yes, and will be till the end of time. They waste away, they fade, but they do not age or die. They will live here, in my domain, forever. That is their reward."

"Their *reward*?" Neridah burst out. Her hands were trembling as she pushed away her plate.

The Guardian nodded, smoothing his beard thoughtfully. "A rich reward indeed, is it not?" he murmured. "Though I fear they are ungrateful. They do not appreciate their good fortune."

Lief forced himself to speak. "How did they earn their reward?" he asked.

"Ah . . ." The Guardian stretched with satisfaction. Plainly, this was the question he had been waiting for.

"The first of my subjects, the largest number, came to me in a great wind, the pride that had caused their fall still fresh within them," he murmured. "Others, like you, filled with envy and greed, have come since. To seek to win from me my most precious treasure. The symbol of my power. The great diamond, from the Belt of Deltora."

11 - The Game

L ief did not dare look at his friends, or at Neridah. He gripped the arms of his chair till his knuckles grew white, in the effort not to show what he was feeling.

But clearly the Guardian was not deceived. He smiled around the table, his red eyes greedily drinking in the expressions on the faces of his guests. Then he took the last few scraps from his plate and carelessly tossed them to the floor. The four monsters scrambled after the food, each fighting savagely for a share. He watched with a smile.

"Envy once nearly killed the greedy one at a dinner such as this," he commented idly, as the tumult at last died down. "Ah well."

Slowly, he pushed back his chair and stood up, the misshapen creatures shuffling and drooling behind him. "And now it is time for the game," he said. "The time I love the best. Come with me."

He had no need to ask them. Their feet followed him, whether they wished it or not, as he swept through one gleaming space after another, the monsters following him closely.

At last they reached a room that was plainly where he spent most of his time. Deep red curtains covered the walls, screening out the mist and the other rooms. Fine drawings and paintings, and a huge mirror in a carved frame, hung from the fabric.

On the floor was a rug rich in flowers, fruits, and birds, with a picture of a humble hermit repeated at each end. One of the Guardian's little jokes, thought Lief. Nowhere else in this valley would simple, beautiful living things be found. Upon the rug, in front of a couch heaped with cushions, stood a low table scattered with books. Hundreds more books packed shelves towering around the walls.

The Guardian did not pause, but walked straight across the room and pulled aside the curtain to reveal a glass door set into one wall. He did not open the door, but stepped aside and, with a wave of his arm, invited the companions to look through to the space beyond.

It was a small room that contained only a glass table set exactly in its center. On the table was a golden casket.

"The gem you seek is in that casket," said the

Guardian. His voice trembled. Plainly, he could hardly contain his gleeful excitement. "Whoever matches wits with me and wins can enter the room and take the prize."

Lief pressed himself against the glass of the door. The Belt of Deltora warmed faintly against his skin, proof that the Guardian spoke the truth. The great diamond was in that room. The Belt could feel it.

Barda pushed at the door with his shoulder, but it did not move.

Again the Guardian cackled. "No force can unlock this door. It is sealed by magic, and so it will remain, until you have won the right to open it. So — will you play?"

"Do we have a choice?" Jasmine muttered.

The Guardian raised his eyebrows. "Why, of course!" he exclaimed. "If you so wish, you can leave here now, empty-handed. Turn your backs on the gem you came to find. Go back where you came from! I will not stop you."

Lief, Barda, and Jasmine glanced at one another.

"If we win the game and enter the room, the diamond is ours to keep?" Lief wanted to make absolutely sure. "You will allow us to leave the valley, taking our prize with us? You swear this?"

"Certainly!" said the Guardian. "That is the rule. Your prize will be yours to keep."

"And if we fail?" Barda asked abruptly. "What then?"

The Guardian spread his hands. The fleshy leads swung free from his wrists and the monsters stirred behind him. "Then — why, then, *you* are *mine* to keep. Then you will remain here, like all the others who have chosen to match wits with me. You will become part of the Valley of the Lost. Forever."

The companions stood motionless beside the door. Outside the small room where the casket lay, despairing grey hands brushed the glass through billowing mist.

"Will you accept the challenge?" murmured the Guardian. His eyes burned like hot coals as he waited for their answer.

"We need to know more before we decide," said Barda evenly.

But Neridah was shaking her head. "*I* do not need to know more!" she exclaimed. "*I* have already decided. These three can do what they wish, but I will play no game!"

The Guardian bowed, though the corner of his mouth twitched with scorn. "Then you may go, lady," he said, carelessly waving his arm.

Neridah staggered as the spell that had bound her was broken. She backed away, then turned and ran from the room without looking back.

The Guardian sighed. "A pity," he muttered. "I thought she, of all of you, would find the diamond's lure impossible to resist. Perhaps, even now, she will change her mind and return. The smell of greed and envy is strong on her."

He turned to the creatures at his heels and petted them, one by one. "*You* sensed it keenly, did you not, my sweets?" he crooned. The monsters grunted and snuffled agreement, rubbing their bloated faces adoringly against his hands.

Without bothering to turn around, he flicked a finger in the companions' direction. With relief they felt their invisible bonds relax. Suddenly they could move freely.

The Guardian strolled to the mirror and began looking at himself with appreciation, smoothing his beard and smiling. Lief's fingers itched to reach for his sword, to attack. But he knew, as Barda and Jasmine did, that it would be no use. Hate, Greed, Pride, and Envy were facing them, jagged teeth bared. At a single warning sound the Guardian would turn and cast another spell — a spell even more powerful, perhaps, than the last.

"It is time for me to sleep," he said at last, turning away from the mirror with a yawn. "Unlike my subjects, I still have these needs of the flesh. What more do you wish to know?"

He is sure that we long for the diamond, Lief thought. He felt our need, as we looked at the casket. Still — his need is great, too. He pretends he does not care, but he dearly wants us to play his game. His pride drives him to prove himself more powerful and clever than we are, to crush and defeat us. That is his weakness.

"We cannot make up our minds to play unless we know more about the game," Jasmine said loudly. "What is it? How is it played?"

The Guardian frowned, hesitating.

"You *want* us to play, do you not?" Lief urged. "And we — we want the diamond, I confess. But we would be fools to endanger our freedom blindly. We need to know that it is *possible* to win."

The Guardian's eyes narrowed. "Of course it is possible!" he snapped. "Do you accuse me of cheating?"

"No," said Lief. "But some games are matters of chance, and luck. *Your* game may be one of these. And if so — "

"Mine is not a game of chance!" shouted the Guardian. "It is a battle of wits!"

"Then prove it," Barda said quietly. "Tell us what we must do."

The Guardian thought for a moment. Then he smiled. "It seems that you are to be worthy players," he said. "Very well. I will tell you. All you must do is find out one word. The word that will unlock the door. And that word is — my true name."

The companions stared at him in silence. Of all the things they might have expected, this was the last.

The Guardian nodded with satisfaction, well

pleased by their surprise. "The clues to the riddle are in this palace," he added teasingly. "And the first, hidden in this very room!"

Barda straightened his shoulders. "We would be grateful for some time alone to discuss our decision, sir," he said, using his most polite and formal voice.

"Certainly!" The Guardian bowed. "I am a very reasonable man, and will allow you that courtesy. But I pray you, do not try my patience. I will return in a short time, and then I must have your answer."

Gathering his creatures' leads in his hands, he turned and left them.

12 - The Search

As soon as they were alone, Jasmine ran to the glass door and stared through it once more. "There is another door in there!" she whispered. "A door that leads to the outside. See? In the corner."

"And so? What is your plan?" asked Barda warily.

Jasmine's eyes were sparkling fiercely. "It is simple. We will tell the Guardian that we will play his stupid game. Then, when he is asleep, we will find a way of breaking into this room. We can steal the gem, leave by the other door, and be out of this valley before he wakes."

"No!" Lief exclaimed impulsively.

Jasmine glanced at him in annoyance. "Are you afraid?" she demanded. "Afraid of his magic?"

Lief hesitated. It was not quite that. It was something else. That niggling memory at the corner of his mind. A warning. Something about the diamond . . .

"We would be foolish not to be afraid, Jasmine," said Barda. "The man's powers are great, and he is plainly mad. Whoever he once was, the Shadow Lord has possessed him body and soul."

He was bending over the low table, sorting quickly through the books that lay there. Lief realized that Barda, practical as ever, was checking to see if the Guardian's name, or part of it, was scribbled in the front of one of the volumes. He moved to help him.

"You will never find out his name that way!" Jasmine hissed furiously. "If it were that simple those poor souls outside the windows would have — "

Lief's gasp of surprise interrupted her. At the bottom of one of the piles of books he had seen something familiar. A small, faded blue volume. He snatched it up and opened it.

As he had half-hoped, half-feared, it was *The Belt of Deltora*. The book he had so often studied, at home in Del. The book he had last seen in the dungeon where his father lay chained and helpless.

And now it was here. Here, in the Valley of the Lost! His heart pounding, he held up the book for Barda and Jasmine to see. Barda frowned.

"That the Guardian has a copy of this book means nothing," he said. "For surely there were many copies made, not just one. They must lie in many forgotten places, all over the kingdom."

"The Guardian is a servant of the Shadow Lord — that much is certain, from what he told us," argued Lief. "And if he has been studying this book, it is because the Shadow Lord has told him to do so. The Guardian pretends to think that we are ordinary strangers, seeking the diamond out of simple greed. But perhaps he has known all along that we are not."

"Then why bother with all this talk of a game?" Jasmine muttered. "He could kill us whenever he chose!"

Lief shuddered. "Perhaps he is just entertaining himself. Playing with us, as a cat plays with a mouse."

"Perhaps," said Barda. "But perhaps not. He did not know *when* we would come. And if he has been warned of a boy, a man, and a girl with a black bird, he may not realize that we are the ones. Kree is not with us, Jasmine is dressed as a boy, and we came here with Neridah."

"At least, then, she was of some use," Jasmine sniffed.

Lief was frantically flicking through the little book. On every page were well-remembered words and phrases, but he was looking for just one thing. The passage about the powers of the diamond.

At last, he found it.

✝   **The diamond is the symbol of innocence, purity, and strength. Diamonds gained nobly, and with a pure heart, are a powerful force for good. They give courage and**

strength, protect from pestilence, and help the cause of true love. But take heed of this warning: Diamonds gained by treachery or violence, or desired out of envy or greed, are ill omens, and bring bad fortune. Great evil comes upon those who gain them without honor.

"This — this is what I was trying to remember," said Lief rapidly, showing the passage to his companions. "*This* is why we cannot steal the diamond!"

His friends looked at the book, then at one another. "This warning is not for us!" Jasmine protested. "Why, we do not want the gem out of greed or envy. We would be stealing it for a good reason. We would be rescuing it from the hands of evil and restoring it to its rightful place!"

Lief shook his head. "The words are clear," he insisted. "The diamond must be gained without force or trickery. Otherwise it will bring us nothing but ill — as it has brought the Guardian!"

"And so . . . ?" muttered Barda.

Lief sighed, closing the book and pushing it back into its place on the table. "The Guardian must give it to us freely. And there is only one way we can make him do that. His pride is his weakness, and this game of his is important to that pride. I believe if we can win it, he will be forced to — "

At that moment, they heard the sound of footsteps. The Guardian was returning. He swept into the room, his pets lumbering behind him.

"Well?" he demanded. "Have you made your decision?"

Lief and Barda looked quickly at Jasmine. She paused, then grimaced and gave a slight nod. Barda stepped forward.

"Yes," he said firmly. "We will play."

The monsters whined and pulled at their leads in excitement. The Guardian's eyes burned.

"Excellent!" he hissed. He pointed at a tall, unlit candle that stood on the table below the mirror. A flickering yellow flame appeared.

"The life of this candle will be the time you have to open the door into the casket room," he said. "If the door remains unopened when the candle dies, you will admit defeat and become mine. Agreed?"

"Agreed." The companions said the word together, without flinching.

The Guardian again rubbed his hands. "I wish you good night, then," he smiled. "Explore as you wish. The first clue is in this room, as I told you. In one way it is hidden. In another, it is as plain as the nose on your face."

He walked to the door, but before going on he turned once more. "A word of advice. You have one chance to open the door, and one chance only. Do not waste your chance on a guess."

He smiled thinly. "I will see you in the morning. To claim my victory."

With that, he swept from the room, with his

creatures following him. But as soon as he was out of their sight, his triumphant, cackling laughter began. It echoed around the glass walls of his palace like a hundred voices, fading slowly into the distance, as he went to his rest.

※

For an hour the companions searched the room, seeking anything, anything at all, that would give them a clue to the Guardian's name.

The books on the shelves were of no use. They crumbled to dust as Barda pulled them from their places. The papers in the drawers of the cabinets were yellowed and brittle. They, too, cracked and crumbled at a touch. The pictures revealed no clue. There was nothing behind the curtains but glass and mist.

"He thinks he has everything — but he has nothing!" exclaimed Jasmine. "His wonderful food is ashes. His beautiful books are dust. His companions are disgusting, drooling beasts. His kingdom is a place of misery. How can he be so blind?"

"It is *we* who are blind," Barda said through gritted teeth, his eyes on the slowly dripping candle. "He said there was a clue in this room, and I am sure he was telling the truth. But what clue? Where?"

"He said there was a clue *hidden* in this room!" Lief buried his face in his hands, trying to concentrate. "We have looked under everything, behind everything, inside everything. So that means it is hidden in another way."

"Hidden by magic!" Jasmine looked around the room in desperation. "And that would make sense of the other thing he said — that in one way it was hidden, and in another it was as plain as the nose on your face."

"The nose on your face! Why, of course!" thundered Barda, leaping to his feet. As his companions watched, astonished, he strode across the room and looked into the mirror. For a moment the others saw his face, strangely softened and youthful, reflected in the glass. Then the image disappeared and words appeared, shining white in the flickering light of the candle.

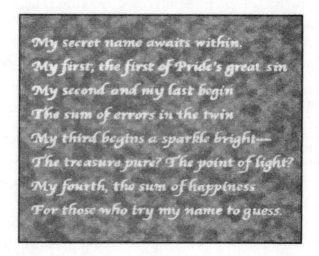

> My secret name awaits within.
> My first, the first of Pride's great sin
> My second and my last begin
> The sum of errors in the twin
> My third begins a sparkle bright—
> The treasure pure? The point of light?
> My fourth, the sum of happiness
> For those who try my name to guess.

"But it makes no sense!" cried Jasmine in dismay. "No sense at all!"

"It does," said Barda. "I have seen things like it before. It is a puzzle."

"The rhyme tells us how many letters are in the Guardian's name," said Lief slowly. "It tells us how to find out what the letters are. But it is more difficult by far than any puzzle I have ever solved."

He gripped the Belt of Deltora, wishing with all his heart that the topaz was at its full strength. Often before it had cleared and sharpened his mind. But its power increased as the moon grew full, and lessened as the moon waned. Tonight there was no moon at all.

If he and his companions were to solve this puzzle, they would have to solve it alone.

13 - Sparkles Bright

After copying the words from the mirror onto a scrap of paper that Jasmine found among her treasures, the companions sat and talked.

"The first line means simply that the name is to be found from clues within the palace," Lief said. "Agreed?"

"Even I can see that!" exclaimed Jasmine, as Barda nodded. "But what of all the rest?"

"The next line means that the first letter of the name we seek is the same as the first letter of Pride's great sin."

"Well, that appears simple, too," said Barda. "The first letter of Pride is P."

"But that is hardly a puzzle at all!" Jasmine objected. "Surely it cannot be so easy."

"It is not," Lief said gloomily. "Do you not see,

366

Barda? 'Pride' has a capital letter. It is a name. The name of one of the Guardian's pets."

"And the Guardian told us that none of his creatures had the fault for which it was named," groaned Jasmine. "Pride's sin must be envy, greed, or hatred. Ah — I begin to see now how this puzzle works. The first letter of the Guardian's name must be E, G, or H."

"But how are we to guess which one?" Barda exploded. "I do not even remember which creature was which! The Guardian is not playing fair, for all he said!"

"I am sure he is," said Lief, tapping the pencil on the paper. "The triumph he hopes to enjoy would be meaningless otherwise. Somewhere in the palace there must be another clue."

"Then we had better find it! Quickly!" exclaimed Jasmine, jumping up with a nervous glance at the candle. It was burning down alarmingly fast.

Her fear was catching. Lief felt his heart begin to pound. He forced himself to be still, and put his hand on the Belt of Deltora. His fingers found the amethyst, and as they pressed against it, his heart slowed and a soothing calm settled over him. He took a deep breath.

"We must not panic and begin rushing around without a plan," he said quietly. "Panic will stop us from thinking clearly. It is our enemy."

"Time is our enemy also, Lief," Barda reminded

him sharply. "We have been at this task hours already, and we are no further ahead."

"But we are," said Lief. "We know that the Guardian's name has five letters, because the rhyme speaks of 'my first,' 'my second,' 'my third,' 'my fourth,' and 'my last.' We know that the first letter is E, G, or H. And we know that the second and the last letters are both the same."

"How do we know that?" Jasmine was fidgeting, anxious to be away.

"The rhyme tells us so." Lief read the words aloud.

My second and my last begin
The sum of errors in the twin.

As Jasmine nodded anxiously, Lief glanced over the rest of the rhyme, and suddenly saw something else.

"And I believe — I believe I know what the fourth letter is!" he exclaimed. Again, he read aloud.

My fourth, the sum of happiness
For those who try my name to guess.

"How much happiness has come to those who have tried to guess the Guardian's name?" he asked.

"None, from what we hear," said Barda grimly.

"Exactly. And because the word 'sum' is used, I would guess that the Guardian is playing a little trick here. The fourth letter is in fact a number. Zero. Which when written down is the same as O."

As the others stared, he began scribbling under

the rhyme. When he had finished, he turned the paper so they could see what he had done.

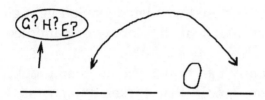

"There," Lief said. "Now we can begin filling in the blanks."

He stood up, wishing that he felt as confident as his words had sounded. "We will search the palace room by room," he said. "Wherever we go, we will look for things that match the rhyme."

Together they left the study and began the search. One room, then another, and another, yielded no clue, though they looked carefully at every piece of furniture, every rug, every ornament.

The palace was vast. They moved on and on, the lilting music following them, trying to keep calm and alert. For a while there were small sounds of movement other than their own — echoing, faraway sounds as of soft footsteps, of doors opening and closing. But at last the music stopped, and the other sounds stopped also.

Now they worked in complete silence. It was hard not to hurry. Hard not to begin rushing, skimping the search. In all their minds was a picture of the candle, dripping, dripping, relentlessly burning away.

Finally they came to a room which, like the Guardian's study, was screened by curtains and sealed by a closed wooden door. Soft light glowed behind the door's small window of patterned, colored glass.

Gently Lief turned the knob and looked in. Despite the candle that flickered on a stand beside the door, the room was dim. It took a moment for him to make out the huge pile of soft cushions in one corner.

The Guardian was lying there, asleep. But he was not alone. His four pets shared his bed, their fleshy leads tangling around them like pale snakes. And the creatures were awake. They turned their terrible heads to the door. Their teeth gleamed as they growled, long and low.

Hastily, Lief jerked backwards and closed the door again.

"We cannot go in there," he whispered. "It is his bedroom. And the creatures are with him."

"We will surely have to face them in the end," Barda whispered back. "How else will we have any hope of finding out what Pride's fault is?"

They stood, undecided, staring at the closed door. Then Jasmine's face grew puzzled. She pointed to the colored glass window. "There is something strange about this," she murmured. "I have just noticed it. Look!"

"It is certainly odd. There is a diamond or a star in every square except the last," said Barda, peering at the glass.

"Yes!" Jasmine snatched the paper from Lief's hands and read out two of the lines from the rhyme:

My third begins a sparkle bright —
The treasure pure? The point of light?

She looked up eagerly, to see if they understood. "Diamonds and stars are both bright sparkles," she said. "The rhyme is asking us which one of them should go in the last square. A diamond, which is a treasure. Or a star, which is a point of light."

"So the third letter of the Guardian's name is the beginning letter of one of those two. It is D, or S." Lief took the paper from Jasmine and made a note on his diagram, gnawing at his lip, fighting down his excitement.

They stared at the panes of colored glass till the pattern blurred in front of their eyes, but with no result.

"There is not any sense to it!" growled Barda at last. "There are sixteen squares in all. But they seem to be arranged simply according to someone's fancy."

Lief agreed. And Jasmine, now that her excitement had died, was growing more and more uneasy.

"Perhaps the mystery is connected with sixteen," Barda muttered, refusing to be beaten. "Sixteen is a useful number, for it divides easily into smaller, equal parts. The platoons at the palace numbered sixteen. Often, when we were marching in formation on the parade ground, we would begin together, then split into eights, then fours, then . . ."

His voice trailed off. His jaw had dropped. He was staring fixedly at the window. "Look!" he said huskily.

His blunt finger drew a cross through the center of the window, dividing it into four equal parts.

"The whole makes no sense," he said. "But if instead of seeing it as one large square made of sixteen smaller squares, we see four squares, each containing four smaller squares, what happens then?"

Lief looked, and it was as if he was seeing the window with new eyes. Now it was made up of four blocks. Two on the top, two on the bottom.

In the first block, there were three stars and one diamond. In the block next to that, there were two stars and two diamonds. In the third block, the one directly below the first, there was one star and three diamonds. And in the fourth block, the one that contained the blank square . . .

"One diamond is added each time," hissed Barda, his eyes alive with relief, "and one star taken away. So the last square must contain *no* stars, and — *four diamonds!*"

"Yes!" Lief could hardly believe how simple it was. But it had not seemed simple until Barda worked it out. And all because he remembered his days as a palace guard, thought Lief, writing a D above the third dash on his paper.

Barda watched with satisfaction. "Two letters filled in!" he said. "Now — shall we face the creatures?"

14 ~ The Name

Gently, they opened the bedroom door once more. The Guardian had not moved, but now the monsters were sprawled all over him. Hearing intruders, all of them raised their heads and snarled threateningly.

"This is impossible!" breathed Barda. "They will not let us near him. How can we find out about them from here?"

"Perhaps we can call them by name," Jasmine suggested. "Each in turn."

"Well, do not call Greed first, that is all I ask," murmured Lief.

"Why?" Jasmine asked.

Lief grew very still. He had spoken without thinking. He had blurted out the half-joking request because of something he had not realized he knew.

"Because," he said, his heart starting to pound,

"because, when we first came to the palace the Guardian told us that the envious monster and the proud one are both afraid of Greed. So Greed cannot be the envious one, or the proud one, itself. And we also know that Greed is not greedy, for none of the monsters has the fault after which it has been named. So — that means Greed must be the most dangerous one of all, the one full of hatred."

He could tell that his friends were thinking of other things the Guardian had said. Things that at the time they had not guessed were important. But which, now, suddenly seemed very important indeed.

Without a word, they backed out of the door for a second time, and closed it behind them.

"He gave us the clues, and we did not realize!" hissed Jasmine. "What else did he say?"

"He said that Envy once nearly killed the greedy one, fighting over scraps from the table," said Barda firmly.

"If Envy tried to kill the greedy one, then it is not greedy itself," said Lief. "And it is not envious, we know that . . ."

"And it is not full of hatred!" exclaimed Jasmine. "For we have already decided that Greed is that. So Envy . . . must be the one who is proud!"

They were walking away from the door, through to another room. By now they were sure that they had no need to face the monsters. They already knew enough to work the puzzle out for themselves.

"What else did the Guardian tell us?" hissed

Lief, racking his brains. "He said . . ."

"He said that Hate is not envious!" said Jasmine triumphantly. "He said it when we first saw the beasts."

"Yes!" Lief remembered. "And Hate is not full of hatred. And it is not proud, for Envy is the proud one. So — Hate must be greedy!"

"And that leaves only one fault for Pride," said Barda slowly. "Pride is envious."

Without a word, Lief wrote E on the first dash on his paper.

And now there was only one letter left to find, for the rhyme had said that the second and last letters of the name were the same. Barda repeated the clue:

My second and my last begin
The sum of errors in the twin . . .

"I have not the smallest idea what this could mean," Jasmine confessed. "I feel I am stupid, but — "

"If you are stupid, then so am I," growled Barda. "It has been a mystery to me from the start."

And Lief could not think what the strange lines could possibly mean, either. All he knew was that somewhere in this glass-walled maze was the last clue, and they had to find it.

Filled with desperate energy, they hurried from room to gleaming room, searching everywhere for some sign that would help them solve the riddle. But they found nothing. Nothing but magnificent emptiness.

Finally they turned a corner and Jasmine groaned. "But we have been here before!" she exclaimed. "We have already searched this room."

Lief and Barda looked around them and realized that Jasmine was right.

"There is nowhere left to look!" Barda's face was lined with weariness, heavy with despair.

Outside the windows, heavy mist rolled in darkness, shadowy figures drifted, fingers trailed across glass, haunted eyes stared. How much time had passed? Lief found he did not know. He clutched at the Belt under his shirt as he felt panic rising within him once more.

"The clue is here somewhere. We know it," he said, managing to keep his voice steady, the amethyst cool under his fingers. "We will simply begin the search again."

They moved on, and on, rechecking every space, till they reached the curtained study where they had begun.

"We searched this room from top to bottom," Barda muttered. "Surely there is no point . . ."

But they had to enter the study. None of them could resist the urge to look at the candle, to know how much time they had left.

Lief had braced himself for what he might see, but even he could not keep back a gasp of horror as he saw how low the flame now burned. The candle was just a stub, almost smothered by a thick mass of hardened drips. It could not last much longer.

"We cannot go on with this," Jasmine said urgently. "We must smash the glass door, take the diamond, and run, Lief, whatever you say. We must do it now!"

"She is right, Lief, I fear," said Barda, his eyes on the flame.

Lief shook his head despairingly. He knew, *knew*, that this would be a terrible mistake. Yet what choice had they? There was plainly no time to waste. No time to search the palace again. No time to think . . .

Jasmine had begun darting around the room, looking for something heavy that she could use to shatter the glass. Finding nothing better, she swept the books off the low table and began dragging it determinedly towards the door.

"No!" shouted Lief. "You must not!"

Jasmine swung around furiously. "I must! Do you not understand, Lief? What is the matter with you? It is too late now to worry about a warning in some old book! We cannot win the diamond. The Guardian's rhyme, with its riddling talk of twins that do not exist, has defeated us. This is the only way!"

She turned again and went on heaving at the table. After a brief hesitation, Barda went to join her. Pushing her aside, he lifted the table clear of the rug and carried it to the glass door.

Lief sprang at him, pulling urgently at his arm. But he had no chance against Barda's strength. The big man shook him off ruthlessly, sending him sprawling to the ground.

"Stand back," Barda said grimly. "The glass will shatter. Cover your eyes."

Lief crawled to his knees, his head spinning. Barda was already swinging the table back, steadying himself, preparing to strike. Lief ducked his head. The rug, with its flowers, fruit, and birds, was soft under his hands. The two hermits stared solemnly up at him. Two pairs of eyes. Two beards. Two long, plain robes, tied at the waist . . .

Lief stared. The blood rushed to his face. "Twins!" he shouted, staggering to his feet. "Barda, stop! The twins! I have found them!"

He pointed desperately at the rug as Barda slowly lowered the table and Jasmine stamped with frustration and anger.

"They were here all the time!" Lief babbled. "We hardly noticed them because they were under the table, and under our feet. But now you can see clearly. The hermits seem exactly alike. They look like twins! But they are not exactly alike at all!"

By this time, Jasmine and Barda were by his side, staring at the rug. Lief snatched out the paper he had stuffed in his pocket.

"The sum of errors in the twin," he read. "That must mean the number of differences between one hermit and the other."

"*Are* there differences?" demanded Jasmine, glancing worriedly over her shoulder at the weak candle flame. "Where?"

"Look at the cord around the waist," Lief urged. "In one picture it is knotted on the left side, in the other it is knotted on the right."

"And the bird!" Barda exclaimed. "In one picture it has a crest, in the other it does not."

"There are more bees coming from the hive in one than in the other," Jasmine added, drawn into the search in spite of herself. "And look — one tree has berries, the other has flowers."

"The toadstools on one side are spotted, the others are plain," Barda pointed out.

"That makes five differences," said Lief. "And there is another. One tree has a branch of leaves on the top left-hand corner, the other does not. Six differences."

"The hermit is holding three stems in one picture, and only two in the other! Seven!" whispered Jasmine.

They looked carefully, but could see nothing more.

"The number is seven," muttered Barda, his voice harsh with relief. "The letter we are looking for is S."

"No!" Jasmine was pointing again at the rug. "Wait, I see something else! The sack beside him. One sack has a tie. The other does not."

"You are right!" Lief exclaimed. "Eight! So the letter we are looking for, the second letter of the Guardian's name, and the last, is not S, but E."

"We have already had an E," hissed Jasmine.

"Ah, he is cunning," growled Barda. "He thought we would be tricked by that. And we nearly were!"

Lief scribbled on his diagram, then showed them.

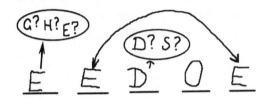

"Eedoe. His name is Eedoe." Jasmine collapsed on the couch behind her. "Oh, we have done it!"

In the relieved silence that followed, Lief suddenly became aware that the soft music that had filled the air the night before had begun again. No doubt that meant that the Guardian had woken.

He glanced at the candle. The wick was flickering uncertainly, swimming in a pool of melted wax. The flame was about to go out. But that did not matter now.

The hermits on the rug looked up at him with sad eyes. No reason for sadness now, my friends, he thought. We have nearly . . .

And then he saw it.

One hermit's arm, the arm on which the bird sat, was held above the tie of his robe. The other was not.

Lief stared stupidly at the paper in his hand. His chest grew tight. He was finding it hard to breathe.

"Lief, what is the matter?" hissed Jasmine. But Lief could not answer. He walked stiffly to the glass door.

"Say it!" Barda urged. "Say, 'Eedoe'!"

Lief wet his lips. "The name is not Eedoe," he said huskily. "There are nine differences, not eight. The missing letter was N. The name — the Guardian's secret name — is — Endon."

15 - The Casket

The door swung silently open. The glass table, the golden casket, lay waiting. But Lief, Barda, and Jasmine stood where they were, gripped by horror.

"It cannot be!" Jasmine whispered. "The Guardian is too old to be King Endon! He looks as old as time!"

"He has lived as the servant of evil for sixteen years," said Lief drearily. "Evil has eaten him from within. Even Father would not recognize him now." His heart ached as he thought of what his father would feel, if he ever had to know what his friend had become.

"Jarred always said that Endon was weak," Barda growled. "Foolish and weak. Protected from the world, and used to flattery and power. But still he loved him, and tried to protect him. He saved Endon from the palace, and certain death. And for what? For this!"

"How could Father know that Tora would refuse to help?" cried Lief. "How could he know that Endon would turn to the dark side, to regain all he had lost?"

"Do not call him Endon," Barda muttered. "He is not Endon any longer, but the Guardian. And he has regained nothing! He is deceived and used. He is unloved, alone . . ."

Jasmine gasped, her eyes wide and alert. "He is alone," she repeated. "Alone! Where is the queen? Where is the heir?"

The others were silent. Their shock had for a moment driven all other thoughts from their minds. But now they saw that Jasmine had seized on the really important question.

"Father said Queen Sharn was strong," Lief said. "Strong — and brave. Not at all the spoiled, petted palace doll she appeared. Perhaps she refused to stay with Endon, once he began to listen to the Shadow Lord, once he began to become the Guardian. Perhaps she took the child, and fled."

He turned to them, his face alight with hope. "And if that is true, if Sharn and the heir are living safely somewhere else, it does not *matter* what Endon has become. The heir has always been the one we had to find."

At that moment, somewhere in the palace, he

heard footsteps and low, growling sounds. Coming closer. His skin crawled.

"Quickly!" he muttered.

He hurried into the small room, with Barda and Jasmine close behind him. Together they approached the table and stood before it.

But before Lief could lift a hand, there was a sound at the door. The Guardian was standing there, his seamed, ruined face writhing with astonishment, fury, and baffled pride. Behind him, the monsters snarled.

"So," spat the Guardian. "You discovered my name. Did it surprise you?"

"A little," said Barda evenly.

The Guardian sneered. But Lief thought he could see, deep in the red eyes, a gleam of reluctant respect.

"Only one other has ever done so," he said. "And he — he found the truth so hard to bear that he refused to enter this room and claim his prize. He left the valley, cursing me. Saying that he and his cause, whatever that may be, wanted nothing that had been tainted by my possession."

With a jolt, Lief realized who that man must have been. The man who had travelled far and wide across Deltora, seeking allies for his cause and money for arms and supplies. The man who had warned them so earnestly against coming to the Valley of the Lost. Who had always said, so bitterly, that the battle for Deltora must be fought without the king, without magic. Who had told them so firmly that their quest was pointless.

"Doom," he murmured, and felt Jasmine and Barda stiffen beside him.

The Guardian laughed mockingly. "I never knew his name, though he, at last, knew mine. It is a shame that he did not stay. There was a bitterness and hatred within him that warmed my heart, and made my creatures glad."

He stroked his beard, looking at the companions slyly. "Will you follow his example, and run?"

"No, we will not," said Barda boldly. "We will take our prize."

Lief put his hands on the golden casket. His neck burned as the Guardian's red eyes stared from the door. The Guardian. His father's friend Endon, hideously changed.

And Doom has known it all the time, he thought angrily. Yet he did not tell us. No, he kept it to himself. As he keeps everything. Trusting no one. No one but himself. Whatever the cost.

The beasts at the door whimpered and growled. Lief knew they could feel his anger. It was like meat and drink to them. This was not the time to think of things that did not matter. He pressed the catch. The lid of the casket flew up.

And inside, nestled on a bed of black velvet, a great diamond gleamed.

Lief snatched up the gem and whirled around, clutching it tightly.

"Get out!" the Guardian hissed. "Take your prize, and go!"

The door leading into the valley swung open. Mist billowed into the room, mingled with the sound of soft, sighing voices.

"Lief!" urged Barda, trying to pull Lief towards the opening.

But Lief stood his ground, feeling the blood rush into his face.

"Why do you stay?" snarled the Guardian. "Is it not enough that you have won? Must you jeer at me, too?"

"You have cheated us," Lief cried, his voice trembling with anger. He held out the jewel, gleaming on the palm of his hand. "This gem may be a diamond. But it is not the diamond from the Belt of Deltora!"

"I never promised you more than what was in the casket!" the Guardian blustered. "I said to you clearly, 'you may take your prize and go.' That is all."

"You told us your treasure was the diamond from the Belt of Deltora," Lief insisted. "And the real gem was here, when first you showed us this room. But now it has gone."

He moved a step forward, ignoring the monsters' snarls. "You moved it, Guardian, once we were safely out of the way, searching other parts of your palace," he shouted. "You replaced it with another gem. So that even if we won your game, your real treasure would not be lost."

The Guardian's eyes narrowed. "How can you know this?" he spat.

"It does not matter how I know," Lief cried. "The important thing is, you have lied and cheated. You, who make so much of following the rules."

"And did *you* follow the rules?" the Guardian jeered. "Yes! I took my jewel from the casket, and hid it outside in the mist. The gem I put in its place should more than satisfy your greed."

Panting with rage, he moved towards them, his creatures growling around his feet. "But who was watching me?" he spat. "Who stole the diamond from its hiding place, as soon as I turned my back? The fourth member of your party. The one who refused to play the game. Who pretended to have left the valley!"

"Neridah?" gasped Lief. "But . . . we knew nothing of this!"

"So you say," sneered the Guardian.

"Of course we did not know!" Jasmine was already at the doorway, almost hidden in the swirling mist. "If we had, would we have wasted our time on your stupid game? Where is she? Which way did she go?"

The Guardian shrugged. "It does not matter to you," he said. "You have your prize."

Lief stepped forward, his fists clenched. The creatures snarled.

"Lief, no!" snapped Barda. "Forget this. We must try to find Neridah's tracks. By now she will be hours away."

But Lief paid no attention. His eyes were fixed on the Guardian. "Where is Neridah?" he asked softly. "She has not left the valley, has she? You know where she is, and the diamond, too."

"And if I do know," the Guardian said, just as softly, "I will not be telling you. Did you really think I would give you the most important thing in my life? The thing that is the symbol of my lord's favor? The thing that has brought me power and riches?"

"It has brought you dust and ashes, Guardian," spat Lief. "It has surrounded you with misery. You gained it through cunning, trickery, theft, and violence. Its curse is upon you. And in your heart you know it."

Something flickered in the red eyes. "Who are you?" the Guardian murmured. "Who are you, that you know so much?"

"I have read *The Belt of Deltora*, as you have done."

"It is more than that, I think," the Guardian said. "I think you are the ones! The ones of whom I was told." He nodded to Jasmine and her hand reached up unwillingly and pulled the cap from her head. Her black hair fell, tangling, to her shoulders.

The Guardian smiled grimly. "And so I was deceived," he said. "The black bird, of course, remained outside the mist. And the fourth member of the party, the thief, was merely following you to profit by your cleverness. Ah — how nearly I let you slip through my fingers."

Once again his red eyes turned on Lief. "Give it to me," he commanded. "Give me the Belt of Deltora!"

Lief felt his hands move to his waist. His fingers found the clasp of the Belt. Sweat breaking out on his forehead, he forced them away from it, pushing them with all the force of his will over the gems that studded the medallions. His hand slid over the topaz, the ruby, the opal . . . and came to rest on the lapis lazuli, the heavenly stone, the talisman. He curled his fingers over it, and held it fast.

"That will not protect you," snarled the Guardian. He strode forward with Envy, Greed, Hate, and Pride growling and drooling around his feet. He reached out, and his hands fastened on the Belt like claws.

His eyes glowed with triumph, then suddenly widened, burning, burning like pits of fire. Staring into them, fixed in terror, Lief seemed to see a thousand pictures leaping in the flames.

But the Belt was icy cold.

The Guardian's mouth gaped in a shriek of agony. And the monsters — the monsters were capering around him, throwing up their heads and howl-

ing, straining at their leads, trying to get away from
him.

Lief staggered. He was released. The spell was
broken. The Guardian fell to his knees, throwing back
his head, still clinging to the Belt as though he could
not let go. Envy, Greed, Hate, and Pride turned on
him in a frenzy, their jaws frothing, their terrible teeth
ripping and tearing at him, shredding his robe to ribbons, slicing into the shrivelled grey flesh beneath.

And then, with a thrill of horror, Lief saw what
the robe had hidden. Saw the four great, oozing
lumps on the Guardian's chest. Saw the pulsing,
fleshy cords that arose from them, twisting and
snaking through his sleeves and on to the swollen
necks of the savage, attacking beasts. The Guardian
had called Hate, Greed, Envy, and Pride his pets, but
they were part of him. Vile growths from his own
body.

"Release me!" screamed the Guardian. "They are
eating me alive! Cut the cords! Oh, I beg you!"

Lief's sword was in his hand. Shuddering, his
ears ringing with the shrieks of the man and the roars
of the beasts, with his companions' shouts of horror,
he swung at the lashing ropes of flesh, slicing them
through.

Yellow-green liquid gushed from the wounds.
The cords writhed, their cut ends flopping horribly to
the ground. The monsters swayed, then fell. For an instant they lay twitching. Then they were still.

The Guardian's fingers loosened. His withering face turned up to Lief's. In the red eyes, the fires were dying.

"The diamond," he croaked. "Take it! It is with her. Where she lies. The stream . . ."

He crumpled and fell backward. Lief, Jasmine, and Barda turned and ran.

16 ~ Answers

Neridah lay face up in the stream, the slow water drifting over her unseeing eyes, her hair billowing over the rock on which she had hit her head. In the open palm of her cold, cold hand lay a great diamond.

"It seems that the Guardian did not kill her," Jasmine murmured, wondering. "It was just ill fortune that she tripped while she was crossing the stream. Ill fortune that she hit her head and drowned."

Realizing what she had said, she glanced at Lief and bit her lip. "I am sorry," she muttered. "If I had had my way, no doubt we would be lying here, or somewhere like it, ourselves. The curse — is strong."

"Strong enough for the Guardian to know that he did not have to fear theft," Barda said grimly. "The diamond could be relied upon to act before the thief escaped the valley."

"Take care!" cried Jasmine, as Lief reached into the water.

But Lief shook his head. "We have nothing to fear," he said. The Belt grew hot at his waist as he lifted the great gem, dripping, from the water.

Mist swirled about him, filled with shadows, filled with whispers, as he took off the Belt and laid it on the ground. The six gems glowed on their steel medallions. The last medallion waited to be filled.

Lief pressed the great diamond down. With a tiny click, it slid into place. Into the place where it belonged. The Belt was complete.

There was a moment's breathless silence. Then the whispering began again. Louder now. Louder. The mist billowed, clumping into columns and spirals, rising from the ground and writhing upward through the trees, as though it was alive. And as it rose, figures were left blinking in the clear air. Men, women, and children looked in bewildered joy at their warming hands, at their slowly coloring robes, and at each other.

Then there was a great crack, a shattering, like the sound of breaking glass. In an instant, the valley was flooded with color and blinding light.

And when Lief, Barda, and Jasmine looked again there were people by the hundreds, by the thousands, rejoicing among the trees, under the blue sky. They were no longer grey, drifting, hollow-faced, but rich with color, warmth, and life.

Most were tall and slender, with long, smooth faces, their dark eyes shining beneath slanting eyebrows. Black, silky hair hung down their backs, the deep sleeves of their robes swept the ground. Staring at them in wonder, hardly able to accept the evidence of his own eyes, Lief remembered the Guardian's words.

The first of my subjects, the largest number, came to me in a great wind, the pride that had caused their fall still fresh within them . . .

And then he knew. These were the lost people of Tora.

✳

The companions walked through the crowd, and everywhere hands were held out to them. But now the hands were open, filled with life and thanks.

The people of Tora had wandered in the Valley of the Lost for as long as Lief had been alive, yet they had not grown old, or changed. Old, middle-aged, and young, they remained just as they had been that day when they broke their vow. Lief, Barda, and Jasmine moved among them, hearing over and over the story of their fall.

The magic of the tunnel had protected Tora from evil for so long that the Torans had come to think they had grown perfect, as their city was perfect, and that any decision they made would be the right one. When the message from Endon came, they considered it as they considered everything: without passion, without hate, without anger. But also without warmth, without love, without pity.

"The decision did not seem a betrayal of trust," murmured a young man who held the hand of a small child. "It seemed sensible, and just. For to us, the king was a stranger. Even the Torans who went to Del with Adin, and those who went afterwards, had long ago become part of the Del palace life. They had ceased to be a bridge between our cities."

"But in our pride we forgot the magic on which our power was based," sighed an old woman, tall and straight in her scarlet robe. "The ancient vow, with the curse it embraced, was still as strong as it ever was. We did not count on that, for we looked forward, but never backward in those days. We have learned better since."

The companions walked back through the trees to the palace clearing, the crowd following silently. As they approached the clearing Lief was haunted by the feeling that he was dreaming. At any moment he might wake. At any moment he might see the palace, gleaming like a jewel, and the Guardian, red eyes staring, beckoning through swirling mist.

But the palace had gone, as if it had never been. In its place was a small wooden hut. Flowers and wild grass grew around it, and standing at its door was a bearded man wearing a coarse gown, tied at the waist with a knotted cord. His sad eyes met Lief's. They were very familiar.

Perched on his arm was a black bird. Sitting on his hand was a small, grey bundle of fur.

Before Lief could say a word, Jasmine was running forward with a cry of joy. Then Kree was flying towards her, and Filli was leaping, chattering, to meet her. They had come down from the cliff edge the moment the mist had lifted. They had waited with their new friend patiently. But now that they saw Jasmine, they would not wait a moment longer.

✳

Together once again, the companions moved to the stranger's side.

"You are the hermit — the hermit in the pictures on the rug," Lief said.

The man nodded.

"And you are the Guardian."

The man put his hand to his chest, close to his heart, as if feeling a tender place. "No longer. Thanks to you," he said quietly.

"But — you are not Endon, are you?" Lief already knew the answer, but he wanted to hear it aloud.

The man smiled. "No, I am not. My name is Fardeep. Once I was a rich man, it is true. A respected man, and very well content. But I was no king. Just the keeper of an inn in a place called Rithmere, far

399

from here. Bandits invaded the town. My family was killed, and my inn was taken from me. The Shadow Lord, it seems, had a use for it."

The companions exchanged glances. "Could you be speaking of the Champion Inn?" Barda asked.

"You know it?" said Fardeep. "Yes. The Champion Inn was once mine. I have always liked games."

His mouth twisted ruefully as the companions shuddered. "Now the games played at Rithmere are of a different sort, I hear," he said. "And the inn is much larger, and run upon very different lines from those in my time, and for a different reason."

He sighed deeply. "But in those days the Shadow Lord's plans were not known to me. It all happened long before he took possession of Deltora. Before Endon ever became king. I knew nothing, and cared nothing, for what was ahead. I escaped Rithmere and fled to this valley seeking refuge, and peace."

He bowed his head. "But peace was denied to me. My misery and anger was felt, and used, by the one who knows how to use them best. At first I did not know he was the one who had caused my trouble. Later, as gifts were showered upon me, it did not seem to matter. I told you how it was. Pride, envy, hatred, and greed grew in me. And as time went on I became — what you saw."

Again his hand crept to his heart.

"But why did your game — the Guardian's

game — make us think your name was Endon?" Jasmine asked. "Why did that name open the door?"

"The Shadow Lord wished it," said Fardeep simply. "From the first, he wanted anyone who came here for the diamond to be deceived. To think that King Endon had turned to the dark side, and become his servant. As the Guardian, I found the idea — amusing. And as I told you, I have always liked games. That part of me had not changed."

He looked up, grim-faced. "Until you came, only the scar-faced man — Doom — had ever solved the puzzle. And the effect on him was everything my master could have hoped."

He glanced across to where the Torans had gathered, murmuring to one another. He straightened his shoulders and went to speak with them.

"We have learned one important thing from this," said Jasmine, as soon as they were alone. "It means that the Shadow Lord does not know that it is Endon's heir, not Endon himself, who is important."

"Or if he does, he does not know that we are aware of it, too," Lief answered thoughtfully.

Fardeep and the people were coming towards them. "We hope that you will stay with us, for rest while you can," Fardeep said rather stiffly, stepping forward. "We can offer you little luxury. But there is wild food enough for all now, in the valley. And friendship in abundance."

"That is luxury enough," smiled Barda. "And we will be glad to stay — for a time. We must bury our companion, Neridah. And we have much to talk about."

Fardeep's whole body relaxed in a shuddering sigh of relief. "I would not have blamed you if you had loathed the very thought," he said. He glanced over his shoulder at the crowd. "They, too, have forgiven me," he said in a low voice. "It is more than I expected. And far more than I deserve."

"We forgive you heartily," called a stout, blue-clad woman at the front of the crowd. "Your fault was only blindness, as was ours. And we will stay here, for as long as you allow it, and be grateful. For we have nowhere else to go."

"Tora is perfect, as it always was," called Barda. "It is waiting for you!"

But the people shook their heads regretfully. "We can never go back," the blue-clad woman murmured. "The stone that is the city's heart is cracked, and its fire is no more. The vow was broken, and that evil can never be undone."

It can, Lief thought. It *can* be undone.

He thought he knew how. But it was not time yet. The heir to Deltora still had to be found.

But where? Where in all the wide kingdom was the hiding place that had kept Endon, Sharn, and their child safe for so long? How could he and his companions find it, with no idea of where to look, or where to start?

For a moment he felt a sinking in his heart. Then, again he touched the Belt, heavy around his waist.

We will find the hiding place, he told himself. Wherever it is, no matter how far. For we are not without guidance any longer. The Belt is complete. And it will show us the way.

Return to Del

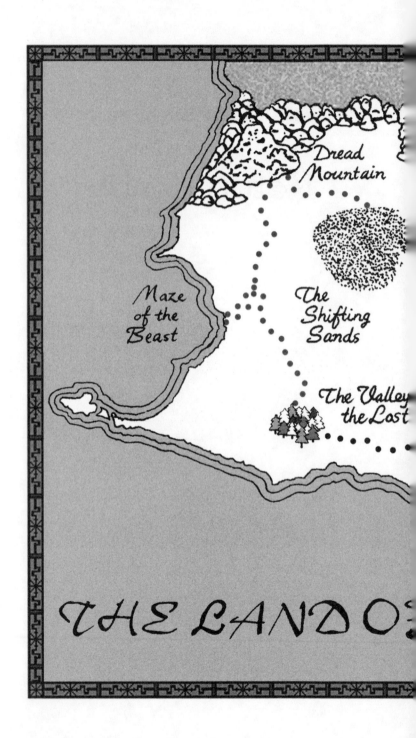

Dread
Mountain

Maze
of the
Beast

The
Shifting
Sands

The Valley
the Lost

THE LAND O

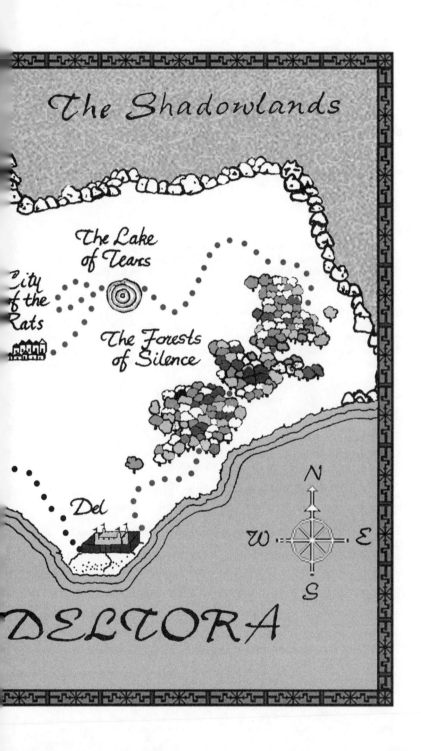

DEDICATION

This, the eighth and final book in the Deltora Quest series, is dedicated to Kate Rowe and Bob Ryan, my companions from the beginning of this long journey. Without their help, advice, enthusiasm, and technical skill, without Kate's graphics and Bob's unfailing support, none of what has been achieved would have been possible. ER

ISBN 0-439-25330-6

12 11 10 9 8 7 6 5 4 3 2 1   1 2 3 4 5 6/0

40

Printed in the U.S.A.
First American edition, November 2001

Contents

The story so far . . .

Lief, Barda, and Jasmine have found the seven lost gems of the magic Belt of Deltora. Now they must find the heir to Deltora's throne, for only when the Belt is worn by the true heir can the evil Shadow Lord be overthrown, and Deltora freed.

    Lief's parents, now imprisoned in Del, told Lief that when they helped King Endon and Queen Sharn to escape the city on the coming of the Shadow Lord, over sixteen years ago, a hiding place was planned for the royal couple and their unborn child. But the companions have learned that this plan failed when the magical people of Tora broke their ancient vow of loyalty, and refused to offer refuge. The Torans were banished to the Valley of the Lost, and the royal family's whereabouts are unkown.

    Doom, the grim, mysterious leader of the Resistance, left the companions in anger when they refused to heed his warning to keep away from the Valley of the Lost. Dain, a young Resistance fighter of about Lief's own age, reluctantly went with him. Now the valley has been freed of its evil enchantment, but Lief, Barda, and Jasmine do not know which way to turn. They must find the heir, but they do not know how. And the Shadow Lord's servants — Grey Guards, hideous shape-changing Ols, and huge vulture-like birds called Ak-Baba — are searching for them.

    Now read on . . .

1 - Toran Magic

The Belt of Deltora was complete. Seven gems glowed once more in its gleaming medallions of steel. It was perfect. And yet . . .

Lief glanced at Barda and Jasmine, walking with him through the sunlit beauty of what had been the Valley of the Lost. In the blue sky above them, Kree sailed on the wind with others of his kind. Many birds had returned to the valley since the evil mist had lifted, the exiled people of Tora had been freed from their living death, and the evil Guardian had returned to his old character of the hermit Fardeep.

The three companions had triumphed. But now they had to face the fact that unless they found the heir to Deltora's throne all their efforts would have been in vain. They had believed that the Belt would lead them to the heir. But so far there had been no sign.

Sighing, Lief flipped open the little blue book he carried. This copy of *The Belt of Deltora* was one of the few things that had survived the destruction of the Guardian's palace. And why? Lief thought. Why, unless it holds the key? He stared again at the words he had read so often.

✝ **Each gem has its own magic, but together the seven make a spell that is far more powerful than the sum of its parts. Only the Belt of Deltora, complete as it was first fashioned by Adin and worn by Adin's true heir, has the power to defeat the Enemy.**

"Reading the words again will not change them, Lief," muttered Jasmine. "We must find the heir — and soon!" She plucked a berry and gave it to Filli. Many little furred creatures now thronged the valley. But all were larger than little Filli, who stayed shyly on Jasmine's shoulder, peering around with wondering eyes.

"If only we knew where to look!" Barda moved restlessly. "We cannot remain here any longer, waiting for a sign. At any moment — " He looked up, and his brow creased in a sudden frown. Lief, too, looked up, and was startled to see that where only moments before there had been clear blue, a swirling mist was gathering. The birds were wheeling, screeching . . .

Sharply, Jasmine called Kree, who broke away from the flock and came hurtling down towards her. At the same moment, Lief saw Fardeep approaching. Two Torans were with him: Peel, a tall, bearded man, and Zeean, a straight-backed old woman in a scarlet robe.

"Do not fear!" Fardeep called. "The Torans are weaving a veil of cloud to shroud the valley once more. The Shadow Lord must not discover that we are free."

"But what of the creatures?" Jasmine exclaimed.

"Our mist will not harm them, little one," smiled Zeean. "It is soft and sweet. Now that our magic has returned, we can do many things."

"Except the thing we want most," Peel said soberly. "Except return to Tora."

"Indeed." Zeean's eyes turned to Lief, Barda, and Jasmine. "And yet," she murmured. "I have hopes . . ."

Lief glanced quickly at Fardeep.

"Fardeep has said nothing, Lief," Zeean said. "But we remember what we saw just before the valley changed. You are carrying a precious thing — a thing that could save us all. Yet you are troubled. We can feel it. Can we not help?"

Lief hesitated. The habit of secrecy was strong. But perhaps, indeed, the Torans could help. Barda and Jasmine stirred beside him and he knew that they, too, felt the impulse to trust.

"Be aware," Zeean said softly, "that to tell one Toran is to tell all. We have no secrets from one another. But this is our strength. Between us we have much knowledge, and our memories are long."

Lief touched the Belt, heavy under his shirt. But before he could say a word, Zeean and Peel stiffened. "Strangers are entering the valley!" Peel hissed. "Walking quickly, along the stream."

"Friends?" Fardeep asked urgently.

Zeean shook her head, puzzled. "We cannot tell. Shape-changers — Ols — we can usually sense. Others of evil will also. But these minds are closed to us."

The light dimmed as the mist thickened. Lief made a decision. "We will go to meet them," he said. "And, on our way, we will talk."

And so it was that, walking in the greenness of the valley floor, the companions told the secret they had kept for so long. It was strange to speak the words aloud. But Lief felt no fear as the Torans drank in the sight of the Belt.

"The amethyst," Zeean whispered, gently touching the purple gem. "The Toran stone, symbol of truth."

"The Toran stone?" exclaimed Jasmine. "What do you mean?"

"Why, the Torans were one of the seven tribes who gave their talismans to Adin when the Belt of Deltora was first made," Zeean said.

"No doubt that is why the amethyst was in the

Maze of the Beast, so near to Tora," Peel added. "Once taken from the Belt, the gem yearned to return to its first place. As far as it could, it bent to its will the Ak-Baba which carried it. Perhaps — "

Two people rounded a bend in the stream ahead. One gave a cry, and broke into a run. Startled, Lief saw it was Dain, and that the man with him was Doom.

"Dain!" Doom bellowed. Dain glanced behind him guiltily, and his flying feet stumbled and slowed.

"Why, this boy looks very like one of us," Zeean murmured. "His hair — his eyes . . ."

"Dain's mother is of Toran blood," Lief told her. "His parents were taken by the Grey Guards a year ago. Now he works with Doom, in the Resistance."

Both of the visitors were now standing quite still. Doom glanced at the cloud above his head.

"All is well, Doom," Fardeep called. "Your friends here are safe. The mist is only for our protection."

Warily, Doom moved closer. He searched Fardeep's face, and his own face darkened. "You!" he snarled, reaching for his sword.

"No!" Lief exclaimed. "Doom, this is Fardeep. He is no longer the Guardian. No enemy of ours, or of yours."

For the first time since Lief had known him, Doom looked baffled. "You have much to explain!" he muttered.

"As you do," said Barda harshly. "Why did you keep your knowledge of this place from us?"

"I warned you against the Valley of the Lost with all my strength!" Doom growled, recovering a little. "Would it have helped if I had told you I had visited it myself? No! You would have decided that if I could escape its dangers, so could you."

"Perhaps," snapped Jasmine. "But you take your wretched love of secrecy too far, Doom! Why did you not say that you believed the Guardian was King Endon?"

Ignoring Dain's gasp of horror, Doom smiled grimly. "Even *I* have some fine feelings. When I left this accursed valley I swore that never from my lips would my people learn what their king had become. They had suffered enough. Far better, I thought, to let them believe he was dead."

"You played into the Shadow Lord's hands, then," said Lief quietly. "He wants the king forgotten, so his own hold over Deltora can never be broken."

Doom flinched, as though he had received a blow. Slowly he rubbed his brow with the back of his hand, hiding his eyes. Dain was staring straight ahead, his face quite expressionless. But it seemed to Lief that behind the calm mask many different feelings were struggling.

After a long moment, Doom dropped his hand and looked straight at Lief, Barda, and Jasmine. "I believe I know why you came here," he said. "Am I to understand that you succeeded in your quest?"

The companions remained silent.

A shadow crossed Doom's face. "Perhaps you are wise not to trust me," he said bitterly. "Perhaps, in your place, I, too, would keep silence." He turned away. "Come, Dain," he said to the boy standing rigidly beside him. "We are not needed here. Or wanted, it seems."

Zeean stirred. "Wait!" she cried.

Doom swung around, unsmiling.

"We cannot afford suspicion and rivalry now," the woman said, standing very straight. "United, we drove the Shadow Lord and his abominable hordes from our lands in the time of Adin. United, we can do it now."

She turned to Lief, Barda, and Jasmine. "The time for secrecy between friends is past," she said firmly. "You are hunted, and you do not know what your next step should be. We need the talents and experience of all who share our cause. Now, at last, it is time to trust."

✳

They returned to the clearing beside Fardeep's hut. There, while bees hummed among the flowers and the sun sank in the sky, the story was told once more. When, at last, Lief showed the Belt, Dain gasped and shrank back, trembling. "I knew that you had some mighty aim," he whispered, "I knew it!"

But Lief was watching Doom. The man's face had not changed. What was he thinking?

"Some of what you have told us I had already guessed," Doom muttered at last. "No one who has travelled this land as I have done could have failed to hear the legend of the lost Belt of Deltora. I came to believe that you were seeking it — but whether for reasons of good or ill, I did not know."

His mouth tightened. "Now I regret my suspicion that you were working against our cause. But — " He ran his lean brown hands through his tangled hair. "Can it be true that this — this legend made real — can help Deltora? Perhaps, long ago, in the years that are dark to me, I would have accepted such a tale. But as it is — "

"You must believe!" Jasmine burst out. "The Shadow Lord himself fears the Belt. That is why the gems were taken and hidden in the first place!"

Doom regarded her thoughtfully. "How many gems does the Shadow Lord know you have?" he asked.

"We have strong hopes that he thinks we are still to reach Dread Mountain, the Maze of the Beast, and this valley," Lief answered.

"Hopes are no basis for planning," said Doom curtly.

Lief felt a prickle of irritation. He was not alone.

"We are as aware of that as you, Doom!" exclaimed Jasmine angrily. "No one would welcome certain knowledge more than we would!"

Looking from one to the other, Zeean sighed, and rose. "Let us rest, now," she said. "In the morning, our minds will be clearer."

As she and Peel quietly left the clearing, Doom shrugged and strode off to where his belongings lay. Dain hurried after him. Fardeep wandered back to his hut to begin preparing food.

"Doom is an uncomfortable ally," Barda muttered. "But he is right in wanting facts, rather than hope."

"Then we will give him facts!" Jasmine snapped. "Lief must use the last of the water from the Dreaming Spring."

Lief nodded slowly. They had been saving the water for when they really needed it, but surely that time had arrived. If he visited his imprisoned father again, the evil Fallow might come to the cell. Then Lief could learn how much the Shadow Lord knew. But what if Fallow did not come?

Lief's heart sank as he saw what must be done. He could not risk visiting his father or mother. Instead, he must use the magic water to spy on Fallow himself.

2 ~ Fallow

Much later, Lief lay still in the darkness. His eyelids were very heavy, but his mind was fighting sleep. He was afraid — afraid of what he would see. Who was Fallow? *What* was he? Lief thought he knew. Words he had heard Fallow say to his father echoed in his mind:

. . . *where one dies, there is always another to take his place. The Master likes this face and form. He chose to repeat it in me* . . .

Lief had not known what that meant, when first he heard it. Now he knew only too well.

Fallow was an Ol, and perhaps — almost certainly — one of the Grade 3 Ols Doom had heard of in the Shadowlands. The triumph of the Shadow Lord's evil art. An Ol so perfect, so controlled, that no one could tell it was not human. An Ol that could mimic nonliving things as well as living creatures. An Ol that was evil and powerful beyond anything Lief could imagine.

Prandine, King Endon's chief advisor, had been one such being. Of that Lief was sure. Fallow, made in his image, had taken up the Shadow Lord's work where Prandine had finished.

Lief turned restlessly. Queen Sharn had killed Prandine — tipped him from the palace tower window to crash to his death. Grade 3 Ols paid a price for their perfection, then. They could die as humans could.

He closed his eyes and forced his mind to go blank. It was time to give in to the Dreaming Water. Time to visit the world of Fallow.

White walls, hard and gleaming. A gurgling, bubbling sound. And in the corner a tall, thin figure — Fallow — shuddering in a shower of sickly green light, bony arms flung high. His mouth was gaping open like the jaws of a skull, its corners thick with foam. His eyes had rolled back so only the whites showed, shining, horrible . . .

Lief choked back his cry of horror, though he knew he could not be heard. His stomach churned, but he could not look away.

Thump! Thump!

Lief jumped violently as the sound, like a great heartbeat, throbbed through the room.

The green light disappeared. Fallow's long arms dropped to his sides. His head fell forward.

Thump! Thump!

Lief clamped his hands over his ears. But still the sound vibrated through him, filling his mind, making his teeth chatter. It was unbearable. But it seemed to compel him. It seemed to be calling him. Wildly he searched the room, looking for its source.

Then he saw it. A small table in the center of the room. A table that looked like any other, except that its glass surface was thick and curved — and moving like water. Lief felt himself drawn forward. The urge to look into that moving surface, to answer the summons, was irresistible.

But, panting, Fallow was stumbling out of the corner, snatching a cloth from his sleeve. Wiping his face hurriedly he staggered towards the table and leaned over it, staring down at the rippling surface.

The throbbing sound lessened, dimmed. The ripples grew smoky, rimmed with red. And deep in the midst of the grey and red there was a hollow darkness.

Fallow leaned closer. A voice hissed from the darkness. Deathly quiet.

"Fallow."

"Yes, Master." Fallow quivered, his mouth still flecked with drying foam.

"Do you abuse my trust?"

"No, Master."

"You have been given the Lumin for your pleasure in your place of exile. But if you neglect your duties because of it, it will be removed."

Fallow's eyes darted to the corner where the green light had showered, then swerved back to the table surface. "I do not neglect my duties, Master," he whimpered.

"Then what news do you have for me? Has the blacksmith Jarred confessed at last?"

His heart wrung, Lief pressed his hands together in an agony of fear.

"No, Master," said Fallow. "I think — "

"Is someone with you, slave?" the voice hissed suddenly.

Startled, Fallow whirled around and scanned the room. His dull eyes passed over Lief, standing motionless behind him, without a flicker.

"No, Master," he whispered. "How could there be? As you ordered, no one enters this room but me."

"I felt . . . something." The darkness in the center of the whirling shadows grew larger, like the pupil of a giant eye widening.

Lief stood still as a stone, trying to keep his mind blank, holding his breath. The Shadow Lord could sense him. That evil mind was probing the room, trying to find him. He could feel its malice.

"There — there is no one here." How strange to see Fallow cowering, those cruel lips trembling.

"Very well. Continue."

"I — have begun to think the blacksmith indeed knows nothing," Fallow stammered. "Starvation and torment have not moved him. Even the threat of death or blindness for his wife did not cause him to speak."

"And she?"

"If anything, she is stronger than her husband. She rails at her tormentors, but says nothing of use."

Mother. Lief felt hot tears trickling down his cheeks. He did not dare move to wipe them away. He held himself rigidly, trying to cut off his mind from his heart.

"They have made a fool of you then, Fallow," whispered the voice from the darkness. "For they are guilty — guilty of everything we suspected. Their son is one of the three. There is no doubt."

Fallow gaped. "Their son is with the king? But the blacksmith laughed when I suggested it. Laughed! I could have sworn the laughter was real."

"It was. The man who is travelling with the boy is not Endon, but a palace guard named Barda. No doubt Jarred found your mistake amusing."

Fallow's face twisted with rage. "He will pay!" he croaked. "And the woman, too. They will wish they had never been born! I will — "

"You will do *nothing*!" The hiss was icy. Fallow grew rigidly still.

"Perhaps you have been living too long among human peasants, Fallow, and have started to think as they do. Or perhaps too much use of the Lumin has weakened the brain you were given by my hand."

"No, Master. No!"

"Then listen to me. You are my creation, whose only purpose is to do my will. Do exactly as I tell you. Keep the blacksmith and the woman safe. I have need of them. While they live, they can be used against the boy. Once they are dead, we have no hold over him."

"Beings in their shapes — "

"He wears the great topaz. The spirits of his wretched dead will appear to him, the moment they leave the world. Ols in their shapes will not deceive him."

There was silence. Then Fallow spoke again.

"May I ask where the three are now, Master?"

"We have lost sight of them. For now."

"But, I thought your — "

"Do not think of what does not concern you, Fallow! Curiosity is for humans, not for such as you. Is that understood?"

"Yes, Master. But I was not asking for myself — only out of concern for your plans. The three may, by some miracle, restore the Belt. And this will — displease you."

The words were humble. But Lief thought he saw a tiny spark of rebellion in the downcast eyes.

Perhaps the Shadow Lord saw it, too, for the swirling red that edged the grey seemed to flare, and a crafty note entered the hissing voice.

"I have many plans, Fallow. If one does not succeed, another will. If you follow my orders exactly, sooner or later you will be free to have what sport you wish with the boy's mother and father. And with Endon himself, if he at last lifts his cowering head and crawls out of hiding."

A chill ran down Lief's spine.

"And the three?" Fallow asked greedily.

There was a long, low laugh. The red swirls deepened to scarlet.

"Oh, no. The three, Fallow, will be mine."

✳

Lief awoke, his heart thumping, his stomach knotted. There was a sour taste in his mouth — the taste of fear and misery.

He was not sure how long he had been asleep. Moonlight still filtered palely through the Torans' cloud, flooding the clearing with its dim, mysterious glow. Lief forced himself to lie still until the pounding of his heart had quietened. Then, quietly, so as not to wake the other sleepers, he roused Barda and Jasmine.

With the ease born of long practice, they were instantly awake and alert, reaching for their weapons.

"No! There is no danger," Lief whispered. "I am sorry to disturb your rest. But I had to speak with you."

"You learned something!" hissed Jasmine, sitting up.

Lief nodded. He glanced over to where Doom and Dain lay, and, lowering his voice still further, told of what he had seen and heard. He made himself tell it all, biting his lip to stop his voice from shaking.

His companions listened in silence till the end.

"So he hopes that we will fall into his hands," Barda muttered. "We shall see about that!"

Lief glanced at him. The big man's fists were clenched and his face was filled with grief and anger.

Jasmine put her hand on Lief's arm. "At least we know that for now your parents are safe, Lief," she said softly. "And Doom can stop his sneering. We were right. The Shadow Lord is not certain where we are."

Barda nodded. "And, plainly, he does not know where Endon, Sharn, and their child are, either. He thinks that we will lead him to the heir's hiding place."

Lief's stomach was churning. "And perhaps we will," he breathed. "For do you not see what else we have learned?"

They both stared at him blankly. He swallowed and went on. "The Shadow Lord has found out who you really are, Barda. And he knows my name as well. How could that be? Unless . . ."

"Unless someone in the Resistance stronghold is a spy!" whispered Jasmine, suddenly realizing the truth. "For it was at the stronghold that Barda's name was revealed to all, by that acrobat, Jinks. And no doubt Dain told Lief's name, and mine, while we were imprisoned. He would not have seen the harm."

Lief gnawed at his lip. "And someone — someone in the stronghold has made contact with the Shadow Lord. Dain told us that Doom suspected there was a spy in the Resistance. This proves it."

"Glock!" hissed Jasmine with loathing.

"Or Jinks himself," Barda muttered. "It could be anyone."

"Yes," said Lief, glancing again at the sleeping figures of Dain and Doom. "It could be anyone at all."

3 - Suspicion

Noiselessly, the companions gathered their belongings and stole out of the clearing. In moments they were moving along the stream, towards the valley's end. They knew that it would be folly to try to escape by climbing. The cliff walls were too steep, too slippery with loose stones.

It was cold and dim under the trees. Everywhere Torans lay sleeping under the shelters they had made.

What will they think when they wake and find us gone? Lief thought. But he and his companions had no choice but to flee. Following Zeean's well-meaning advice, they had revealed their precious secret to two people whose friendship was now far from certain.

Lief bitterly regretted that he had not been more wary.

We cannot tell, Zeean had whispered, when Fardeep asked her if the visitors to the valley were friends or foes.

Why could the Torans not tell if Dain and Doom were of good or evil will? Surely only because one or both of them were skilled at veiling their minds. This could be habit — completely innocent. Or —

I have many plans . . .

The evil whisper swirled in Lief's mind like a foul mist.

He looked ahead, and realized that they were nearly at the end of the valley. The space between the rocky cliffs was closing. They were reaching the narrow pass through which Doom and Dain had come.

"There is something across the valley entrance," Jasmine breathed. "Something is blocking our way."

And indeed now Lief could see for himself a large shape lying across the stream. As he crept closer he saw that it was a caravan. On the driver's seat, rolled in a blanket, lay a man, gently snoring.

"Steven," breathed Barda. "He must have come with Dain and Doom. No doubt he is to follow them into the valley if they do not return within a certain time."

The caravan hulked before them. Its back doors were pressed close against one rocky cliff wall. They would have to pass it at the other end, right under Steven's nose. But he was still snoring gently under his blanket. Surely he would not wake!

They began moving forward. *One step, two . . .*

They were almost opposite the caravan now.

Three steps, four . . .

The snoring stopped. Lief looked over at the rolled bundle on the driver's seat. It was silent, and absolutely still. Too still.

Lief's heart seemed to freeze. Then, abruptly, there was a terrible growling sound, and the blanket began to heave, as though the body inside was swelling, doubling in size.

"Here!" A voice from the trees split the air. Lief whirled and saw Doom pounding towards them.

On the caravan seat, something snarled like a huge animal. Hot, heavy breathing grew louder, louder . . .

"Nevets, go back!" Doom shouted. "This is Doom! There is no danger!" Roughly he pushed Lief, Barda, and Jasmine back into the trees and stood in front of them.

"There is no danger!" he shouted again.

Slowly, the growling faded. And when Lief managed to focus his eyes on the caravan once more, the form under the blanket had shrunk back to a normal size. As he watched, it turned over as if settling once more to sleep.

Doom began hustling the companions back the way they had come. "What game do you think you are playing?" he hissed furiously. "Do you want to die? If I had not woken and found you gone — "

"How could we know you had set your pet mon-

ster to guard the valley?" Jasmine flashed back furiously.

"And are we not free to do as we please?" Lief
was boiling with anger and shock.

Doom's eyes narrowed. Then he turned on his
heel and began walking back down the stream.

"I suggest you stay in the valley for now," he
called back over his shoulder. "Even I would not risk
troubling Steven again for an hour or two. And Zeean
and Peel are very anxious to see you. It seems they
have something to tell you."

✳

By the time the companions reached the clearing once
more, dawn was breaking. Zeean, Peel, Fardeep, and
Dain were gathered around a small fire, sharing a
breakfast of hot, flat cakes dripping with honey from
Fardeep's hives. They looked up as the companions
approached with Doom, but asked no questions.

Perhaps they know that they will get no answers, thought Lief, taking his place at the fire with
Barda and Jasmine. He felt a mixture of emotions: re-
sentment at having had to return; curiosity as to what
the Torans had to say; frustration at the thought that
whatever it was would be heard by Doom and Dain
also. Yet Doom had saved them from Nevets. Did that
not mean . . . ?

"It is good you have returned," Zeean said,
pushing the plate of cakes towards the newcomers.
"We have an idea to discuss with you."

She paused, her brow creasing as she saw Barda, Lief, and Jasmine glance at Doom and Dain.

Lief gripped the Belt around his waist. The calm of the amethyst, the strength of the diamond, flowed through him. And suddenly he knew what must be done. He and his companions must act as though they had no doubts about their allies. At all costs, the knowledge they had gained through his dream must be kept secret. This would be their strength.

He smiled at Zeean, and casually reached for a cake. The woman seemed to relax, and began speaking once more.

"Your father told you that the Belt would lead you to the heir, Lief. But your father knows only what he has read. And that is perhaps not all there is to know."

"What do you mean?" Lief asked, frowning. He took a bite of the cake. It was warm and sweet on his tongue.

"The book — *The Belt of Deltora* — is a work of history, not of advice," said Peel eagerly. "The writer could not foresee that one day the gems would be torn from the Belt, and would not know what should be done in such an event."

"The Belt is a thing of great mystery and magic," Zeean added. "The gems have been restored. But perhaps this is not enough."

There was a muffled sound from the edge of

the group. Dain was leaning forward, as though he wanted to speak.

"Dain?" said Zeean.

Dain blushed as he always did when attention was drawn to him. "I was thinking of — of the story of how the Belt was made," he stammered. "And of what happened after."

He fell silent, glancing nervously at the silent Doom.

"Yes?" urged Zeean encouragingly. Her eyes were sharp with interest. Lief's skin began to tingle. Somehow he knew that they were on the edge of something momentous.

He pulled out the copy of *The Belt of Deltora* and flipped through it. In moments he had found what he was looking for — the words that told of how the blacksmith Adin had persuaded each of the seven tribes to allow its gem to join the Belt.

✝ The tribes were at first suspicious and wary, but, one by one, desperate to save their land, they agreed. As each gem became part of the belt, its tribe grew stronger. But the people kept their strength secret, and bided their time.

✝ And when at last the Belt was complete, Adin fastened it around his waist and it flashed like the sun. Then all the tribes united behind him to form a great army, and together they drove the enemy from their land.

Slowly, he read the words from the book aloud.

"The victory depended not only on the Belt, but on the union of the seven tribes, and their loyalty to Adin," said Peel slowly, when the reading was finished. "Is that what you are thinking, Dain?"

Dain nodded. Doom regarded him curiously.

"Why, you are quite a scholar, Dain," he said mockingly. "How did a farmer's boy learn so much of the history of Deltora?"

Dain flinched, but would not be cowed. "My parents taught me," he said quietly. "They never lost hope that one day Deltora would be free. They said its story should not be forgotten."

Doom shrugged and turned away, but Lief thought he saw a flicker in the dark eyes. Was it anger? Regret? Or something else?

"Your parents were wise indeed, Dain," Zeean was saying. "Your mother had Toran blood, did she not? What was her name?"

Dain seemed to tremble. "Her name is Rhans," he said, so softly that Lief could hardly hear him. "*Is*, not *was*. Why do you speak as though she is dead?"

Zeean looked distressed. "I am sorry," she said. "I did not mean — "

"So the seven tribes united under Adin and the Belt," Barda growled. "Why is this important to us?"

"Who knows?" muttered Doom. He got to his feet and moved a little away from the group, turning his back. Dain looked desperately at Lief.

"You must have been helped on your journey, Lief," he said in a low voice. "Throughout Deltora you met people willing to defy the Shadow Lord. Surely they will help you again. Help you to . . ." He glanced at Doom, and again his voice seemed to fail him.

Lief took a deep breath. "I think Dain's idea is that the uniting of Deltora formed part of the Belt's magic," he said. "Dain thinks that we should bring the seven tribes together once more."

4 ~ The Seven Tribes

Jasmine was the first to break the silence. "But the seven tribes existed in ancient days — or so I was told," she said. "Surely they are long gone, now."

"No, they are not," said Zeean. "Certainly, many in Deltora would not know from which tribe they sprang. The Del tribe, whose gem was the topaz, has spread far and wide. Other tribes have done likewise."

"But some tribes have remained the same," Peel put in. "The Torans, for example. And the Dread Gnomes."

"The Dread Gnomes were one of the seven?" Lief's heart began to pound.

"Indeed," nodded Zeean. "The great emerald was the gnomes' talisman."

Lief shook his head in amazement. Fa-Glin and

439

Gla-Thon had said nothing of this. Did they not know it?

Or had they just decided to keep silent, until the time was right?

He felt in his pocket for the gnomes' farewell gift, pulled out the little Boolong wood box and opened it. "If we send this token, the gnomes will come," he said quietly, as all stared in awe at the golden arrowhead.

"You have powerful friends indeed," breathed Peel.

"Now we have three tribes," said Fardeep, with satisfaction. "What of the others?"

"The Ralads are an ancient race!" Barda exclaimed. "Are they, perhaps — ?"

"Yes," agreed Zeean. "Do you know them?"

"One of them, Manus, helped us to find the ruby at the Lake of Tears," said Barda. "The ruby must have been the Ralad stone!"

Lief searched his jacket again, this time for paper and pencil.

"What of the people of D'Or?" Jasmine asked.

"Their ancestors came to Deltora from across the sea," Doom called over his shoulder. "It was long ago, but after the time of Adin and the seven tribes."

So he is listening after all, thought Lief, scribbling at the list he had begun to make. He pretends to think this is foolishness, but still he cannot move away.

"The Plains people were another tribe," said Zeean. "Their gem was the opal. Then there was the Mere tribe of the upper Broad and beyond — "

"Whose talisman was the lapis lazuli!" Lief broke in, still writing.

Zeean nodded. "The last of the seven, the Jalis, lived in these parts. They were the wildest of all the tribes, and great warriors. Their gem was the diamond."

Lief held up his list.

Tribe	Gem	Where found
1. Del	Topaz (faith)	Forests of Silence
2. Ralad	ruby (happiness)	Lake of tears
3. Plains	Opal (hope)	City of the Rats
4. Mere	lapis lazuli (heavenly stone)	Shifting Sands
5. Dread Gnomes	emerald (honour)	Dread Mountain
6. Tora	amethyst (truth)	Maze of the Beast
7. Jalis	diamond (purity & strength)	Valley of the lost

"All along I have felt that we were being guided on our quest," he said. "Now I am sure of it. We must have met members of all the tribes."

"Except the last. The Jalis," said Jasmine. "We saw no one at all on our way here."

"There was no one to see," said Doom, turning to face them. "When the Shadow Lord came, the Jalis defended their lands ferociously. But even they had no hope against the Grey Guards. They were slaughtered — their children with them. Only a few escaped."

"So you, too, know some history, Doom," said Jasmine pertly.

Doom frowned. "Enough to be sure that if you hope to raise a Jalis army, you will be sadly disappointed."

"We do not want armies," said Zeean. "Armies would be seen and destroyed at once. We need just seven souls — true descendants of the tribes that once allowed their talismans to be joined for the good of all — to put their hands on the Belt, and renew the oath of loyalty to Deltora."

"Yes!" Lief exclaimed, feeling a great surge of hope.

Dain said nothing. But his eyes were shining.

"Torans we have in plenty," Barda said. "Lief and I are of Del. We know Ralads, and Dread Gnomes. But what of the Plains people? The Mere folk? Let alone — "

"I am of the Mere tribe," said Fardeep quietly. He raised his chin as all eyes turned to him. "Rithmere has been my family's home since before the time of Adin."

"What of the Plains people?" asked Peel.

"The people of Noradz must be descended from the Plains tribe," Jasmine murmured. "We have a friend among them — Tira — "

Barda shook his head. "Tira would certainly be killed if she tried to escape Noradz," he said flatly. "Dain? Could your father have been a Plains man?"

"No," Dain said huskily. "Our farm was not far east of here. My father's people were of Del. But . . ." He glanced pleadingly at Doom. Doom sighed, came back to the group and sat down with a weary groan.

"You spoke of fate guiding you," he said to Lief. "I find it hard to believe in such things. But, as it happens, there is a Plains man close by. His family is . . . unusual, but of the Plains nonetheless. I am sure that he would be willing to help. He — and his brother."

Lief's heart sank. "Steven?" he asked faintly.

Doom's face creased into a mocking smile. "And Nevets. For you cannot have one without the other."

"All the better!" exclaimed Fardeep heartily.

Barda, Lief, and Jasmine looked at one another. They were not at all sure of that.

But already Fardeep was speaking again. "Now all that remains is to find a Jalis," he said.

Zeean turned to Doom. "I think that you can help us here, also," she said shrewdly. "I think you were told the Jalis story by one you know. One of the Jalis who escaped. Is that not so?"

Doom's smile broadened. "Indeed it is," he murmured. "And if you want him, you shall have him. He will liven up proceedings, no doubt. Almost as much as Steven will."

"Indeed?" asked Fardeep, beaming.

"Oh, yes. He is a charming fellow," said Doom. "A charming fellow, by the name of Glock."

Barda, Lief, and Jasmine exclaimed in horror.

"We cannot have Glock!" snapped Jasmine.

"Then I fear you cannot have a Jalis," said Doom. "Glock is the only one I have ever seen. The others who escaped are dead, I fear. This is Glock's belief, also."

"Then, whatever this Glock is like, we must ask him to join us," said Zeean quietly. "Where is he now?"

Doom sighed again. "At Withick Mire, a Resistance stronghold near to Del. He was causing trouble where he was. Withick Mire is less — confined."

"So, we have the seven," said Zeean. "Now even you, Doom, must admit that we are being guided."

The lines on Doom's hard face deepened. Then he seemed to come to a decision. "Once you said that when the time was right we would join the fight for Deltora together," he said to Barda. "It seems that time has come. Not, perhaps, in the way I would choose, but —"

"Perhaps we do not even want your help!" snapped Jasmine. "Have you considered that?"

"I cannot say I have," Doom murmured. "I would not think you would be so foolish."

"Indeed we would not," said Barda, frowning at Jasmine, warning her to silence.

444

Doom's mouth twisted into a wry smile. "Then let us plan," he said. "First, secret messages must be sent to Raladin and Dread Mountain."

"How?" demanded Jasmine.

"You can leave that to me," said Doom. "The Resistance also has useful friends. I suggest the meeting place be Withick Mire."

Lief felt a stirring of unease. Why did Doom want them so close to Del, and their greatest danger?

Because Withick Mire is a Resistance stronghold, the voice of suspicion whispered in his head. *Because there, Doom's word is law.*

Plainly, Barda was also filled with doubt. "Why Withick Mire?" he asked bluntly.

Doom sighed. "It seems that all this will be in vain if we cannot find the heir," he said. "So the closer we are to the possible hiding place, the better. Endon and Sharn were travelling from Del to Tora, but they could not have gone far before they received the Torans' message refusing sanctuary. It was sent at once, I imagine?"

Zeean and Peel nodded, their faces shadowed by this brutal reminder of Tora's broken vow.

But Doom had no time for sparing feelings. "The Kingdom was filled with danger," he went on. "The queen was expecting a child. It is quite likely, then, that the pair sought refuge nearby — somewhere between Del and the Valley of the Lost."

A shiver ran up Lief's spine. Their quest had

taken them in a great circle, bringing them back to the area where the heir was most likely to be. Somewhere to the west of Del. A quiet place, where Endon and Sharn could bring up their child unnoticed.

Something twitched at the corner of his mind. A memory of something he had heard, not very long ago. He could not quite catch hold of it . . .

"But surely it is better to remain here," Fardeep was arguing. "If Lief, Barda, and Jasmine move from hiding, they will draw the Shadow Lord's attention."

"We can travel hidden in Steven's caravan," said Jasmine, who was plainly burning for action. "Besides, despite Doom's doubts, we are certain the Shadow Lord's search is being concentrated in the west."

"Perhaps we can make doubly sure." Doom swung around to Peel. "You are about Barda's height and coloring. And among your people there must be two who resemble these young ones," he said, pointing at Lief and Jasmine.

Peel nodded silently, his eyebrows raised.

"We need decoys," Doom explained. "To show themselves near the River Tor. A girl, a boy, and a man, a blackbird flying with them. Steven can provide clothes that will — "

"No! It is too dangerous!" exclaimed Jasmine.

"Are you the only ones who must face danger?" Peel asked gently. "The plan is clever. And it is fitting that Torans should carry it out. If we must live in ex-

446

ile, we can at least try to repair the great wrong that caused it."

"One day you will be able to go back to Tora," Lief cried, his heart torn. "The heir's forgiveness will surely undo the curse."

Zeean raised her head. "Perhaps," she said gravely. "But first the heir must be found. And we will do our part." She looked carefully at Lief and Jasmine. "Your friend Steven will not have a cloak like that," she said to Lief. "The cloth is very rare. Worthy of the looms of Tora. How did you come by it?"

"My mother made it for me." Lief touched the rough fabric of his cloak.

Zeean's eyebrows rose in surprise, and Lief felt a flicker of pleasure mixed with pain. Pride at his mother's skill. Fear for her.

✳

The rest of the day passed in a blur. When Lief thought of it afterwards, he remembered only pictures:

Dain hurrying away to fetch Steven. Fardeep packing food. The eager faces of Kris and Lauran, the young Torans chosen as the decoys. Lauran having her silky hair curled and tangled so that it looked like Jasmine's. Kris's long black hair being cut to match Lief's own. The golden arrowhead on the palm of his own hand. Blackbirds waiting silently in the trees.

Then Steven's cart trundling through the valley. Steven nodding, studying the message Barda had written. Steven sitting alone by Fardeep's beehives, murmuring, drawing in the dust. The bees swarming up through the mist that shrouded the treetops, and speeding towards Broad River . . .

Evening. Three people moving into the clearing. A big, roughly bearded man, a boy wearing a long cloak, and a wild-looking girl, a blackbird on her arm. Like looking in a mirror. Doom nodding with satisfaction. Zeean, very proud and upright, her eyes dark with fear. Peel, Kris, and Lauran embracing their families before slipping away to begin their perilous journey . . .

Night. Air thick and hard to breathe. The slow slipping into sleep, and dreams. Dreams of desperate searching. Of legs that could not run. Of tied hands and blinded eyes. Of veiled faces and smiling masks that slipped aside to reveal writhing horrors. And, brooding over all, a crawling mass of scarlet and grey, the darkness at its center pulsing with malice.

Calling him.

5 - Messages

The caravan jolted on the rough road. Inside, it was dim and stuffy. Hour after hour Lief, Barda, and Jasmine sat, listening to the sounds of jingling reins, creaking wheels, and two voices singing.

Do I spy an Ol-io,
Ol-io, Ol-io?
Hello, wobbly Ol-io!
You don't bother me!

It had been decided that it would attract too much attention if the whole party travelled together. Dain, Doom, Fardeep, and Zeean were moving overland.

"Steven and Nevets are more than capable of defending you, if need be," Doom had said.

Lief was sure this was true. Still, his skin crept as he thought of the strange brothers singing together on the driver's seat at the front of the caravan.

Barda, like the trained soldier he was, had taken the chance to sleep. Propped against a pile of rugs, he dozed as comfortably as if he were in a soft bed. But Jasmine was wide awake. Kree hunched beside her, his feathers ruffled indignantly. Filli slept inside her jacket. She frowned as the singing voices were raised once more.

"It is all very well to be jolly," she muttered. "But must they sing such nonsense?"

Lief sighed agreement. Despite himself, he found he was following the foolish words.

Time to stop and take the air,
Ol-io, Ol-io.
Trees ahead, the sky is clear,
No more Ol-io!

Lief sat bolt upright, his eyes widening. He had suddenly realized that the song was far from nonsense. All along, Steven had been sending them messages!

"Soon we will be able to get out and stretch our legs," he told Jasmine gleefully. "There are trees ahead, and no sign of Ols or Ak-Baba."

Jasmine stared at him, her frown deepening. Plainly, she thought he was losing his wits.

✳

Far away, a round old woman, her face as red and crinkled as a wizened apple, bent over clear water. Around her head swarmed a black cloud of bees.

The woman was listening. Large silver fish hung in the water below her. Bubbles streamed from their mouths, making strange patterns on the surface.

At last, the woman straightened and turned, settling her many shawls around her shoulders. The bees swirled before her. The patterns they made in the air mimicked the trails of bubbles that marked the water.

"So," she said to them. "You have learned your lesson well. Passed on from your sister bees in the south, to the fish, to you. Go, then!"

And the bees were off, a humming black arrow, carrying the message on.

✳

Jinks emerged from the Resistance stronghold of the west and shivered in the cold wind. The sky was clear except for a flock of blackbirds, dark specks against the blue. Jinks shaded his eyes and peered at them.

Birds? Or Ols? Ols did not usually fly so high. But, on the other hand, the flock was heading for Dread Mountain. And what real bird would go there?

Suddenly Jinks saw a tiny flash in the center of the flock — as if the sun had struck something made of bright metal. But what would an Ol — or a bird, for that matter — be doing carrying such a thing?

451

My eyes are deceiving me. I must be tired, Jinks thought. Yawning, he returned to the cavern.

✳

Tom the shopkeeper was serving ale to Grey Guards in the little tavern he kept beside his shop.

"There are many of you about at present," he said lightly. "Some of your fellows were here only yesterday."

One of the Guards grunted, reaching for a brimming mug. "They are ordered to the west," he said. "And many others, too. We are to stay in the northeast, worse luck. We will miss the real fighting."

"Fighting?" Tom's lean face creased into a broad smile as he passed the other mugs around.

"You talk too much, Teep 4," grunted a second guard.

Tom raised his eyebrows. "Old Tom is no threat!" he exclaimed. "What is he but a poor shopkeeper?"

"A poor innkeeper, too!" snarled Teep 4. "This ale tastes like muddlet droppings."

Amid loud guffaws, the shop bell sounded. Tom excused himself and went through a door, closing it behind him. Waiting in the shop were a man and a woman, well muffled against the cold.

"Greetings! How can I serve you?" Tom asked.

Without a word, the woman made a mark on the dust of the counter.

Tom casually swept the mark away as he pulled a package from under the counter. "This is your order, I believe," he said. He gave the package to the woman, then glanced quickly at the tavern door.

"I have news," he murmured. The customers bent towards him, and he began speaking rapidly.

High on Dread Mountain, Gla-Thon saw a flock of blackbirds approaching and fitted an arrow to her bow.

The gnomes still placed filled glass bottles at the base of the mountain for the Grey Guards to take to the Shadowlands. The fact that the liquid in the bottles was now water and Boolong sap instead of deadly poison was something the Guards would discover only when they tried to use the blisters made from it.

Perhaps, at last, that time had come. Perhaps the blackbirds were the first sign that the Shadow Lord had discovered the Dread Gnomes' treachery.

If so, we are ready, thought Gla-Thon grimly. She heard rustling behind her and spun around. But it was only Prin, the youngest of the Kin.

"Birds!" Prin gasped. "Blackbirds — "

"I have seen them," grunted Gla-Thon.

The flock was wheeling close, now. Gla-Thon's arrow strained against her bowstring. Then one of the birds separated from the rest and plunged towards her. In its beak was something that flashed golden in the sun.

And even before the bird had landed, Gla-Thon was shouting. Shouting that the sign had come.

✳

Manus lifted his head from his work in the vegetable beds of Raladin to swat the flies that were swarming around him. Then he stared.

The flies were not flies at all, but bees. The air seemed full of them. As Manus watched, easing his aching back, he frowned.

The bees were acting strangely. They were not hovering around the flowers, but buzzing in the sky. They were clustering together, making patterns. And the patterns . . .

Manus's jaw dropped. The spade fell from his hand. With his long, blue-grey finger he began tracing in the soil the patterns the bees were making, black against the blue.

Manus sat back on his heels and read what he had written. The message was clear. "One person — travel to — friends — quickly. For freedom!"

✳

Many days passed. Slow days for Lief, Barda, and Jasmine, cooped up in the caravan. They knew from Steven's songs that Ak-Baba had flown overhead and Ols in all shapes had stared as the caravan passed by. But the caravan was a familiar sight to the Ak-Baba, and the Ols were not interested in it. They had been ordered to keep watch — but not for that.

> *Road forks just ahead I see,*
> *Ol-io, Ol-io!*
> *Night is falling, we seem free*
> *Of Ol-i, Ol-ios!*

Steven was singing again, giving the news.

A few minutes later, the caravan stopped, the back doors were thrown open, and the companions scrambled out. It was just past sunset. A rocky hill rose in front of them. The main road curved around the hill to the right. Another track wound off to the left. A signpost stood at the fork. Lief's throat tightened as he read it.

"We must take the Del road, but it will be a journey into the unknown," said Steven. "I know nothing of it, and neither does Doom. He always travels overland in these parts. The hills that hide the coast are treacherous, he says. But he prefers them."

"I would prefer them, also," muttered Jasmine.

"And I," growled Barda. "But we must stay hidden. If we are sighted here, the decoys in the west will have risked their lives to no purpose."

Lief was looking at the Del road. Endon and Sharn had no doubt followed it from the city, the night they escaped. They would not have tried to go overland, with Sharn so close to giving birth to her child.

He tried to imagine how it would have been. The road would have been crowded. Many fled from Del that night. He remembered his father's sad voice, telling him about it. "Your mother and I stayed shut up in the forge all through the uproar. When at last we opened our gates, we found ourselves alone. Friends, neighbors, old customers — all were gone. Killed, captured, or fled."

"We had been expecting something of the sort," Lief's mother had added. "But the confusion was worse than even we had imagined. It took a long time for life in Del to begin again. When it did, we were ready. And so grateful — because we were safe, and so were you, my son, for by that time you had been born, and were the light of our lives. But . . ." Her strong voice trembled. "But we feared for those who had fled."

Those who had fled.

Unrecognized in their humble working clothes, Endon and Sharn would have lost themselves in the panicking crowd. They would have hurried along with others moving west, suffering who knew what terrors. Then, when the blackbird carrying Tora's message reached them, they would have realized that there was no point in continuing.

What would they have done then? Moved off the road. Found a place to hide. Endon knew the Belt would never again shine for him. Deltora's only hope lay with his child. He and Sharn had to find a place where the baby could be born in safety. Where?

Lief was roused by Jasmine's sharp voice. "Lief! We must go, so we can find a place to stop for the night."

Lief turned to the caravan. But his thoughts still dwelled on a time before he was born, and on two desperate people he had never known, searching for refuge.

6 ~ Dangerous Road

Rain threatened as they set off the next day. The companions cared nothing for that, cheered by Steven's assurance that they would reach Withick Mire before sunset. But they had not gone far before his voice reached them with bad news.

> *Be prepared for flight or fight.*
> *Ol-io, Ol-io!*
> *Gripper field lies to the right,*
> *Ahead are Guard-ios.*

"What is a gripper field?" whispered Jasmine, as the caravan jerked to a stop.

"It cannot be worse than Grey Guards, in any case," growled Barda. "And Guards, it seems, are ahead."

The caravan doors were thrown open, and Steven looked in.

"The road is blocked," he hissed. "The Guards must be searching all carts that pass." He heaved a barrel from a corner as Lief, Barda, and Jasmine scrambled out onto the road. They were hidden from the Guards because the caravan had stopped in the middle of a bend. But once it moved on . . .

Lief looked quickly for a way of escape. On one side was sheer, high rock. On the other was a field, bordered by thickly wooded hills.

"Make for the hills," muttered Steven. "With luck, the Guards will not notice you. We will meet further on. Take care. The stones are hard to — "

He broke off as a hoarse shout came from the road ahead. He slammed the doors and moved to the front of the caravan, carrying the barrel. "I am coming, sirs," he called. "With ale, for your pleasure."

The companions heard him climb onto the driver's seat. Then the caravan began to move.

Kree soared towards the hills. Lief, Barda, and Jasmine rolled into the ditch that edged the road.

"I see no sign of grippers, whatever they may be," Barda whispered, scanning the field.

Indeed, the field appeared quite empty. The only unusual thing about it was its bright green color, caused by a multitude of large, flat weeds. Like round mats made up of circles of broad leaves, the weeds pressed closely together, almost choking out the grass.

Lief glanced along the road. The caravan had almost reached the Guards. There were ten — a whole pod. The road was blocked by fallen trees. Heaps of rubbish, empty barrels, and boxes lay everywhere. Plainly, the Guards had been on duty here for months.

They will be bored, eager for entertainment, Lief thought, his heart sinking.

"And what do we have here?" one of the Guards shouted. "A big, ugly tick with a horse to match!" There was a gale of laughter as his brothers gathered around the caravan, their eyes fixed on Steven.

"Now!" hissed Barda.

Keeping together under the shelter of Lief's cloak, the companions began scrambling forward. But almost at once Barda staggered, with a muffled cry of pain. At the same moment, Jasmine gasped and fell to her knees.

Lief whirled around, crouching to help them. But when he put down his left hand to brace himself, the ground gave way beneath it, and his hand was dragged down by something that bit and burned.

His hand had sunk into the center of one of the flat weeds. The center was widening, sucking at his arm, drawing it down . . .

Wildly, Lief tore himself free. His hand was covered in blood. The center of the plant gaped like a huge, flabby-lipped mouth, flecked with red. With horror, Lief looked down at the rows of vicious teeth lining the green throat that plunged deep into the earth.

The plants! Grippers! Steven thought we knew . . .

Beside him, Jasmine struggled to free her trapped leg as Filli squealed in terror, trying vainly to help her, and Kree flew back to her side. Barda floundered in agony behind them, both legs caught and sinking.

Lief seized Jasmine's arms and heaved. Her leg came free dripping blood, and all around her grippers opened their hideous mouths wide. Cheers rang out from the road, and for a moment Lief thought they had been seen. But when he looked, he saw that the Guards had their backs to the field. They were gathered around the barrel, filling their mugs.

"Barda!" choked Jasmine. Barda was pinned to the ground. All four of his limbs were trapped, now. His neck strained as he fought to hold his face away from a pulsing, greedy green mouth gaping just below it. Every moment he sank deeper, deeper . . .

Why am I not sinking? thought Lief. He looked down. He was standing on a patch of pale grass. Then he realized that the grass was covering a flat stone. Steven had begun to say something about stones . . .

The stones are hard to — to see!

With a moan of frustration Lief saw pale patches making a line through the field. Stepping stones! A path that would always be safe because, though grass could overgrow a stone, grippers could only grow in deep earth.

He and Jasmine were standing on stones right

now. Barda lay in a seething mass of bright green. But the line of stones snaked beside him.

"Jasmine! The pale patches are safe!" Lief hissed. "Move back along them!" As she sprang to obey, he snatched his rope from his belt and followed.

When he reached her, Jasmine was stabbing viciously at the grippers holding Barda. The plants were quivering and recoiling a little. Lief pushed the end of the rope under Barda's chest. Then, leaning over perilously, he pulled it through on the other side and knotted it, pulling it tight under the big man's arms.

"Help me, Barda!" he gasped, pulling with all his might. And Barda, making a final, anguished effort, groaned and arched his body.

His arms came free. The sleeves of his jacket were torn to ribbons, soaked with blood. The greedy mouths beneath him yawned wide.

Her teeth bared in disgust, Jasmine began attacking the leaves around Barda's trapped legs. Again Lief heaved on the rope. This time Barda could help little. Blood flowed freely from his torn flesh, and he had almost lost consciousness. But at last, with agonizing slowness, his legs began to ease out of the ground, till he was free.

Jasmine and Lief rolled him onto the stepping stones and began half carrying, half dragging him towards the hills.

The noise from the road rose to a gleeful roar. The Guards had thought of a new entertainment. Five of them were holding Steven at dagger's point. The other five were pulling the horse towards the gripper field. The creature, sensing its danger, was rearing and plunging, screaming in terror.

The Guards were cheering. Steven was shouting at them to stop, to stop! His huge brown figure with its crown of golden hair was almost hidden in a jostling crowd of grey uniforms.

Lief's blood ran cold. "Jasmine, faster!" he cried. The trees were not far away now. A few more steps . . .

There was a spine-chilling bellow. Lief looked up. The Guards were falling to the ground, their hands pressed to their eyes. Steven was staggering back, blinding yellow light pouring from his body like smoke. Then another figure was rising in front of him, taking shape in the glare. A golden giant, with a wild mane of dark brown hair.

"Nevets," Lief whispered.

The giant's body was covered in golden fur. His yellow eyes glittered with cruel fury. His massive fingers were tipped with viciously curved brown claws. He lunged for the terrified horse and swung it to safety. Then, growling like a beast, he began snatching up the screaming, writhing Guards, shaking them like dolls, and tearing them apart.

Lief and Jasmine stood frozen in horror. Steven crawled to his feet, and saw them. "Go!" he roared. "Once he has begun, I cannot stop him! Get out of his sight!"

✳

Safe under the trees, Lief and Jasmine bandaged Barda's terrible wounds, wrapped him in blankets, and gave him Queen Bee honey. But the bleeding would not stop, and Barda did not stir. Rain began, soaking, icy.

Desperately, Lief looked for shelter. Then he gave a cry of amazement. Not far away, like the answer to a prayer, was an old stone hut, almost hidden by bushes. Of course! The stepping stones had once led to someone's home.

With Kree fluttering anxiously above them, Lief and Jasmine hauled Barda to the hut. Inside, it was dark, for the small windows were filmed with dirt. There was a musty, unpleasant smell. But it was dry, and its fireplace was piled with sticks and dead grass.

They dragged Barda inside and Jasmine ran to the fireplace. In moments she had started a fire. The tinder-dry wood crackled as flames leaped up. Light began to flicker around the tiny room.

And it was then that Lief saw what lay in a corner.

Two skeletons were propped against the wall. Scraps of clothing still clung to the bones, and hair to the skulls, so Lief could see that it had been a man and a woman who had crept in here to die. Then he saw that the woman cradled in her arms, in the tatters of a shawl, another small heap of bones — the bones of a tiny baby.

Sweat broke out on his forehead. He forced himself to take a step forward, then another. There was something lying at the man's feet. A flat tin box.

"No!" Jasmine's hushed voice was filled with fear, but Lief did not stop. He picked up the box and opened it. Inside was a scrap of parchment covered in black writing. He squinted at it, the terrible words dancing before his eyes. He took a deep, shuddering breath.

"What is it?" whispered Jasmine.

Lief read the note aloud. His voice sounded thin, like the voice of someone he did not know.

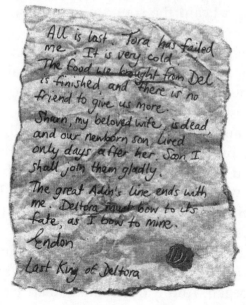

The note crushed in his hand, Lief stared at the bones. He could not take in what he was seeing.

The heir to Deltora was not safe in hiding, waiting for them. The heir had been dead all along.

"This Endon was a man who did not deserve to be king," Jasmine said harshly. "Weak and peevish, filled with pity for himself. It is what I always feared."

Lief forced himself to speak. "You are cruel, Jasmine!" he whispered. "He had lost all he loved when he wrote this note. He was in despair."

"He caused his loss himself!" Jasmine spat. "If he had been brave enough to depend on himself for once, they would have survived, as my parents did. There is wood here. I heard the sound of a stream. There are berries and other wild foods."

She shook her head angrily. "But oh, no! Still looking for others to hold his hand and make his life easy, he could not even try to help himself or his family. And so they ended in this barren place, starving and cold, and his wife and her little one died." Her eyes were brimming with tears as she stared at the tiny, ragged bundle resting on the woman's breast.

"We will never know the truth of it," Lief said heavily. "But one thing we do know. Without the heir to wear it, the Belt cannot save Deltora."

His chest was tight, his stomach churning. Barda is dying, he thought. Dying for a cause that was lost before it began. And Mother and Father! How much have they suffered? All for nothing. Nothing! Father's plan to help his friend and hide the heir led only to death and misery. Who told him the lie that the Belt would remain whole only while the heir lived?

Was it stated in *The Belt of Deltora*? Lief searched his memory. No! He was sure — positive — that the little book had never mentioned any such thing. Why had he not thought of that before?

Because I simply believed what Father told me, he thought dismally. As no doubt Father believed someone else. Prandine, perhaps. Or even Endon himself. He bowed his head, in an agony of despair.

7 - Withick Mire

The caravan swayed. The bells on the reins jingled. But Steven was not singing. Inside, in the dimness, Lief and Jasmine sat with Barda lying between them, trying to protect their injured friend from the worst of the jolts.

They had spent a miserable hour by the hut fire before Steven came looking for them. Lief shivered, remembering what had happened when Steven saw the skeletons and read the note.

Steven's face had darkened. His face had begun to heave. Suddenly he had screwed his eyes shut and pressed his lips together. "No! No!" Lief heard him mutter as he turned away, beating the stone wall with his fists. And Lief knew he was struggling with Nevets, trying to keep his savage brother in check.

After a few moments, the battle was won. Steven turned back to them, his face weary, but calm. "What cannot be changed, must be endured," he said grimly. "Our duty now is to the living."

He bent over Barda. "Ah — this is my fault," he murmured. "I thought you knew of gripper fields."

"Will Barda live?" Lief's throat was tight as he asked the question.

Steven gnawed at his lip, hesitating. "At Withick Mire he will be warm and comfortable," he said finally.

He bent and lifted Barda as easily as if the big man were a child. Then he strode from the hut without a backward glance. Lief and Jasmine trailed after him, both very aware that he had not answered the question.

They walked in silence through the trees to where the stepping stones began, then picked their way back across the gripper field. Ahead, the caravan stood alone, the horse waiting beside it. The trees that had blocked the road had been cast aside. The cooking fires, the stores, and the rubbish had been swept away as though blown by a great wind.

Of the Guards there was no sign except for a few scraps of bloodstained grey fabric scattered here and there. With a chill Lief realized that Nevets had chosen the easiest way to dispose of the remains of his victims. The grippers closest to the road had been well fed.

✳

Hours later, they began to notice a vile smell. The stench of rot and decay seeped into the caravan till the still, dusty air was thick with it. Jasmine wrinkled her nose in disgust. "What is it?" she whispered.

Lief shrugged, then steadied himself as the caravan rocked violently as though it was travelling over rough ground.

He looked down at Barda. The rough bandages that bound Barda's legs and arms were soaked with blood. He had taken a little water, and when they smeared Queen Bee honey on his mouth, he licked it from his lips. But he had not opened his eyes or spoken.

The honey is all that is keeping him alive, Lief thought. But for how long? How long? Oh, let us reach Withick Mire soon!

So that Barda could be cared for properly. So that his wounds could be washed and freshly bandaged. So that — Lief forced himself to think of it — so that if Barda had to die, he could die peacefully, comfortably, on a warm couch, instead of in this cold, shaking, stinking caravan.

At that very moment, to his surprise, the caravan came to a stop. The back doors were flung open, and Lief and Jasmine scrambled out.

The rain had stopped. The sun was setting, flooding the sky with dull orange light that lit a strange and horrible scene. The caravan was in the middle of a giant garbage dump. Giant, stinking mounds of rags, bones, broken furniture, and household goods, twisted metal and rotting food scraps rose on all sides. Among the mounds, ragged, miserable people bent and shuffled, searching the refuse.

Lief spun around angrily to Steven. "Why have you brought us here?" he demanded. "We must get Barda to Withick Mire!"

Without a word Steven pointed at a sign that stood just beside where the caravan had stopped.

Before Lief could say anything, one of the ragged scavengers came shambling towards them, leaning heavily on a stick. A black patch covered one of his eyes and he had tied a scarf around his mouth and nose, no doubt to protect him from the stench of the mounds. He bent forward, leering at the newcomers with his one good eye.

"What do you seek here, may I ask?" he rasped, his voice just a croak. "Here, amid the leavings of Del?"

Lief and Jasmine hesitated, not knowing what to say.

The scavenger cackled. "Perhaps you seek shelter?" he asked. "Then come with me. All are welcome in Withick Mire."

He hobbled off, threading his way through the mounds with the ease of long practice. Not knowing what else to do, the companions followed, Lief and Jasmine on foot, Steven leading the horse carefully through the maze.

As they walked, they passed many pathetic hovels made of pieces of wood, tin, and cloth. People crouched outside these hovels, sorting through the pickings of the day, or starting cooking fires. Some grinned up at the strangers. Others did not bother to raise their heads.

At the back of one of the larger mounds, a more substantial shelter had been built. The scavenger beckoned, and Lief and Jasmine, with a backward glance at Steven, followed him inside.

And there a surprise awaited them. Beneath the thin layer of tin and board was a sturdy building. It was far larger than it had appeared from the outside, because all but its entry was buried deep under the mound. It was not only large, but clean and well organized, with many stretchers arranged neatly around the walls, each topped with folded blankets, and with possessions stacked below.

The scavenger turned to them, straightened, and threw off both the eye patch and the scarf.

"Doom!" Jasmine exclaimed in amazement.

"Did you not know me?" asked Doom, his lips

tweaking into a smile. "That is excellent! You did not expect the Resistance stronghold to be in a garbage dump, no doubt. But what better place to hide? No one comes here willingly — not even Grey Guards. And who cares for or about poor scavengers? Some of the people you saw on your way here are true scavengers — sad souls from Del whose livelihoods have been taken from them. Others — many others — are our people. Glock, Fardeep, and even Zeean are out there somewhere, with all the rest. Dain is away fetching water."

Leif nodded slowly, taking it in. So nothing is as it seems, even here, he thought.

"Doom," Jasmine said urgently. "Barda is injured. He needs care. And . . ." She glanced at Lief. "There is other news. Very bad."

Lief fumbled in his pocket and drew out Endon's crumpled note.

Doom's dark eyes grew even darker as though, somehow, he knew what was coming. But he did not take the note. Instead, he turned swiftly to face the door once more.

"Time enough for that when Barda has been seen to," he said roughly. "Bring him in. We will do what we can for him."

✳

Later, Lief and Jasmine sat by Barda's bed. Their own wounds had been washed and bandaged, and the big man lay peacefully at last. The bleeding had stopped, and for this they had to thank a strange ally — Glock.

"You won't heal this with bandages," Glock had mumbled, grabbing Lief's wrist and inspecting it. "Grippers inject something that keeps the blood flowing."

He went over to his own stretcher, rummaged beneath it, then came back holding a grubby jar filled with grey paste. "Smear this on the bites," he ordered.

"What is it?" asked Jasmine, smelling the paste suspiciously.

"How would I know?" snarled Glock. "Those who made it are long dead. But my tribe always used it in the old days — for half-wits and infants who blundered into gripper fields."

Jasmine bit back her angry response and turned to Barda.

"Do not waste it on him," Glock growled. "He is finished."

Jasmine did not bother to reply. Already she was smearing the paste on Barda's cleaned wounds. Glock spat in disgust, and lumbered away. Now he was nowhere to be seen.

Lief looked up wearily. Zeean, Fardeep, and Doom were standing together not far away, with Steven beside them. Their heads were bent. Their faces were grave. They were reading Endon's note.

"So," Lief heard Doom say heavily. "That is the end of that."

They looked up, saw Lief and Jasmine watching, and moved to join them. Doom handed the note back to Lief.

"The Dread Gnome and the Ralad will arrive to find they have made their journey for nothing," he said.

Lief nodded. "All our journeys have been for nothing," he replied through stiff lips.

Zeean's face was shadowed with grief. "It is very hard," she murmured. "I had — such hopes."

"It is well for our hopes to be dashed, if they were false." The old bitterness had returned to Doom's voice. "Soon we will all return to our places. And every step we go, we will tell what we know, so no other fools will be tempted to risk their lives in a useless cause."

There was a sound beside Lief. He looked down, and his heart thudded. Barda had stirred. His eyes were open.

"What is — the matter?" Barda asked weakly.

Jasmine stroked his forehead. "Nothing is the matter," she said soothingly. "Rest, now."

But Barda moved his head impatiently and his eyes fastened on the note in Lief's hand. "What is that? Show it to me!" he demanded.

Lief knew Barda too well to think he could refuse. Reluctantly, he held out the note so that Barda could see it, explaining how it had been found.

Barda blinked at the terrible words. Then, to

Lief's amazement, he smiled. "And — is this what is troubling you?" he asked.

Lief and Jasmine exchanged alarmed glances. Barda's mind was wandering. Jasmine bent over the bed once more. "Sleep," she whispered. "You need rest, Barda. You are very weak."

"Weak I may be," Barda said softly. "But not so weak that I do not know a falsehood when I see it."

8 - Arrivals

Barda gazed wearily up at the ring of astounded faces, and again he smiled. "The note is a good forgery, oh, yes," he murmured. "The writing is very like that on the note we saw in Tora. But the mind that framed these words was not Endon's mind. I — "

His voice faltered as he was distracted by a noise. Lief quickly turned to see Dain hurrying towards them from the door, his eyes wide with questions. But before the boy could speak, Doom frowned and raised his finger to his lips. Lief turned back to the bed.

"How can you tell the note was not written by King Endon, Barda?" Jasmine asked gently. "You did not know him."

"Perhaps not," muttered Barda. "But Jarred did. Time and again Jarred has told me of Endon's terrible feelings of guilt. It brought tears into his own eyes to tell of Endon's agony when he realized how he had failed Deltora. Yet this, which is supposed to be Endon's last message, written not long after the escape from Del, says not one word of that."

"You are right." Lief felt that he was slowly waking from a nightmare. "Not one word of apology or grief for anyone other than for himself and his family. And this cannot be. The note — the skeletons — were planted to deceive us! That is why the Guards were placed where they were. To force travellers off the road, up to the hut. It was all a Shadow Lord plan."

I have many plans . . .

"But . . ." Like Jasmine, Doom was plainly not convinced.

Barda tossed his head restlessly. "Look at the seal at the bottom of the message. It should not be there. The note in Tora did not bear the royal seal. And why? Because Endon did not have the seal ring in his possession when he escaped. He could not have done so. The seal was always kept by Prandine, and brought out only when messages had to be signed."

"How do you know this?" asked Zeean curiously.

Barda sighed. "My mother, rest her soul, was nursemaid to both Jarred and Endon. She was a great chatterer, and told me many things about palace doings. Often I only half listened, I admit. But it seems that I learned more than the Shadow Lord suspects."

"And what a blessing you did," breathed Far-deep, his eyes goggling. "If it had not been for you, we would have abandoned all our hopes."

"I have stayed alive to some purpose, then," said Barda, with the faintest of smiles. "But now I am very weary." His eyes closed.

Jasmine drew a sharp breath and pressed her ear to his chest. When she straightened, her face was very pale. "He is only asleep," she whispered. "But his heart beats very faintly. I fear he is slipping away from us."

Blindly she put out her hand to Lief, and he clasped it, his eyes filling with tears. How much our journey has changed us, he thought, dazed with grief. Jasmine shows feeling, and reaches out for comfort! I am not ashamed to weep! How Barda would smile at that.

Steven touched his arm. "Do not grieve before you must, my friend," he said gently. "Barda is strong, and a fighter. He will not give up easily. And Queen Bee honey has performed miracles before."

Lief felt Jasmine's hand tighten on his own. Then there was a sudden movement beside him. He looked around and saw that Dain had pushed his way to the bed, and was kneeling at his side. The boy's eyes were wet, but his face was determined. "Barda must not die," he said. "If we tend him carefully, surely he will recover."

Jasmine's face was glowing with gratitude as she

looked at Dain. But this time Lief felt no jealous pang. If Barda was to be saved, he needed all the hope and help he could get.

※

That night, and another day, passed in a dream. Lief, Jasmine, and Dain watched over Barda in turns, coaxing him to take honey, water, and spoonfuls of broth. At times Barda seemed to strengthen a little, rousing himself and even speaking. But soon the weakness would take hold again, and before long he would be worse than ever.

It was as if he was on a gradual downward slide that could not be halted. The stirrings were coming less often now.

Barda is dying, Lief told himself. I must face it. But still he could not make himself give up hope. Jasmine certainly had not. And Dain was a tower of strength, taking longer and longer turns at the bedside, sparing them as much as he could.

At sunset, Lief had just stood up from the bedside, giving up his place to Dain, when a shrill cry was heard outside.

"Ak-Baba! Beware!"

Suddenly all was confusion as people began streaming through the door into the shelter. Lief looked around frantically. Where was Jasmine?

Then he remembered. Jasmine had gone with Zeean and Fardeep to collect water. He pushed his way through the throng in the doorway and ran outside. Almost at once he saw the three he was seeking. They were standing with brimming pails, looking upward at the dark shadow approaching through the orange glare of the sky.

"Jasmine!" Lief shouted. "Run!"

But to his surprise Jasmine simply turned and smiled wearily at him. He looked up once more, then realized what the shadow was.

It was no Ak-Baba. It was a Kin! Ailsa, if he was not mistaken. She was surrounded by a wavering cloud of blackbirds. As they came over the Mire, the birds swooped away and Ailsa began dropping to earth. A small figure in her pouch was waving vigorously.

Gla-Thon, Lief guessed, squinting up at the sky and waving back. Quick-thinking, sharp-tongued Gla-Thon. He recognized her sturdy body, her frizz of brown hair. And who but Gla-Thon would have thought of asking a Kin to fly her speedily to the meeting? Old Fa-Glin may have agreed to make peace with the gnomes' Kin neighbors. But Lief thought it unlikely that he would have consented to ride with one.

Now six of the seven tribes are represented here, Lief thought, as he ran with Jasmine to welcome the newcomers. I should be excited. I should be filled with hope.

And in a way he was. Celebration, and much talk, would follow this arrival, he knew. He looked forward to explaining everything to Gla-Thon. He

481

was overjoyed to see Ailsa again. But the fear of losing Barda hung over him like a cloud, blurring every thought, every feeling.

✳

A few days later, Lief was sitting beside Barda's bed, half drowsing, when there was a light touch on his shoulder. Startled, he spun around and met two solemn black button eyes set in a wrinkled blue-grey face.

"Manus!" he exclaimed, leaping up and bending to fling his arms around the Ralad man. "Oh, Manus! You came!"

"Of course," said Manus. He turned to the golden-maned man standing behind him, with Jasmine. "Our friend Nanion, chief of D'Or, was the means of my arriving so quickly. Nanion has a way with horses which I do not. His feet reach the stirrups, for one thing! But I must say it was an uncomfortable journey. I was terrified half out of my life, and bruised from head to toe!"

Nanion laughed. "To follow a swarm of bees over rough country is no easy task," he said. "And this Ralad complained from the beginning of the journey to the end. I am relieved to have arrived at last, and to be free of his nagging." But his eyes were warm as he spoke. Plainly, he and Manus had become good friends.

"How did you come to have a horse?" Jasmine asked. "And such a fine one!"

Nanion shrugged. "A certain shopkeeper made it available to me," he said. "I only hope he has a good explanation ready for its owners when they come seeking it."

"I daresay he has," said Doom dryly, strolling up behind them. "Good explanations are Tom's specialty. So — he finally decided to take sides, did he?"

Manus smiled. "Not quite that, I think," he said. "He warned Nanion that lightning does not strike twice in the same place. Meaning, I suppose, that we should expect no more favors from him."

"But I think he had forgotten that he had already done us one good turn," Nanion put in. "Shortly before I saw him, he had given two of my people some news. Grey Guards are being ordered to the west. Fighting is expected."

Doom's eyebrows shot up. "Indeed?" he muttered. He drew Nanion aside, leaving Manus alone with Barda, Lief, and Jasmine.

"This is a sorrowful thing," Manus murmured, looking down at the big man lying so still on the bed. "Can nothing be done?"

Lief shook his head. "He has not stirred since sunrise," he said, all his grief flooding back. "I think — it cannot be long."

Manus bowed his head. "Then I am glad I arrived when I did," he said softly. "For it means much to me to see him again. He has a great heart."

He looked up, meeting Lief's eyes squarely. "He

has not given his life in vain," he said. "Jasmine has told me why I was summoned, though I think I had already guessed. You three have worked a miracle."

"Part of a miracle," Lief answered. "The heir is still to be found."

"And is that not why we are all here?" Manus asked quietly. He stood up. "The moon is rising. It is time for the seven tribes to join once more. It is time for the heir to be summoned."

9 - The Heir

Candles flickered around the walls. Faces — grave, excited, afraid — formed a half circle around the seven. All eyes were on the Belt, lying in shadow, on the table where Lief had set it.

They were standing by Barda's bed. Jasmine had insisted on that. "In whatever twilight world he is wandering, he may hear us," she said. "And even if he cannot, it is his right to be present."

No one argued with her. But it was clear to all that Barda's long struggle for life was almost done.

Zeean stepped forward. "I, Zeean of Tora, am here," she said gravely, laying her hand upon the amethyst.

Gla-Thon was next. "And I, Gla-Thon of the Dread Gnomes," she said, her head held high as she caressed the emerald.

Lief watched, holding himself rigidly, as one by one the others moved forward.

"Fardeep, of the Mere." Fardeep's usually hearty voice was shaking. Humbly, he touched the lapis lazuli.

"Steven, of the Plains." Steven towered over all the rest, his golden hair gleaming as he bent to the opal.

"Manus, for the Ralad people." Manus brushed the ruby with gentle fingers.

Glock lumbered forward. His face was fierce and proud as he stretched out his huge paw to the diamond. "I am Glock, last of the Jalis," he growled. And Lief caught his breath as he saw tears spring into the savage eyes.

Then it was his turn. He squeezed Barda's hand and moved to the Belt. The faces of the watchers in the front row swam before his eyes.

Jasmine, solemn, Filli and Kree on her shoulder. Ailsa, paws clasped to her mouth. Nanion, chief of D'Or, eager. Doom, watchful. Dain, pale and intent.

Lief placed his hand upon the golden topaz. For you, Barda, he thought. For Mother and Father, and all at home. "Lief, of Del," he said clearly.

He looked down. The Belt was almost hidden by the hands that touched it. Seven hands of every color, every shape, pressed together in one purpose.

Zeean was speaking again, saying the words that had been agreed.

"Together we, representatives of the seven tribes, renew our ancient vow to unite under the power of the Belt of Deltora, and swear loyalty to Adin's rightful heir."

"We swear," the seven said as one.

And Lief felt the Belt warm under his hand. A thrill ran through him. The topaz was gleaming golden through his fingers. His mind sharpened. The Belt grew hotter, hotter until he was forced, like his companions, to draw his hand away. But by that time, he knew.

The heir was here, in this room.

He looked up. His gaze swept over the people in front of him. Fixed on one. One whose body was trembling, but whose face was shimmering with light as he stepped forward.

Dain.

How could I not have seen? Lief thought, staring in wonder as gasps of shock sighed through the crowd. How could I not have guessed?

Dain, whose very name was a clue, an anagram, made up as it was from the letters that also formed the name "Adin." Dain, who had grown up on an isolated farm, not far from where they now stood. Who had learned the ancient royal art of archery, and as much as his parents could teach him of Deltora's history. Dain — who was quiet, obedient, and dutiful like his father, dark and delicate like his Toran mother. The name he had given his mother — Rhans

487

—was only Sharn in another form. Yet no one had seen it.

How well he had kept his great secret! Only once had he come close to revealing it. When he had lain by the cracked stone in Tora's heart, stunned and broken by shock and despair.

The tension in the room seemed to crackle as Lief picked up the Belt and moved slowly forward.

Dain waited. The trembling had stopped. He was holding his head high, now. A quiet dignity seemed to have settled over his shoulders like a fine cloak. The smooth skin of his face and hands glowed with light.

My father served and protected his father, thought Lief. Now I will serve and protect him.

He stretched out his hands. The Belt hung loosely between his fingers, for the first time catching the light. He felt a strange reluctance to let it go. He glanced at Jasmine. She nodded, her eyes shining.

This is what we have striven for, Lief thought. This is what was meant to be. He stared at the Belt, taking one last look at the stones that gleamed in the steel medallions. So hard-won, so beautiful . . .

Then he blinked. The ruby was not red, but palest pink. The emerald was dull as a stone. The amethyst had paled to soft mauve. The blood rushed to Lief's head, and his heart begin to pound.

"Danger! Evil!" he gasped. "Here — "

A bloodcurdling shriek split the air. Something

huge burst, slavering, through the door. Then, with a sound like thunder, a blast of wind tore through the room, blowing out the candles, throwing Lief backwards into darkness. He scrambled blindly on the hard floor, clutching the Belt, crying out for Jasmine, for Dain. The wind beat in his face. He could hear crashing and thudding as people fell and furniture flew, splintering against the walls.

"Lief! The Belt!" he heard Dain screaming. "To me! Oh, quickly — "

His cry was drowned out by the wind, by screaming, by something roaring with savage fury.

Lief staggered to his feet and began battling through the howling darkness in the direction from which the voice had come. Something flew through the air and hit him in the chest with tremendous force, hurling him back against Barda's bed. He slumped over it, gasping for breath, struggling to rise.

Then there was a tremendous, rumbling crash from the doorway and the wind stopped, as suddenly as it had begun.

A ghastly silence fell, broken only by the moans and sobs of injured people. His head spinning, Lief pushed himself away from the bed. As he did so, Barda stirred.

"Cold . . ." Barda whispered. Lief realized that his fall had dragged the blankets from the bed. Feverishly feeling around in the dark, he found them and did his best to spread them over Barda once more.

Then, wincing at the pain in his chest, he managed to stand. "Dain!" he heard Doom shouting. "Dain! Answer me!"

But there was no reply.

Someone lit a torch, using the coals of the fire. Glock. Lief caught a glimpse of his brutish face, weirdly lit by flickering light. Glock had a great bruise on his forehead. One of his eyes was swelling and darkening. But still he held the torch high, sweeping it from side to side so that great shadows leaped around the walls.

Lief saw Ailsa, curled on the floor like a great stone; Gla-Thon, staggering from among the remains of the table that had held the belt; Doom, his face smeared with blood; Zeean clutching Manus for support; Jasmine murmuring to Filli. The door was torn from its hinges. The opening was blocked by a mass of collapsed wood and rubble . . .

And Dain was gone. His dagger was lying on the floor where he had dropped it. Dazed, Lief walked over to it. Then he bent and picked it up. The tip of the blade was stained with blood. Dain had tried to fight his attacker. But he had stood no chance.

Sliding the dagger into his belt, Lief thought of the moment he had hesitated before handing over the Belt of Deltora. Perhaps if he had not given in to that feeling of reluctance — if he had passed the Belt to Dain at once — none of this would have happened. Dain would have been safe. They would all have been safe.

Sick with pain and guilt, he looked down at his hands, and his stomach lurched as he realized he was no longer holding the Belt. He looked around wildly, then realized that, of course, he must have dropped it on Barda's chest when he fell against the bed. It was safe there, covered in blankets. He would get it in a moment. When his head had stopped spinning. When he could breathe properly again. When this sickness passed.

He slid to the ground and crouched there, like a wounded animal.

"Dain has been taken!" Fardeep was whispering.

"It was a creature of darkness that did the deed," snarled Glock. "I saw it, as it burst in. A wolf — huge — with a yellow mouth. Then, it changed to a fiend. Even larger. And slimy red, like blood!"

A terrible thought came to Lief's mind. He wet his lips, afraid to put it into words.

Glock's eyes narrowed. He pointed a stubby finger at Lief. "You know something!" he growled. "I see it in your face. What was this thing?"

The words caught in Lief's throat as he spoke. "It sounds — like . . ."

"Like the last and most wicked of all the sorceress Thaegan's children," Doom finished for him. "The only one of that foul brood that still prowls the northeast. Ichabod."

"We have been betrayed," hissed Gla-Thon.

Glock bared his teeth and glared around the

room. His eyes fixed on Manus. "You came from the northeast, Ralad man," he snarled, clenching his fists. "You led the monster here! Admit it!"

Quaking, too shocked and afraid to speak, Manus shook his head. Nanion of D'Or moved to stand beside him. "If we were followed, we were unaware of it," he said sternly. "Keep your insults to yourself, Jalis."

"Do . . . not . . . fight." The words were soft, mumbled. But they broke the angry silence like a shout. For it was Barda who had spoken — Barda, struggling to sit up, to look around him. Jasmine shrieked piercingly and flew to his side, her hair wildly tangled, her small face pale in the glow of the lantern she had coaxed to life.

"Fighting . . . will profit us nothing!" Barda said, his voice growing stronger.

"It is a miracle!" Zeean breathed, staring.

It is the Belt, Lief thought. The Belt. It must be.

But already Doom was striding towards the door. "We must dig our way out of this place and give chase," he snapped. "Every moment we delay means that Dain is closer to death!"

"He is dead already," Glock growled. "The monster will by now have torn him limb from limb."

Doom's head jerked up, as though he had just remembered something. "Where is Steven?" he asked sharply.

In the silence that followed, they heard a faint

sound. A scratching sound, coming from the rubble that blocked the doorway.

"Steven!" Doom shouted.

"Yes!" a voice answered weakly. "I am here. Trapped. The building collapsed upon us as we tried to give chase. Even Nevets could not free us. Doom — it was Ichabod. Ichabod has Dain!"

"We thought as much," said Doom grimly.

"I could see nothing, but I could hear him laughing as he ran away," the faint voice called. "Laughing at Dain. He was saying — that if Dain was king, it was only right that he take him to where the king belonged. To Del."

10 – The Road to Del

Had Ichabod been under orders to capture the heir? Or had it been his own idea to snatch Dain? There was no way of knowing. But of one thing Lief could be sure. He and his companions had done exactly what they had sworn not to do. They had led the Shadow Lord to the heir.

And another thing is certain, Lief thought, as he and the others dug their way out of the shelter that had become their prison. If Dain is being taken to Del, we must follow — alone, if necessary.

But there was no doubt in anyone's mind. The seven tribes would remain united. At dawn, a party left for Del, Ailsa farewelling them tearfully. Doom had made his plans without delay.

"We will travel in small groups, far enough away from one another not to be seen," he said. "This is our best chance of reaching Del unnoticed."

"We will not reach it unnoticed if there is a spy within our ranks," muttered Gla-Thon.

Doom's face hardened. "No one is to be left alone for an instant, except for Steven, who will drive the caravan," he snapped. "Does anyone wish to question Steven's loyalty?"

Not surprisingly, no one dared do that.

The caravan went first, with Barda hidden inside. He was still weak, but he had refused to be left behind. On the right flank moved Manus and Nanion. On the left flank were Gla-Thon and Fardeep. Bringing up the rear were Doom, Zeean, and Glock. And in the center walked Lief and Jasmine, with Filli and Kree.

Lief still carried Dain's dagger. It had been precious to Dain. It would be returned to him — that, Lief had sworn. The point of its blade was deeply stained. No matter what Lief did, it would not come clean.

In the distance, Del-io,
Del-io, Del-io!
Two hours' rest, then on we go,
To Del-i, el-io!

Steven's voice sounded as jolly as if he really was just a simple pedlar. But his message was clear. He could see the outskirts of Del. He was stopping to rest.

"Why must we stop?" Jasmine muttered crossly.

Lief glanced at her. "Because it was agreed we would," he murmured. "Because we want to arrive in Del after dark. And we are tired. You sleep first."

They had been moving by the road's edge, where thick bushes gave plenty of cover. Lief watched as Jasmine settled herself for rest. He knew she would be asleep in moments. That was her way, no matter how uncomfortable the place, or how dangerous the time.

He sat with his back to a tree and touched the Belt, once again fastened around his waist. The Belt had halted Barda's slow drift towards death. But how? Surely none of the gems had the power to cure weakness due to blood loss. Perhaps the diamond . . .

Quietly, he drew out *The Belt of Deltora* and found the section on the powers of the diamond.

† **Diamonds . . . give courage and strength, protect from pestilence, and help the cause of true love.**

Still Lief was unsatisfied. Restlessly, he skimmed the pages, glancing at phrases here and there. A few he had forgotten. Most were very familiar to him.

† **The amethyst . . . calms and soothes. It changes color in the presence of illness, loses color near poisoned food or drink . . .**

† **The topaz protects its wearer from the terrors of the night. It has the power to open doors into the spirit world. It strengthens and clears the mind . . .**

✝ The emerald . . . dulls in the presence of evil, and when a vow is broken. It is a remedy for sores and ulcers, and an antidote to poison.

✝ The great ruby . . . grows pale in the presence of evil, or when misfortune threatens its wearer. It wards off evil spirits, and is an antidote to snake venom.

✝ The opal . . . has the power to give glimpses of the future, and to aid those with weak sight . . . The opal has a special relationship with the lapis lazuli, the heavenly stone, a powerful talisman.

Suddenly impatient, Lief snapped the book closed. Jasmine stirred, then abruptly her eyes opened.

"I am sorry — " Lief began. But she shook her head.

"Something is coming," she hissed, sitting up. "A horse-drawn wagon. Travelling away from Del."

Soon Lief himself could hear the sound of plodding hooves and rumbling wheels. He peered through the bushes and, to his amazement, saw Steven's caravan trundling towards them. There was no jingling sound, for the bells had been taken from the horse's reins.

Steven was singing, but very, very softly. No one but people very near the road could have heard him. As he came closer, Lief could hear that he was crooning the same verse over and over again.

Come out, Twig and Birdie-o!
Little creatures lying low?
Others rest, but we must go,
Twig and Birdie-o!

"It could be a trap," Jasmine breathed. "He could be Ol."

"I do not think so," Lief whispered back. "He is calling us by the false names we used in Rithmere. Barda must have given them to him."

"Glock knows them also!" Jasmine hissed. But already Lief was crawling out from the bushes. She sighed and clambered after him.

Steven saw them, smiled broadly, and stopped the caravan. "So there you are," he said in a low voice, climbing down. "Into the back with Barda, quickly."

"But this is not the plan!" Lief objected. "We are to meet with the others in the grove of trees outside the Del wall, just after dark. If we go with you now, we will arrive before sunset, and alone."

"Indeed," Steve nodded. "Barda will explain all to you. He and I have been talking. I opened a fresh jar of honey for him before we began our journey, and it seems to have done him good. See here!"

He flung the caravan doors wide. And there was Barda, sitting up and grinning.

"Barda! You are well!" Jasmine exclaimed.

Barda shrugged. "Not completely. I would not

relish a fight with an Ol." His grin broadened. "But I could certainly give a small pirate something to think about. Now, get in, quickly. We must be off."

"Why?" demanded Lief, as he and Jasmine reluctantly obeyed.

"If we reach Del before sunset, Steven can drive straight in. He will look like any pedlar hurrying to reach home before the laws against being on the streets at night come into force," Barda explained rapidly. "The gates are always crowded at that hour. The Guards will not bother to search the caravan. And standing with the other carts in the yard beside the market square, it will not be noticed. When it is dark, we can slip away."

"But why change the plan?" Lief was confused.

A rueful expression crossed Barda's face. "First, because the important thing is to get the Belt to Dain, wherever he may be imprisoned. The three of us, I believe, can do this better alone. Second — " He broke off.

"Second," said Steven quietly, "we are both certain that there is a spy in our party. That spy may have a secret way of communicating with the Shadow Lord — a way no one would suspect. If so, our plan could already be known in Del. We could be moving into a trap. We cannot risk that. We cannot risk losing the Belt."

"So we decided to go our own way," said Barda. "Without telling another soul."

"Not even Doom?" asked Jasmine, wide-eyed.

Again, Steven and Barda exchanged glances. "No," said Steven soberly, closing the doors. "Not even Doom."

11 - The Square

A nother stuffy, jolting hour. Steven's voice, singing softly, telling what he could see. Terrifying, tense minutes as the caravan slowed to join a line of carts passing through the city gates. The shouts of Guards. Then the sudden, achingly familiar sounds of Del. Wheels, bells, people shouting, jostling one another, bumping the sides of the caravan as it rumbled slowly over cluttered, cobbled streets.

And at last . . . stillness. The smell of rotting vegetables. Footsteps moving slowly to the back of the van.

The click of a latch. The doors opening a crack. Steven's face, tense, peering in, the sky a dimming orange glow behind him. Steven climbing into the van, pulling the doors closed behind him and holding them shut.

"All seems quiet," he whispered. "The streets are empty. There are no Guards about."

"Then where are they all?" Jasmine hissed. She put her hands up to Filli, who was whimpering, nuzzling into her collar.

"Del is a big place," Barda growled. "Perhaps they are guarding the walls. Perhaps they are around the palace . . ."

"Or perhaps they are waiting outside the walls, in the grove of trees — for us!" said Steven.

Lief shuddered. That would mean that there was indeed a spy in their ranks. It would mean that their friends were at this moment walking into a trap. He began to speak, but Barda held up his hand.

"If that is so," he said harshly, "we must only be glad that the Belt is safe here. But our friends will not be unprotected. Steven will go now to the meeting place, if he can escape the city."

"I will escape, one way or another," Steven said grimly. "And I will attend the meeting. To explain — or to settle a score." He clasped Barda's hand, then Lief's, then Jasmine's. "Good fortune," he said huskily. "May I see you again, and soon."

Silently, the four companions climbed from the van. Rats gnawing on piles of vegetable scraps shrilled and scattered around their feet. Steven patted the old horse, which was nibbling at a wilted green leaf. "Wait," he murmured. The horse nodded, snuffling softly.

Threading their way through a crowd of battered carts, they stole to the end of the small yard. But before they could enter the market square, there was a sudden commotion. A door was flung open with a crash. Rough voices and heavy boots burst, echoing, into the night. The light of many torches lit the darkness.

Hastily, the companions drew back into the shadows of the yard. The sound grew louder. There were crashes, grunts, the chink of stone. What was happening? Unable to contain his curiosity any longer, Lief peered cautiously around the corner.

Torches were blazing everywhere. Ten Grey Guards were working in the middle of the square. They were heaving huge blocks of stone into place to make a stepped pyramid with a flat top. Through the center of the pyramid rose a tall pole, towering high and held in place by the blocks that surrounded it.

"Where's the freak?" one Guard bawled. "The Ichabod?"

"It's in the palace, feeding," growled another. "It'll be down here presently, for more. It prefers its meat cooked, they say."

There was a gale of harsh laughter. Lief's skin began to crawl.

"Get up to the top, Bak 6!" barked another Guard. "There'll be trouble if we aren't ready when they bring the others." He strode over to the shadows and came back hauling what looked like a bundle of rags.

"They got them, then, Bak 1?" called the first Guard, climbing to the top of the pyramid. He had a length of rope and an oil jar in his hand.

"Easy. Knew exactly where they'd be, and when, didn't they?" Bak 1 was heaving the bundle up the steps towards the pole. "They got the old woman first, so she couldn't try any of her hocus-pocus. After that it wasn't too bad. The big, ugly one took a bit of time. And the gnome gave some trouble, they say. Killed three Quills and a Pern on her own. But they fixed her in the end."

Lief's heart seemed to stop. He heard the sharply drawn breaths of his companions behind him, but did not turn. Rigid with horror he watched as Bak 1 pulled the bundle upright against the pole and Bak 6 began tying it into place.

It was Dain. Dain, silky hair flopping forward, the side of his pale face flickering in and out of view in the light of the torches. As Lief watched, he slowly raised his head. His eyes opened and widened in terror.

There was a heavy, panting sound behind Lief, and a rough movement. "No!" Steven's voice rasped. "Nevets! Not while the Guards are close to Dain. They have daggers, blisters . . . They will kill him at once, if you strike now. Wait, I beg you!"

There was a moment of struggle. Then the panting eased. The movement stopped.

"Awake at last, your majesty?" Bak 1 was sneer-

ing. "That's good." He beckoned, and his fellows began toiling up towards him, their arms full of dead
branches. As they dumped the wood around Dain's
feet, piling it high, Bak 6 sprinkled it with oil.

"This'll keep him nice and warm," he sniggered.
Then he looked up, squinting into the torchlight. "The
others are coming with the prisoners," he said. "Party
can start anytime. Someone had better get Fallow. Bak
3 — you go."

"He won't come," whined Bak 3. "Ever since he
heard that story about the three being sighted in the
west, he's stopped worrying. He's locked in that room
with his green light. You can see it under the door.
And you know he — "

"He'll come for this," growled Bak 1. "There'll be
trouble if he misses it. Go on!"

As Bak 3 grumbled away, there were shuffling,
clinking sounds from the side of the square nearest
the city gates. The next moment, a group of stumbling
figures came into view. Some were being dragged by
Guards, other were walking alone, their legs weighed
down with heavy chains.

Lief searched the faces. There was Gla-Thon, her
hair sleek, wet with blood, her left arm hanging use-
lessly by her side. Manus, shivering with fear, came
next. Behind him, Fardeep and Nanion supported
Zeean, who hung limply between them. And, dragged
on his belly behind the last of the Guards, his body
thumping over the cobbles, wrists bleeding freely as

the straining chains bit deeply into his flesh was . . . Glock.

Only one person was missing.

"So now we know," muttered Barda.

Steven's great body had begun to tremble all over. Lief glanced at him fearfully.

The huge man's eyes were fixed on Dain. They were changing from yellow to brown, brown to yellow. His mouth was twitching, his flesh quivering, as he fought Nevets for control. "When I give the word, Lief must run to the boy," he growled thickly. "You others — guard Lief as best you can. We will do the rest. But keep away from us. Keep away!"

Lief tore his eyes from the terrible, writhing face, looked around again. Only Bak 1 and Bak 6 stood beside Dain, now. But both still had their daggers drawn.

Lief's fingers felt numb as he reached for Dain's dagger. If he managed to reach Dain alive, he would use the dagger to cut the ropes. That would be fitting. That would be . . .

But the dagger had gone. Lief looked down, blinking stupidly. The dagger must have fallen from his belt, unnoticed. Probably when he was climbing into the caravan on the road to Del.

A lump rose in his throat. Somehow this small loss seemed a symbol of his great failure. He had thought of himself as his king's protector. What folly!

He glanced at Jasmine, rigid beside him. Her eyes were narrow and intent. Her lips were firm. Behind her, Barda towered. He had drawn his sword. His face still showed signs of his illness, but his brow was furrowed with determination.

Lief shook himself. This was no time for weakness. He turned back to face the pyramid and drew his own sword. The sword his father had made for him. That, too, could cut ropes. Could free his king. That, too, was fitting.

Bak 1 grinned cruelly as the chained group came to a stop in front of the platform. "You've got a rare treat in store," he snarled. "You're to witness a great event, before you die."

He looked down, annoyed, as Bak 3 hurried into his view. "Where's Fallow?" he snarled.

Bak 3 shook his head. "He wouldn't answer the door!" he panted. "I told you!"

"Then we'll begin without him!" Bak 1 snapped. "And he'll face the consequences when the master comes!" He jerked his head at Bak 6, who sprang down to the ground, snatched up a torch, and held it up to him.

The prisoners struggled vainly in their chains, their faces masks of horror. Dain leaned back against the pole and closed his eyes.

Lief held himself ready. Ready . . .

"Now, traitors," snarled Bak 1, raising the torch.

"Watch your puny king scream for mercy as he burns." He touched the torch to the wood, then jumped to safety as flames began to leap.

"NOW!" The roar echoed around the square. Not just one voice, but two. And both of them like thunder.

12 - Desperation

L ief ran like the wind, dodging every hand that clutched at him, every blister that flew at him. He did not look behind him. He barely heard the screams, the snarling fury, the shouted orders that ended in shrieks of terror. Jasmine and Barda were on either side of him, but they could not keep pace. In seconds he had reached the platform. Alone he leaped up to the top, sliced through the ropes that bound Dain, pulled the limp body from the flames.

Eyes streaming in the smoke, he swung the boy further down the platform and let him go. Dain staggered, then stood, swaying, on his own feet. Lief grappled with the clasp of the Belt of Deltora. At last it slid apart. He pulled the Belt from his waist . . .

There was a mighty crash, a bellowing roar. Lief spun around. Jasmine and Barda stood teetering on the edge of a gaping hole that had opened in the square. Flaming torches were scattered around them. Nevets, Steven, and a host of Guards had disappeared. The Guards' screams echoed hideously up into the night for a single moment, then were choked off. The ground shook as Nevets raged against the walls of his prison.

Rats poured from the little yard where the caravan stood. As they ran they shimmered and paled, rising into wavering white flames with coals for eyes and gaping, toothless mouths. And in the core of every one was the Shadow Lord's mark.

Lief whirled back to Dain, the Belt dangling from his hand, his mind blank with horror and confusion. A trap had been set for Nevets. They had been betrayed! Their plans had been known. But how? No one knew of Barda and Steven's scheme. No one . . .

And then he saw the dagger on Dain's belt. Unsheathed, the dagger gleamed in the fire's fierce light. Its tip shone bright silver. Lief looked away from it. Up into Dain's dark, dark eyes. And in those eyes, unveiled at last, he saw the answer to all his questions.

"You," he said quietly.

Dain smiled. "I made an error," he said. "I should have put the dagger aside when I returned to this form. How fortunate you did not notice it before you ran to me. That would have spoiled my plan."

His hand swung, striking Lief's arm a tremendous blow, knocking the Belt into the fire. With a cry, Lief grabbed for it. But Dain had his wrist in a grip of icy steel. Dain's eyes narrowed, and suddenly Lief's sword was white-hot. It fell from his blistered hand and clattered, useless, down the steps of the platform.

"Still, I am glad you know, human," Dain hissed. "I want you to know what a fool you have been. And it does not matter now. For now the Belt of Adin cannot harm me. Soon it will be nothing but melted scrap."

He pointed at the remaining Guards. They were open-mouthed, devastated by what had happened to their companions. "Take the prisoners to the palace!" he shouted shrilly. "They have served their purpose."

"No! Let them go!" Lief cried. "You have the Belt! What more do you want?"

Dain's huge, dead eyes glittered. "When I call him, my master will come," he sneered. "He will see you, and your companions, and all the other traitors I have found and brought together here. Then I will be his favorite, ruling this land for him as the soft, Lumin-soaked failure in the palace never could. And you — you will die in torment amid the ruins and ashes of all you love."

His mouth twisted in scorn at the expressions on Lief's face. "You fool! You never dreamed that Ichabod was acting under my orders. That he had not carried me away, but was running alone in the dark, babbling of Del! And when you found the dagger I had become, you did not suspect it for a moment — even though you knew that Grade 3 Ols could take any shape they wished. You put it in your own belt, as I knew you would, snivelling for my loss, little knowing that you were carrying me with you from that time on. I was watching your every move. Listening to your every plan. Waiting to see how best I could destroy the devil Steven and that accursed Belt. And when I knew enough — I left you, and came here to prepare . . . this."

He waved his hand at the seething square. But Lief held his gaze, and did not look away. Lief had seen a movement behind Dain. Someone crawling up the steps of the platform towards him. A hawklike face. A pale, ragged scar. Tangled black hair. Slowly, slowly . . .

"I trusted you, Dain," said Lief. "I thought you were the heir."

Dain sneered. "As you were supposed to do from the first, human. It was what I was created for. I acted my part perfectly, did I not? I made no mistakes."

"You did," Lief said. "You should not have entered Tora. That was your vanity — and it was nearly your death, was it not?"

For the first time, Dain's eyes flickered, and dread brushed his face. But he did not answer.

Keep him talking. Keep him looking at me.

"And you failed to kill Barda with the poison you fed him, little by little," Lief went on doggedly. "Of course, I should have known why he was weakening. I had forgotten. When the amethyst dims, that is a sign of poisoned food. But you had forgotten something, too. The emerald is an antidote to poison. It cured him."

Dain's lip curled. "When he is facing my master, he will wish it had not," he spat.

Nearer . . .

"You feared Barda," Lief said. "He knew too much about the king, and the palace. You realized he was a danger to your scheme when he saw so easily through the false note left with the skeletons. Another of your precious master's plans that fell in ruins!"

By now Dain was breathing heavily. His twisted face was hardly recognizable as that of the delicate, modest boy Lief had known so long.

"My master had many plans, human," he rasped. "And I was the most deeply hidden one. How often I wished I could inform on you, or kill you while you slept! But that was forbidden. My master had ordered me to peace and silence. I was his final weapon, to be used only if every other plan failed,"

"You contacted him once," said Lief. "You told him our names."

Soon . . .

Dain clawed at his chest in remembered pain. "I was — corrected, for that," he said sullenly. "So then I made my own plans. And now my time has come."

Without warning, he threw his head back.

"Master!" he screamed. "It is time!"

A clap of thunder shook the earth. Great red clouds began to roll across the sky from the north, blotting out the stars. Dain faced Lief, eyes gleaming.

"The armies of the Shadow Lord have risen!" he shrieked. "Those throughout the land who have dared defy him will be destroyed. And *you* have brought his wrath down on all their heads. You and your companions have done it all, Lief of Del!"

Doom!

With a cry, Doom leaped upon Dain, knocking him down, his sword plunging for the heart. But Dain twisted like a snake, his body dissolving, rising again in a column of sickly white. Icy mist coiled around him. He whirled around, his fingers reaching for Doom's throat. Long, thin fingers, bringing with them the chill of death.

Lief staggered back, shuddering in a cold that was beyond imagining. The fire wavered, and went out.

Doom was on his knees. The Ol that had been Dain was laughing, laughing, pressing forward, intent on destruction. Shouts and groans rang from the square as Jasmine and Barda, torches blazing, held back a hundred crawling Ols, and the prisoners were dragged away. The sky was a mass of scarlet cloud.

Sobbing, Lief crawled to the fire. He scrambled among the dying embers, his fingers burning and freezing by turns. He found the Belt, staggered to his feet. The Belt was covered in white ash. But it was whole. The ash dropped from its gleaming length. The gems flashed under the red sky.

Now!

With the last of his strength, Lief threw the Belt around the Ol's waist. With both hands he pulled it tight.

And the Ol screamed, throwing up its arms so that Doom fell heavily down the stone steps. Smoke rose from the place where the Belt gripped, and beneath the smoke the shuddering white flesh began to melt. The Ol twisted, trying to break free. But already it was dying. One face alone loomed from its melting white. The face of Dain, in all his moods: timid, beseeching, tearful, laughing, teasing, dignified, brave . . .

Lief bent, choking, as his stomach heaved. But he held tightly to the Belt, squeezing his eyes shut. And when at last he opened his eyes, there was only an ugly puddle of white dripping down the stone steps.

He clasped the Belt around his waist and threw himself down to the bottom of the pyramid, to where Doom lay. Doom was muttering, shuddering with cold. His lips were blue. Great red marks wound around his neck. There was a swelling bruise on his brow.

"Lief!"

Lief looked up wildly. Jasmine and Barda were racing towards him. The Ols in the square were not coming after them. They were wavering, aimlessly clustering together, as though they were confused. It was as though the source of their power had been struck a blow by the destruction of the great one among them.

But already some of them were starting to recover. And the red clouds were tumbling, boiling, as they raced towards the city.

Frantically hauling Doom to his feet, Lief tried to think. Where could they go? Where could they hide?

Then the answer came to him. Where he had always gone when he was in trouble.

Home.

13 - The Forge

The forge was dark, desolate. The Shadow Lord's brand was on the gate. But there was shelter, heat, water. And, for the moment, there was safety.

They lit a fire and wrapped Doom in blankets. They gave him Queen Bee honey and bathed his wounds. At last he seemed to rouse. His eyelids flickered, opened. He stared blankly at the flames leaping in the fireplace.

"Where . . . ?" he mumbled huskily. He put his hand to his throat, and then to the swelling on his forehead.

"Do not try to speak," Lief whispered. Doom turned his head to look at him. His eyes were confused, without recognition.

"The blow on his head was severe," said Jas-

mine, pacing the room restlessly. "He needs to recover."

"Time is what we do not have." Barda moved to
the window and peered cautiously through the curtains. "When they realize we have escaped, they will
look here, for certain. We must move very soon."

But Lief was watching Doom. The man was staring around the room, his brow creased in a puzzled
frown as his gaze lingered on tables, chairs, cushions.
It was as though the place was somehow familiar to
him. Then he caught sight of Jasmine. His face light-
ened. His lips moved.

"Jasmine!" Lief hissed. "Come, quickly."

Jasmine hurried to the fire and crouched beside
Doom. He raised a hand and touched her cheek. His
lips moved again. The words were faint, so faint they
could hardly be heard.

"Jasmine. Little one. You . . . have grown so like
her. So like . . . your mother."

Jasmine jerked away from him, shaking off his
hand as if it was a spider. "How would you know
this? My mother is dead!" she cried angrily.

"Yes. My dear love . . . dead." Doom's face
creased with grief. His eyes filled with tears. Lief's
heart gave a great leap.

"Jasmine . . ." he whispered.

But Jasmine, half sobbing, had turned away.

Doom's eyes had closed once more. But again he

spoke. "They . . . refuse refuge, dear heart," he mumbled, his fingers curling as though he were crumpling a note in his hand. "We . . . must turn back . . . go east of Del, instead of west . . ."

Lief held his breath, realizing that Doom was reliving a time long forgotten. The blow to his head had unlocked the door in which memory had lain.

"We must," Doom murmured. "The news . . . Guards . . . waiting on the western road. All the women with child — killed. We will go east . . . to the Forests. They will not think of looking for us there." He paused, and seemed to listen. His mouth curved into a tender smile as a beloved voice spoke to him in memory.

Jasmine had turned around. Tears were rolling down her cheeks. Filli made tiny, worried sounds and Kree clucked unhappily. Absently, she put her hand up to her shoulder to soothe them, but her eyes were fixed on Doom.

"Danger?" Doom sighed. "Yes, dear heart. But all is danger now. We will take care. We . . . will survive. Our child will be safe. Grow strong, until it is time . . ."

Lief's heart was hammering in his chest. He could scarcely breathe. He saw that Barda had turned from the window and was staring in wonder.

Doom's head moved restlessly. "Little one . . . Jasmine . . ."

Jasmine put her hand in his. "I am here, Father," she said softly.

Doom tried to open his eyes once more, but his lids were heavy. "Poor, brave little girl child," he murmured. "No playmates but the birds and animals. No playthings but the ones the Forests could provide. No books, no comfort. And fear . . . always fear. So many times we wondered if we had done right. We did not regret our choices for ourselves. But for you . . ." His voice trailed off. He was slipping once more into sleep.

"I was happy, Father," Jasmine brushed angrily at her tears. "I had you and Mamma. I had games, songs, rhymes." She tugged at Doom's sleeve, trying to rouse him. "One rhyme I loved especially, because it had pictures," she babbled. "You gave it to me, Father. Remember?"

Doom made no reply. Desperately she released his hand and began rummaging in the pockets of her jacket. Her treasures spilled upon her lap — feathers and threads, a broken-toothed comb, a scrap of mirror, coins, stones, bark, scraps of paper . . . At last, she found what she was looking for. The oldest paper of all — grubby, and folded many times.

Carefully she unfolded it, and shook it in front of Doom's unconscious face. "I still have it," she cried. "See?"

Scarcely able to believe what he was seeing, Lief looked up to meet Barda's eyes. Endon's childhood rhyme. The rhyme that told of the secret way into the palace. Repeated in this very room by Lief's father when the story of Endon and Sharn's escape was told. Here was the one proof that could not be denied. And Jasmine had been carrying it, all along.

His mind flew back to that moment at Withick Mire, when the seven tribes had sworn on the Belt. He had known then, *known*, that the heir was present.

And he had been right.

With shaking fingers he took the Belt of Deltora from his waist. He touched Jasmine's arm. She turned to him, her face anguished. He held out the Belt.

Her eyes widened in shock as she understood him. She shrank away, shaking her head.

"Jasmine, put it on!" Barda thundered. "Doom is Endon. You are his daughter. You are the heir to Deltora!"

"No!" Jasmine cried. She shook her head again, scrambling away from Lief as Kree screeched, fluttering on her shoulder. "No! It cannot be! I do not want it! I cannot do it!"

"You can!" Lief urged. "You must!"

She stared at him defiantly for a single moment. Then, her face seemed to crumple. She crawled to her feet and stood waiting. Lief went to her and, holding his breath, looped the Belt around her slim waist, fastened it . . .

And nothing happened. The Belt did not flash, or shine. Nothing changed. With a great, shuddering sigh Jasmine pulled at the clasp and the Belt dropped to the floor at her feet.

"Take it back, Lief," she said dully. "I knew it was wrong."

"But — but it cannot be wrong!" Lief stammered. "You are the heir!"

"And if I am," Jasmine said, still in that same, dead voice, "then all we have been told about the Belt is false. Doom — my father — has been right all along. We have pinned our lives, and our hopes, on a myth. An old tale made for people who wanted to believe in magic."

Barda slumped into a chair and buried his face in his hands.

Lief stooped and picked up the Belt from the floor. As he fastened it about his waist once more, he felt numb. Why had the Belt not shone? Was it because Jasmine was unwilling?

Or — was the Belt itself at fault? Could one of the gems be false? No. The Belt had warmed to each of the gems in turn. It had sensed them. It knew them.

He moved away from the fire, away from the silent Barda, and Jasmine kneeling beside the sleeping Doom. He wandered out of the room, into the darkness beyond. Then he felt his way to his own small room, and lay down on the bed, hearing its familiar creak.

The last time he had woken in this room, it had been his sixteenth birthday. The boy who had lain here then seemed a stranger . . .

He leaped up, shocked, as there was a crash and a shout from the front of the house.

"I have him!" bawled a rough voice. "Now, the girl! The girl!"

Lief stumbled blindly towards the bedroom door, drawing his sword, hearing with horror the sound of smashing glass, cursing, the thumping of heavy boots. Kree was screeching wildly.

"Mind the bird!" roared another voice. "Ah — you devil!"

Desperately, Lief hugged the wall, feeling his way towards the sound.

"Keep away!" shrieked Jasmine. "Keep away! There are only three of us here, and there are ten of you! Ten!"

Lief froze. Jasmine was warning him that it would be useless to try to interfere. Warning him to keep away, and at the same time making the Guards think that only she, Doom, and Barda were in the house.

He heard a grunt of pain, then the sound of a sharp slap. "That'll teach you to bite!" a Guard snarled. "Three of you, yes! Just where Fallow said you'd be. And one of you out cold. Easy pickings!"

There was a shout of laughter, and the sound of bodies being dragged across the floor. Then . . . there was silence.

Lief waited a few moments, then crept to the living room. The fire still crackled brightly. Warm light flickered over a scene of ruin. Furniture had been thrown everywhere in the struggle. Both windows had been smashed.

Kree hunched on an overturned chair. As Lief approached him, he turned his head and squawked hopelessly.

Lief gripped the hilt of his sword till his knuckles turned white. Suddenly, he was full of a cold anger. "I could not save them, either, Kree," he said. "But it does not end here."

He held out his arm, and Kree fluttered to him. At almost the same moment, through the broken windows came the sound of loud, clanging bells. Lief's stomach churned. He knew what that meant. He had heard the bells before.

"The people are being summoned to the palace, Kree," he said grimly. "And we must go there, too. But not to stand outside the walls with the rest. We must get inside."

He walked to the fireplace and picked up the worn scrap of paper that Jasmine had dropped on the rug. Carefully he refolded it and put it in his pocket.

It was time for the bear to be woken once more.

14 ~ The Place of Punishment

The chapel was cold and empty as Lief crawled from the secret tunnel and slid the marble tile that had concealed it back into place. Shivering, he pushed open the chapel door and climbed the dark steps beyond, with Kree perched firmly on his arm.

Lief had no plan. No plan at all. But somehow it seemed right that he was here. Where this story began, so it will end, he thought. One way or another.

He peered from the darkness of the steps into the huge space beyond. The ground floor of the palace seemed deserted. But echoing down the vast stairway which wound up to the top floors was a distant, murmuring sound. The sound of a huge crowd.

Lief knew where the sound was coming from. It was floating through the huge open windows of the great hall on the first floor. The people of Del were thronging the hill beyond the palace garden. They were looking up at the Place of Punishment. This was a wooden platform supported on great poles, stretching all the way from the windows of the great hall to the wall that ringed the palace garden. The flag of the Shadowlands, a red hand on a grey background, hung from a flagpole directly above it.

The Place had been built when the Shadow Lord came. The sight of it, even from a distance, had chilled Lief from babyhood. For even tiny children were forced to witness the executions that took place there, and forbidden to turn their heads away. The Shadow Lord wanted all in Del to know the price of rebellion.

And so they did. Once or twice a year they saw terrible sights at the Place of Punishment, and in between those times it remained a constant reminder. The ground below it was heaped with bones. The wall was spiked with skulls. And the edge of the platform itself was hung with a thick fringe of dangling, rotting bodies, each branded with the Shadow Lord's mark.

"People of Del! Behold these traitors!" Lief gripped his sword as the thin, penetrating voice echoed faintly down the stairway. Fallow himself was standing on the Place, addressing the crowd. Usually, one of the Grey Guards conducted the executions. But this, of course, was a special occasion.

Running the secret way, Lief had reached the palace very quickly. Toiling the long way, up the hill, the Guards who had raided the forge could not yet have arrived. But Fallow had six other examples to show the crowd while he waited for news of the capture of those he wanted the most.

Rapidly, Lief looked around him. He knew that there was no chance of reaching the Place from inside the palace. Guards and palace servants always clustered in the windows that edged the platform.

But from what his father had told him, he knew that the kitchens were near. And they would be empty, for all the servants would be upstairs. He could run through the kitchens, outside, and around to where the Place towered. He could climb one of the poles that supported the stage from below.

But — the Place was always well lit. The Guards who stood at the platform's edge would see him the moment his head appeared. They would all have blisters ready in their slings, too, and plentiful supplies in boxes behind them. It was their task to hurl blisters into the crowd at any sign of disobedience.

"If only I could fly like you, Kree," he muttered, glancing at the bird perched rigidly on his arm. "Then I could surprise them from above."

Kree blinked, and cocked his head. Then Lief saw what he must do.

❋

In moments he was in the open air. The dark red clouds hung heavily overhead, casting an eerie glow over the earth. He could hear Fallow's voice clearly.

". . . joined in a plot to overthrow our great

leader. A plot doomed to failure, as all such evil is doomed."

Lief shut the sound from his mind.

Hurry!

The palace loomed above him. Dark, but with plenty of windows, ornaments, and other footholds.

He began to climb. Up, up, past the first floor windows, then up again to the narrow ledge that ran under the windows on the second floor.

The servants who cleaned the windows sat on the ledge often, no doubt. But Lief was standing, and his stomach knotted as he carefully turned until his back was to the wall. Then he began to move, edging along to the corner of the building, around to the side . . .

And below, far to his left, the Place of Punishment stood in a blaze of light.

He edged close. Closer . . .

The Place was thick with Guards. Torches flamed, lighting the darkness. Large red cones stood on each end of the platform. Lief had never seen their like before, and could not imagine their purpose. To one side was a huge metal pot of burning coals. Lief gritted his teeth. He knew *its* purpose only too well.

Fallow was in the center of the stage, holding two chains that were fastened to the necks of a pair of prisoners sprawled at his feet. Six more chained figures stood in a ragged line behind him. Glock.

Zeean. Manus. Nanion. Gla-Thon. Fardeep. All were wounded. Zeean was swaying. Glock could barely stand. Fallow stabbed at them with a bony finger.

"See them, people of Del?" he shrieked. "See these strangers? See their ugly bodies? Their twisted, evil faces? Monsters! Invaders of Del! Double branding, and death!"

A sickening wave of dizziness seized Lief. He pressed his back against the wall, panting. His throat had tightened so that he could hardly breath.

Six Guards strode forward and plunged iron branding rods into the pot of coals. They laughed and spat on the heating metal. Their turn for amusement had arrived.

The Guards facing the crowd raised their slings threateningly.

"Double branding and death!" chanted the people.

Lief gazed desperately over the sea of upturned, shouting faces. He saw no grins of glee or scowls of anger. The faces were absolutely blank — the faces of people beyond hope, beyond despair.

Suddenly, Fallow glanced behind him, at the windows of the great hall. Guards were moving there, stumbling out of the way of another Guard hurrying through. The newcomer signalled to Fallow, nodding excitedly, pointing behind him. Fallow's face changed. A triumphant smile spread over his face and he glanced upward. Lief caught his breath and flattened himself even further against the wall.

But Fallow did not see him. He was looking much higher — to the tower. Seven huge birds perched on the tower roof, their cruel, curved beaks outlined against the scarlet sky. Inside, where once the Belt of Deltora had lain in its glass case, red smoke swirled. And a shadowy figure stood motionless. Watching. Waiting . . .

Lief sidled further along the ledge. Now he was exactly where he wanted to be — on a small stone platform directly above the Place of Punishment, and beside the metal pole that bore the flag of the Shadowlands. Forcing his shaking hands to do his bidding, he pulled his coil of rope from his belt and tied one end of it to the flagpole. He tugged it gently, and knew it would hold.

Fallow swung back to face the crowd. He gestured, and the Guards pulled the six condemned prisoners roughly back, to stand against the palace wall.

"Their punishment can wait!" Fallow cried, his voice cracking with glee. "I can now announce, that, by my orders, our three greatest enemies have been captured! I knew it would be so!"

His face dark with spite and anger, he bent to heave up the crumpled figures at his feet.

And Lief's breath caught in his throat as he saw that the helpless couple were his mother and father.

Ragged, gaunt, they sagged in Fallow's cruel hands.

He shook them by their iron collars, as a dog shakes a rat, then set them back on their feet. They stood, swaying. "These two wretches will see their son before they die!" he snarled. "Behold them! The father and mother of treachery! Now they will pay for the evil they have caused, the lies they have told!"

There was a terrible roaring in Lief's ears. He saw the crowd staring at the prisoners. He saw many of the blank faces crease with pain as they recognized the kind, quiet man and the sweet, lively woman from the blacksmith's forge. Some, perhaps, did not even know their names. But they knew their natures. And so they grieved, hopelessly, for what was to come.

And Lief — Lief slowly unclasped the Belt of Deltora and put it down at his feet. It would have helped him in the fight ahead, but he knew that this was a fight that in the end he could not win. If he was to die, he would not die wearing the Belt. He would not allow it to be part of his defeat and pain. Or let his parents see it trodden into the dust.

He stared down at the precious, mysterious thing that had brought them all to this. It was complete. And it was powerful. Powerful enough to kill Dain. Powerful enough to feel the presence of the heir. And yet . . . somehow it was not perfect. Somehow, they had not discovered its final secret. He was tormented by the feeling that the answer was before his eyes, if only he could see it.

The gems lay gleaming in their steel medallions. The topaz. The ruby. The opal. The lapis lazuli. The emerald. The amethyst. The diamond.

Lief remembered the winning of every one — what he had felt as each stone was added to the chain in turn.

Added . . . in turn . . .

His scalp began to prickle. Well-remembered words from *The Belt of Deltora* swam into his mind:

✝ Each gem has its own magic, but together the seven make a spell that is far more powerful than the sum of its parts. Only the Belt of Deltora, complete as it was first fashioned by Adin and worn by Adin's true heir, has the power to defeat the Enemy.

. . . complete as it was first fashioned by Adin . . .
. . . together the seven make a spell . . . a spell . . .
SPELL!

Lief pulled out his dagger, crouched over the Belt. His fingertips tingled as quickly, quickly, he used the dagger's tip to lever the gems from their places, one by one. It seemed to him that they came easily, helping him. Helping him again as he replaced them — but this time in a different order. The right order.

Diamond. Emerald. Lapis lazuli. Topaz. Opal. Ruby. Amethyst.

DELTORA.

With a great sigh, Lief stood up, the Belt of Deltora gleaming in his hands. His breathing had slowed. His hands were steady. He knew, beyond doubt, that at last the Belt was as it should be. Now it was as it had been when first fashioned by Adin, who had used the first letters of the seven tribes' talismans to form the name of their united land. Now it was ready to be claimed by Adin's true heir.

And Jasmine was coming. At any moment she would be dragged onto the platform. Now Lief knew why he had been led to this place. Now he had a plan.

15 - Fight to the Death

There was a sudden confusion of noise from the windows below him. The newest captives were coming through. Fallow shrieked an order. Guards touched torches to the red cones. The crowd gasped in shock as blinding white light hissed and flared. Light flooded the Place, lighting the faces of the prisoners, banishing every shadow, illuminating the whole of the side of the palace almost to the roof.

Bathing Lief in brilliance.

He shrank back, but there was nowhere to hide. And the people of Del, looking up, could see him. See him clearly. His stomach heaved as he waited for them to call out, pointing and exclaiming. Waited for Fallow to turn, for Fallow's eyes to follow the pointing fingers, to sight him, to shriek to the Guards . . .

But there was utter stillness. Utter silence. Lief saw a wide-eyed little child in her mother's arms began to lift a hand. But the mother quickly pushed the hand down, murmuring softly, and the child stilled.

Lief stared, holding his breath. The people of Del stared back, their faces intent. Many knew him well — his friends, their parents, those who had visited the forge while he worked with his father. Others knew him only by sight — as a nuisance, a wild boy running with his friends through the city. Some did not know him at all.

But they knew he was one of them. They saw what was in his hands. And none of them was going to give him away.

Fallow had noticed nothing. He was watching as Jasmine, Barda, and Doom, blindfolded with hoods and heavily chained, were dragged to his side.

Lief measured the distance to Jasmine with his eyes. He took the rope in his right hand. Grasped the Belt firmly in his left . . .

The people watched. Silent. Wishing him well. He felt their thoughts as clearly as if they had shouted them aloud. Flowing through him. Giving him strength.

"Now!" Fallow cried. "Now I show you three traitors who nearly escaped, because a vain and foolish creature, bloated with pride, thinking to be my rival, put his own secret plans into action while I was — occupied with other important duties."

Grinning, he snatched off Jasmine's hood. Then Barda's. But when he saw Doom, the grin vanished.

He took a step back, his face a mixture of fear and rage.

Wait . . .

Leif saw his father turn, look at Doom. He saw his father's eyes light with mingled joy and pain. Saw him stretch out a trembling hand to his boyhood friend.

And saw Doom staring back, his ravaged face suddenly blazing with consciousness, with memory. Then turning this way and that, looking around him, searching urgently for someone he could not find.

Searching for me.

"You fools!" Fallow hissed savagely to the Guards who had brought the prisoners. "This is not one of the three! Where is the boy? The *boy*?"

The Guards mumbled in confusion and backed away.

Now!

Lief jumped, Kree screeching above his head. He swung outward, then let go of the rope and landed just beyond Jasmine, stumbling, then regaining his feet. He lunged for her, the Belt in his hand. He saw her face, wild-eyed with shock, heard Barda shouting, the crowd roaring, Fallow screaming to the Guards. And from the tower, a cry of rage that pierced his flesh, melted his bones, forced him to his knees.

Lightning cracked the boiling sky, streaking towards him. He threw himself aside, rolling, stunned, as it struck the place where he had been kneeling.

With the shriek of splitting wood, the front of the platform collapsed as though a giant had smashed it with a mighty fist. Its two halves tipped towards one another like giant slides, and the nearest Guards toppled, scrambling, shrieking, into the yawning gap between, white hot coals spilling after them.

Lightning flashed again, and again. Roaring thunder shook the trembling earth. And out of the thunder swooped the seven Ak-Baba, their unearthly, wailing cries chilling the blood.

Lief clung desperately to the tilting boards. The crowd was screaming now, screaming to him . . .

But Fallow — Fallow had him. Fallow's icy hand was on his neck, wrenching him upward. The hated, writhing face was close to his, lips drawn back in a snarl of triumph as Lief struggled to draw his sword.

Then, abruptly, the face jerked backwards, eyes bulging. Lief was hurled backwards once more as the icy hand loosened, flew to the thin throat, and clawed desperately at the strangling chains biting deeply into the flesh.

Did Fallow know who had seized him? Did he know who were behind him now, using the last of their strength to heave him, choking, away from his prey?

The ones he had thought too broken to be a threat. Whose chains he had dropped without a thought.

"Father! Mother! Beware!" Lief screamed, clawing his way up the slope towards them. Fallow was feeling for his dagger. He had found it! Lief lunged forward.

"No, Lief!" his father cried. "The Belt! You — "

His voice was silenced as Fallow struck. He crumpled and fell. Lief's mother caught him, and together they crashed onto the groaning boards. She flung out a hand and clutched the edge of the platform to hold them both, her scream lost in the raging of the wind, the shrieking of the Ak-Baba.

Fallow was dragged down with them, caught by the chains wound around his neck. He pulled himself free, writhing on the tipping boards, struggling for breath, struggling to rise. Then he saw the red cone of light sliding slowly towards him. He grabbed for it, seized its base, then saw his danger.

Too late. Slowly, slowly, the cone tipped. Burning white liquid light poured over him, covering him, sizzling, sizzling as he screamed.

There was a roaring, rushing sound above. Lief looked up. Red smoke was gushing from the tower. Red smoke, thick and edged with grey, heavy with menace. Grey light circled and swirled in its depths. And in its center a huge shape was forming. Hands, reaching. Eyes, hungry for revenge.

Lief spun around. He saw Jasmine and Barda facedown on the other side of the platform, clinging on for dear life as the planks tipped more and more steeply. Above them flapped an Ak-Baba, talons outstretched. Kree was darting at the monster's head, yellow eyes flashing as he pecked again and again. The Ak-Baba was screeching in fury, twisting its neck, trying to rid itself of its attacker.

Lief gritted his teeth. Prepared for the jump of his life. Could he do it? Jump that yawning gap and climb up those steep, slippery boards? With the sword in one hand, the Belt of Deltora clutched in the other?

Once, he would have tried it. Now, he had learned wisdom. Steadying himself, he sheathed his sword. He clasped the Belt around his waist . . .

And — time seemed to stand still.

What . . . ?

A rush of heat swept through Lief's body. There was a strange, crackling sound. Then the Belt seemed to explode with light.

A furious roar shook the palace to its core. Red smoke recoiled, hissing, into the boiling clouds. But the gems of the Belt of Deltora blazed like fire, their rainbow brilliance streaming outward, filling the air, banishing the night, dancing on the faces of the cheering, weeping people. And in the center of the light stood Lief. Lief, the true heir of Deltora, revealed at last.

Shrieking, panic-stricken, the Ak-Baba wheeled away, soared upward to the tower. But the tower was empty. And already the red clouds were rolling back to the Shadowlands, a raging malice growling in their depths. A malice that would not die, but which knew that this battle, at least, it could not win.

Astounded, Lief looked around him. Saw his mother smling, sobbing, cradling his father's head in her lap, and Doom kneeling beside them. Saw Jasmine and Barda, clinging together, their faces wild with joy and relief while Kree screeched above them and Filli danced on Jasmine's shoulder. Looked behind him at the shrieking, cheering Manus, Gla-Thon, Nanion, and Fardeep. Saw Zeean raising her head, her eyes shining. And Glock — Glock! — grinning all over his face.

They are safe, Lief thought, his heart swelling. All will be safe now.

The remaining Guards were tearing blisters by the dozen from the boxes and hurling them into the celebrating crowd. But the people had already learned that water and Boolong sap were not harmful. Soon, the Guards would realize their own danger.

For they had been ruthlessly abandoned. As had the Ols, who, their source of power withdrawn, lay with burst and shrivelled hearts in the market square, where at last Steven was climbing from the pit. As had Ichabod, sprawled like a drained sack of red skin over the gnawed bones of his last meal.

And so it would be now, all over the land. As the radiance of the Belt filled Lief, his eyes seemed to pierce darkness and distance. From Raladin to Rithmere, from Dread Mountain to the Valley of the Lost, from Broad River to Withick Mire, fear was vanishing.

Throughout Deltora people were seeing their enemies falling, the clouds of evil in flight. The people were throwing down their weapons in joy, creeping from hiding, embracing their loved ones, and looking up at the sky. Knowing that suddenly, amazingly, a miracle had occurred. And at last they were free.

Lief knew all this. He knew, he accepted, that he was the heir to Deltora. The Belt had proved it beyond doubt. But how? How could this be?

16 ~ The Last Secret

Dazed, Lief climbed to his parents' side. As he knelt, embracing his mother and bending to his father, he met Doom's eyes. Doom's mouth twitched into a ghost of his old, mocking smile. Do you not yet understand? the smile seemed to ask.

Lief shook his head. Dimly he heard the crowd cheering still. He felt Jasmine and Barda, freed from their chains, sinking down beside him. But he could not move. He could not speak. He could only stare at Doom, his eyes filled with questions.

"The perfect hiding place," Doom murmured. "Was it not? For whoever would suspect? Whoever would suspect that the man and woman who ran from Del that night nearly seventeen years ago were laying a false trail? That they were not the king and queen at all?"

His eyes warmed as he looked at Lief's parents.

"Who would suspect that the king of Deltora could live as a blacksmith? And a queen, a fine lady of Toran blood, could grow vegetables, and spin common yarn? Yet, what was Adin, but a blacksmith?

Then he turned back to Lief, and raised an eyebrow. "And what should be more fitting than that the heir to Deltora be brought up as a common boy, learning without trying the ways of his world, and its people?"

Then, in wonder, Lief saw it. Saw the plan in all its simplicity. A plan based on sacrifice. Based, also, on the confusion and chaos that Del had become. When neighbor lost sight of neighbor, friend lost touch with friend, and no face was familiar.

Doom's plan . . . Doom, who was not Endon, but Jarred. Jarred who, with his beloved wife, had given his identity, his home, and his life to his friend, for the sake of the land they loved. Jarred, who had fled Del that dark night, with the little rhyme that had led him into the palace still in his pocket. No wonder Jasmine was as she was, with parents such as these!

"You had the idea of decoys once before, then, Doom?" he murmured.

Doom nodded. "So it seems. Though I did not know it, when I sent our Toran friends to the west. It is good to think that they, also, are safe." He glanced behind him, and Lief heard the sound of fighting in the palace.

"The Resistance has arrived," Doom said casually. "They will take care of the last of the Guards. Like Barda and Steven, I thought it wise to make a special plan, known to no one else. There is a certain drain-tunnel in Del, that leads to the palace kitchens . . ."

"I think I know it," Lief muttered. "I found it once. On my birthday . . ."

His mother squeezed his hand.

His mother. Not Anna of the Forge, practical and wise in the ways of herbs and growing things. But Sharn, of Tora. The one who could weave like a miracle. The one whose wit and courage had taught him so much.

Lief looked down at his father, the tender, soft-spoken man whose name, he now knew, was not Jarred, but Endon. How could he have not guessed?

How could his gentle father have done the things Jarred was said to have done? Why would the true Jarred have been so bitter about Endon's foolishness?

The face seemed smoothed, softened. It was very calm. The eyes were warm and peaceful. The mouth curved into a smile. Lief heard Barda's quickly indrawn breath, and felt his own eyes burn with tears.

"Do not weep for me," his father murmured. "I am happy. My life is fulfilled. Here, now, at the moment of my death, I have what I have longed for. The knowledge that the evil caused by my fault has been undone. The knowledge that, with my dear wife, I have raised a son who can lead his people wisely, know their hearts."

"Why did you not tell me, Father?" murmured Lief. "Why did you not tell me who I was?"

"While you did not know, you were safe," his father whispered. "And — you had to learn — to love and know the people, and be one of them. That — I had sworn."

"But . . . Barda?" Lief glanced at the big man kneeling so silently beside him.

His mother shook his head. "Barda did not know the truth. He had seen Jarred and Anna leave. He thought they were the king and queen, for that is what we told him. At the palace he had only ever seen us from a distance, dressed and painted in palace fashion. We never told him the secret. We had sworn to keep the plan between the four of us. And when you went on your quest — why, we thought that as soon as the Belt was complete, there would be no need for explanation. We thought it would shine! We did not know . . ."

"We did not know that the order of the gems was important," Doom finished. "How could we? The book told nothing of that."

"It did," Lief said quietly. "But it told it in riddles."

Endon smiled. "That is fitting," he said. "For all along, Lief, this has been a story where nothing is as it seems. I have always liked such tales. For such tales usually have happy endings. . . . As does this one."

His eye closed. Lief clasped his mother's hand, and bowed his head.

❋

Lief, Jasmine, and Barda stood together, looking out into the dawn.

"I am glad it was you, Lief," Jasmine said. "So glad."

Lief looked at her. Her face was smudged with mud. Her hair was tangled. Her mouth was set in a strong, straight line.

"Why?" he asked.

"I could have offered the people nothing," she said, moving away from him. "How could I be a queen? What am I but a wild girl, quick-tempered and troublesome, more at home in a forest than a walled garden?" She tossed her head. "Besides, I cannot stay here. This city is hideous to me. And the palace — a prison!"

"Prison walls can fall," Lief said softly. "Gardens can become forests. Del can be beautiful once more. And as for what you can offer, Jasmine . . ." For a moment, his voice failed him. This was so important. He had to choose his words carefully. But whatever he said must be the truth. Not the whole truth, perhaps, but at least part of it.

"Well?" Jasmine demanded, her shoulders rigid.

"There is much to do," Lief said simply. "So much to do, Jasmine. All over Deltora. Barda, Doom, and I cannot do it alone. We need your courage and your strength. We need you, exactly as you are."

"Indeed," said Barda gruffly.

Jasmine glanced at them over her shoulder. Filli chattered in her ear. Kree screeched on her arm.

"Then, I suppose I will stay — for a while," she said, after a moment. "For, certainly, you need me. As your father needed my father. To get things done."

Lief smiled, and, for once, did not argue.

He was well satisfied.